VANQUISHED
BREATH OF DEATH

BOOK ONE

THE VANQUISHED TRILOGY

BOOK ONE
VANQUISHED: BREATH OF DEATH

BOOK TWO
EMERGENCE: BREATH OF LIFE

BOOK THREE
RECLAMATION: FINAL BREATH

Book Two and Three in the series are coming soon…

VANQUISHED

BREATH OF DEATH

BOOK ONE

ANITA R. ESCHLER

Content & Trigger Warning: This novel may be inappropriate for younger audiences under the age of eighteen. Additionally, it may potentially harm the reader mentally by triggering stressful episodes, panic attacks, depression and anxiety. There is course language, sparse scenes of strong violence and gore, horror, and implied sexual violence.

Please note this is a work of fiction. Names, characters, incidents, and places are either a product of the author's imagination or are used fictitiously, and any resemblance to actual persons, living or dead, events, or locales is entirely coincidental.

Vanquished ~ Breath of Death
Book One: The Vanquished Trilogy

Editor ~ Chloe's Chapters
Cover design ~ CoverDungeonRabbit
Formatting ~ Evenstar Books

First Edition
Paperback ISBN 978-0-6450769-0-5
Hardback ISBN 978-0-6450769-1-2
E-Book ISBN 978-0-6450769-2-9

For those struggling to survive in any way; please do not give up. You are precious. Know that you are loved—even if it does not feel that way.

A Note for Readers

This book is written in United Kingdom English.

This means words like *color* and *favorite* are spelled *colour* and *favourite* as is standard in UK English. This also means you may see phrases such as: *she walked towards the door* rather than the US *she walked toward the door*.

VANQUISHED EARTH
A Poem

*Possessions matter not in this world for moths and corrosion will
eventually destroy their worth;
Money has no value in death, only floating upon the wind — lost when
their owners are buried deeply within the earth.*

*Bones and flesh are gnawed on by beasts then slowly eaten by worms
until evidence of existence has perished;
Status crumbles, like the dilapidated buildings that once flourished —
like a being's prized belongings that were once cherished.*

*Invisible monsters ravish the earth, their forms disguised as greed and
vanity — the vanquishers of this civilisation;
Humans fall for their alluring deceit and glamour, the nature of us
causing the downfall of each nation.*

*We are our own demons, causing the grief of others — our egotism
disregarding the poor;
We do not deserve mercy, for it is the innocents of this world neglected
of their need — it is them we choose to ignore.*

*Life is but a fragile zephyr — gone with an instant, yet worthwhile on a
scorching day as a valuable contribution;
Just as each breath is a waste of oxygen — air that could be implemented,
unless helping those in destitution.*

*So those reading this message... you are provided with the knowledge
of the utmost importance;
That this earth is in despair and in great need of kindness — in need of
less greed and riddance of malicious influence.*

*Otherwise, the downfall of humanity will be imminent, and love will no
longer bloom;
Evil will prevail our species — vanquishing the kind nature of people
until all that remains is doom.*

- ANITA R. ESCHLER

PROLOGUE

THE BLOODCURDLING, RESONATING SOUND *of a woman screaming during childbirth pierces through the silent night's air. Deep within a dark, damp cave leading into the bowels of a desolate mountain, lies a beautiful raven-haired woman with bright cerulean eyes; eyes that are filled with tears of excruciating pain.*

"I won't make it to the other side of this birth, my love," the woman gasps through the agonising pain of contractions.

Tears stream down the young man's face as he shakes his head fervently in denial.

"No, Riona, you will survive. You must survive!"

Peace fills the blue eyes of the woman named Riona and she stares lovingly at her husband.

"You must be strong for our little girl; she is to be a queen and her name will be Raine."

A scream rips from Riona's mouth again and her husband looks nervously at the entrance of their sanctuary. He holds his wife's hand and soothingly strokes her hair, before situating himself between her bent knees.

"Did you have a vision about our daughter?" The husband asks in a strained tone to distract Riona from her excruciating pain. He tells himself to chat to her as if it is just another normal day.

Riona jerkily nods her head, her expression tightly crumpled, eyes clenched shut as she battles through the violent labour. "Yes. Raine means queen." Riona suddenly gasps and her eyes snap open. "The baby is coming; please take care of our daughter, my love."

Riona's husband nods once in a promise and puts his hands between her legs, dread filling him at the copious amounts of blood pooling beneath her. Rain batters the ground outside, the coincidence of weather and his daughter's name not escaping him. Trepidation coils low in his abdomen at the feeling of evil closing in on them.

The baby must be born soon, or they will all die.

Riona lets out one last bloodcurdling scream and their blood-covered baby slides into the world. The father efficiently cuts the umbilical cord with a sterile dagger and instantaneously wraps the precious bundle in a swathing of cloth. No sounds come from her sweet little mouth, yet her face is red and screwed up. He quickly places the child over his shoulder and gives her a firm pat on the back, resulting in the tiniest hiccup, then a loud, ear piercing cry.

Raine is breathing, though her mother, Riona, is fading quickly as her loss of blood swiftly drains the life from her, but she still manages to hold out her arms for their little daughter. "Let me hold her once before I leave this world."

Her husband nods, tears streaming down his face at his wife's strained whisper and places the bundle carefully on her chest.

"Raine, y-you are the light of this world, y-you are a queen," Riona whispers with jagged breaths against her newborn's bloodied face. "You have b-been bought into this life to s-save this f-fallen world."

The husband hears multiple noises closing in on the entrance of the cave and his heart pounds erratically. He unsheathes his trusty sword in preparation to protect his loved ones.

"My love, it is time," Riona whispers, the last of her strength fading, and her husband whips around, falling heavily to his knees by his wife's side. Tears continue streaming down his face and he nods once, pressing a tender kiss to his beloved's once rosy lips.

"I love you, Riona, and I promise to protect our daughter from the evil eradicating this world. I promise to raise her into a strong warrior — into a queen."

A soft smile graces Riona's face as she stares lovingly into her husband's eyes for the last time. "I love you," she gasps through her last breath. "Go with peace, my love." The life in Riona's once vivid blue eyes dims until she stares blankly into space. A mournful cry rips from the mouth of her husband, yet he does not hesitate to grasp the precious bundle, binding her to his chest with a long strand of material as the scalding tears stream down his face. He will need his hands free to slaughter any creatures that dare to steal his daughter's precious life. The rain and wind continue assaulting the once flourishing earth outside and pale flashes of flesh dart back and forth in the distance. With both baby and father clothed in waterproof leather, the time has come to start their treacherous journey to safety.

Gripping the sharp sword in his hand, he trudges out of the deep cave and away from the protection it affords. The tiny human squirming against his chest is his utmost priority now... even if it eventually kills him.

RULE ONE:
DON'T SLEEP

1

RAE

RUNNING THROUGH THE MANGLED OVERGROWTH in utter darkness is not my preferred option to start the night, but here I am, currently being hunted.

By Breathers.

My teeth grit as the images of them plague me, monsters that resemble zombies derived from the old-world fiction, as cliché as that sounds, but more heinous. Really, I wish they were such creatures because *these* things are not brain dead like those fictitious zombies. No, they are smart. They hunt in packs. They lurk in the darkness and study their prey.

If a human is *unlucky* enough to see them, then they would be traumatised for the rest of their short and dismal life. That is *if* they endured the encounter. But providing they implement common sense, which effectively are a set of rules I abide by, survival is possible.

In short, a few centuries ago, governments across the world became united and decided that chemical weaponry was the only solution in rectifying the increasing population of humans causing the rapidly decreasing resources. They did it so no one suspected anything. The united government's Treatment was fabricated to slowly kill, attacking one's immune system. It was the beginning of our impending downfall.

The beginning of The Vanquishing.

Each generation produced more and more birth defects, subsequent of the chemical weaponry disguised as medicine. Eventually the government decided these defects, these *mistakes*, if that is what a person can call deformed children and adults, needed to be eradicated once and for all. So, they produced a final Treatment; one meant to treat humans of all disease and sickness. Thankfully, my family line did not succumb to their deception being leaked into the ears of the unsuspecting and naïve.

No one is certain if the outcome of this medicine was an accident, but either way, the aftermath was atrocious. It spread much too quickly to stop. But that did not prevent the government from firing nuclear missiles at every major city riddled with the consequences of *their* creation. Hence the wasteland I am currently sprinting through.

My mother's ancestors sailed across from Old Ireland, in search of a prosperous land, though they had no sense of direction and happened to land on the continent of Old South America. The land I was raised on and am presently surviving on.

These tales have been passed down through each generation, to eventually my own father who had gifted the knowledge of my family's origin and the downfall of humankind to me. My mother apparently died with me at childbirth.

My kin did not accede to the deception that this treatment would be the mother of all treatments. So, in effect, they survived the wave of mutations that spread like wildfire through the continents and then they survived the aftermath of nuclear warfare by implementing gas masks. Unfortunately, survivors that had no means to acquire such sought after equipment perished from radiation.

The masks are no longer required for the radioactivity these days—as time has slowly diminished its prevalence—but Pa mentioned the rich residents residing in thriving cities will still brandish them if leaving the safety of their walls. These cities were founded after the nuclear fallout and are known as *Segments*— walled sanctuaries that only the privileged can live in. I have never seen such civilisation and would rather die an agonising death than be associated with *these* humans and their luxuries of running water, accessible food, electricity, and gadgets. My father encountered them once in Segment Three and said their power and privilege stripped them of their human decency.

I know he was putting it mildly.

I know they rape, murder and steal, taking advantage of the less fortunate souls who have survived The Vanquishing of mankind. They took advantage of my father. Now it is just me. But I will avenge his death. If I can ever find Segment Three.

If I survive the horde of rabid Breathers on my trail first.

Sweat trickles down the sides of my face and my forehead creases with panic.

Keep focused, Raine, I think as I place my hand on the cold pendant around my neck. It is the only thing that I have left from my father apart from my trusty sword. Before Hunters caught up to us, he thrust the pendant and chain into my hand and said to never take it off. So, I have worn it for three years straight. It has kept me safe somehow, though I believe it is just coincidence, but I will not risk taking it off just to see how well it works.

I'm additionally adamant on avoiding these creatures at all costs, even if it means leaving my shelter and few belongings behind.

I *really* do not want to see one of these *things* ever again.

The bones and organs on these deformed creatures have mutated further from the nuclear fallout, so the proportions of each body part are no longer symmetrical. Each creature is unique, with diverse deformities and irregularities. Some of their bones have evolved into long points and clubs, as if the mutation has worked in their favour and provided weapons. Their sinewy flesh has permanently melted and fused into a grotesque mound of horror—milky translucent flesh, the skin a by-product of the Treatment's influence on the human genetics and immune system. And that is just their *body*. The faces on these things will haunt the bravest of human's dreams... if they ever dare to sleep.

To survive in this post-apocalyptic wasteland *outside* the walls of a Segment, the first rule that my father passed down to me—though they are not particularly in any order of importance—is to ensure not to sleep during the night. One hour *at most*, at a time, during the day is acceptable. Most survivors have figured this out... the rest are likely dead.

Humans have adapted to the minimal sleep schedule, as have I, though it is all I have known. We either evolve and adapt... or die. My father said residents in the Segments sleep up to eight hours a night. I inwardly scoff. The idea seems preposterous.

The sound of heavy crunching behind me pulls me from my musings and I whimper, pushing my adept, lean legs to sprint faster.

Breathers.

Just the mere idea of witnessing the abominable face of one, sends a new rush of adrenaline coursing through my veins. They are certainly not like the zombies that were depicted in movies all those centuries ago that Pa told me about.

No. These have the faces of pure death. Pure *evil*.

I unfortunately had the displeasure of encountering a stray one just before this horde came after me.

Since they are living creatures, unlike zombies, they age like humans, and the one I encountered must have been in its final days since I was able to defend myself quite easily. But that did not make its face any less horrifying. Its jaw unhinged in a supernatural way, wide enough that its mouth could envelop an entire head. Ligaments of sinewy flesh tethered its jaw to its skull. The skin was elasticated, translucent-white flesh that stretched unnaturally without tearing. Its teeth had evolved into long, ragged points to hunt and tear into flesh.

Human flesh, unfortunately.

So, when I witnessed this creature's jaw unhinging to reveal a large gaping hole of deathly razors; I froze momentarily. This Breather did not have a nose, just an empty gaping hole in the middle of its face, though that is not to say others do not have their human features still, as each mutant is uniquely different.

Either way, the worst of all features on this Breather's face were its soul-sucking eyes—midnight-black orbs bulging from the sunken voids of its sockets. Amid those glistening, sinister spheres, were its pupils; two flickering specks of glowing amber.

They peered within the depths of my own soul, metaphysically reaching in and grasping around my essence with its long bony claws to paralyse me. The sensation was hard to comprehend and I wondered if demons had possessed its body because of the indiscernible *feeling* that weighed heavily on my chest when it stared deeply into my eyes. The sensation was akin to my *spirit* being sucked from my body, and it immediately paralysed me where I was standing. Thankfully, the training that Pa had permanently imprinted in my mind paid out, and I had managed to snap myself from the trance and swing my sword down to eventually hack off the Breather's head before I was its dinner.

A chill suddenly races up my spine at the memory of the Breather, urging me to push myself harder as my feet pound the dead earth. The recollection of its horrifying form causes my hand to drift to the hilt at my waist, resting over the metal pommel of my only companion, though my stride does not waver and remains consistent.

Pa handed me this sword as soon as I was big enough to hold it and it has been passed down through generations of women in my family. It was my mother's prior—apparently, she was a phenomenal warrior. The tarnished, battered gold pendant around my neck was also hers.

Sudden thoughts of the mother I never met afflict me, and the unknown reason of why she named me Raine—an entirely depressing name—spears through the forefront of my mind. A scowl crosses my face. Pa claims that, even though it was a storming night when I was born, and coincidentally my name was the very weather they experienced, I was still his ray of sunshine peering through the dark, stormy clouds. I'm still unsure if *stormy clouds* were his metaphor for my mother's death. Additionally, he always said I was a ray of sunshine for this broken and desolate world, though, perhaps he was just biased. So, he had always called me Rae instead. His peculiar description still perplexes me to this day, and I'm remorseful to have lost any chance of finding out his meaning behind it. I never thought to pester him prior, irrationally thinking there would never be a day where I was without him.

A sad smile teases my lips at the memory of his stern yet kind face. Even though I was his daughter, he always trained me to fight and survive like a warrior from the day I could walk. I'm thankful for the skills he's imparted on me, since they will come in handy if these Breathers ever catch up to me.

There is also this weird buzzing I've always had, and I feel it gushing through my veins right at this very moment. I cannot discern what it may be since I have no one to compare symptoms with, but it becomes more prominent when I'm feeling threatened. Perhaps that is just adrenaline, though. The buzzing feeling is at its most severe right now.

The description of these creatures elicits the very same buzzing running through my veins and is the reason I'm currently sprinting *farther* away from my shelter, across the desolate wastelands. Though, there is also one other motivation for my relentless sprint, bringing me to my second rule of survival; a rule that will save the *essence* of any human life.

RULE TWO:
HOLD YOUR BREATH

2

Rae

THE SOUND OF A TWIG SNAPPING in the silent night has me freezing and I'm thankful now, more than ever, that my generations of family have evolved their night vision over hundreds of years. Straining my eyes, I peer from the safety of my makeshift fort, in the branches of a tree five meters tall.

My sprint across the wasteland to escape the pack of Breathers on my trail landed me in an overgrown jungle on the outskirts of a nuclear hit zone. I was certain I had lost them until that blasted twig snapped.

Slow and small breaths, Rae. They can hear you breathing.

I inwardly laugh at the thought that they can hear us breathing, yet if they breathe on us, *and* we inhale, then we die. Well, our human essence dies apparently, and we transform into the very devils themselves. My knowledge is predominantly second-hand, imparted from what Pa taught me. Their breath is seemingly contagious, and is the origin of their name, reminding me of the second vital rule.

Hold. Your. Breath.

If a human is lucky enough to survive an encounter, meaning that their heads are not decapitated in one bite; it is imperative they do not inhale. Though, residents from Segments are fortunate since they all have gas masks and brandish them if leaving their sanctuary. These respirators have been modified so they only cover the nose and mouth, seeing as eyes are safe in being exposed, with two filters protruding on either side where one's mouth would be. Somehow, they prevent the effects of the monster's breath.

I'm positive I survived my earlier encounter with a Breather by holding my breath, although proceeding to hack my blade through its neck was a likely factor too.

The sound of another twig snapping echoes through the jungle canopy, once again wrenching me from my musings, and every muscle in my body tenses. Frowning into the abyss below the makeshift floor of my shelter for the night, my eyes strain to pick up any threats looming nearby. A sigh of relief rushes from my lungs as no flashes of milky skin alert me to Breathers. Though, that is not to say whatever is down there is not just as deadly.

Hunters, the surviving humans, are just as dangerous. Hunters are mostly hordes of men who rape and pillage their way through the lands and tend to work for the Segments, stealing resources and women for breeding.

My brows furrow deeply, and the thought has consternation crawling up my spine.

I wait for a few moments more and conclude the twigs snapping are likely the nocturnal animals going about their business, seeing as I can hear their eery, forlorn calls echoing throughout the thick greenery. Nestling into the warmth of foliage I collected from the jungle floor, I bunker down for a night of rest. Not *sleep*, but rest.

My muscles are aching and are in desperate need of rejuvenating from the long distance I sprinted, so I will spend tonight doing just that. My feet are worn and cut up badly, but they will heal quickly as they always do. Thankfully, Breathers cannot climb *high* distances due to their deformities, but in the back of my mind, I'm still concerned by other species that *can* climb.

Like my own.

Twinkling stars peek through the scattered leaves of the trees' canopy, like a smattering of diamonds hanging delicately from an expanse of obsidian velvet, and a smile graces my face at the little offering of beauty.

"Absolutely breathtaking," I whisper to myself, a habit I need to restrain from, considering any noise can alert predators to my presence.

I'm lonely, and it has been roughly three years since my father was murdered, which means it has been possibly three years since I've had someone to talk to.

The concept of time is vague, and I rely on the change of seasons to keep track of each year, so my estimate of three years may be inaccurate.

My social skills will also be sorely lacking since my father was the only person I constantly conversed with for five and twenty years. If that estimation is correct and he has been dead for three years, then that would make me eight and twenty.

Quietly snorting at the absurd calculation, I nestle further into the foliage. Knowing how old I am is pointless in the given situation. Give me a blade, though, and I will be the most adept fighter anyone has ever witnessed. I do not fancy finding a man to settle down with or to protect me since I've been told they're all pigs in this generation anyway. The few I have encountered throughout my life certainly were. Pa did everything in his power to keep me away from men in general, so I have nothing to compare them to.

Taking a deep breath, I inhale the crisp, clean air of the jungle, relishing the relief it offers my lungs. Wastelands are dry and dusty, wreaking havoc on any survivor's respiratory system.

I focus on sighting the glittering stars above the canopy, cataloguing each cluster of diamonds for directional purposes. My heart constricts at the thought of Pa, teaching me every morsel of knowledge for me to survive. Subconsciously, I reach for the cold pendant hanging around my neck and hold on to it. I would not have made it this far in life if it were not for him.

Those bastards will pay.

My eye twitches, becoming suspiciously prickly at the reminder of the Ruler who murdered him in cold blood. Well, the Hunters murdered Pa on *behalf* of the Ruler, just so they could capture me and drag me back to their walls of Segment Three and demand me to spread my legs for his son to *breed* me.

It tore the very heart from my chest when my father screamed for me to run when they seized him. I was already farther ahead, scavenging for carcasses of dead animals. My uncanny speed was advantageous then, but I knew it meant leaving Pa behind. The guilt of making that split second decision of running will weigh heavily on my conscience until my last dying breath. I had whirled around when hearing my father frantically yelling at me, only to see him struggling in his final moments with two sneering Hunters holding his frame up by a fistful of hair. That last glimpse of the valiant man who raised and protected me will always haunt me, and the image of one of those men violently slicing his throat in a severe, red smile is seared permanently into my mind.

I stifle back a sob at remembering the thick spurt of blood and the beady eyes of the Hunters as they laughed menacingly, letting Pa's limp body drop to the ground with a thud.

My decision to run was made when their malicious focus then drifted to me.

"You are a coward, Rae," I whisper to myself, choking back a cry.

Tears cascade over my cheeks from the memories tormenting me, and the relentless question of whether I could have saved him from those vile human beings storms my conscience. Shame pierces through me, because like a coward, I did not stop running for days and left my father rotting in his own puddle of coagulating blood.

The endless days of tears, sweat, and blistered feet eventually led me to a musky cave high in a large mountain, affording me shelter and protection.

That was roughly three years ago.

I became slack in covering my tracks on outings to hunt for food though, all for the chance of a stray rat or vulture, and Breathers consequently must have discovered the tracks and started stalking me. Which is precisely why I sprinted across a vast, barren wasteland for countless days to land here in this beautifully lush jungle.

My ability to run long distance at uncanny speeds has always baffled me, and Pa never explained it, only saying I'm *special.*

Do other humans have the same ability?

A noisy insect buzzes around my head and I prop up on

my elbows to swat at the creature, irritation bubbling up at its interruptions of my musings. Serenity once again fills my surroundings and I attempt to nestle back down, only to find the new position distractingly uncomfortable.

The various twigs and leaves of my makeshift nest poke me through my thin, deteriorating shirt and I huff my annoyance, turning on my side. My new position provides me a different view of the jungle, the towering height indicating how perilously perched up in the tree I am, with its gnarled branches as the only support for my refuge.

Ignoring the increasing apprehension niggling me, I scan the dark jungle, appreciating the beauty of chaotic vines and leaves sparsely illuminated by thin streams of moonlight filtering through thick vegetation.

Large, fan-like leaves provide little relief from the biting chill of the night's air and I curl into my frame with the efforts of generating more warmth. Exhaustion sweeps over me, and my lids begin to flutter shut, even though I must stay alert. Sleep beckons, and I wearily drift towards it, unable to remain alert after such a harrowing, strenuous journey.

A twig suddenly snapping below, its sharp and distinct sound piercing through the night, has me darting upright with my hand over the hilt of my sword, ready to fight.

I will never rest at this rate!

My annoyance simmers, boiling just below raging point at the constant interruptions. Heat suffuses my cheeks as I narrow my eyes, peering out into the darkness, nostrils flaring with irritation. A metallic taste fills my mouth from painfully biting my tongue to refrain from swearing loudly at the insects. It is imperative to remain quiet.

This temper has always been my worst trait. Pa said I inherited it from my mother, just like my piercing electric-blue eyes, black wavy hair and porcelain skin. Once it was unblemished, but now is peppered with fine, silver scars and a few thicker ones from the hazardous life of surviving in the wild.

My complexion has remained pale, bar a cluster of freckles over my nose. The lack of weathered skin is due to Pa ensuring I was protected from the sun's harsh rays. He fashioned many head coverings over the years, using scraps of discarded material and the flexible stems of plants to effectively rest on my crown and shade my face during the day. Additionally, he had handed down his long-sleeved shirts and pants, once acquiring extra attire, for further protection—but they always engulfed my tiny frame and generally hindered my ability to hunt and defend myself.

They still do.

I shift on my hands and knees to peer over the edge of my makeshift platform, cleverly crafted with fallen branches and long lengths of vine, only to see a clear and peaceful jungle floor.

Hmm. The air seems too still and the animals too quiet.

I stay deathly silent, my ears straining in hopes of hearing any suspicious sounds… but I hear nothing.

"I suppose I'm just being paranoid," I murmur to myself and settle in amongst my foliage.

I'm too exhausted to listen to my instincts, and I speak much too soon. Before I inhale my next breath, a shadow flashes past me, permeating my senses with a scent of something enticingly aromatic. I'm not afforded any moment to regain my bearings and as I turn to follow the shadow, a sharp pain shoots through the back of my head, instantaneously causing my world to fall into utter darkness.

RULE THREE:
LISTEN TO
YOUR INSTINCTS

3

RAE

MY HEAD THROBS AND I OPEN MY GRITTY EYES, wincing at the blinding sun that streams in through the open window. *Wait, window... What!?*

I attempt to bolt up, only to realise my efforts are in vain when noticing my legs and arms are bound. Frantically, I take stock of my surroundings and conclude I have been transported to some sort of house.

Human.

With a strained groan, I twist my neck to peer out the window behind me and am greeted with the familiar greenery of the jungle I was taking refuge in the night prior.

"I should have listened to my instincts," I whimper in regret.

I had felt deep down that something, or rather some*one*, was stalking me.

Fear coils low in my abdomen at the potential scenarios of what might happen to me. My neck strains as I glance down to study my clothed body, the tattered, oversized attire thankfully still covering me and reassuring me that I have not been violated. *Yet.* Steeling myself for whatever I'm to face, I take some deep, calming breaths and start plotting my escape.

And the demise of whoever stole me during the night like a thief.

No one can walk away from laying a hand on me.

The single bed I'm lying on provides me some options, so I roll over with a groan to make my way to the edge. It takes all my strength to roll my body over so that I am precariously perched on the edge of the mattress. The full effects of sprinting for so long is finally taking its toll.

My efforts are still successful though, and I swing my bound legs over the side. Once my feet hit the wooden floor, I push myself to standing, causing my tired thighs to burn with the exertion. I then scan the room for any sharp objects. My heart sinks as I find the room is completely bare, and the door is shut. With an exasperated sigh, I hop over and lift my bound hands in the challenge of opening the doorknob. It does not budge. Of course.

It's locked. I roll my eyes. A second sigh of exasperation leaves my chest and I shuffle around on my feet until I'm able to peruse the entire room from one standpoint.

The bed is adorned with a frilly, yet faded cover—something that would still be classed as a luxury in these times—and the frame itself appears to be a section of a carved tree trunk with its surface stripped back, flattened where the mattress rests. The clever construction fashions a base approximately two metres in length, with two holes on the lower side, perhaps for one's hand to grasp and move the wood. The base is seemingly hollow as the holes enable me to see darkness underneath.

That looks heavy.

The notion of *who* may have constructed the bed causes dread to pool in the pit of my stomach.

Movement of trees waving in the wind outside the window attracts my attention and I shuffle forward to attain a better glimpse. The closer I get, the more I come to realise I'm seeing the tops of trees.

"Oh, we're in a tree house!" I exclaim to myself with surprise, then quickly snap my mouth shut, knowing I should stay quiet. Momentary relief fills me at discerning I'm safely above any Breathers or predators lurking below.

Not safe from this human predator, though.

A delicious scent of savoury meat wafts through the house, causing my mouth to instantly pool with saliva at the savory aroma. My stomach violently protests with a loud rumble.

I have not eaten in several days.

Even though I *have* endured longer without sustenance and am used to long periods without food, I'm simply ravenous. And thirsty. I painfully swallow the dry lump at the thought of clean, cool water trickling down the back of my throat and I silently note to make water my next priority once I escape.

Clean water is another luxury.

What I would give for some food and clean water.

My loud exclamation must have alerted my assailant as the door slowly opens behind me. I whirl around on bound feet with my tied wrists defensively raised in front of me to see a face cautiously peering around the corner.

I almost faint at the sight, but indignation overrides the shock of seeing the rare gender, irritated that I have been taken against my will and by a *woman*, who would have no use for me.

"What do you want with me?" I croak out sharply, my throat

unused to speaking and my social skills poorly lacking. My eyebrows furrow deeply when she does not reply, and the oddity of the situation surfaces once again.

A woman kidnapped me?!

The thought races around my head as we stare at each other. Seeing another woman is rare as the partners they are bound to generally keep them safely locked away.

My gaze skims the unbelievable sight in front of me. Her skin is tanned from countless days in the sun and her features appear exotic. A mass of curly dark hair frames a heart-shaped face with large brown eyes that blink back at me. Her full lips curve into a tentative smile. I stumble back at the sight, my eyes widening at her pointed teeth poking through the deceptively feminine lips. The female notices my apprehension, and quickly shuts her mouth into a tight line.

Since my wrists and ankles are *firmly* tied, I cannot fight her, so I am left with one other choice. To talk.

I have no idea how to start a conversation with a stranger.

"So, uh, do you speak Old-English?" I ask, implementing the old yet common tongue. I'm too curious not to take a chance on conversation and besides, I haven't had company in an excruciating amount of time.

The woman's almond shaped doe-eyes brighten at my question and she opens the door wider to step tentatively in the room. My jaw hits the floor at what her movement reveals.

Tight fitting leather pants, and leather bindings around her forearms. A snug leather vest sits over a loose shirt. *Leather!*

Leather is extremely rare and expensive to trade, but it is also handy when in battle as it provides another layer of protection. My suspicion hits the roof seeing a *woman* in possession of the commodity without any indication of a male partner visible. I narrow my eyes at her, and she sees my change of attitude, quickly deciding to dart back behind the door.

I should be happy she has removed herself from the room since I do not trust her as far as I could throw her, but I'm more curious than wary.

"Wait," I call out to her, my voice only coming out as a hoarse whisper. "I'm just suspicious of any strangers... and you are wearing highly sought-after gear."

My explanation seems to appease her, and she glides back into the room like a panther.

Ah. Perhaps she is a female Hunter. That would explain the leathers. She would have slaughtered an animal for them.

It would also explain why I did not see her when she knocked me out. The thought of a solitary female besting me irks me somewhat, but I push the irritation aside.

As the woman walks in, she surveys my stance dubiously, ascertaining whether I'm a threat or not. This lady, if that is what you can call her, has skills.

"I'm Alayah," her sudden silky voice startles me, forcing my legs to buckle as I heavily sit onto the bed in shock. Luckily, it was directly behind me, otherwise I would have a bruised backside.

I have not heard a voice in three years.

I have not heard a *woman's* voice, apart from my own, my entire life.

The voice is sweet and melodic, like music to my ears, and I'm unable to reply, the words stuck on the tip of my tongue as she intently looks at me, waiting for me to speak.

She probably has not heard a woman's voice in a long time as well. Women are... rare... in these male-dominated times. Only the fittest survive.

My mouth gapes open and shut like a fish gasping for air and she slides down the wall into a seated position, waiting patiently for me to discover my wits.

"I'm Rae," I manage to stammer out.

The smile that illuminates her face is as blinding as the sun, even with her beastly teeth glinting in the light.

"I'm just as shocked to hear a woman's voice as you are," Alayah says with a quiet giggle.

The sound is so foreign to me that I just nod mechanically. I suddenly remember my involuntary situation, causing a frown to tug at my eyebrows, and I pin her with an intimidating stare.

"Why am I here?" I manage to demand the question with an assertive voice.

A soft smile tugs at the corner of her mouth and her dark, golden eyes soften at my change in tone.

"I honestly don't know why I *kept* you," Alayah explains slowly, as if judiciously weighing her words. "I smelt a human, though the scent was different to all the men I have encountered, so I didn't know if you were a threat or not." Her shoulders lift in uncertainty. "That's why I didn't approach you first. And why I tied you up."

My eyes drop to the makeshift rope binding my wrists and ankles and I momentarily appreciate her craftmanship of entertaining vines to create a durable binding. Her reasoning makes sense and I soften slightly... but only slightly, because I still do not trust her.

"I can untie you if you like?" Her voice is uncertain, and I know it is paining her to offer this liberty. "Only if you don't immediately kill me."

I hear the undertones of a *joke* in her words and my mouth twitches.

"Well, I did promise myself I wouldn't let my kidnapper walk away alive," I say light-heartedly in attempt to joke back. I have no idea how to converse, but I obviously say something correct as a smile extends across her face once more and she pulls a dagger from her waist. The movement seems ominous and I reflexively tense at the visual of the deadly sharp blade.

"Relax, I'm just cutting the ropes," Alayah says reassuringly, and somehow, I trust her.

Odd… I have never trusted anyone before — except Pa.

I admire the intricate markings on her blade as she effortlessly slices my bindings and quickly steps back — perhaps in caution — once the last one falls from my wrists.

Rubbing the red marks around my wrists, I stand and stretch out my tight muscles and then sit back down on the mattress, taking advantage of the luxury.

We stare at each other solemnly for a few moments before a hysterical laugh bubbles up within my chest at the absurdity of the situation. The sound echoing throughout the small room is foreign and contagious, instigating Alayah's own laugh as she throws her head back and belts out her own belly wrenching laugh.

Tears continue to stream down our dirty faces, leaving dark, streaky marks as we roll onto our sides, laughing and clutching our aching stomachs. We must look like madwomen, but the relief of having another woman's company is overwhelming for both of us. I guess my father's fourth rule to survival in this desolate world is why we are both in hysterics right now.

Rule Four:
Rely Only
On Yourself

4

RAE

IT IS UTTERLY BIZARRE being in the company of another person, particularly a woman. Humans are taught from the moment we can walk to only rely on ourselves for survival. Most survivors will live out their short lives as hermits, with only their thoughts as the sole company to keep them sane through the long and lonely nights.

Safety does not derive from numbers in this world. The more people there are in a group, the higher the chance of Breathers tracking their movements. Hunters are different as they possess sheer power and weaponry to demolish any Breathers who cross their paths, thanks to the advocacy and aid from the Segment they work for. Segments are afforded with the protection of impenetrable walls, so their numbers do not matter.

Us lowly outsiders rely on independence to survive.

This is the precise reason why Alayah and I are currently in hysterics.

"I cannot remember the last time I laughed," I wheeze out as we both slowly calm down.

"I don't think I've *ever* laughed," Alayah adds and my heart squeezes at her confession. Her story will be just as, if not more, heart-wrenching than my own.

We sit in silence for a few moments, both of us enjoying the presence of another human being—of another woman. I assess Alayah's lean muscle mass and my curiosity gets the better of me.

"How did you lug me down from the tree I was in then up here?"

Alayah's eyes glow with pride and excitement as she stands up and gestures for me to follow her outside the room.

I'm momentarily dazed and in awe of the spacious construction of her private sanctuary when I follow her from the room. The bedroom leads out to an opening on a deck-like structure that surrounds the house, with the roughly crafted wooden planks weaving in between large branches. Clay, rubber, and stone fill the gaps that any of the obscure planks have created, reinforcing the overall structure of the flooring. The edges of the decking have sturdy logs placed intermittently around the border and thick vines have been tied horizontally in the same fashion, creating a fence-like barrier. The same materials have also been used within the house to fill in the gaps, forming a sturdy, fortified wall around the perimeter. Each space of the flooring has been effectively segmented into uses; a flat plank of wood and simple rough cupboard has been fashioned to create a kitchen bench for preparing and storing food. A makeshift pulley with a bucket attached hangs loosely to a vine in order to lug water up and down the tree.

Water!

I swallow the dry lump down my throat and wait patiently for the impending liquid gold I know I will eventually guzzle down.

"Here, you will need this for the onslaught of bugs," Alayah says.

My forehead crumples with confusion as I look down at her outstretched hand, offering a handful of long, bladed grass. She gestures the length of me at seeing my uncertainty and elaborates. "It secretes an oil that repels mosquitoes, so you might want to rub it over your skin. Every time we go to the ground, we will collect more."

My fingers twitch happily at the reprieve she offers. "Ah, thank you," I gratefully say, grasping the handful and rubbing it over my already assaulted, hived skin. The rough motion relieves the insistent itchiness bothering me, satisfaction rising as my movements become more urgent.

After covering myself with the scented plant, I hand her the now wilted remains, which she discards, and I resume admiring her dwelling.

I crane my neck to see an opening in the roof above with a clay and stone cylinder leading up and out of the ceiling void. Below it lies a simple structure that holds remnants of ash and coal which has also been created using the same materials as the cylinder. A woosh of air leaves me in amazement as my mouth drops upon realising its use.

That is incredible!

It is a fireplace to sterilise water, cook food, and keep warm on freezing nights.

I look at Alayah with newfound respect at her innovative abilities and smile widely with appreciation at her luxurious home.

"This is amazing," I reverently say, and she gushes with

pride. "Do you not worry the smoke from your fire might alert unwelcome visitors though?"

"I have created a filter with multiple leaves that disperses the smoke in smaller puffs, so a large billowing cloud doesn't signal my location."

"That is brilliant," I laugh before pointedly staring at her. "It still doesn't explain how you managed to lug me up here though." Alayah's eyes brighten and she gestures for me to follow her to a hatch-like section crafted into the floor.

"This is how I hauled you up," she explains, gesturing at the pulley system before reaching up to pull on a wooden lever crafted from a small branch. The thick, plaited vines creak and groan, and the hatch we are standing on lurches and starts slowly descending. I glance at the vines holding onto the four corners of the platform we are on and realise how sturdy the whole construction is. A laugh bursts out of me and a dorky smile expands across my face as I turn to Alayah. "You're ingenious."

My words light up her face and she shyly looks at the ground. "Thank you, Rae."

We both share the rare moment of forming a silent bond before Alayah looks up and gestures to the platform. "I use this for when I need to carry up larger items, like a dead animal or stones. Or in this case—you."

I nod in understanding then gaze in awe at our surroundings, taking in the captivating beauty of life flourishing around us. My balance slightly hitches when Alayah pulls the lever and we start ascending slowly.

We are suspended at least fifteen meters in the air, and though I'm not terrified of heights, I have never been comfortable with them. The view surrounding us is enough to settle my nerves and

I rotate in a circle to continue absorbing the breathtaking sight of the jungle canopy.

"You can see the ridges in the tree that I use to climb up to the house," Alayah points out, breaking through my wonderment. I look closely at the tree we are slowly ascending next to and see the most subtle handmade grooves chipped out of its trunk, creating a hidden ladder up to her home. The grooves lead into the bottom of the hut's flooring, to a hatch door that opens with a flick of a latch.

"All of this is the most innovative engineering I've ever seen," I say with amazement, and a blush tinges Alayah's olive, high cheek bones.

With better visibility outside, I'm able to study my captor-turned-companion more thoroughly. Her stature is tall and solid, built for hunting in this environment, and it hits me that this jungle is probably the home of her ancestors, explaining the exotic look of her appearance. The origin of her sharpened teeth is still questionable.

"Thank you."

I meet Alayah's eyes with surprise, baffled for the second time that she has used good manners, a social etiquette that is rare in these bleak times. A smooth, honeyed laugh escapes her lips and I raise my eyebrow in question. "What?"

"Nothing," she chuckles. "It is ridiculously bizarre using manners after so long."

I'm surprised we are using them at all considering the current world we reside in but smile and nod in agreeance just as we enter the opening of the tree-hut floor.

"So, now that you see I'm not a threat, or a man," I direct at Alayah and her expression becomes curious, "what will you do with me?"

The question stuns her momentarily and she just stares at me with her mouth agape.

"What do you mean?" Her face fills with confusion.

"Well, will you imprison me, kill me, or kick me out?" I doubt I need worry about the first two options, but one can never be too sure.

"I just found you!" she exclaims in disbelief. "Why on earth would I get rid of you?"

"Oh." That answers my concern. "Well, I'm used to being solitary, much like other survivors. We only ever rely on ourselves and seldom make connections or relationships other than with our own kin if they're still alive."

Alayah's expression turns to one of understanding and she nods in agreeance. "Yes, it is less complicated having only one's self to reply on."

I nod, pleased she unknowingly abides by the rules my own family established over many generations. Even though the rules I live by are not openly known, Pa had mentioned many survivors would be implementing them in their own lives to some extent, seeing as they are mostly common sense.

"Well, as much as being solitary is effective in our survival, don't you feel there should be more to life than a lonely existence?"

Her quiet words punch through my chest, resounding so deeply within my own subconscious that my eyes start to feel suspiciously itchy and hot.

I'm sick of being alone, and even when Pa was alive, we lived a lonely existence.

Something deep in the recesses of my mind hovers at the edge of my awareness—a feeling that reassures me that life has more purpose than just surviving day to day. Alayah must feel the same.

"I agree." My words act as a truce; a silent communication that forms an instantaneous bond between two humans. We are essentially breaking the fourth rule that has been hounded into my mind growing up.

It does not escape my notice that we are forming more than just an alliance as some survivors may do to benefit themselves. We are forming a *friendship*. The notion is such a foreign concept to me, and a hot tear scalds my skin as it rolls down my cheek, my eyes overflowing with the relief of finding *someone*. That mere morsel of hope flickers like a beacon through the dismal darkness that has blanketed the face of the earth.

Alayah's own eyes overflow with the same salty emission, and she hesitantly walks towards me with her arms stretched out, the stance familiar to my Pa's own rare embraces. I nod once and we collapse, clutching each other tightly. The need for human contact is too unbearable. Compelling sensations expand the cavity in my chest at experiencing the touch of another human. I know Alayah feels the same.

The sounds of our sobs break through the silent jungle air as we cry in consolation from the discovery of something so precious.

Sorry for breaking Rule Four, Pa, but I need this more than you will ever know.

We both sit in silence for hours, holding each other tightly as we make up for lost years of physical affection and mere human contact. Darkness blankets the jungle around us, and we reluctantly break apart, rubbing our puffy, dry eyes as we do so.

My vision adjusts to the absence of light, as if a switch has turned on, and I bask in our tranquil surroundings, appreciating the sounds of the jungle coming to life as animals begin their journey for food. My stomach grumbles at the reminder of sustenance and Alayah's dark eyes glint with humour at the sound. "Lucky for you, I only went hunting yesterday."

My body rejoices at the news of much needed fuel, my mouth watering at the idea of meat, and I send back my own toothy smile. My grin falters as I see Alayah's wide smile, the length and sharpness of her teeth glistening in the moonlight. I remind myself that she is not a Breather. No, their teeth are much more frightening.

I need to ask her about the teeth.

Any notions of proper conversational etiquette no longer matter in this Vanquished civilisation, so I'm not worried about offending her.

Rule Five:
Eat in
Moderation

5

Rae

MY EYES BULGE when Alayah pulls a large chunk of steamy, dripping meat from the dilapidated pan resting over the dying embers of the stove's fire, and she glances over with a wide smile. "Tapir."

As if that explains anything.

"I had to cut it into smaller chunks, otherwise there was no possibility of hoisting it up here since my elevator would not be able to handle the weight. Because I have no way of preserving my leftovers, I discard most of the meat, otherwise it would rot, and if I left it laying around, the smell would attract unwelcome predators." Alayah must notice my blank face and deduce it is regarding the animal itself, so she quickly adds, "Sorry, the tapir is quite a large pig-like animal."

Searching my memories of Pa's overt lessons regarding edible animals, I fail to recall him mentioning such a creature and I remain staring at Alayah vacantly. Sensing my confusion, she runs to her room, bringing back a sketch of a weird looking hog with a narrow snout. It is quite cute, and I *almost* feel terrible eating the creature. Almost, but not quite since my self-preservation is paramount over any sentiments.

"That's a really good drawing," I point out, and Alayah blushes.

"I have a lot of time to pass, so I keep myself occupied with drawing when I'm not hunting, using dye from fruits and plants for the colour and charcoal for the outline."

"Well, you are clearly talented either way," I tell her and she smiles in return. "So, this is what we're about to eat?"

Alayah nods in confirmation. "Yes, it is a large mammal native to South America, or to what South America would have been prior to The Vanquishing. We are in the Amazon—what is left of it."

"You're Amazonian?" That explains her strong frame.

"Mm-hmm," Alayah hums affirmatively through a mouthful of meat.

I take the piece she offers to me and bite into the juicy and tender slab, moaning in pleasure at the bursts of robust flavours dancing across my tongue. I know to savour this tasty morsel due to Rule Five.

Eat in moderation.

Unfortunately, an apocalypse not only wipes out the land's apex predator on the food chain—humans—but because of the decrease in overall human activity, other predators become more prominent. Therefore, the rise of those remaining predators has caused a rapid decrease of animals we humans survive on—such as the Tapir, the population dwindling to the point of extinction. Pa had mentioned when we stopped seeing a certain species, generally that meant it was threatened or had become entirely extinct.

I wipe the juice trickling down my chin, silently hoping this delectable creature never reaches that point, and continue my reflections.

Not only do humans need to fight each other for food now, but we also compete against animal predators. So, in order to stretch out our resources, we eat in moderation, ration our food and only eat when necessary. Like when our bodies need to heal, or we become sick. Or when we are close to starving to death, though it seems life near a jungle such as this one proves more abundant than the desolate land Pa and I roamed, for there is ample fruit and edible vegetation here one could exist on. But otherwise, survivors inadvertently follow Rule Five... unlike the privileged of Segmented cities who tend to eat whenever and whatever they want.

Gluttony is high up there amongst greed as Pa told me repeatedly, and if his assumption that most cities were erected near flourishing forests for their source of food or water is correct, then that would mean there is likely a Segment not far from this jungle's border.

Meaty juice streams down my arms as I slowly chew and savour the hunk of delicious meat.

The fact that Alayah is sharing her *livelihood* with me resonates deep within my soul. Kindness is rare and I have only ever experienced it from Pa when he was alive.

"Thank you for sharing this with me," I tell Alayah, and she smiles brightly, her joyous expression quickly becoming my favourite visual.

"Think of it as my contribution in trade for your companionship and company."

"Deal."

We finish our small morsel of stewed meat and Alayah takes a handmade bowl carved from wood, dipping it into the bucket hanging by the vine. Without any hesitation of parting with the precious commodity, she offers me a drink and I almost cry at the prospect of hydrating myself.

"Thank you, Alayah." I grasp the bowl and take tentative sips, moaning at the cool, clean water gliding down my parched throat. Tipping my head back, I gulp the remainder of the water down, careful not to spill any precious drops, then hand the empty bowl back to Alayah who takes it and fills it with more water for herself.

"Help yourself whenever you're thirsty," Alayah says, and I gawp at her. There must be a supply of water nearby for her to offer unlimited access to the liquid gold. Her sharp gaze sees my blatant astonishment and she offers further explanation. "There's a stream not too far from here that runs from the mountain— it's perfectly safe and has been untainted for some time by the radiation that spread all those centuries ago. And it rains a lot here, so we also have access to fresh water."

My eyes widen at the rare gift of running, clean water. It explains her cleanliness and hygienic state. I must smell a fright compared to her and I lift my arm to take a whiff, retching at the sweaty odour emanating from my armpit.

Alayah chuckles at my reaction. "Well, I wasn't going to mention it," she says teasingly, "but you're welcome to wash yourself with the water that's stored up here. I try and wash once a week."

Once a week.

I almost faint at the idea of such indulgence.

"Wow, yes, I might bathe *now* so I don't subject you to any further violation of your nose."

"Yes, please do," Alayah laughs. "I will set up the tub I carved from a fallen tree."

My curiosity peaks at her words and I follow her back into the bedroom, wondering what tub she is talking about considering I did not see one when I first woke in the sparse bedroom. I tilt my head when she pulls the bedding off the bed base, knowing whatever is revealed will once again amaze me. Her innovative mind never ceases to astound me.

Effortlessly, Alayah drags the bed base out and then crouches down to grip the holes situated on the side.

My assumption about the holes' use was right.

But when she lifts the entire thing and flips it over without breaking a sweat, my heart accelerates, and I instantaneously realise she must have a special ability much like my own. *Strength?*

Alayah senses my observation and freezes, wary as to what my reaction might be to her slip of displaying a constantly hidden trait.

"I have uncanny speed if that makes you feel more comfortable with me knowing," I gently tell her, and she visibly relaxes.

"My mother always told me to never let anyone see, otherwise they would use me for their own gain. Or kill me if I was a threat to them."

I nod in understanding, relating to her caution. "My Pa was the same for me. I was only to use my speed in a life-or-death situation."

We smile at each other, our similar abilities bonding us even further, strengthening the connection we recently forged.

My gaze drops to the underside of the beautiful piece of wood, carved out and hollowed like I had originally suspected, enabling a volume of shallow water to fill the base. Rubber and clay have been smoothed over every inch of its surface to provide protection from moisture seeping in, which would have caused the wood to rot over time.

"Wow," I whisper with awe. I've never seen something of its like before.

I have not bathed in a long time and the only time I washed was when I resided near an ocean, though salty water does not prove to be sufficient to wash with.

"If you don't mind the cold water, we will pull the covering off that bamboo over there and fresh water will flow from the rain tank on the roof."

My wide eyes dart up at Alayah in pleasant surprise. "Rain tank? As in fresh rainwater?"

"Yeah." Alayah's toothy smile sparkles in the dark once again and I refrain from letting a happy squeal burst from my mouth; a foreign feeling that I have only ever experienced as a little girl.

I remain silent and observe as Alayah moves the wooden tub towards the corner of the wall where bamboo vertically hangs from the roof. Clay and rubber seals the gaps where it protrudes from the ceiling, likely connecting to the rain tank above.

Once the bamboo is positioned so its tip rests inside the tub, Alayah removes the animal skin tied to the end with some smaller bindings. Crystal clear water immediately flows into the wooden base and I laugh with glee at the simple luxury, only stopping when concerned thoughts dance in my foremind.

"You aren't using all your water supply on my bath, are you?"

I ask her, a frown marring my face. "You've already done so much and shared your sustenance with me."

Alayah's razor-sharp teeth appear as she smiles broadly at me and shakes her head. "Not at all. The rains here are constant and almost too much at times, so there will always be plenty of water. And if it ever did run out—which it won't—then we can just get more from the stream."

"I still find it odd that the water source has been untainted by the radiation for some time, not that I am complaining since you have just made me the happiest woman on Earth."

Alayah chuckles and clasps her hands together, pleased at my reaction, then she covers the hollow bamboo to stop the water flowing out. "I assume it's because it has been centuries since the original fallout, so the radiation that dispersed through the atmosphere at the time, plaguing the lands, has slowly diminished over time. This jungle—though now much smaller than it was hundreds of years ago—is only standing because this part of the area was not targeted by the nuclear missiles. Well, from what my mother told me as a child, anyway."

"Ah, that makes sense," I say, her mention of a mother causing slight curiosity to rise, though I do not pry and continue theorising with her. "The wastelands must have been where the missiles hit, explaining the lack of water and life in those areas. So, you are saying the radiation eventually vanishes over time?"

"Yes, well, that is what we learnt growing up in this area. It takes hundreds and even thousands of centuries for it to completely dissipate. The world we live in today is slowly healing, but for the most part, radiation is much less, if existent at all in some areas. I do remember my mother mentioning this jungle was much larger prior to the fallout—stories of its previous magnificence were passed down through our family's generations. It seems, even though this area was not directly hit, the radiation that may have spread over the atmosphere still impacted the vegetation and life here."

Sadness flickers in her eyes at the mention of her mother again, though she quickly forces a smile and gestures to the half-filled tub. "What are you waiting for?"

Coercing my inquisitiveness aside, a foreign squeal manages to escape me—my toes curling with anticipation at the impending luxury. The forlorn ambiance from Alayah's story dissipates as we strip our dirty, tattered clothes off until we are standing bare. Bumps litter my skin from the chill of the cool night air and a shiver racks my frame. Modesty is irrelevant and neither of us are uncomfortable by our naked states as we confidently stand before each other.

I look to Alayah who gives me the thumbs up and steps in the shin-deep water, her long limbs folding into a cross legged state, enabling me to sit at the other end. The iciness is refreshing, and I sigh as my weary muscles relax into the blissfully cool liquid, already feeling the weeks' worth of thick grime peeling off me.

"You can use these leaves to wash the dirt and odour away," Alayah says as she hands me a bunch of sticky, aromatic leaves. I recognise the sweet fragrance and realise the familiar scent is what assailed my senses before she knocked me out the night prior.

"Thank you," I reply, and rub the slimy leaves over my soaking body, instantly feeling revitalised.

Alayah uncrosses her long legs and places them either side of me, bending her knees as she slides down until her head is submerged. I watch inquisitively as she emerges and rubs the leaves through her dripping hair that is no longer curly from the weight of the water. Alayah then repeats the submerging motion to wash any remaining grime out.

Once she comes back up, I copy her routine, sliding down until my legs have encircled her sides and my head is submerged. When I rise, I rub the leaves through my tangled wet hair and then repeat the motion, washing out the residue. The aromatic slime acts as a conditioner and I'm able to comb my fingers through the tangles as I rinse for the last time.

My torn feet sting from the open cuts I endured on the sprint across the wasteland, but I know how beneficial it is for them to be cleaned in such a thorough manner.

We sit for a few moments in the tub and continue chatting like old friends.

"So, are your teeth naturally pointy?" I ask, curiosity getting the better of me. Pa always said my curiosity would end up being the death of me, but so far, I'm still alive.

Alayah seems unphased by my blunt question and ponders her answer before answering quietly.

"My mother sharpened them for me when I was little, once my adult teeth came through."

I nod at her morsel of information and wait silently as Alayah sombrely plays with the water around her, reminiscing on her lost loved ones.

"We were constantly on the move, hiding from the hordes of Hunters that would plague the forest. They were always in search of females who would be sold to the highest bidder for breeding. Mother always said; *'your bite should be worse than your bark. It will be what saves you in a time of desperation.'*"

Apprehension fills my spine at the ominous undertones of Alayah's story. Something awful clearly happened here.

Alayah sighs wearily, a vast contrast to her usually bright demeanour, and continues her story. "I remember the fear in her eyes when she first saw the Hunters close in on us. I think she knew they would dispose of her since she was past the prime of bearing children and she knew once they did, she wouldn't be able to protect me."

I lean over and squeeze Alayah's shoulder in comfort, and she smiles weakly at me in gratitude, my gesture giving her the strength to continue.

"Mother said, '*If they get a hold of you, tear out their throats and don't let them live to see another day.*'" An angry tear trickles down her face as her expression turns deadly.

"She hid me in the base of a hollow tree and started running to lure them away, but they caught her within seconds, and I saw... *everything.*"

Alayah expels a rough, shuddering breath and a chill races over my skin at the sinister denotation behind that one word. Horrifying events have always happened regularly during and after The Vanquishing, but that does not make it any more normal or endurable for a little girl to witness.

"From where Ma hid me, I could peek through the gaps of the high tree roots and see the men wearing gas masks throw her to the ground, tearing her clothes from her body simultaneously. They were yelling at her, asking her where I was. If they were tracking us, they would have seen evidence of a little girl on the run with her. Every time Ma denied my existence, the four of them would hit and kick her concurrently, and I just remember Ma lying naked on her side—looking at me through the gaps of my cover within the tree roots, with pleading, swollen eyes. Silently begging for me to stay hidden." Her teary gaze drops to the floor and her voice drops to a mere whisper.

"They broke every bone in her body, but she still didn't give me up. And then, they all forced themselves on her, one by one. Brutally and violently. There was so much blood—" Alayah's words are cut off by a harsh sob and her body shudders in the moonlight as she suppresses her mournful cries, "—I couldn't help the scream that tore from my mouth when they started cutting her limbs off in front of me. I think she was well past dead at that point, but my twelve-year-old mind could not comprehend that. I realised my mistake when they turned at the sound of my scream and left Ma, limp, broken, and scattered across the ground. I had not used my strength at this point of my life, but the anger and fear that surged through my veins pulled the ability from its hibernation. When the Hunters easily tracked me and found me in the base of a tree, their arrogance and underestimation of the small girl before them was their first mistake."

Alayah's voice gains a determined and formidable strength as she progresses, no longer wallowing in the grief of her mother, but filling with a quiet rage. I intently watch a range of emotions flash across her face as she continues, her body seething with the internal wrath against these bastards.

"The four men surrounded the tree, and one of them dragged me kicking and screaming. I hadn't thought to implement my sharpened teeth just yet, but as soon as I was out in the open, this haze of red fell over me—it's hard to explain—as if it were inhuman. Something awoke inside of me when that man laid his hand on me, unleashing this inner beast that I had no control over. I don't remember a thing after that. When I woke up the next day, there were male body parts surrounding me, their throats and internal organs scattered over the bloodied jungle floor—I couldn't even salvage their gas masks. I was drenched in blood, head to toe, and could taste the metallic hint of it on my tongue. I will never forget that rancid taste."

Alayah falls silent as she reminisces on the morbid memory and I remain quiet, my own heart heavily weighed down with the hurt and anger I feel on behalf of her injustice.

Her eyes meet mine, and I return her determined gaze, full of resolve.

"I want them to all die. Every. Single. Hunter." Her words are like a balm to my soul and I nod once in finality.

The memory of Pa grasping his severed throat fills me with renewed vengeance and I reply vehemently. "Yes. They will all die."

Rule Six:
Knowledge is
Powerful

6

Rae

WE MAKE A SILENT PACT to kill every Hunter; to take from them what they took from us.

Maybe this is the purpose I felt I had. Maybe this is my reason for surviving, for living.

Alayah rises from the tub and shakes the residual water from her body, much like an animal would. I stand and do the same, feeling stripped to my soul, but a sense of peace descends over me in conjunction with my cleanliness. The serene feeling overrides the strange sensation of my lack of grime. This must be what the privileged humans of Segmented cities feel like permanently.

We will tear them all down.

One by one. Taking out their Hunters will be priority, their first defence. Pa always said most cities rely on Hunters for food and new supplies since they are too lazy to do it themselves— paying them for their services with items such as gas masks and weapons.

Eliminating the Hunters from the equation will ensure the

corresponding Segments will be void of regular resources.

"We must rest, train, and gain our strength before we take on groups of men," Alayah says, her mandate pulling me from my musings.

I murmur my agreeance, watching her as she effortlessly tips the tub over in a corner where rubber has been smeared across the floor to provide a drainage system. The hollow ends of various bamboo pokes up through the floor of the sealed corner, allowing the water to drain out from under the hut. I shake my head at her ingeniousness again—I must have been too preoccupied from the stress being kidnapped when I first woke to even notice it.

Alayah makes her way through the room, returning the bath back into its bed-base form. "Let's rest for the night, we are safe up here to sleep for a few hours."

"Oh, I thought the Breathers sensed us more strongly when we slept?"

"They do, but not when we're this high up," Alayah reassures me, and once again I'm astounded by how different her life is to mine.

"Well, I suppose I will attempt to sleep but I'm not sure how I will fare since I've never actually slept during the night."

Alayah laughs at my comment. "You will grow accustomed to it, but perhaps just concentrate on your breathing first. Deep breath in and count to seven while you hold, then exhale for seven counts. Hold your breath for four counts and exhale for four counts then repeat the whole process. I promise your eyes will feel heavy after a few minutes."

"Oh, thank you... I will try that. Where did you learn that trick?" I ask Alayah curiously.

"Ma."

The painful silence after her sad answer squeezes my heart and I'm overcome with the emotions of Alayah's palpable grief at the reminder of the horrors her mother endured at the hands of Hunters.

"We will kill them all, Alayah," I reassure her quietly and step forward to pull her into a tight embrace. "All of them." But even as I say the words, I cannot help the niggling feeling clawing at my chest at the idea of slaughtering humans, even if they are evil. My brows furrow and I push the unsettling feeling deep down.

After we both squeeze into Alayah's bed—with me at one end and her at the other—I attempt her breathing technique and am amazed at the sudden lethargy that settles over me like a weighted blanket. I feel a gentle squeeze on my leg and smile, squeezing Alayah's leg in return. The gesture comforts me strangely; perhaps because of the reassurance of another soul being present, and I'm able to fall into a deep, blissful sleep. It is something I have not done since my Pa died, as he was the allocated watch whenever I did sleep during the day.

The calls of early rising birds and animals rouse us both from sleep and we sit up, simultaneously stretching our arms above our heads. I smile sleepily at Alayah who returns a bright smile. Her pointed teeth are no longer disconcerting now I know the story behind them, alongside the knowledge that they saved her life.

"Good morning, sleepy-head," Alayah says, her voice laced with mirth.

"Hey, be nice," I playfully remark back. "I'm still adapting to this whole night-sleeping business. It makes me feel unusually tired."

Strange, since I thought I would feel more energetic after a long sleep.

"Oh, it's just your body telling you that you slept *too* much, but it doesn't know any better—once you have a few weeks of sleeping several hours a night, you won't ever want to go back!"

I laugh at the absurdity of how different my life is now. All thanks to the horde of Breathers chasing me across the wasteland.

"So, have you ever encountered any more Hunters? Or seen the Segment where the privileged citizens live?"

I heard many stories growing up, of the Segments and their unlimited food, water, electricity—something I've yet to encounter in my lifetime—and many other luxuries most outsiders could not even begin to comprehend.

"I have encountered other Hunters," Alayah says, her expression darkening. "But they didn't see me when they passed through. I thought of trying to wipe them out, but there were so many of them and I didn't want to risk any taking me."

I nod in agreeance with her sensible decision at the time.

"I have also seen a Segment up close when I was much younger. Ma made me study it back in the day when the security was not as prominent. From what I recall, the city borders the edge of this jungle, though is still a fair trek away... I prefer to keep my distance from it though, so haven't made any attempt to find it again."

This piques my interest. Knowledge can be a powerful tool. Which is the Sixth rule.

Knowledge. Is. Powerful.

"This is perfect, Alayah!" I exclaim, and confusion falls across her face.

"Why? It's been so long that most of my knowledge isn't current anymore."

"Bah, don't be pessimistic. This is my father's Rule Six! *Any* knowledge is powerful. So, *any* knowledge is better than *no* knowledge. We can use it to our advantage. Maybe we could catch a Hunter and torture him for information, providing you don't think the noise would reveal this location."

That unsettling feeling rises in my chest again at suggesting such a violent act, but I once again suppress it by reassuring myself.

No. These Hunters deserve *to die.*

Alayah's expression becomes thoughtful and she nods as she slowly comes to agree with my reasoning. "Yes, that is perfect, though it may be a good idea to find somewhere secure to torture him, like a cave in the mountains upstream. Like you say, it would draw attention to our location if we did it here. My strength will be convenient since I would have to carry him up there."

"How often do Hunters pass below you?" My question gives Alayah pause and her eyes squint as she calculates the last sighting.

"Probably a few weeks ago. One Hunter went past, which is strange as they are usually in packs. Then perhaps a month prior to that, a full group passed through, though they looked different to the usual Hunters I have seen... less savage."

"Mm, well I suppose that gives us time to train and prepare," I say thoughtfully. "Do you think we could manage to snatch one without the others noticing until it's too late?"

"Maybe," Alayah replies slowly. "Only if we're careful enough."

"This will be good for us. We can both take back a life from those that took from us."

"Yes!" Alayah yells, raising her fist in the air.

I chuckle. "We should probably be quiet if we don't want to attract unwanted attention."

Alayah laughs and we listen to the echo of our promise reverberating through the peaceful treetops. "I never thought of having to be quiet before. I did not have reason to since I've been by myself for so long. I suppose being alone means you're silent normally, as you were probably trained to be."

"Well, I suppose being noisy is one way to attract the Hunters sooner," I playfully say, then suddenly pause with a gasp, realising it is a valid idea. "That might work actually." Alayah leans forward, studiously listening as I continue, "And making noise during the day won't matter since Breathers hunt predominantly at night."

Alayah twirls a strand of her hair around one finger as she ponders the suggestion. "It is risky, but would be worth the chance if it were successful. We could set up traps to kill them without us lifting a finger or alerting them to where our base is."

Exhilaration fills me at the prospect of our plan, though a strange disquiet unfurls deep within my abdomen once again. I remind myself that all Hunters deserve to die, regardless of who they are, and force a smile up at Alayah. "Yes, perfect. Where do we start?"

Alayah taps her chin thoughtfully. "Well, I need to show you the area first, so you become familiar with it and don't ever lose your way. It is your home now, so knowing your surroundings is pretty important."

I nod, my chest expanding at the mention of a *home,* then follow her to our room. Pulling on my tattered clothes and adorning my sword, once again admiring Alayah's weapon as she slides the dagger into its sheath overtop her leathers.

We make our way to the exit where Alayah opens the hatch door.

"What better time than now?" Alayah says gleefully, starting the deathly descent down the tall tree.

I peer over and look down through the hatch. My stomach drops at the sheer magnitude of what I'm about to do and a sweaty sheen breaks out over my skin.

"Here goes nothing," I mutter and force myself to turn around, placing my first foot in the hand-carved groove. The excitement of being shown the residence originally must have distracted me from the sheer height as now my heart is pounding erratically against my chest, though I suppose descending on a platform is somewhat different to climbing down.

The grooves are large enough to slide a foot in yet small enough to create a snug fit for extra security, and I loudly exhale with relief, cautiously continuing my descent.

Alayah has already monkeyed her way down, swift and graceful, and I glance down to see the reduced version of her form, waiting patiently at the base of the tree.

"I really need to practice this so I'm faster," I mutter to myself.

Particularly if we encounter a life-or-death situation.

After a few painstaking minutes, I descend the last leg of the tree's thick base and leap onto the ground next to Alayah.

"That was *not* enjoyable," I whisper to her, my hands shaking, and she laughs quietly with twinkling eyes.

"You will get used to it," Alayah whispers back. "As you can see, the last two metres don't have the carved ridges and you will need to use the few knots in the tree to make your way up."

I turn to see her pointing at the tree's natural gnarls protruding in various places.

"It's to ensure Hunters don't notice anything out of the ordinary when they pass through here. Thankfully, there is a fair amount of foliage at the base here so it covers any traces of our coming and going, but we will need to cover our tracks from here on out."

I snap off a wiry branch from a nearby shrub to use as a rake and lift it up in question. Alayah nods keenly at my idea of covering our footsteps as we go. I attach it behind me, so it hangs down while we are walking, and Alayah stays in front for my process to work on her footsteps as well.

"Let's cover our feet with skins so if we happen to miss covering any tracks, the Hunters can't tell if the prints are human or, more importantly, female," Alayah whispers, pulling out some leather skins from the band around her waist. "It will also protect your poor, battered feet from infection."

"Okay, thank you," I whisper back and take two skins along with some bindings from her.

We hastily cover our feet with makeshift shoes and I look to Alayah for further instruction.

"We have to be extremely aware of our surroundings," Alayah whispers and I nod, agreeing with her unknowing citation of Rule Seven.

Alayah pulls back the thick foliage and we start our journey into the thick of the jungle. One of my hands constantly rests over the cold, metal hilt of my sword, its presence comforting me on this risky venture.

RULE SEVEN:
BE AWARE OF
YOUR SURROUNDINGS

7

RAE

AS WE MAKE OUR WAY THROUGH THE DENSE UNDERGROWTH, my eyes attentively dart around, looking for any possible threats and additionally cataloguing each plant, tree and land marker. It is not long before I hear the trickling of running water and smell the sweet scent of blossoming flowers and thriving greenery.

A smile stretches across my face at the fresh air and I inhale deeply, absorbing as much of the jungle's essence as I can. My previous dwelling consisted of a damp, musty cave by the salty oceanside and my hunting ground was sparse wilderness beside the barren wasteland, so this is a pleasant change.

Alayah swiftly makes her way through the thick foliage and leads me to a wide opening, though we remain cautiously hidden amongst the tall plants and their umbrella-like leaves. My mouth drops at the scenery before me and I inhale sharply at the vision of crystal-clear water bubbling over large rocks, making its way into a ravine down farther.

A colourful abundance of fruit and flowers protrude from the river's edge, decorating the dark green backdrop with bright specks of reds, yellows, and oranges. Alayah enables me to absorb the beautiful sight momentarily before resting her hand softly on my shoulder to grasp my attention. I glance sideways at her, still dazed from the profound awe washing over me as we communicate silently with our eyes and hands. Alayah gestures to a small sack around her waist and then to the succulent looking fruit.

We are going to collect some food.

My mouth instantly waters at the prospect of eating such juicy, colourful delicacies that could only cause bursts of sweet flavours to dance across my tastebuds. They are similar to the fruits Pa sometimes brought back from his foraging trips throughout my childhood, though these ones appear much plumper.

We spend a few minutes darting out from our protection and grabbing handfuls of fruit, each of us taking turns to keep watch of our surroundings. Five minutes pass and I watch as Alayah darts out to grab a branch consisting of juicy, deep red berries, when I hear a twig cracking not too far from us. My head snaps around frantically, searching for a visual as to what created the sound, but fail to see anything.

I wave urgently at Alayah, signalling we need to make haste and get out of here and her eyes widen with fear as she scurries back over to me. We stand deathly still with our backs against each other, hands over weapons, straining our ears in hopes of ascertaining what may be nearby.

Both Alayah and I are implementing Rule Seven. Be aware of your surroundings.

Neither of us speak as we silently conclude the creature

making the noise must have passed through, so we start hastily retreating to the tree-hut.

Shit-fuck-shit!

I rarely curse as Pa bestowed me with courteous manners for some unknown reason—seeing as we never conversed with people for it to be useful—and an extensive vocabulary to replace the colourful words. Even without any lessons on reading and writing, my knowledge of many subjects is considerable. He said that words and knowledge are just as powerful as one's weapon. Though, right now, words will be disadvantageous.

Adrenaline surges through my veins like raging lava and my heart beats erratically against my chest. In our haste of retreating, the makeshift rake pulls free from my waist, but we have no time to stop and reattach it. The coverings on our feet will hopefully deter any Hunters on the prowl for humans since our footprints will be obscured by the reduced imprint of our toes and soles.

"Let's imitate the gait of an animal, so try to keep your steps synchronised with mine," Alayah urgently whispers.

"Okay," I reply quietly.

We remain close together and our two sets of legs scurry, almost graceful as we find our rhythm to create the illusion of a four-legged animal. Covering a vast amount of ground with the fear of any lurking creatures, it is not long until we see our ancient tree looming in the distance.

Almost there!

I keep my eyes peeled on my peripheral in case there are any unsuspecting animals lurking in the thick undergrowth around us, but the greenery is deathly still from the lack of breeze. The air is thick and damp with humidity, causing a layer of beaded condensation to cover every surface of the jungle's greenery and our own skin. We arrive within a few metres of the base of the tree when a white blur zips past us, causing us to freeze. Alayah's wide eyes dart around quickly before meeting mine and she unsheathes her dagger in preparation.

My stomach clenches at the knowledge that we have been hunted by something and whatever it is, it will be making a move soon.

I pull my short sword from the makeshift sheath tied around my hips and take a defensive stance. We can only stand and wait for it to make its move.

Thank goodness it is daytime.

The jungle floor is eerily quiet as we stand back-to-back, deathly still and not a single muscle twitching as we hold our breath.

Excruciating moments pass and before we can blink, the creature darts out of thin air to loom before us. I momentarily freeze with crippling horror at the unimaginable. It's a Breather.

What on earth is a Breather doing out during the daytime?

Its asymmetrical limbs protrude crudely into twisted claws, and its mouth unhinges to reveal the dark abyss of deathly razors, dripping with blood and saliva. I study its milky skin, noting the black veins running under the surface, pulsing with each beat of its blackened heart. I can feel fiery energy buzzing through my veins, igniting my ability within as the Breather weighs us both up. Its sunken black eyes flash, the glowing pupils burning into our souls as we hold our breath.

I feel the icy grip of its fingers, imagining them sliding around my chest, reaching for my essence and, unprepared, I exhale suddenly at the sensation. The heat of my breath causes the Breather to throw its head back in an ear-piercing scream, the dissonant sound eliciting bumps over the surface of my skin.

Gobsmacked, I stare at its reaction to my exhale and feel Alayah stiffen beside me. Without further reluctance, I implement its current state to our advantage, knowing it will not take long for the creature to come back to its senses and resume its attack. Knowing Alayah's dagger will be inefficient against the atrocious creature, I lunge forward with my sword swinging in the air and use the sideways momentum in attempts to decapitate its head. My blade wedges in the spine of its neck, blood spraying in my face, and I grit my teeth painfully at the jarring impact. The intensity and effort of the movement causes me to scream continually, spittle spraying everywhere as I hack at its flesh vigorously in a sawing motion.

The sound of metal against bone and muscle makes the fine hairs smattered over my arms stand on end until the head finally falls to the ground, along with its body. My scream dies and I reluctantly lower the sword, the grip of my hand around it still relentless—the sounds of my rapid panting being the only noise in that harrowing moment.

I watch more blood ooze out from its exposed, deformed neck, gurgling over and sizzling with a bout of steam as it hits the forest floor.

We stare at the offensive heap of twisted flesh and shock begins to settle deeply within me as the adrenaline leaves my system. My mouth goes slack, and I clench my free hand tightly into a fist to stop it from shaking. The blood leaves my face in a rush.

"What just happened?" I grit out and look to Alayah, her usual cheery expression filled with disbelief and horror.

My eyes travel back towards the ground and we stand for a few more moments gawking at the carcass until I snap out of my hypnotised state.

"We should probably dispose of it, so Hunters don't find it and realise there are humans living in the area," I tell Alayah and she nods, though not tearing her eyes from the dead Breather.

"I've never seen one before."

My eyes broaden and brows fly upwards at her whispered admission. "Oh."

That explains her frozen state when it jumped out at us.

Nothing more is said as I swing my sword down over the Breather's midsection. I yell in exasperation as the blade becomes stuck, catching on the bone and sinew once again, then proceed to viciously hack away at the colossal mound.

The muscles in my arms burn from the exertion and sweat pours down my forehead, the salty liquid burning my eyes, but after a few arduous minutes, the sword eventually cuts through and I release a sharp cry of victory.

"Good work!" Alayah exclaims. "Let us burn this under the cover of the jungle's canopies so the smell doesn't permeate our home. The canopy should prevent the smoke alerting any Hunters of our location. But we need to be quick. I'm nervous another Breather will stumble across us."

"Agreed. Where do you have in mind?"

"Here is fine," she replies. "Gather as much dried vegetation as you can and meet back in this spot."

After collecting dead leaves for kindling and larger sticks from our surroundings, we dig a slight ditch in the soft ground. Placing the kindling down first, Alayah crouches and retrieves some flint from a small pouch hanging from a cord around her neck. Once again, her skills impress me as she makes quick work to spark the flint, using a small rock nearby, then leans closer to blow on the smoke beginning to seep from out of the pile.

Within moments, glowing flames engulf the tinder and I resume hacking up the Breather into smaller portions, feeding bits into the contained fire with each section. Alayah clears the remnants of flesh and thick blood splattered over the forest floor, scattering vegetation and dirt around to cover any visible evidence.

Once every inch of mutated flesh has been burnt, we fill the shallow pit with dirt to extinguish the fire, then cover it with leaves.

"Unfortunately, the blood will likely attract a few wild animals since I could only cover it with dirt, but hopefully some rain will come soon and wash it away," Alayah says as she wipes her filthy hands over her pants. She picks up the bag of fruit one of us had dropped in the moments of panic when the Breather appeared, to then sling it over her back.

"Thankfully, it isn't overly close to the hut since Hunters might track the residual blood," I say grimly. "Let's get out of here." The palms of my hands sweat at the idea of encountering any more threats, Breather or otherwise.

We both quickly cover the tracks behind us, using large leaves to erase our footprints and reach the base of our tree after several minutes. I scrupulously but efficiently follow her up the side of the towering trunk, my face paling the higher we go.

As I pull myself up through the base of the hut, flopping onto my stomach with shaking arms and legs spread out, I then twist my neck to look at Alayah who has sprawled out beside me in the same fashion.

"Well, I hope to never repeat that again," she says drily, and I cannot help but laugh, earning me a playful glare. "Don't mock me, Rae, that was awful."

"Aw sorry, Lay," I apologise, bestowing her with an endearment. "I think it was just my shock wearing off into a bout of hysteria."

Alayah nods in understanding as her expression quickly turns thoughtful and she glances at the ceiling then back to me. "Did you notice how it reacted to *your* breath?"

Her question takes me by surprise, and I take a moment to recollect the sequence of events. My forehead puckers as I remember the Breather screaming as if it were in *agony* after I had suddenly exhaled.

"Yeah, that is odd," I slowly say, wiping at the sticky blood beginning to dry on my face. "Do you think that happens with everyone who encounters them?"

The noxious smell of blood makes my nostrils wrinkle in distaste and a slight burn where it covers my skin concerns me, but I quell the worry and focus on our current conversation.

Alayah shakes her head. "I honestly haven't heard many stories of people that survive encounters with the things, so I couldn't say."

My mind races with the possibilities of the discovery. "It slightly makes sense," I think out loud. "If they can infect us with their breath, only if *we* inhale, then maybe it's the same for humans. Perhaps we can infect them with our breath if *they* inhale."

Alayah's expression turns sceptical and I realise that saying the words out loud makes them more nonsensical than just thinking them.

"No, that can't be it," Alayah says, her analytical mind working in overtime. "I'm positive we would have heard about that over the years if it were possible." I nod in agreeance and she pauses as if hesitant to say something.

"Spit it out," I tell her playfully, though her expression remains serious.

"Do you think… that perhaps it's something to do with *your* breath—*your* physical self?"

The question is like a fist to my chest, and I inhale sharply at the notion.

The strange sensations I feel when threatened. The energy running through my veins.

Perhaps I'm not *just* imagining things. Maybe it is not *just* my adrenaline going into overdrive.

Alayah observes the thoughts racing across my face and taps her foot impatiently with her arms crossed. "Come on, what is it? I can see you've concluded something of importance!"

The anticipation must be killing her, but I'm tentative to rattle off theories without validating them first.

"I don't know," I tell her cautiously, "I don't want to be making it into something it's not."

"Ah, that's nonsense and you know it," Alayah scolds me. "The only way we can get to the bottom of this is if we brainstorm, but I need to know what you know first. Just like you said, knowledge is power, remember?"

She is right.

Sighing, I glance down at my bloodied attire and gag, feeling nauseous at the sight of blood caking over me. "Let's wash first, so I'm not constantly getting whiffs of this stench."

Alayah looks at her own clothes and purses her lips with revulsion, then nods abruptly. "Best idea I've heard all day."

Not before long, we are stripped down in the freshly filled tub, washing the remnants of Breather and grime off our skin with the scented, slimy leaves. The clear water rapidly turns a murky black and we jump out. Alayah drags the tub to the waterproofed, irrigation corner then carefully tips it over, allowing the discoloured liquid to discreetly drain to the jungle floor below, evidence of its residue shrouded by the thick foliage.

We clean out the grime from the bottom of the tub with some clean water from a bucket, then Alayah moves the tub back over for us to step back in. We take turns in kneeling under the hanging bamboo, allowing fresh clean water to flow over us in order to rinse off any residual blood left from the dirty bath water.

Alayah throws our disgusting clothes in the tub once we get out and then runs from the room. Peering out of the door curiously as she plucks something from the little shelves, my eyebrows shoot up in surprise as she retrieves a bar of discoloured waxy substance and hands it to me.

"I made it from animal fat and ashes," she explains, and her eyes twinkle. "It is useful in removing blood stains."

"I guess you must be covered in blood regularly if you are creating something specifically to remove it," I tease her, wriggling my eyebrows.

Alayah laughs and we kneel in front of the tub after she lets fresh water continue to flow for a few moments before sealing it off. I join her furious scrubbing, cleaning my own disintegrating clothes, but the worn materials tear from my efforts and a stifled sigh leaves me. I'm in desperate need of new attire.

"Where did you get your leathers?" I ask Alayah, eager for a set of my own.

"Ha, you'll be telling me *your* little secret first—and *then* we can concentrate on a set of leathers for you."

Seems fair.

We hang our clothes over the windowsill to dry and make our way back to the little stone seating area near the fireplace. I have never had the chance to laze around nude, but now that I've experienced the liberty, I conclude it is quite enjoyable.

Alayah dices up several pieces of tropical fruit from the day's venture and gives me a full bowl. How one of us had managed to retain it during the frantic run away from the Breather that was stalking our movements before it caught us—I do not know—and simply cannot bring myself to care.

My mouth waters at the sweet, citrus aroma wafting up from the bowl and I pop one in my mouth to moan at the burst of tang across my tongue.

Alayah laughs at my reaction and slides a piece in her mouth as well. "They were known as Camu-Camu prior to The Vanquishing," she informs me while chewing, and I nod at the titbit of information. "So, do you think you're ready to tell me your thoughts on the Breather's reaction to your breath?"

I roll my eyes playfully at her tenacity. "You are seriously like a beast with a bone," I tease, and she giggles. My eyes widen at hearing her laugh, as do hers.

"I forgot how pretty a giggle sounds," I say wistfully. "I used to giggle when Pa played with me as a little girl—chasing me around as if he were a monster."

A soft smile tugs at my lips from the fond memory and my eyes glaze over as I transport back to the moment. Alayah's voice reverts me back to the present and I direct my attention to her as she reminisces.

"I generally giggled when Ma tickled me as a little girl."

Her face becomes pensive as she briefly recollects her cherished memories, then looks at me. "I didn't realise I still had the ability to giggle now."

"Clearly not," I laugh. "Oh, well, it is pleasant to hear, so don't hold back on my account."

Alayah smiles brightly at me, her sharp teeth glinting in the sunlight streaming through the small openings in the walls.

"Now, now," she teases, her dark eyes sparkling, "don't think you can be changing the subject."

A giggle escapes my own mouth at her clever awareness, and I slap the palm of my hand over my mouth to stifle the unexpected sound, my eyes widening with surprise. Alayah throws her head back to start laughing and I join in with her, tears streaming down our faces.

"Being in the company of another female must be awakening our femininity?" I wheeze out in question and Alayah nods her head fervently.

We take a moment to catch our breaths and settle down, my brows drawing together solemnly as I begin reciting my theories.

"I have always had a strange feeling wash over me when threatened, though it's much more vigorous when Breathers are nearby. I assumed it was just adrenaline," I start slowly, and Alayah encouragingly nods for me to continue. "It's like a fiery sensation that I can feel running through my veins, energising me. Generally, I only experience it while I'm using the full extent of my speed."

My hand goes to the pendant around my neck and Alayah's curious eyes drop to it.

"I wondered what it was, but didn't feel right asking you," she says softly, meeting my watery eyes.

I clear my throat of the tears lodging there. "Pa gave it to me just before the Hunters got to us and murdered him. He said it was my mother's, that I was always special and to always have this with me. I never really thought to question what he meant when he called me special since I thought he was just being biased—because he was my father."

"That's really sweet," Alayah says quietly, tears thickening her own voice.

"Well, all sentiments aside, perhaps he was meaning something more? Perhaps that is why my breath affected the Breather?"

Alayah quietly contemplates the information and nods once. "I think it's exactly what we were thinking—and your father knew all along."

Flashbacks of the unrelenting training flashes through my memory and it dawns on me that Pa may have been preparing me. I shove away the conflicting thoughts of betrayal and dishonesty, relaxing the tightening balls of my fists, and exclaim, "Oh!"

He was not just training me to protect myself against Breathers, he was training me for something more crucial. But what?

RULE EIGHT: KILL OR BE KILLED

8

RAE

BOTH ALAYAH AND I CONCLUDE we need to test our theory, though unfortunately, this means encountering another Breather.

"Do you think it odd that the Breather was out hunting during the day?" I suddenly ask Alayah while we clean away the scraps of fruit and her face fills with concern.

"Yes, it did cross my mind. I'm hoping it was just a random occurrence. It appears that way since it was hunting by itself and not in a usual pack."

"Mm. I hope so." I fall silent momentarily, deliberating before adding, "I'm also thinking that we start taking down the packs of Hunters now. The sighting of a Breather during the day changes our urgency in case we start seeing more."

Alayah's eyes gleam wildly with vengeance, the usual amber flecked irises glinting a dark shade of brown. "Yes. I think we need to start setting traps. If we kill most of the Hunters in a pack, we can capture the last one."

I tamp down the unsettling feeling of murdering humans.

They deserve it.

The justification does not change the fact that we would be assisting in the dwindling population of our species.

We spend the next few hours sitting on the edge of the slightly lowered platform, plotting our plan of attack, and the sky fills with swirling pastel pinks and oranges of the setting sun. Birds and animals begin calling across the tree canopies and forest floor, an increasing flurry of activity for the impending night life.

"You can hear a distinct call in the distance," Alayah points out and I nod at the mournful call of a bird. "It means there is rain coming." My brow shoots up and she continues, "I've learned over many years to recognise certain calls and their meanings," she explains. "It's prevented my demise several times, and will continue to do so, particularly if the call indicates imminent flooding or predators."

"Please teach me," I say. "It will benefit both of us if there are two pairs of ears tuning in to the calls of animals."

"That's exactly what I was thinking," Alayah says excitedly, keen to share her way of life with me. "We can start with the call you just heard; a macaw."

She jumps up, pulling the lever of the platform to bring us back inside before eagerly running to retrieve her pile of charcoal sketches, some tinged with colour used from flowers or fruits.

We sit down on the floor and she slides an image of a colourful large bird in front of me. My mouth parts in adoration. I instantly fall in love with its bright blue and red feathers and intelligent eyes peering back up at me.

"It's so beautiful," I whisper reverently as I gently trace the lines. "Do you ever see them?" I glance up to see a mischievous glint enter Alayah's eyes and she darts up, striding over to grab a piece of fruit, returning to lean down and hand the yellow flesh to me.

"Don't eat it, just come to the window and hold it with your arm outstretched."

My heart beats erratically with anticipation as I push up from the wooden floor and make my way to the window, stretching an arm out with the offering. Alayah cups her hand around her mouth and I almost cry at the beautiful caw that emanates from her, the sound echoing across the tops of the tree canopy.

For a few tense moments, we wait silently, my extended arm shaking with both eagerness and wavering endurance, until ever so slightly, I hear the faintest sound of large wings flapping.

"Have your palm open with the fruit sitting freely," Alayah whispers, contagious enthusiasm tinging her tone, and I immediately comply, feeling the similar effects of her feverishness.

A massive bundle of blue, red and yellow feathers swoops in and plucks the fruit from my hand. My jaw drops wide open at the precious encounter of something so beautiful and exotic, and I watch in admiration while the majestic macaw gracefully flies away with the fruit gripped tightly in its claws.

I stay frozen with my arm outstretched, my awe momentarily stunning me, and I stare into the distance, watching the coloured bird become a tiny, dark speck until it disappears into the thick trees. Reluctantly, my arm drops, and I close my mouth, turning around to see Alayah beaming at me. Joyous emotion bubbles up within me as my eyes fill with tears at the beautiful experience. I fling myself at Alayah, embracing her with a tight hug.

"That was so special, thank you for sharing it with me," I whisper.

"I'm so glad to finally be able to share the best parts of my life with someone, so thank *you*."

We both giggle, embracing the new, feminine sound, and break apart to stare back out the window.

"We should probably prepare for the storm that will hit tonight," Alayah's concerned voice breaks through my trance and I notice the ominous, black clouds billowing in the distance above the trees. She takes our clothes from the windowsill and hands mine over, both of us hastily slipping into our attire.

I follow her as she makes her way around the tree-hut, securing items and reinforcing walls with extra clay, and hatches with stones that were stored against the walls outside the bedroom. The stifling humidity coats my skin with more sticky sweat when the slight breeze suddenly and completely stills, a troubling indication of the calm before the storm.

"Is there anything I can do to help?" I ask Alayah, who shakes her head.

"No, we are all secured. This tree is large enough to withstand fierce winds and rain, but unfortunately it won't prevent other trees falling onto us."

"Oh. Has that happened before?" Fear coils low in my abdomen at the prospect of being crushed so high in the air.

"It has, but years ago, and I adjusted the design of the walls, so hopefully it withstands whatever the storm throws at us."

"Well, hopefully Hunters get caught in any flood waters and drown," I joke, not really wishing such a cruel death on anyone, though Rule Eight floats in the back of mind.

Kill or be killed.

9

XANDER

CROUCHING LOW IN THE FOLIAGE, sweat drips down my neck, drenching the tight, threadbare shirt I borrowed from one of my guards prior to leaving the Segment for this lengthy mission. The humidity is stifling, but I'm adamant on showing my men how devoted I am. I may be Ruler of Segment One, but I still get my hands dirty from time to time—much to the distaste of my Council members. But since I'm Ruler, I do as I fucking please.

Right now, that is finding enough meat to bring back to the city and additionally tracking the beast that tore out the throats of some Hunters I contracted nine years prior—not that I would hire Hunters again since I despise their greed, but those were harrowing times.

Yes... I hold a grudge.

Anything that poses a threat to my city and my people, I make a personal goal to track down and destroy. Even if it were only those rough Hunters who were slaughtered.

My Segment has its own group of men—husbands and sons

residing in my city—that venture out to hunt for meat. But nine years ago, there was a shortage of food that not even my own men could rectify, so I hired outside help to travel across vast wastelands in search of meat.

Now, for the past nine years, my own men have been venturing out to scope the lands but have unfortunately scoured the total area to come back empty-handed every single time. Over these years, the dangerous threat of a beast still resides in a jungle near the walls of *my* city. Even if it is a long trek through the thick foliage to the other side where a river separates the jungle and Segment; the threat is still valid.

I'm fucking sick of their lack of results. *"If you want a job done properly, do it yourself,"* my father always said. He was a tyrannical man, so I would rather not follow in his footsteps but either way, here I am. Balls deep in sweat, mosquitoes, and millions of other little fuckers that want a piece of me.

"Do you want to keep moving or set up camp for the night?"

The gruff whisper of my second in command, and only friend, cuts through my seething thoughts and I glance at Lucas with an abrupt nod. He pulls down his gas mask, letting it hang loosely around his neck, and I do the same, my nostrils flaring appreciatively as I inhale fresh, uninhibited air.

The other men will keep theirs on since everyone is paranoid about encountering Breathers, but both Lucas and I detest the stifling masks and would rather take the risk.

"We need to find a high place to camp the night," I tell him with a hushed voice. "Breathers will be out in force, since the jungle is full of meaty meals."

The last round of citizens that came back from a hunt informed me the Breathers are getting desperate; sightings of them are becoming more and more common, particularly through the day. The presence of Breathers would not concern me normally, but now they pose a threat to possibly breaching the city wall.

Lucas moves stealthily ahead of me, implementing hand gestures for the men who work under his command to spread out and advance forward. Tension runs high and energy buzzes angrily through the thick air as we quietly move through the jungle floor. This is only my second attempt at finding the beast myself, but we discovered disturbed foliage not far from here by a small running stream. It could just be an animal or a Breather, but the way the greenery had been cut indicated human blades.

I look up to see Lucas gesturing me over to where he is standing, and I move surreptitiously, cautious not to make any noise. A smile expands across my scarred face as I study the set of what appears to be outlandish animal prints at our feet. Four legs, prints large enough to indicate its ability to take down several men.

We found the fucker.

It only took nine years, but surely, we found it.

I slap Lucas on the back, silently thanking him for a job well done and he shoots his own victorious, moronic grin back at me. We may not be holding the beast physically in our hands, but we are closer than ever before.

I hear a rumble of thunder in the distance and a fat raindrop lands on my face, its presence portentous.

"Fuck," I hiss, the tips of my ears burning with anger. The storms in these forests are not only deadly, but the rain will wash away the fresh tracks. "Work quickly, Lucas. Have your men follow these prints before the rain sets in. Then our priority is shelter. Have someone scale a suitable tree and set up for the night."

Lucas nods, concern darkening his face as he whispers to the men, issuing orders to different groups. The two burly guards carrying gear and equipment strain their necks, looking up to ascertain suitable trees. They select a massive Pará rubber tree nearby, then efficiently begin chopping down bamboo and piling it to the side. The remaining men start creating platforms using vines, and I smirk at their drenched shirts coated in sweat.

They knew this mission would be challenging.

I tilt my head back to scan the trees above us, noting the sturdy branches protruding horizontally in a convenient manner. Gnarled limbs twist together to create perfectly reinforced structures to hold the weight of various men. They will secure the platforms high enough that we will be safe from Breathers for the night.

Nothing will protect us from this storm rolling in, though.

I roll my tense shoulders and force myself to concentrate on the task at hand when I am called over by Lucas.

"Look up there, at the side of this tree," Lucas whispers, and my eyes follow the direction of where his finger is pointing. My eyebrows rise at the man-made grooves in the side of the tree, the first notches starting two metres or so above the bottom of the trunk.

Well, well, well. This just got more interesting.

"It's probably just a survivor living up there, not your beast," Lucas points out, and I nod.

He may be the closest and only friend I have—my regimented way of ruling ensures this—but his skills and intelligence have always been the foremost reason of him being my second in command. That, and we grew up together since he was my stable boy. I used to get flogged by my father when he found me playing in the stables with Lucas and our wooden swords as a child.

We had both made another friend, but my father immediately threatened to *kill* him when he found out, since he perceived the boy as even more unworthy than Lucas. So, we both immediately stopped playing with him. *Gideon.* I never see him, but he leads one of my city's hunting parties and I hear from Lucas that he is doing fine.

"People like us don't associate with people like him," my father always said. I ignored him when he quoted the words when finding me with Lucas since he never threatened to kill him. I guess Lucas was too useful in cleaning the stables.

After disregarding my father repeatedly and tolerating his thrashings, Lucas quickly became my best friend. We constantly defied my father and when I was old enough—and big enough—to stand up to him, the constant beatings stopped. Then, his reprimands ceased altogether when I shot up past six feet, reaching adolescence and bulking up with muscles built from hard labour. Twice as wide as the lazy coward himself.

"I think we should still go up and ensure the *resident* is non-threatening to us while we're nearby for the next few days," I tell him, and hesitance fills his face. Crossing my large arms over my wide chest, I roll my eyes. "Nothing's stopped you speaking your mind before, so don't hold back now."

He nods and scratches his stubbled chin in deliberation, gazing up the tree's length. "I think you should keep the men on our night platform while we go up. They're all hopped up on adrenaline and I wouldn't want them accidentally butchering an innocent." Lucas tears his gaze from the treetops and meets mine. "Not that they wouldn't do as ordered, but if they feel we are threatened, they will strike first and ask questions later."

I nod at his reasoning and he turns to sternly provide his men orders.

"Lads, if you could bunker down for the night up on the platform. Xand–, uh, the Ruler and I are doing further recon and will join you later. If you hear my call, then I will only need two of you to come after us."

I smirk at his slip of my first name. No one calls me that but him since I'm *Ruler* to all citizens and guards.

The men acknowledge their commands and climb the various makeshift shelters for the night while Lucas and I make the treacherous climb up the giant tree. Another ample raindrop lands on me and my eye twitches at the crack of thunder close by. Nothing generally phases me, but I don't fancy being hit by winds or lightning while this high above ground.

With the impending storm looming, we make quick work to swiftly ascend the side of the tree, utilising the man-made grooves to assist our climb and make it to the underside of a large platform. Just in time, as the heavens open their gates and torrential rain begins bucketing down. I snicker at the image of the men below on their metal sheets, surely looking like drowned rats from the heavy downpour.

Lucas attempts to open the small hatch leading to the other side of the platform, but it does not budge. He looks back down at me and rolls his eyes.

Of course, we climb this high up and get stuck.

I chuckle and tilt my head at his sword, and he nods affirmatively. We will pry the hatch open.

Lucas unsheathes his sword and slides the long, sharp blade through the gap in the edge of the hatch. Using one arm to cling to the groove in the side of the tree, he uses the strength of his other to pry the hatch slowly open. There must be something heavy on it, but the steel of our swords contains titanium, a rare metal that can withstand anything.

My father's greed was at least practical in some senses, as everything he left behind is useful for the most part.

Lucas manages to open the hatch enough for him to squeeze his shoulders through, reaching over to move the stone weighing it down. He pauses to scan the space above for any threats then hoists himself through to stand on the defensive as I climb in.

My eyes instantly travel to the one room on the farthest side, secured with a large plank covering the entire opening. Lucas looks to me for instruction and I nod silently to the room. He slightly tilts his chin in reply, and we start moving stealthily towards the entrance, our gaze keenly darting around the open space as we go.

The thunder and heavy rain thankfully create enough noise to cover any creaking from our heavy weight as we make our way across. I take note of the fireplace that has recently been used, and I frown at the indication of a human presence nearby. Lucas silently gestures at the pulley, lever, and platform someone has cleverly built. All suspicion of where the human or *humans* are, dissipates as I inwardly applaud whoever resides here for their innovation.

That must have been what they used to lift the heavy stones used to make the fireplace and reinforce the walls.

The hut is built to withstand hectic weather and I'm suddenly grateful we discovered it. Concern briefly fills me for the men exposed to the elements below, but I push it aside, reassuring myself with the reminder that they are highly trained for any situation.

We reach the entry to the room and keep our weapons raised in front of us, our stance ready for whatever or *whoever* may be lurking on the other side. Lucas studies the plank and slowly starts sliding it sideways so he can peek through the gap.

He turns back to me, frowning, and I move forward to peer through as well, seeing nothing but an empty, makeshift bed on the far wall. The window beside the bed has been boarded shut and reinforced with fresh clay and rubber from a Pará rubber tree in preparation for the storm.

Suspicion and wariness climb my spine as my eyes narrow at the view of the empty room.

They probably heard us and are hiding somewhere.

Possibly to the side of the entrance to ambush us. I indicate my thoughts to Lucas, gesturing behind the door with numerous hand signals. He nods in agreement then gestures that he will burst through the plank first.

I shake my head at him. I may be Ruler, but no one needs to risk their life for me, especially my closest friend.

Lucas rolls his eyes at my obstinacy and bows mockingly as he motions me to go first.

I bite my tongue, so I don't laugh at his idiocy. Now is not the time for dicking around.

Effortlessly, I rip the planks from the entrance, causing rubber and clay to fly everywhere at the sheer force. Jumping through the opening with my sword raised, my nostrils flare as I'm instantaneously greeted with a feminine, floral yet citrusy scent. My head snaps around the room to ascertain if there is any sign of life but to my confusion, it is completely empty. Lowering my sword, I spin on my heels to check the empty room once more and turn to Lucas who enters with a frown marring his face. His eyes go to the empty bed and they narrow as he walks warily towards it. I follow him with the comprehension that he is certain someone is hidden there. Brandishing my sword in preparation for anything, Lucas grips the man-made holes in the side of the wooden base and uses his sheer strength to quickly flip it over with a loud grunt.

Neither of us are prepared for the shadowed blur that flies at Lucas's throat, but his reflexes kick in and he shields his vulnerable jugular by crossing his leather-bound forearms in front of his face and neck.

In the peripheral of my vision, I see a glinting shortsword coming at me and I efficiently block the blow with the tilt of my longer blade. With a wide, low kick of my leg, I sweep the assailant's feet from under them. My action causes them to land on the floor with a satisfying thud and groan. Quickly glancing at Lucas, I'm content to see he has his own blur of an assailant under control, so I look back down at mine.

My whole body stiffens at the image splayed before me. My assailant is a *woman*. And her electric blue eyes are boring into the depths of my soul with such hatred and vengeance that I'm momentarily worried for our safety. But as we are twice her size, the concern is transitory.

"I'm not here to hurt you," I tell her reassuringly, placing my sword back in its sheath and holding my hands out in a passive pose, but I wonder if she can even understand what I'm saying.

Her soft, ivory skin, striking azure eyes and long black hair suggest she isn't from around here, but the flare of understanding and suspicion that crosses her face says otherwise—that she does understand our language.

Fuck, she's breathtaking.

And intelligent. I can see those beautiful eyes of hers shifting quickly over me, then Lucas—assessing and weighing options.

I tilt my head at her, curious of what her story is and how an unpaired female is surviving without protection of a man. I glance at the other woman.

Two unpaired women. Intriguing.

My probing gaze makes her uncomfortable and she becomes increasingly wary, slowly sliding on her arse as she backs up against the wall. The beauty crosses her arms over her pert breasts in protection and defence.

Or defiance.

The flare in her bright eyes indicates the latter and a smirk tugs at the corner of my lips.

Being the Segment's Ruler, I don't lack for company of women—but none show any attitude or spirit for fear of my rejecting them. They all act exactly how they *think* I prefer women. It's fucking boring and getting old.

I glance over to Lucas, who has managed to bind the hands and feet of his feisty female, and I kick myself for being distracted by my own woman. Pulling rope from my belt, I stalk towards the petite pixie of a woman, her eyes widening at my movements and obvious plan. I shrug at her silent protest and firmly grab her as she pushes up to dart away. Her legs and arms flail about and the wind leaves me as a hard elbow sharply connects with my abdomen.

A wild smile extends across my face at her fight and I pull her back against me, instantly groaning at the softness of her behind and the feminine scent raiding my senses. In hopes she doesn't feel my arousal and instantly think I'm a pig, I efficiently bind her legs and arms with my free hand. I then carry her with my arms supporting the underside of her legs and back, placing her in the cleverly crafted hollow of their upturned bed base, alongside her companion.

Two angry faces, albeit beautiful ones, glare back at us with murderous expressions and I look to Lucas with a wide smile. Blood is dripping from his forearm and my brows pinch, smile instantly wiped from my face. "What the fuck, man, how did that happen?"

Lucas's own eyes are bright with mirth, clearly enjoying the company of his angry female. "Believe it or not, she *bit* me."

A scowl crosses my face at the unlikely thought niggling in the back of my mind. "That's a deep gash for human teeth to create. Did you see her teeth?"

Lucas nods affirmatively but smiles like a man who has found a bountiful chest of treasure. "I did, and somehow they make her even more beautiful!"

He must have received a knock to the head.

I glance over at the subject of my suspicions and she hisses at me. My eyes widen at the razor blades filling her mouth and my face whips back to Lucas who still has a goofy grin plastered across his face.

"See? Utterly breathtaking," he says as if everything is normal.

I roll my eyes at his one-track mind and grab his bleeding arm to study the bite marks. My heart drops when I do. "Fuck!" I yell, and Lucas jumps back, startled at my outburst.

"Calm down, man, it's not that bad!" Concern is etched across his face, but my mind is racing with the possibilities of our discovery.

"Your arm shows the exact same markings on the body parts

of the Hunters who were torn apart nine years ago," I tell him bluntly, and shock fills his expression as it dawns on him.

"Shit, you think *she's* the one?"

We peer down at the woman, if you can call her one, who starts trembling as tears streak down her mournful face.

"They raped and brutally murdered my *mother*," she says with quiet rage in a hoarse voice. "I was only a child! They were going to do the same to me!"

Sobs rack her sturdy frame, and my eyes shift to the pale female who wraps her bound arms over and around the back of her companion's neck. Through the efforts of comforting the distraught friend, the discernibly angry blue-eyed woman shoots murderous daggers at us.

I look at Lucas, my own thoughts reflecting his grim face, and his eye twitches as he meets my gaze. Tension and violence emanate from his large frame.

"Did you know about this? Did you know the Hunters *you* hired did this kind of thing?" His words are accusatory, and I flinch at the insult.

"I would never condone violence against women," I tell him, my voice low and even. A loud scoff tears my attention from Lucas, and I turn to see the slight female rolling her sapphire orbs at me with tangible disgust and disbelief. Her reaction amuses me, and I stride over to her, kneeling beside the tub so I'm level with her face. A smirk spans my own.

"Something bothering you, little one?" I ask her condescendingly, purposely attempting to evoke her temper. I inwardly cheer when her astounding blue eyes flare with vehemence.

But then she spits at me.

Lucas freezes beside me, and I look up at him with disbelief. I'm uncertain whether to spank her or laugh. Though my fingers temptingly twitch, I decide the latter, and my smile widens impossibly as I focus on her—the demented reaction visibly disconcerting her.

"Y-you're a pig! And you're ignorant if you think groups of men under *your* ruling *don't* rape, murder and pillage their way through the land!" Her hands ball into fists and her frame shakes angrily. If it wasn't for the sinking feeling in my gut at her ominous words, I would tease her spluttering start to the accusation. But I don't. I fear there is truth to her words and though I know Hunters can be ruthless and are generally greedy men, I had no idea they were taking advantage of the innocent and weak.

Fuck.

My shoulders droop and the light-hearted friskiness within me deflates.

Something needs to change.

RULE NINE:
DON'T TRUST MEN

10

Rae

ILOATHE THE STRANGE FEELING fluttering low in my abdomen when he stares intently at me. I'm disgusted by his mere presence and that makes my body's reaction all the more infuriating.

He's a man.

Though a strangely beautiful one.

I instantly reprimand myself at the ridiculous thought, though I cannot help but catalogue his expressive dark chocolate eyes, the scars that run down his forehead and cheek and the rough dark stubble that frames the enticing lips and well-defined jawline. His skin is not as dark as Alayah's, but it is olive and somehow sensual. I have seen few well-built, fit men—only from a distance thanks to Pa—but *he* is almost unhuman. I've never seen someone tower over me like that—and I'm tiny. And I *felt* him against my back when I elbowed his hard stomach. He is pure stone.

Gah!

I have no idea why these thoughts are appearing suddenly,

when I've experienced nothing like this in my entire life.

Stay focused. These men are a threat.

Sharply tilting my head to crack my neck, I repeatedly remind myself of the important fact.

All men are a threat.

Which is why Rule Nine is so important for survival against humans, particularly the male gender. Don't trust men. No matter how breathtakingly good looking they are and no matter how charming.

Do *not* trust men.

They only work for their own personal gain and will use and abuse women and innocent people as per my father's stern teachings. He was certainly adamant on keeping me away from them. And this man is the worst of them all!

My lip curls when I glance at the gas mask hanging around his neck, confirming my belief. He has the most power, the most resources—and he does nothing with it. Unless it benefits him directly. I heard his friend address him as if he is a Ruler, so I *know* my assertions of him to be correct since Pa hounded into me the awful and greedy ways of every Ruler.

My gaze travels to his soft, inviting lips again and I tilt my head when I notice them moving.

"What's your name?" His smooth voice cuts through my distraction and heat rises to my face as I meet his twinkling eyes. The corner of his lips twitch.

Don't tell him your name.

"Rae."

Blast.

I could not help it. It is as if his eyes placed me under a trance, forcing the words from me. And my stomach tightens when he flashes a handsome, roguish smile revealing a full mouth of white teeth.

Alayah elbows me sharply and I glance at her, momentarily dazed. She quickly shoots me a look that is both disapproving and full of warning before re-focusing on her own male adversary.

"Rae," he says softly, "like a ray of sunshine."

I gasp at the use of my Pa's nickname for me and anger fills me at the reminder of his death.

"You don't get to say that." I seethe through clenched teeth, and concern fills his hard features.

He tentatively lifts a large hand to my face, and I flinch at the contact as he wipes a stray tear from my cheek. The tender gesture confuses me—contradictory to what I have been taught about all Rulers' hardened, evil character—but I reinforce the walls around my heart in order to protect Alayah and myself.

Feelings are a weakness. Pa always said that *all* men lie and deceive to gain what they want.

This man is no better.

"I'm sorry for your pain, Rae," he says sincerely, his voice still gruff but quiet, and my hackles rise with indignation.

"*You're* the one that caused it, *Ruler*," I spit out, enunciating the last offensive word in mockery.

A look of surprise and concern fills his face again and I roll my eyes. I believe him incapable of sympathy and empathy. Yet my brows crease as confusion clouds my mind. His behaviour has gone against everything Pa taught me.

It must all be an act.

"Explain." His gruff order should not surprise me, but it does.

I pause before deciding to tell him, knowing that disclosing such information will not cause me any harm. "Three years ago,

Hunters I believe to have been *yours* tracked my Pa and me down. They slit his throat and would have done worse to me if I had not escaped. I ran and did not stop. They were hunting *me* to steal away so one of your men could use and keep me."

An array of emotions flitter across his face; anger, surprise, then confusion. All of them muddle my feelings more.

"Firstly, I did not order them to hunt you both down nor did I order them to kill your father. Those orders would most likely originate from one of the neighbouring Segments," he says, his voice low and threatening. "Secondly, I am not the fucking keeper of *any* Hunter's actions. They are free people who can do as they please. I only employed their services *once* when the city ran out of certain resources."

It bothers me that everything I knew about Segments and their Rulers is not entirely true.

But however true his reasoning might be, I laugh dryly at his excuses. His brow rises at my deliberate disrespect.

"You have the *power* to punish and make an example of these people who murder innocents and rape women and children, yet you still choose to remain ignorant." My face hardens with renowned defiance as I grasp on to anything that justifies my hate for the man.

His jaw clenches tightly in annoyance at my truth, and he looks to his man who nods slightly in agreeance.

I quickly peek at Alayah, whose angry stare is fixated on the man standing in front of her, and it briefly crosses my mind that they have probably been arguing with each other too.

Oh well, she's tough enough to look after herself.

There is not much we can do with our feet and hands bound anyway.

Rain continues to batter heavily against the roof and my attention swings back to the insufferable oaf in front of me. My palms sweat nervously at the calculating expression on his face as he studies me. His ability to abruptly switch temperaments—from roguish, to angry, then to serious—gives me whiplash and is frankly disconcerting.

Looking down to break the uncomfortable connection, I concentrate on the tight rope around my ankle and an idea suddenly pops into my head at the sight.

We can charm them to untie us and then we can escape. Perhaps poke a few holes in them first.

I take a deep breath and paste a sweet smile on my face as I look back up to the man kneeling in front of me. His dark eyes narrow suspiciously at my change in attitude but a spark of interest flickers across them.

Who knew something as simple as a smile could do damage?

I laugh inwardly at myself.

"So, what is your name?" I ask him sweetly. "I assume it's not *Ruler* since all Segments call their leaders that."

He studies me curiously, his eyes momentarily assessing before he decides to answer. "Xander."

My stomach flutters at knowing his personal name, one that suits his authoritative and handsome aura.

Focus, Rae! Remember to charm *him.*

I clear my throat. "I like it," I say awkwardly, and realise there is no hope in me charming *any* man let alone *this* one. I have *zero* experience in the art of seduction.

Xander's lips tilt into a half smile, producing a dimple on one cheek. My belly flips at the sight.

"Well, I like your name too," he says flirtatiously, then glares up at the man beside him when he snickers. "Shut up Lucas, I see you've made *no* progress with *your* woman."

Alayah tenses beside me, and I shoot her a troubled look, though she responds with a quick shake of her head, silently begging me not to worry. When I glance back to Xander, his eyes pin me and have darkened even further, filling with something I don't recognise. I squirm under his attention until finally he gets to his feet, the other man he calls Lucas following him to the other side of the room where they whisper quietly to each other.

I take the opportunity to quickly whisper into Alayah's ear. "If we act sweetly enough, maybe they will untie our feet and hands..."

Alayah clues into my plan and smiles wickedly at me, nodding at the implication.

The two men stop talking and glance at us, their expressions conflicted, and concern fills me at this change in their demeanour. Thunder rumbles outside with an instantaneous crack of lighting that makes me jump, and I stifle a scream.

I hate storms!

My clear discomfort must show as Xander swiftly strides over to me and kneels, his hand brushing the hair back behind my ear that had fallen across my face in a curtain. "You alright?" he asks gently, and I realise I can use *this* to our advantage.

"I'm scared," I tell him, attempting to fake a timid voice. I feel Alayah shake as she stifles a laugh beside me. Xander thankfully doesn't notice and places his hands under my armpits. I tense at the physical contact and he stands, lifting me to my feet as he does so. Without a word, he lifts me from the tub, cradling me in his arms as he carries me to the bedding on the floor.

Lucas watches with amusement as his large friend lies me

down on the bed and sits at the end, so my head rests on his lap. My eyes widen with disbelief at both being manhandled and at the oddly nurturing action. Alayah's own disbelief flickers across her shocked face, her jaw dropping widely open. Our plan almost worked, with only our bound limbs the remaining obstacle.

"Uh, my wrists and ankles are hurting from the tight rope," I say tentatively, in hopes of appealing to the empathetic side of Xander. He chuckles, the rich, deep sound reverberating in his chest, and I roll on my back to look up at him.

Those dark eyes twinkle until his mirthful expression suddenly drops as he meets my gaze. A crease forms in the middle of his brows and his enthralling eyes momentarily drop to my lips. I feel my cheeks heat at the blatant interest flaring in the brown swirling depths and squeeze my knees together to relieve the strange pressure between my thighs. My movement doesn't escape his notice and his jaw clenches as his breath visibly quickens with the rise and fall of his wide chest.

Is this what seducing a man is?

I glance over at Alayah who vaguely nods with encouragement, and I sigh in relief at the chance of success.

"If I untie your wrists, you only get one chance. Fuck up and I'll tie you back up *and* gag you." Xander's tone is hard and my mind spins at the sudden change of mood. But it doesn't matter, because the plan *worked.*

Lucas shakes his head, clearly disagreeing with Xander. "Shit, man—if they escape, what's stopping the men below from doing what they want with them?"

Both Alayah and I stiffen at the new information and glance at each other, our faces crestfallen. *There are more?*

"Well, if they escape us, they won't escape the men. You know our men are harmless and won't hurt women, but they will tie these ones up for me," Xander replies with a hard tone and looks down at me, his expression threatening.

His ominous words and sudden cold demeanour remind me once more of Rule Nine.

Never. Trust. Men.

I internally reprimand myself for falling under the influence of his charms, like a moth to a flame, and harden my heart so I don't make the same imprudent mistake again. Rolling back over to my side, I shift to prop myself up into a seated position—any position *away* from Xander—and lift my wrists up to him as he grudgingly takes a dagger from his boot and slices each rope with a swift motion. The rope leaves a dark red imprint on both my wrists and ankles and I rub the soreness from them, jumping when large, capable hands reach for my own to continue the massaging.

The sensation of his rough palms and fingers sends an electrical charge suddenly shooting up my arm, triggering me to reflexively yank my hands away. My eyes dart up to meet his own, and I swallow nervously at the penetrating look that has befallen his face.

"I'm sorry the rope hurt you," he says, voice thick with the same unfamiliar emotion I see reflected in his eyes. "Let me massage the circulation back into your hands and legs for you."

I clear my throat and pull my knees against my chest. "No, it's fine, but thank you."

I need to keep my mind alert and clear so I can plan another way out of this mess.

RULE TEN:
I REPEAT,
DON'T TRUST MEN

11

RAE

XANDER INSTRUCTS BOTH ALAYAH AND ME to lie on the bedding situated across the floor against the far wall. We huddle close together as we rest, keeping our eyes fixed on the two large men spread out on the floor adjacent to us... in front of the doorway.

I twist my neck and look behind me at Alayah, who rolls her eyes exasperatedly at the ceiling, clearly as frustrated by the intrusion as I am. Sensing a sharp gaze searing the back of my head, I turn to see Xander staring raptly at me. His riveting eyes pierce through my chest and the breath hitches in my throat. My brows knit together as he slowly peruses the length of me, his leisurely yet assessing scan leaving a scalding trail from head to toe. His nostrils flare and I wriggle slightly to alleviate the pressure growing in my abdomen; the movement not going unnoticed as his pupils dilate.

Irritated by the effect he has on me, I send him a flaming glare and roll to my other side so I'm facing Alayah. Her eyebrows rise and she glances over my small frame at the men, her eyes becoming thin slits when they rest on Xander.

"I don't trust them," she hisses.

"Same, but it's pissing me off, the effect Xander's having on me." I whisper the words so quietly she leans in closer, straining to hear. Her eyes widen at the realisation of what I'm saying.

"Don't fall for his deceptive act," Alayah gently says. "I've had a man do the same to me before and he was only using me. I thought he loved me. I was lucky he wasn't violent or forceful."

Oh. Am I the only inexperienced female in the world?

I kick myself at the meaningless thought. Father always said survival is much more important than settling down with a man. Which is why I'm still *unbroken* as the pigs call it. A disgusting term for virginity.

Again, Rae. Don't. Trust. Men.

"Have you *been* with a man at all, Rae?" Alayah whispers, her eyes wide with disbelief. My mouth gapes at her ability to read my thoughts, but she smirks. "You sometimes think out loud."

I groan and slap my palm to my face. "That's mortifying," I whisper, my tone brandishing discomfort, and she chuckles, snuggling in closer to me.

"What is? That you speak your mind or that you're an innocent?"

I swat her playfully, shushing her as my face flames a bright red. "Shh! They will hear you—imagine how much I would be sold for as an *unbroken* woman!"

Our whispers draw the men's attention as they move from their guard at the door and stand intimidatingly in front of us, towering over where we lie. Alayah's eyes widen at the two formidable shadows behind me and I sigh. Rolling over, I smile sweetly at them and clasp my hands together like a saint would, speaking in my most saccharine, slightly mocking voice. "Oh, big men, is there anything we can do to help? Perhaps we can cook you some food? Perhaps you would like us to open our legs for you?"

Alayah gasps at my brazen words, but I ignore her, focusing my attention on the emotions flashing across Xander's face, only to become annoyed when he smirks with amusement, the action dangerous. The puckering of his facial scars as he smiles makes the expression even more ominous.

"Well, if you're offering, we accept all of the above." His predatory smile contradicts his low, smooth voice and I swallow the lump in my throat, not expecting his reply. "What, have you changed your mind already?"

My lids partially lower and his eyes challenge me, but I quickly reinforce my seductive pretence, looking at him from under my lashes then peruse his large frame suggestively until I reach his crotch.

An idea sparks in the recesses of my mind and I turn my head slightly and glance at Alayah, my eyes hinting as they flicker up in the direction of their groins. Xander and Lucas are both standing vulnerably, their nether regions right in the paths of our feet if we were to kick our legs up. In an instantaneous decision at seeing the affirmation glinting in Alayah's eyes, I fling my leg up with all my strength, with her following suit closely—and my foot connects with Xander's crotch as does Alayah's with Lucas's. Both men groan and heavily drop to their knees, though Lucas's groan is louder. Alayah is stronger than I am, but I do not feel any remorse for Lucas and his manhood.

We spring to our feet and I grab the bindings the men used to tie us up. Throwing half to Alayah, I snatch Xander's hands and bind them, though not without struggle, using his hindered state to my advantage. Chancing a peek at his face, my progress halts at seeing the feral expression that has fallen over it, his eyes blaring with the heat of a suns solar flare.

He is thoroughly excited.

I glance at Lucas who appears to be in the same state with Alayah.

The terrifying notion that these ropes will not contain them has dread settling heavily in the pit of my stomach.

We need to run.

The urgency to escape fizzles as I remember the pounding storm outside and the possibility of running into hunting Breathers... or Xander's men below.

Blast.

I gnaw the inner flesh of my cheek as I consider what to do, and in my moment of inactivity, Alayah has already tightly bound Lucas and is rushing over to commence restraining Xander more securely. He realises this is no longer a game and starts struggling to break free.

Stepping back, I watch Alayah effortlessly push him back to the ground and efficiently re-bind his arms behind his back just as she did Lucas. Sucking my lower lip between my teeth with thoughts of our next steps, I make the mistake of glimpsing at Xander. His eyes have fallen to my mouth, his jaw tightening and nostrils flaring at what he sees.

His expression reminds me of a wild animal, and the reaction causes an abundance of additional nerves to flood my stomach, raging through as rapids would a ravine. I storm away, incensed once again at my response to him.

"What do we do now?" Alayah asks, walking over to me after successfully securing the two massive men. I scratch my chin in deliberation and a devious smile tugs at the corners of my mouth. Xander is at *my* mercy now.

"Well," I begin slowly, my tone as serious as I can manage, "we were wanting to spill some Hunter blood, but this is even better... we can bring down the whole city by removing its Ruler."

Not that I'm serious... if Xander wasn't previously lying about not dabbling with Hunters, then his city is likely different to the other wicked Segments.

I watch his every expression as I say the words and he glowers at me.

Good, I have your attention.

Alayah laughs with mirth at my words, though she does not seem to grasp my false threat. "Oh, that's perfect!"

My eyes dart to her and I communicate with a look that says *just play along for now.* She nods curtly in understanding and I sigh in relief. We might just benefit from this situation—from these men.

Knowledge is power.

The arbitrary thought reminds me to wheedle as much information out of them as possible. I continue my devious plan by addressing Xander.

"Well, we *won't* kill you *if* you provide us with some exchanges... and information."

Xander becomes enraged, the vein in his forehead pulsing as he struggles against the ropes around his wrists while sending me a withering glower.

"I won't even consider blackmail from a *woman*. We *will* break free, and once we do... well, you'll want to run as fast as you can, little mouse." His threatening words come out as a growl and I nervously crack my knuckles, compelling myself to not exhibit any fear.

"Oh, big bad wolf, I'm so scared," I say mockingly, my faux confidence unwavering. His expression turns predacious again as a smirk spans widely across his face.

I ignore the disconcerting smile and continue with my devious plan, relishing this back and forward between us. "And why would I want to run? What should I be so *afraid* of?"

Xander's smile grows even more, and I swallow nervously at the challenge that has entered his dark eyes.

"You will have to wait and find out," he says, his voice baritone and husky. Shivers run up my spine at the evocative promise behind his words.

I spin around to an extremely concerned Alayah and see Lucas smiling cheekily at us both. It suddenly hits me, and I realise *why* she is so concerned.

We have just painted a substantial target on our backs.

12

Xander

MINE. It's the only word running through my one-track mind. I watch her lips move while she talks—while she mocks me—and I cannot help the compelling urge to take her over my knee and spank her. Then make her mine. Then do it all over again. I've never had a woman drive me to the point of insatiable need.

Fuck, I love her attitude.

My body tightens, coiling in desire when a blush graces her soft, creamy skin—the gravity of her inexperience becoming clearer. My mouth waters at the movement of her plump, rosy lips, unintentionally yet seductively inviting my own to join them. Fear flashes through her piercing blue eyes and I... frown. No, that's not right. I don't want her to fear me. I don't like that feeling.

But you do *need her fearful. That's how you control.*

It's how I rule so effectively and why everyone follows my orders, hanging on my every word.

But it's different with Rae. For the first time, I don't want someone to fear me.

I don't want *her* to fear me.

"We would like you and your men to leave us alone and not bother us again," Rae's sweet voice interrupts my perplexing thoughts. "And we won't slit your throats." She pauses and quickly adds, "Also, we want leathers."

A smirk teases the corner of my lips, but I refrain from yielding to the urge of smiling to appear serious. Her sass is the most foreplay—the best foreplay—I've had since I was an adolescent. Maybe ever.

"So, let me get this straight," I ask her, and she raises her chin defiantly, "you want us to leave, pretend we never met *and* give you our leathers?"

Her curt nod sends a curtain of silky black hair swinging across her face and my hands twitch with the need to wrap the wavy locks around them.

Like hell I'll pretend we never met.

But I'll play along.

I pretend to think over the ultimatum, scratching the rough stubble on my chin thoughtfully before looking to Rae with a serious expression. "We accept; if you let us stay for the remainder of the storm." I'm lying through my teeth, but the relief is apparent on Rae's face and it's a punch in the gut since I thought my feelings were at least marginally reciprocated. I look at Lucas who is visibly biting his tongue to refrain from arguing with my decision.

Rae glances to her friend in question, both women blatantly worrying about the possible consequences from accepting my counteroffer. Moments pass after shaking their heads negatively at each other, in perhaps a silent argument, when Rae suddenly throws her arms in the air with an exasperated groan then glares at me. "Fine," she narrows her eyes suspiciously at me. "But we will be keeping an eye on you all night and if you do not leave in the morning, you will be sorely regretting it."

"We will leave."

Little does the pretty mouse know, I won't let her slip through my fingers now I've had a taste of her spirit and beauty.

As for her friend—it appears the nine-year mystery of the beast that ripped apart those Hunters has been solved. The *beast* is just a woman, though she is still dangerous, brutal *and* intelligent. Perhaps I should be somewhat concerned at her unnatural show of strength and power—she easily wrestled Lucas and me down. My brows furrow at the perplexing reflection.

I should feel somewhat relieved my search is over, but it was the only thing keeping me amused in my boring life as Ruler. Any excuse to get out of the city walls and *hunt.*

Glancing back at Rae, I catch her staring at me and notice her nipples straining through her cloth. My body instantly stiffens, and she blushes furiously, quickly looking away.

She wants me.

Yet her indifference baffles me. As if her body knows what it wants but her head hasn't received the message yet. It's comical watching the internal battle with herself; particularly as it pisses her off that she's attracted to me. That attraction will be the only weapon I can use against her… use to trap her.

My thoughts jump to the issue of surrounding Breathers becoming more active—and during the day. The city walls have been fortified to withstand any attack, human or not, but something is unsettling me. What we always knew about the Breathers is rapidly changing and the underestimation of the accursed creatures might be our collapse.

I sigh and roll my head, thankful when a loud crack releases the tension mounting in my neck and shoulders. Having the burden of a whole city causes the worst knots in my back.

I will need to see Nelinha for another massage.

The sudden thought makes me wince. Nelinha is the Segment's masseuse but four years ago, she was seeing to my more... base needs. I soon stopped that because of her unsavoury intentions to weasel her way into my life as my queen.

Though, maybe one last fuck will be beneficial.

A quick roll in the hay might rid me of this overwhelming and distracting urge to claim this jewel-eyed woman as mine and permanently—which frustratingly, is a foreign feeling.

I glance at Rae and desire coils low. All women pale in comparison. The petite, feisty woman ignites something in me, though I can't quite place my finger on it.

Possibly the hope for something more.

I shake my head to rid myself of the senseless thought. There's no hope left in this desolate world; not even in the form of a beautiful, raven-haired temptress with adorable freckles scattered over her nose. But that still doesn't stop the one thought repeatedly whirling through my already chaotic mind.

I will make her mine.

It would at least appease the Council's nagging for me to choose a wife and produce heirs. *Fucking Council.*

Lucas's dim voice pulls me from my considerations, and I glimpse at him as he speaks to his own subject of desire. I can see it in his eyes. The wild woman does it for him; just like what my pretty prisoner does for me. Challenge.

Rae's friend is attractive in her own exotic way, with dark skin and untamed hair, though the teeth are somewhat off-putting, but Lucas doesn't seem phased by them at all. I study the woman's long, strong legs and make my way up to her pretty face.

Strange. Nothing happens. I don't feel a thing.

Usually, any attractive female is enough to ignite my blood.

I glance back over to *my* little captive and am pleasantly surprised to see jealousy raging in the depths of her stormy swirling orbs. Jealousy is a good sign. Not that she has any reason to be jealous of her friend.

"Perhaps you should both leave now," Rae spits out, and I smile widely at her.

Fuck, she's so much fun.

"No, that wasn't a part of your ultimatum, but thanks for offering," I reply, and she becomes irritated at my pert comment, an adorable scowl transforming her face.

There is no way I'm leaving. This tree-hut has served to be a sanctuary from my burdens. A possibility to escape my responsibilities even just momentarily. I'm not leaving any sooner than we need to and I'm certainly not leaving my little mouse here yet, if ever.

"While we're here together, we may as well get to know each other," I say diplomatically. Rae scoffs, crossing her arms angrily over her chest as she turns away, causing my eyes to dip to her perky behind.

Fuck.

My fingers itch to spank her yet again and I struggle to tear my eyes away, eventually forcing my gaze up.

"I will start," I continue, piquing her interest, and she turns back to me with scepticism, curiosity imprinted across her features. "I'm around three decades old. Both my parents are dead, and I have no siblings." Her eyes widen with sympathy and I detect grief flashing across her soft face.

Ah, so she has no family either. I knew her father died—apparently this is my fault—but now I know she has no mother, no family left.

My ability to read people's facial expressions and body language has been honed over my ten years of ruling. People do not even need to speak, and I still learn everything I need about them. It has proved useful when negotiating with enemy Segments. Like Segment Two and Three.

"Wait, so if you died, who would be heir?" Her question hits me like a sledgehammer and Lucas overhears, his face whipping away from his tense conversation with Alayah... I overheard the sharp-toothed woman say her name.

Everyone's eyes are on me and I shift uncomfortably at the age-old question that has been asked consistently for at least five years. A Ruler is supposed to produce an heir. What the Council members don't know, is that I purposely spill my seed when lying with women, so I don't impregnate them.

I don't want to bring a child into this world only to subject him to the horrors and responsibility I had inflicted on me as a child. My father didn't allow time for a childhood—I was trained to be Ruler from the day I could walk.

Resentment settles low within my abdomen at the reminder of the man who was barely a father to me. Thank fuck I had Lucas otherwise I would be even more mentally unstable than I am now.

I clear my throat to deliver the same answer I always do, then pause momentarily.

These people aren't my Council members. I could use this opportunity as a confessional, hopefully releasing some of the burdens that plague me at night. "I purposely don't have children."

Everyone gasps at my emission except Lucas, who would have known this deep down.

A weight lifts from my chest and I smile widely at Rae. "Well, I could never find the *right* woman to have children with," I say to her pointedly, and her eyes widen at my meaning.

I'm only partially joking.

I *couldn't* find a suitable woman because they're all leeches, only interacting with me to serve their own selfish purpose. I don't want someone like *that* raising my child.

But oddly, I can envision Rae running around with a little blue-eyed child. The image tightens my chest, causing my breath to hitch momentarily, and I frown.

What the fuck?

No. Priorities: I must keep the city safe first.

"I refuse to spread my legs for you just so you can produce an heir," Rae fires back, cutting through my conflicting thoughts. *Okay...* our hypothetical just became real.

"You wouldn't just be a vessel. You would be a *mother,* a *wife,*" I say, just as surprised by my sudden rebuttal—an underlying offer—as Lucas is.

He looks at me with an incredulous expression then looks to Rae adamantly, waiting for her response.

I suppose this is happening now. My plan to make her mine...

"No."

The singular abrupt word is not what I expected to hear, and Lucas raises his eyebrows at me, amused by the refusal. I have never been told no in my life. It's also unheard of for any survivor to reject this opportunity at a new life—one filled with security and endless resources.

"No?" I echo slowly, repeating her answer in disbelief. "Explain."

Fuck, I should throw her over my shoulder and force her to be my wife.

I scowl at the sudden thought spearing through my mind and shake my head to rid myself of the absurd notion. *Wife.* I never thought in a million years I would utter or think the word.

Shit, I would be the worst husband to any woman, which is another reason why I still haven't taken a wife.

"I am more than *just* a woman. More than *just* a wife. More than *just* a mother. So, my answer is no. I chose my freedom; my own path." Her words are delivered with such conviction that I stare at her with adoration.

Fuck, I want her to warm my bed so bad. Perhaps if I coax her with a softer approach...

"I agree," I tell her, and surprise crosses her face—she was clearly expecting an argument. "You are more than just a wife, mother, and woman. You would be a *queen,* so to speak. It may be an odd label considering we no longer have kings in this world... but the title remains valid for women of such positions. My point being that you're defiant, stubborn, and courageous. You pursue what you want. These are all qualities expected in a Ruler's queen. Which—as my wife—you would be." I'm extremely efficient at smooth talk when I want something. Lies come naturally for me, particularly when it involves women.

You can't deny it; everything you have said about the little mouse is the truth.

Rae glances to Lucas and Alayah who are watching the whole ordeal transpire with a curious tilt of their heads. Blue steel suddenly meets my gaze, the strength in her eyes leaving me breathless.

"I would never *just* be a Ruler's queen."

I don't expect this turn of attitude. It's almost as if she is *contemplating* the idea. It's fun pretending with her about this topic. I don't believe I need a queen. Ever. But I want her in my bed... permanently... and her presence by my side will keep the Council at bay, so it is essentially two birds with one stone. And I hate losing in general, so now she has unknowingly established this challenge, I will do everything in my power to conquer her. It will be fun convincing her to become my lover eventually, but she clearly needs to ponder the idea of being a queen first to soften to me.

I frown as I study Rae. Somehow, the spirited female seems like she should be more than a mistress—*more* in general, and I can't quite identify what that is. This pisses me off that I'm unable to figure it out; I generally know *everything.*

"Explain," I order her, and Rae rolls her eyes at my brusque tone.

"Well, if *I* were to be queen," she starts slowly, "I would be the *only* one leading. With no man beside me."

Lucas guffaws then coughs to cover his outburst of amusement, and I narrow my eyes at Rae.

I don't take the insinuation of treason lightly and I'm not sure I appreciate the direction this hypothetical conversation is now heading in.

"What makes you think you would be the only one leading?" I ask with a growl.

Rae doesn't blink or smile as she answers bluntly, "Because you would be dead."

Lucas tenses beside me and a deeper growl reverberates in my chest at her threat.

Alayah's eyes widen at her friend and looks back to me. "Rae, we agreed not to kill them, remember? Their men are below and would execute us."

My roar of objection at her words startles both Rae and Alayah momentarily before they continue talking as if we aren't in the room. Now I'm *really* not liking the turn of their conversation — nor the turn of Rae's attitude towards me. Anger bubbles up dangerously within me as my blood boils and my nostrils flare as I stare at her.

"No, of course not," Rae scolds Alayah, "I would off him in his sleep once I was his wife. *Hypothetically*. I'm not *actually* considering being queen — we have too much at stake, remember?"

The angry buzzing in my ears intensifies at her talk of treason and I narrow my eyes at the vague last sentence, pissed that I don't know what they're talking about.

"What's at stake, Rae?" I ask her, my voice low and threatening. Little does she know, Lucas is currently sawing through the bindings of my hands behind our backs with a small, sharp switchblade that was hidden in the upper back pocket of his breaches.

Her eyes become shifty, darting towards her fidgeting hands at my question which makes me more curious. Whatever they have been discussing is clearly of importance, so once Lucas and I have our hands free, she will tell me everything.

"Nothing that concerns you," Rae replies abruptly, meeting my gaze, and I smirk at her sass.

My hands finally break free from the bindings behind my back and I stealthily grab the switchblade from Lucas to start sawing through his ties. I continue talking with Rae to distract them both as we surreptitiously free ourselves from the tight knots.

The women seem highly intelligent, but in the stress of securing us, they forgot to check for hidden blades. Or perchance they just didn't want to touch us more than necessary. Either way, it works to our advantage.

"We could help you with whatever you need," I tell Rae sincerely, and her eyes constrict into distrustful slits.

"We don't need your help."

I shrug my shoulders. "Suit yourself."

Rae's lower lip catches in her teeth as she bites the plump flesh in thought. The action isn't meant to be sensual but every muscle in my body tenses, buzzing with lust when she does it. Her hand goes to a tarnished gold pendant around her neck—must have fallen out from under her shirt in our scuffle—and I squint to see its intricate detail. The symbol looks somewhat familiar, but I cannot place it.

Once we have them tied up, I can interrogate her.

I cut through the last of Lucas's bindings and as it snaps silently, I look to him with a nod. We lunge now. My heartbeat increases, beating faster than the stampeding hooves of a hundred beasts.

Like lightning, Lucas and I spring up and dart over to the two women, their faces frozen in surprise.

I'm somewhat disappointed we don't receive a proper fight but relish the soft feeling of Rae's skin under my palms. Lucas struggles more with Alayah—her strength apparent—and Rae wriggles in my grasp.

"The more you struggle, the more I enjoy it," I whisper with innuendo into Rae's ear and she stills against me. I take the opportunity to firmly secure her wrists with rope in front of her and sit the seething beauty down comfortably on the bedding. Her eyes drill me with such hatred that I smile softly in return. As much as I love her spirit and defiance, but more so as much as I don't want her to hate me, I need to concentrate on the welfare of my city.

RULE ELEVEN:
OKAY, MAYBE
TRUST ONE MAN

13

Rae

MY CHEST HEAVES WITH RESENTMENT towards Xander and my mouth turns dryer than the dust found in wastelands. I shoot him my most withering look, but he only returns it with a soft, handsome smile.

Curse him!

Glancing at Alayah, she looks just as infuriated as I feel—her angry eyes blaze at Lucas, who appears to be thoroughly enjoying himself.

"Take Alayah out of the room and keep watch on her there," Xander tells Lucas as his eyes remain intently focused on me. "We need to keep them separated since they like to conspire against us together."

A growl of frustration leaves my mouth and Xander smiles widely, albeit more predatory than the gentle smile he afforded me earlier. I swallow deeply.

"So, little mouse, little Rae," Xander starts slowly once Lucas has carried a struggling Alayah from the room. "Tell me what it is that's *so* important you can't be my wife."

I nervously look at the ground, needing to break the intensity of his gaze. "Nothing that's any of your business." My words sound stronger than I feel and he chuckles, amused by my defiance.

"Well, clearly there *is* something, otherwise you would simply be suicidal to pass up an opportunity such as the one I've offered."

I scoff and roll my eyes at his arrogance. "You're quite sure of yourself, aren't you? You think *you're* my best option at survival, even though I've survived the past three years *by myself* just fine."

"It's only a matter of time before your luck runs out," he says more softly, and I scoff again.

"I'm insulted you think I survive by luck. I can assure you it is one hundred percent skill and ability." I tilt my chin up defiantly and Xander smiles widely.

"In that case, what kind of *skills* and *abilities* do you have?"

His question feels like a trap, so I don't answer.

"Well, since you don't want to answer that, let's talk about that pendant around your neck."

My body hunches over at the mention of Pa's gift to me, and my bound hands protectively clasp it, hiding it from view as I tuck it back under my shirt. "There is nothing to talk about. It is also none of your business."

Xander's expression turns feral and a spark of dominance fills his dark chocolate eyes, churning my stomach into a nervous ball of lead. He shifts closer to me and all my instincts yell for me to bolt. But I can't. My hands are inconveniently bound. I detest the flutter of excitement igniting the strange sensation in my lower abdomen, but all I can do is meet Xander's searing gaze.

His silence is disconcerting, and I keep my mouth tightly shut to remain calm, which only serves as an opportunity for him to study me attentively. Stubbornly, I maintain the fixated stare, drilling him with my eyes, regretting the action after some time.

My lack of human interaction means I have not ever stared into someone's eyes before and it is extremely... intimate. But Xander does not waver. Instead, he shifts slightly closer, his muscles rippling with each movement under the thin, black material serving as a shirt. I frown.

Doesn't a Ruler wear better clothes?

"There's so many thoughts and emotions flickering across your pretty face," his husky voice interrupts me, and I feel my face heating. "Ask any question and I promise I'll answer truthfully."

I doubt it. But I take the opportunity to possibly learn some useful information.

"How impenetrable are your walls if Breathers were to orchestrate an attack?"

My question momentarily surprises him, and his eyes widen with slight interest.

I guess *proper* ladies of a Segment do not bother themselves with such topics. It is undoubtedly a man's world.

"Why would that concern you?" He seems genuinely interested in my answer, albeit still slightly suspicious.

I pause a moment to prudently measure my words before answering. "Well, I encountered a Breather yesterday. During the day. And the horde I escaped from in my homeland was larger than normal—more aggressive than usual. It suggests desperation."

Xander's face remains impassive at my revelation and I briefly wonder if I've revealed too much information.

"I agree." His serious reply surprises me. "I have noticed an increase in activity and am working on ensuring the city walls are efficiently fortified against any surprise attacks."

I blink slowly.

Did he just agree with me? And openly discuss matters of defence?

"If you don't mind me asking, so I can understand you better," Xander asks gingerly, "how the fuck did you manage to escape a horde of Breathers? And what happened to the one you encountered yesterday?"

I bite my lower lip, calculating if revealing the information would be harmful to Alayah and myself. Coming to the deduction it should not, I clear my throat and meet his gaze dead on. "I ran. Across the wasteland until I escaped them."

Xander tilts his head, curiosity and intrigue flashing across his face. "You're fast." He delivers the words as more statement than question and I stiffly nod once.

He shifts suddenly and his arm snakes out, grabbing one of my ankles—I yelp, the movement sliding me on my back along the bed.

"What are you doing?! Put my leg down!" I attempt trying to kick my leg out of his grasp, but he holds on firmly as he studies the underside of my foot. His expression is one of concern and fascination. Satisfied with his conclusion he gently drops my foot and looks at me. "Your feet are cut up, as if you were running barefoot for days, weeks even. Do they still hurt?"

Confusion fills me at his caring words and observation, so I just nod again, emotions tightening my throat.

My wellbeing has not been anyone's concern since my Pa died.

I sit up awkwardly—a difficult feat when one's hands are tied—and tuck my feet away from view.

Xander's eyes soften, his granite, scarred face becoming more handsome with the change, and I purposely look away to avoid the foreign feelings welling up inside.

"Rae," he says softly, and his large hand tilts my chin. "I won't ever exploit your ability if that's what you're worried about. I would protect you in *every way* if you were mine."

His words are so sincere and gentle, I almost believe him.

"I don't belong in a Segment or cooped up in a tower, Xander," I whisper, and his jaw clenches at my rejection.

He rubs his hand exasperatedly over his face and studies me for a few moments.

"Let's talk about something else for now," he says, his tone back to business. "What happened to the Breather you encountered yesterday?"

Ah, so he hasn't forgotten.

"I hacked its head off."

Xander's lips tip in an amused smirk. "I'm not surprised, but my only quandary is that they're known for their speed and stealth..."

I pause at his insinuation. It *is* rare for a human to survive an encounter with a Breather unless one is with a pack of well-equipped Hunters. But I survived *two* encounters.

I don't want to trust him, but I feel if I give him something— anything about me—he may offer his assistance if I ever needed it.

Fat chance of that happening.

Sighing in defeat, I know I have nothing left to lose at this rate. "My breath stunned it." I barely whisper the words but Xander's look of astonishment—an expression that doesn't suit his smug face—indicates he heard clearly.

"You're saying you just *breathed* on a *Breather* and it, what... froze?"

"Uh, kind of," I say warily. "It screamed? I'm not quite sure, but it threw its head back when I did and let out an awful, grating bellow."

Xander just stares at me and I become uncomfortable under his scrutiny, fidgeting with the rope around my wrist in uncertainty.

"It might have been coincidence... maybe it was just calling its pack." Xander seems to be talking to himself rather than me, reassuring himself of the normalcy to my account.

"It has happened before," I say quietly, suddenly recollecting the first encounter correctly, and his head snaps up. *Well, I'm all in now.* "So, it cannot be coincidence."

Xander continues staring at me again and frowns, his eyes dipping to my chest, filling me with fear.

"Your pendant," he growls, and I automatically place my bound hands over my shirt where the cool metal lies underneath, hanging between my breasts. "I've seen that symbol before."

What?

"Where have you seen it?" I demand.

"In the Segment's library. We have a section dedicated to symbols, including that one," he says, pointing to my neck, "I believe I've also seen it in my seamstress' shop."

Knowledge is power.

His words pique my interest and I hope he isn't using them as a trap. "What do you know of it?"

Xander holds his hand out and raises a brow. "Show me first and I will tell you all you want to know."

I narrow my eyes. There is no way I'm handing the last reminder of my Pa to him.

Xander seems to read my mind and chuckles darkly. "I *could* just take it from you, but I'm choosing to *ask* first."

My eyes widen at his underlying threat. "You wouldn't dare," I whisper, half frightened and half thrilled.

He moves so fast; I barely have time to blink and I'm on my back with his large body looming over the top of me. I'm frozen, entranced with his nearness and the spicy, pepper-like scent of him as his warm, rough hand travels beneath my shirt and slowly up my stomach to rest on the pendant between my cleavage. My breathing hitches and becomes shallow as I squirm under his touch, confused at the inordinate sensation of my core tightening with sudden tingling.

Xander closes his eyes, inhaling deeply, and my eyes widen at the realisation of what he is doing. His eyes snap open, pupils dilating, and all breath leaves me completely at the heady emotion I see violently swirling in their depths.

My nipples painfully harden, causing his gaze to drop down, and I whimper as a wolfish grin stretches across his face.

"My little mouse," his voice comes out low, "glad to see you want me as much as I want you."

A frown mars my face at his words. *NO.* "I don't know what you *think* you see, but I do *not* want you." I spit the words out in distaste and challenge flashes through his eyes. His hand on my bare chest softly glides across the slope to a nipple and he pinches, causing a sharp, pleasurable sensation to shoot down into my toes and I gasp.

"Stop it," I whisper, not entirely certain I want him to. The sound of heavy rain fades completely, and my pulse quickens at the increasing ache between my legs.

"I will stop if you really want me to," Xander growls. "But do you?"

My body is betraying me, but all I want is for the ache to go away. So, I shake my head jerkily. "No."

What are you doing, Rae? This isn't right!

Ignoring the reason fluttering in the recesses of my mind, the chance for me to change my mind dissipates swiftly like a sword slicing through one's flesh. My whisper of permission has Xander swooping down to capture my mouth in his own with a needy groan.

I whimper at the new sensation as he worships my mouth, sucking and nipping my lips. As I tentatively open my mouth, his tongue slides in and sensually massages my own. I moan at the sensation and feel my hips rolling on their own accord.

What is happening to me?!

All coherent thoughts quickly dissipate as Xander's rough hand caresses down my shirt and slips under the seam of my pants. I whimper at the building sensation that I cannot seem to stop and gasp into his mouth as his coarse finger trails over my most sensitive flesh, spreading my own moisture around the entrance of my centre. My mind's too far gone to entirely comprehend what is happening, and I cry out as his thick finger slowly enters me. I can feel myself clenching around him at the intrusion and Xander curses.

"Fuck, you're so tight." He continues slowly pushing his finger in until I feel him pressing against my unbroken barrier and he freezes—his eyes snapping to mine.

My haze of arousal subsides as dismay and shock fills his expression. "You're unbroken." His words are more statement than question, so I don't answer, but my face heats with mortification as I look away from his fervent stare.

I whimper as he abruptly removes his finger and pushes off me as if I've burnt him. Tears fill my eyes at the reaction and I angrily reprimand myself for the useless emotion.

"I won't take you on a floor in the forest if you're unbroken," he gruffly says as he stands and adjusts the bulge in his pants.

A foreign emotion fills me at his display of consideration and I suddenly realise—maybe I *can* trust *this* man. It's a stab in the dark and I grasp the flicker of hope growing within me. Maybe Xander is not selfish and self-gratifying like all men my father made out to be. Maybe he is different or maybe I can fix him. I can only hope it is not the unfamiliar lust burning within me that is muddling my good judgment.

14

XANDER

I NEARLY FUCKED HER ON THE FLOOR with people just outside the room like she's some woman of the night—like she's Nelinha—and she's fucking unbroken! I knew she was somewhat innocent, but not *that* innocent.

Taking deep, calming breaths, I rub a hand over my face and look down at Rae, my chest tightening at the vision of her dark, wavy hair fanning around her like a halo. Those bright eyes, so heavy with desire, and the deep blush tinging her fair skin further affects me.

Mine. She will *be mine. But not yet and not like this.*

The visual of her doesn't help extinguish the burning lust, so I force myself to concentrate on more pressing matters.

The pendant. Her Immunity. Her ability. She is more of an asset to you now.

The thoughts manage to tamper my raging desire until her strained whisper breaks through my thoughts.

"Xander, I'm aching."

Rae's words are a desperate plea, laced with confusion as she struggles to comprehend her own body's reaction and need. As much as I want to be deeply inside her, I somehow know she needs a gentle first experience. I won't be gentle right now—I'm too tightly coiled.

Not that I'm ever gentle with any woman I'm with.

I grimace at the thought. My blackened heart will probably break Rae... but I'm too selfish to let her go completely. The need to have her in my bed, in my life, is too acute to ignore. Regardless of any consequences.

And to think I should have learnt my lesson from the last time all those years ago.

I glance down at Rae's slightly parted mouth and shallow breathing, indicating her unbearable need. Maybe I can offer her some reprieve from what she's feeling *now* though.

"What do you need, mouse?" I ask her softly, and a whimper escapes her swollen lips.

"Please," she whispers. "Something... relief?" Her innocent sky-blue eyes pierce through my soul and I catch my breath from the zealous feeling washing over me.

The feeling to protect her from everything terrible in this world.

The need to tear anyone in half that tries to hurt her.

Fuck, I can't be thinking like this, not when the Segment is at risk. Not when every female that becomes intertwined in my life, suffers.

That's why Rae can *only* be a lover. If I had any sense, I would walk away from her and not look back so as not to ruin her. But... I just can't.

My eyes trail along Rae's luscious, feminine body, her slight curves swathed in old attire, but my own body still constricts in response.

Her legs and thighs are tightly pressed together to relieve the pressure she feels there, so I gently pry them apart and peel her pants down, ripping them clean off her. I ignore the conscience niggling in the back of my mind, screaming at me to stop. My eyes dart to the opening, thankful Alayah and Lucas are out of sight, situated farther around from the entrance.

Shit, that was reckless of me.

They could have seen all of that.

Standing up, I stride to the opening to peer around and see them up against a far wall to the left of the room. I move into their view to place the plank back up but pause, growling at Lucas who gives me a knowing look. Alayah cottons on to what I'm doing, panic becoming apparent in her eyes.

"What are you doing?! Stay away from her!" she yells, struggling against her bindings.

I don't know why I bother appeasing Rae's friend—I never would have cared before, but I shoot her a gentle look.

"I won't hurt her, Alayah," I tell her, and her expression becomes doubtful. "I won't do anything that she doesn't ask me to do."

Alayah hisses at me, palpable rage falling over her face. "If you hurt her in *any way,* I will hunt you down and tear out your throat like I did your men."

Lucas stiffens at the threat but doesn't interfere.

"And I would allow it if I hurt her," I tell her bluntly. I would *want* someone to tear my arms from their sockets before I hurt this woman.

But that's what you'll do eventually if you take her back with you.

Without waiting for any reply, I place the plank in its place, my eye twitching in annoyance at the lack of a proper door, and turn to Rae, the mere sight of her leaving me breathless.

I've seen plenty of beautiful women—ones that throw themselves at me every day—but none of them compare to this enigma, this breathtaking woman. The purity of her heart and soul; the spirit and fight that shines through her already spectacular physical attributes. I could stare at her all night.

No. She is just a challenge for you, to lure her into your city and bed.

It is essential to keep reminding myself of this, no matter how much my mind protests each word.

Rae's eyes remain glued to me, wide and aroused, and her glistening lips are parted as little breaths come out in slight pants. Her silky hair fans messily around her head as if she were floating on her back in the water, and my eyes travel down to her bare waist, eliciting a groan from me. Her lean legs are spread open, displaying beautiful pink flesh like a platter for me to feast on.

My legs automatically pull me towards her, like a moth to flame, and I kneel between her spread thighs. It's taking all my power and self-control to not slide into her tight heat.

"Please, Xander," Rae whispers, tearing my attention away from the glistening of her wetness. Hearing my name softly dancing on her tongue is like poetry, and I decide then and there that I never want to hear my name on any other woman's lips again.

Not wanting Rae to suffer any further, I lean down between her legs and lightly lick her sensitive core, making her cry out with intolerable ecstasy. Slowly, I moisten my index finger with her wetness, trailing it around the entrance of her clenching centre before carefully entering. Her moans are like music to my ears and I look up to see her staring down at me, her snowy skin flushed and her chest heaving with anticipation.

"Do you want me to take the ache away?" I ask her one last time, giving her any opportunity to come to her senses and push me away.

Rae nods frantically and I feel a dangerous smile grow, my blood heating, scalding the surface of my skin with prickling awareness.

She's *mine* now. Her one little action sealed her fate. She *will* be in my bed and in my life soon.

Without any hesitation I slide my finger in and reach her unbroken barrier, pausing as her breath hitches from the uncomfortable sensation. It's odd that her barrier is still intact with how active her life is, but I won't complain.

Leaning down, I softly lick her bundle of nerves, making her jolt and cry out. I continue swiping a few more times before her cries become more insistent and she tenses—her release imminent. I slowly but firmly press against her barrier as she hurtles towards the edge and then sharply tear through the thin membrane with my finger once she reaches that blissful peak. Watching her beautiful face fill with fleeting pain then profound gratification and relief almost breaks me. Her cries of pleasure drown me, and I groan as her walls clench and flutter around my finger.

"Fuck," I whisper hoarsely.

Rae eventually comes down from the climax, her pulsing core slowly fading, and I cautiously remove my finger, quickly wiping the remnants of blood on my shirt to not concern her. Her skin is flushed and the inner lips of her sex a rosy pink, glistening with the moisture covering them—tinged with crimson from the mixture of blood. It's the most amazing sight ever. I can't help but lower my head and inhale deeply, relishing the sweet, honeyed scent of her mixed with the metallic hint of blood. My own arousal pushes painfully against my breaches, but I pay no heed to it, only staring up at Rae in the attempts of capturing the image before me. Her eyes are heavily lidded, her skin covered in a sheen of perspiration, with pink splotches smattered over her pretty skin from her peak of euphoria. A sated smile illuminates her face and my eyes nearly pop out of my head. This is the first time Rae's smiled at me. I'm utterly addicted. Silently, I make it my main mission to ensure she smiles like this every day.

No, she is only to warm your bed. She will never love you, so don't bother trying.

I push the dark thought from my mind and tell myself lies instead.

You don't need her love—you don't need anyone's love. Take her back with you for your own pleasure and for the sake of the city—you need her for her Immunity. You just need her as your bed mate.

Yes, that's why I will take her back with me.

Satisfied for a valid reason to steal Rae and take her with me, I crawl over her, pressing a soft kiss to her lips. Her tiny arms loop around my neck, her wrists still bound, and she kisses me in return. Something shifts in my chest and my eyebrows lower.

I pull away from her luscious lips, standing and scratching the side of my head, attempting to identify the increasingly unsettling feeling. My arm drops heavily, and I spin around to avoid meeting Rae's eyes, removing the plank at the door.

"Thank you, Xander," Rae whispers, and I turn back to see her softly smiling at me.

My previous thoughts float up again, but I push them back and force a smile in return. "Any time."

As I remove the plank, Lucas gives me a questioning look and glances at the clear arousal still in my pants. He will know this is the first time ever I have *not* received any relief in return. I shake my head at him slightly, warning him to keep his mouth shut. Alayah only transfixes me with her fiery glare.

"I hope you didn't sign your death warrant in there," she says threateningly, and I tilt my head at her, curious as to why she's being so protective in this situation. Perhaps she knows of Rae's innocence as well, which would make sense if they have been living together for some time. The thought makes me wonder how long they have lived up here.

I don't reply but turn, leaving Lucas to deal with the angry woman. It feels strangely unnatural being away from Rae.

Fuck, man, stop this ridiculousness.

I roll my eyes inwardly and stride over to where my precious little mouse lies. Time to ruin the contentedness and trust.

"We need you in the city, Rae," I tell her softly, crouching down to slide her pants back on. Her sharp gasp indicates how she feels about my words.

"No, I won't live a life of imprisonment and dictatorship," she says defiantly, any trace of climactic afterglow rapidly fading, her lips pursing with contempt.

I need to make her think she has a choice, so I don't appear to be the bad guy in this situation.

"What if you were free to come and go as you please? Free to do whatever you like?"

Rae squints at me as she weighs my words. "I don't see how I could *come and go* from a *fortified* city, Xander."

"The guards would have my orders to freely let you in and out when you please."

"What's in it for you though?" Her tone is becoming more

mistrusting and I decide to be honest. I have nothing to hide.

"I couldn't bear the thought of not seeing you again."

What the fuck?

My words are unexpected, and I inwardly kick myself for lowering my defences—not wanting to lay my feelings bare. But Rae's look of pleasant surprise when her brows rise and eyes gleam ecstatically at my declaration, is worth it.

"You also could work with the senior scientist. Your encounters with Breathers possibly indicate a rare Immunity, one that has been written about in a book I have read."

Maybe I shouldn't have suggested she live in the city so soon. Her expression immediately becomes guarded and I inwardly swear at my inability to read the situation.

"I don't want to be a lab rat—subjected to prodding and who knows what else," Rae says in a low, angry voice, her face turning red. "You promised that you wouldn't tell anyone about my abilities!" Her anger dissipates suddenly as her eyes widen.

"Wait, are you saying I'm Immune? And in what way?"

"Yes, and from what I recall, you would be Immune to their breath rather than their bite. You could read about it in a Celtic book that the Segment's seamstress keeps."

I wait silently for her to absorb the information and an array of emotions flash through her eyes as she blinks rapidly.

"What does that mean? Could I somehow be a cure? A prevention? A treatment?"

I cringe at the mention of such medicine—*treatment* was the downfall of humankind.

"We would find a way to utilise your genetics within my armed forces." I think. I haven't been afforded enough time to properly ponder the opportunities. Not that the Segment has armed forces, only a battalion of guards and our blades of choice.

"So, you would *weaponise* me." Her words are delivered bluntly, clearly unimpressed, and my mind races to find a way to smooth over her negative connotations of the idea.

"We would only be able to use it against the Breathers—in defence—*if* the scientists can find a way."

I become restless, rising from my crouched position to pace around as she silently weighs her options, her intelligent mind working all angles of possibilities, all negative and positive outcomes.

Fuck, she'd make an amazing queen.

The sudden thought stuns me, and I frown. No, I can't seriously deliberate the idea. Even if I did, Rae's not ready for that.

Fuck, I'm not ready for that.

I just need to break her in slowly within Segment One first and get her used to the idea of a permanent life there as my mistress.

She's more than a lover and you know it.

My denial is cowardly, but the dire consequences of her being a part of my life officially would weigh heavily on my shoulders. After the only two women that I cared for deeply died brutally, all because of *my* selfishness, I vowed to never love again.

My gaze rests on the angel's face in front of me. I have a sinking feeling that this vow will be broken one day.

Just leave her behind and save her from yourself. And you from her.

I push the thought deeply down and ignore it. Fuck that.

"I want to live here with Alayah—and I will only come inside the city walls when the scientists need to do their work."

I stare at Rae, my jaw clenching at her answer. I should be satisfied that she's willing to work with the labs to protect the city. That I will still see her occasionally. But I'm not. Because that means she's not *mine*.

Patience, Xander. You don't need her to be yours, *just a warm body in your bed.*

I'm beginning to accept that my internal reassurances are blatant lies and remind myself not to throw her over my shoulder to *force* my life upon her. I know I probably will anyway since my patience is sorely lacking.

I'll see how I feel in the morning, as soon as dawn cracks and the storm passes.

RULE TWELVE:
POSITION IS POWER

15

Rae

MY HEART THUMPS EXCITEDLY at the current opportunity presenting itself; a way into the city *and* a way to defeat Breathers. The thrum of hope running through my veins—the *feeling* that there is more to my dismal life as a survivor, is more dominant than ever now.

Though, I'm unsure if the original idea of bringing the city down in order to restore balance to humankind in the area is the *right* way to go about this all. Alayah had wanted to bring down the privileged and greedy Rulers, making them kneel before us, begging for mercy. I agreed with her, but only because Pa had taught me that all Rulers were the same. Yet, despite Xander's hardened yet smug exterior as a Ruler, I witness glimpses of compassion, care, and proof of a leader who rules with an iron fist, but also fairly.

My thighs ache blissfully, and I squeeze them tightly together. I still feel the remnants of pleasure flowing through my veins and I'm hoping it is not clouding my common sense. My mind whirls with the possibilities that being inside the Segment would provide. But then, as a *queen*, I would have more ability to make the changes Alayah and I crave. We would have more resources at our fingertips to use against the Breathers and bring down the Hunters.

So, do I aim to become a queen, the only *Ruler? Or do I sacrifice my freedom and become* Xander's *queen?* What would serve my purpose better?

My conflicted thoughts violently race around my head and I bite my lower lip as I deliberate the best course of action. Xander silently yet patiently waits for me to come to a decision. I think of what Alayah would want and realise she probably would not want to relinquish her way of living within the jungle.

The mere idea of leaving Alayah just after we have found each other causes my chest to painfully constrict, and I make my decision instantly. "I want to live here with Alayah—and I will only travel inside the city walls when the scientists need to do their work."

As soon as I speak the words, Xander becomes deathly still. His dark, piercing eyes stare through me as if he did not hear anything, and my nerves run high as I wait for his reply.

"If that is what you want," Xander finally says slowly, his voice low. I swallow nervously and his eyes remain fastened on me, their ominous depths swirling with... something I cannot place.

I feel like his prey.

Glancing out the opening, I see that Lucas has moved Alayah to the far side of the platform, perhaps by her request to keep an eye on us, and she watches me intently.

This is for her too.

So, I nod. "Yes, this is what I want."

His expression instantly darkens, his jaw clenching at the confirmation of my answer, but I lift my chin defiantly.

He will fail in intimidating me and compelling me to do what he wants.

"We will leave at first light then," he gruffly says. "Get some rest."

Without waiting for my reply, he gets up and strides out to Lucas, talking with the two of them as he gestures towards Alayah and I simultaneously. Alayah's wide eyes shoot towards me in question—Xander's clearly telling her our plans—and I nod in confirmation. Her tense posture visibly relaxes, and Lucas picks her up, carrying her to lay her back down beside me.

Our feet are not tied, so Lucas could have just helped Alayah to her feet and let her walk over, but I don't comment and refrain from smiling.

Lucas and Xander make their way back inside the room and place the wooden board up against the entrance, sliding down to sit in front of it for the night. Xander's eyes remain glued to me, the dark depths swirling with intensity, and I shift uncomfortably, turning to my side so my back is to the two men.

Alayah's knowing gaze assesses me and compassion fills her expression. "Are you okay?" she whispers, and I smile softly at the reminder of the passion and rapture I experienced. Relief fills her face, and she huddles closer to me. "You should accept Xander's offer."

Her hushed words break through my pleasant memories and I frown at her.

What?

"I want to stay here with you and Xander says we can come

and go as we please. And what about your need to defeat all Rulers and Hunters?"

Hopefully, she has changed her mind… at least about the Rulers.

I'm still unsure on how I feel about wiping out all Hunters, even if they *did* murder my father.

Alayah shoots me a strained look and whispers so quietly that I can barely hear. "You would be better off permanently within the walls of the city. Imagine a life where you would never want for *anything*. And I don't think we should try and destroy the Rulers of Segments in the areas or bring down the walls; but rather control the city from within."

I tilt my head at her sudden change of heart, and she clears her throat awkwardly, glancing over my shoulder at Lucas. "Lucas explained a lot to me—about the inner workings of the city. He implied that *everyone* is equal in their Segment—the privileged don't have any hierarchy and the Council members ensure the Ruler is fair. There are many survivors who have been allowed through the gates and given refuge as well as a fair place to work and live. The stories we have heard are still true for other Segments though. Other Rulers and cities seem to be greedy and violent."

I nod thoughtfully as I absorb the information. Pa was not entirely correct in his teachings.

Perhaps I can be Xander's Queen?

I shake my head at the silly notion. I barely have the social skills for talking to *one* person let alone a *city* of people.

Alayah must see my doubt and whispers softly again. "I think you would be content by his side, even if you have only just met him."

Frowning, I glance over my shoulder at the subject of my dilemma. His dark eyes remain fixated on me, and bumps break out over the surface of my skin. Could I relinquish my freedom to have unlimited access to resources? Can I sacrifice my independence for the welfare of mankind?

I don't know.

Perhaps that makes me selfish, but I have had my independence—albeit under protection of my father—for my entire life.

I turn back to Alayah. "I cannot surrender my freedom and independence, Alayah." The strange feeling burning deep within my soul intensifies as if protesting my words, but I ignore it.

Understanding dawns over Alayah's face and she nods once. "My tree-hut will always be your home."

My eyes fill with tears. "Thank you."

We lay in silence for a few moments, absorbing the possibilities and imminent change within our lives and I quietly laugh, causing Alayah to look up and raise a dark eyebrow.

"I can't believe I spread my legs for him like some wanton… hussy."

Alayah's eyes widen and she glances over my shoulder briefly before huddling in closer to me.

"Did you…?" Her question is left unfinished with implication of the unsaid words.

I shake my head, forehead creasing. "No, he didn't… please himself. Just me."

Surprise fills Alayah's face and realisation brightens her expression. "That explains why he came out with a…uh…bulge after. I thought he was just insatiable and wanted another go."

My cheeks turn red at the insinuation and I glance over my shoulder to see both Lucas and Xander's faces filled with what I have come to learn is lust.

Oh.

"They can hear us, Alayah," I whisper. Loud chuckles behind us cause me to turn back over. Both Lucas and Xander's expressions are amused as they attempt to stifle their laughs.

"Yes, we can hear you, mouse," Xander says, his voice low. "But don't stop on our account." Lucas laughs and his eyes spear Alayah, who shifts uncomfortably beside me.

Argh! Why does he have to be so infuriating?

I blow out my cheeks in an irritated huff. "We will just go to sleep, thank you," I bite back before rolling over to face Alayah again. Even through her dark skin, I can see the blush staining her cheeks.

I close my eyes and attempt to ignore the piercing look I can feel burning through my back, hoping that sleep comes swiftly. Within moments, my reality begins to waver, and I become weary with the need for rest, my muscles aching from the sprint across the wastelands and my feet throbbing from their torn condition. But the bliss Xander gifted to me has turned my body into a boneless pile, so I'm able to relax through my aches. Along with the sounds of heavy rain, I'm easily lulled to sleep.

The crack of dawn arrives much too quickly, and I slowly wake to bright rays streaming through the newly uncovered window. Frogs croak their delight from the blanket of moisture covering the forest and the shrill call of happy birds echoes throughout the canopy. I deeply inhale the fresh scent of damp foliage and raise my bound wrists above my head in order to stretch my stiff back. A growl startles me and I dart up to see Xander standing in the entrance, his large body tightly wound like a coiling snake ready to strike. Heat pools between my legs and I frown at the constant need that plagues me now that I have experienced such indulgence.

Clearing my throat, I nervously glance around, and notice Lucas and Alayah are nowhere to be seen. I stiffen and my head snaps to Xander, all previous desire rapidly dissipating. "Where's Alayah?" I say accusingly.

Xander stalks over to me and I shuffle backwards like a worm on the bedding until the wall behind me halts my progress.

"Lucas has taken her and some men to hunt down a pack of Breathers that were seen prowling around their trees last night."

I gasp at the news and concern fills me for the safety of my friend and *why* Lucas took her with him.

"Lucas won't let anything, or anyone, hurt her, Rae," Xander says reassuringly, though his words do nothing to calm my anxiety.

"You should have let me go with them," I protest, and Xander's eyes darken. "I have killed two Breathers and my *Immunity*, if that's what it really is, would have been useful!"

"Like hell I'd let you put yourself in harm's way," Xander says, his voice low and quiet. "You're too valuable to me; too valuable to the city, to put you at risk."

My eye twitches at the hint of dominance and control he is already starting to display.

"*This* is why I won't be your *wife* and queen," I seethe. "You have already asserted your authority over my choices!"

Xander growls and lunges at me, his last thread of patience at my defiance snapping.

"Well, you won't have a choice in that matter either!"

I scream as he grabs me by my waist and effortlessly hoists me up, throwing me over his shoulder to carry me like some barbarian. Flourishing fear threads through my every fibre at the notion of what he is doing.

I never had a choice.

He was always going to steal me away and force me into his life—into a role of wife, queen… and prisoner.

"Put me down you monster!" I scream, kicking and punching him anywhere I can manage. My fists and feet bounce off his hard body, not affecting him in the slightest, but he recoils at my name for him.

His scarred face is no doubt an instigator for the harsh words of his people. I push my sympathy deep down to erect stone walls around my heart, seething with hate at the man who, with each step, pilfers a grain more of my freedom. The feeling of my independence slipping through my fingers overrides my common sense and all rational thoughts. This is what captive animals must feel like. I continue kicking and writhing over his shoulder when a hard smack to my rear has me momentarily frozen.

"What the… you can't just *smack* me!" I yell, my temper reaching its boiling point. "I will slay you in your sleep if you don't put me down this instance, you insufferable dick!"

Xander's deep laugh riles me more and I twist around and bite him on the arm, suddenly wishing I had Alayah's teeth. My teeth do not penetrate his leather, only serving to amuse him more so.

"You better stop struggling, otherwise we will both fall to our deaths."

I feel the lurch of the platform slowly descending as Xander pulls the lever and I instantly stop struggling with the fear of falling from such a height.

I will unleash all hell as soon as we hit the ground.

My stillness on the ride down has my thoughts swirling violently in my head like a writhing beast; the feeling of betrayal and hurt at Xander's primitive actions—and *deception*—are unfamiliar and overwhelming.

"I will always *hate* you," I whisper in defeat, my words more a defence mechanism than truth, but Xander's frame still becomes rigid beneath me.

"Don't make promises you can't keep, Rae," he replies, his voice deadly.

A tear slips down my cheek and falls onto his lower back as the feeling of hopelessness overcomes me. But I must remain steadfast, so I quickly suppress the despair and barricade the walls of my heart with resolve.

Xander's actions have sealed his death warrant. I *will* become queen. But not *his* queen.

We reach the ground, but I don't struggle or fight Xander, only focusing on thoughts of Rule Twelve.

Position is power.

Though, I am twisting it to signify a different context because in the world of survival against Breathers, it means *physical* position. Like placing one's self or shelter on a higher position to afford protection and advantage. Position provides survivors the power to endure the lethal nights in the Breathers' hunting ground.

But now, Rule Twelve means something entirely different.

It means the position of *authority* enables power, with authority being a Ruler in this case.

I can do this, I reassure myself. *I can lead humankind towards a safer world, free of Breathers; free of the lawlessness created by the anarchy of Rulers.* Starting with Segment One. *Even though Xander's Segment is not necessarily overrun by anarchy.*

The platform hits the ground and Xander steps off, walking towards a group of burly guards. "Men, this is Rae, she will be your queen in the near future," he states confidently, placing me on the ground, and his masked men glance at me with shocked expressions before they swiftly revert to their impassive professionalism.

"Touch her and you die a brutal death."

Shivers crawl up my spine at his merciless words and I realise he is one to follow through with his threats.

How many people has he killed? Has he murdered?

"Let's make a move so we arrive at the city before darkness falls," Xander barks, and his men spread out into formation, creating a barrier of protection around Xander and me. He grabs me and pulls me beside him as we start walking. I wince at the tenderness of my almost healed feet—though my body's quick recovery baffles me slightly—and Xander doesn't hesitate to swing me up into his burly arms. They rest under the crook of my knees and under my back, sending a tingling sensation racing over my skin.

"Put me down, I can walk," I whisper furiously into his ear, and he turns his head to give me a withering glare.

"No."

I inhale to let out a scream, in hopes he immediately sets me down, but instead he quickly tilts his head down to whisper, "Unless you want me to spank you in front of all the men, I suggest you keep your mouth shut."

His threat instantaneously fills me with a burst of desire, only serving to fuel my temper, but I keep my mouth shut, aware that he is one to follow through with threats. I look away, focusing on our surroundings in order to avoid looking at his frustratingly handsome face. Resentment fills me upon realising I have not been able to say goodbye to Alayah, and tears fill my eyes.

"Don't cry," Xander's tender yet stern tone cuts through my internal despair, "you will learn to love your new life."

"What about Alayah?" I furiously shoot back, my tears dissolving at my sudden anger. "She will never be safe now that so many men know where she lives."

"Lucas has marked her as his, so she will be living under his protection now."

I frown at this news and concern fills me for the wellbeing of the female who showed me so much kindness. "But what if she doesn't want to live under his protection? Does she even have a choice? Or was it taken from her just like mine?"

Xander's hold on me tightens and he growls, "You are too stubborn to know what's best for you *and* the people of Segment One, so I've had to enforce the correct course of action."

I scoff at his ignorance and shift in his arms, attempting to relieve the coiling feeling low in my abdomen from the constant press of his warm, firm body against my own.

"Anarchy and dictatorship are neither the way to a woman's heart nor those of civilians," I whisper, and his eyes snap from his constant perusal of the jungle around us to bore me with a severe look.

"And what do *you* know of matters of the heart?"

I sense possessive undertones in his words and glance away uncertainly. "I have never known or interacted with a man other than my own father." I don't know why I tell him the truth, but he visibly relaxes, and relief fills his face.

"Good."

I roll my eyes. He acts and speaks as if he possesses ownership of me *and* my past.

"Are you not going to wear your gas mask?" I change the subject, seeing the half-faced mask hanging around his neck still.

"No, I hate wearing it and am capable of defending myself against a Breather if need be." He looks down at me with a close-lipped smile and I roll my eyes at the smug expression. Tilting his head, he adds, "I was going to make you wear it but am thinking you don't really need it."

He is right. If I *am* Immune to Breathers' breath, then there is no use for a gas mask. My eyes glaze over as I stare off into the distance, happy that at least something is working in my favour today.

Xander's muscles strain as he adjusts his hold of me—frequently as time passes—but he does not place me down. We rapidly make our way through the diminished jungle and hours elapse before we eventually reach a narrow bridge crossing a raging river. My heart quickens at the distant sight of the looming walls of a city. My neck has started to cramp from the hours of holding it away from Xander's shoulder, avoiding touching him as much as possible, and relief fills me as he places me on my feet. I wince at the pressure upon my healing, battered soles and instinctually recoil when Xander swiftly pulls a dagger out to cut the ties around my wrists.

"We need to walk across carefully," he says in warning, concern etched across his face. "Make sure you don't make any sudden movements and hold on to the ropes tightly."

I nod at his instruction and he relaxes at my compliance. I'm only doing as I'm told this once because I do not want to fall to a watery death.

My heart beats erratically as we approach the narrow, rickety wooden bridge, and my eyes widen at the groaning noise it produces, protesting at the weight of two men beginning to cross it. I look at Xander with concern and he nods, indicating to keep moving. I take a deep breath and pull back my shoulders, inwardly cajoling myself to be brave. My first step on the swaying bridge causes the rope securing it to groan in protest and I tense, only to have Xander reassuringly place a hand on my lower back.

"It's okay, the bridge has been crossed many times."

I nod stiffly and force my feet to move, continuing the slow journey across the terrifying and swaying, rickety structure. My legs are like jelly by the time we reach the other side, but I quickly jump to solid ground, glancing down to see the water violently churning below the bridge.

Thank goodness that is over.

The remaining men wait behind until the four of us have crossed before beginning their slow journey over the perilous bridge, and Xander does not hesitate to swing me up in his arms again, shooting me a warning look as I open my mouth to protest. I snap my jaw shut.

My eyes travel to the looming, mismatched wall as Xander strides up to it, and I cannot believe the sight in front of me. All my worries dissipate as I gape at the tall structure that seems to stretch for eternity in both directions. The wall is comprised with a chaotic mixture of stone, various metal—both rusted and untarnished—and wood. My jaw goes slack at its tumultuous beauty. It would have taken years to build and appears to have been altered with added materials over many decades.

Where the sections of slightly rusting metal are visible, hints of reflective surfaces sparkle in the setting sun and I stare, mesmerised by the raw beauty.

A heavy clinking sound of chains draws my attention to the thick, rusted iron gateway as it slowly rolls up. I study the materials as our convoy begins to move through it. Iron is a difficult commodity to mine, and this iron looks ancient, suggesting the age of its birth and history.

My breath hitches once we are through the other side. The hindered sunlight obstructed by the soaring walls does not detract from the magnificence of the bustling city within, and I gasp in delight at the various buildings. Both tall and diminutive structures border the maze of endless dirt roads disappearing into the distance. What appears to be the main street leads directly ahead of us in an unwavering, infinite path. The magnitude of how large a city is does not escape me and Xander chuckles at my wonder.

He probably does not realise I've never seen the exterior of a city that has withstood the fallout, or been erected after the fallout, let alone the inside of one. I have only ever found ruins of desolate and defeated civilisations.

It feels like we walk for miles until we arrive at the entrance of the towering, tarnished metal building that I assume is the centre of the city. Its sheer, threatening presence suggests this is where the Ruler lives. Where Xander resides.

Where I will reside.

The guards quickly assess the area, key in the code on the exterior of the tower and then usher us both in. We walk through to a large foyer and I look around the vast interior of the dark building, noticing how austere and impersonal it is. Large, dark metal sheets cover each section of the walls, hints of rust only partially visible from the lack of lighting, and the floor appears to be made from a cloudy-grey, hard substance. The space is void of any dirt or smell and I strain my neck to look up, my jaw immediately dropping. The sudden inability to move any muscle grips me as awe floods my being from witnessing such impossibly skyward ceilings. Not once do I tear my eyes away from it, even as Xander moves.

He carries me to the bottom of a looming staircase and begins a slow ascent up the cloudy-grey stairs in silence, indicating his need for rest after carrying me for hours.

I catalogue a first then second floor that we continue past, each consisting of a long hallway and singular door, though each floor is silent without any bustle of human activity.

It seems like we have been ascending endlessly when Xander comes to an abrupt stop before a heavy, metal door. Peering up at the ceiling, I note that we are at the top floor, though this level does not contain a lengthy hallway as the two below do.

Xander gently places me down and I roll my stiff neck and shoulders as he effortlessly pushes the large door open. Placing his large hand firmly on my lower back, he ushers me inside and my eyes travel around the spacious yet uninviting room. The interior imitates the foyer below, with the walls consisting of large, rusting metal sheets, and lacking any windows bar a small pane to our left. The space feels just as ruthless and calculating as Xander himself.

"It suits you," I deadpan, and the corner of his lips tip up, transforming his exhausted and slackened face. His eyes darken with desire as he stares at me, and I stand awkwardly in his residence, shifting nervously on my sore, battered feet, my eyes darting around as I lick my lips.

I'm in the privacy of his home now. To do as he pleases with me.

The thought both frightens and exhilarates me, but I push both feelings deep down.

I'm only here for one reason.

Position is power.

16

XANDER

Y BODY COILS WITH DESIRE AT THE IMAGE OF RAE, vulnerable, and standing in *my* home.

Everything about this feels *right* and I stalk towards her, filled with the immense urge to have her in my hands. Rae's eyes widen at my sudden advance and she steps back to evade me. I slow my pace at the display of her fear.

Fuck.

Coming to an abrupt stop only a metre from her, I lean back to briefly look at her, then wearily sigh while rubbing my face roughly.

"I just need to hold you." My voice is gruff but sincere, and my words cause her eyes to momentarily squint before something indecipherable flashes through them. But she only nods affirmatively, and I'm instantly filled with relief.

I move forward, lifting my hand to tuck a strand of dark, silky hair behind her ear. She flinches at the contact and looks away, so I grip her chin and tilt her delicately shaped face towards me. Her breathing becomes shallow and the pupils of her startling eyes dilate as I lean in ever so slightly to brush a soft kiss across her lush lips.

I don't know what urged me to do so, but instant need fills me at the sensation of her full lips against mine, and the entire quantity of my blood rushes south.

The slightest whimper escapes her, snapping my thread of control and I growl, crushing her against my chest as I ravish her lips more urgently. Her soft moans vibrate against me and I groan into her mouth at the pleasurable essence of her feminine body against my own hard, unrelenting one. My hands greedily roam over her lean curves and I grind my hardened length against her stomach. I grip the bottom of her shirt and begin lifting it over her head when an urgent rapping against the door suddenly halts my progress.

This better be fucking important.

Pulling Rae's shirt back down to cover her, I stomp angrily to the door and yank it open. My irritation at being interrupted ramps up at the sight of a scantily clad Nelinha, posing against the frame seductively.

"What are you doing here?" I grit out through clenched teeth, and she flinches at my tone before maintaining her facade of seduction.

This woman is the *last* person I want to see. Especially with Rae in my life now.

"Xander, my darling," she coos in a sickening voice, "I thought perhaps you would need a massage after your long, tiring journey." Nelinha doesn't wait for my reply and attempts to move past me into my living space.

I push her firmly back and stand with my arms crossed, my

stance widened, irritation rapidly increasing at the fact that she would dare to overstep her position. The reminder of sleeping with this snake only angers me further. What was I even thinking when I let her into my bed all those years ago?

Loneliness. Though, I would never admit it aloud.

Even though I stopped fucking her, I stupidly kept her on as masseuse, which seems to have encouraged this illusion of hers.

Nelinha's eyes fill with hurt at my rejection, and she peers suspiciously around me, reeling back at the sight of Rae standing there awkwardly. My hackles rise at the venomous look Nelinha sends Rae and I remind myself to keep a close watch on the sneaky woman. I don't trust her. The woman's superficial beauty does nothing to conceal her noxious character and I will no longer be deceived by the wiles of her green eyes, long dark hair and smooth olive skin.

"What is *she* doing in your residence?" Nelinha hisses and looks back up at me expectantly, her expression sour. I don't *ever* hit women but suddenly feel the need to clench my fists by my sides at her blatant disrespect.

"Firstly, you have overstepped your *position,*" I growl, and her eyes widen. "I did not request your services, yet you had the audacity to invade my privacy anyway. Secondly, who I involve myself with is *none* of your business and it would be in your best interest to keep your nose where it belongs. If I ever see you even *looking* at my future *queen,* you will suffer greatly. Do you understand?"

I decide in that moment that even if I must first convince Rae to be my lover, everyone else need only know that she will be my queen. I can't have people tainting her innocence with harsh slander.

Nelinha's eyes widen at the mention of a queen and her mouth gapes open and shut unattractively before she squares her shoulders and looks me dead in the eyes; her sickeningly sweet facade falling back into place. "Of course, Ruler, I apologise with my whole heart and sincerely hope you will forgive my error."

I won't.

Nelinha shoots a quick glare at Rae, curling her lip before spinning hastily on her preposterous heels and striding angrily away. The sheer, red material billows out around her long legs and I scoff at her attempts of seducing her way into my life, silently promising myself to never use her massage services again.

Not that I would with Rae here now.

My eyes have suddenly been opened to the reality of Nelinha's surreptitious scheme. With a weary exhale, I turn around to see a flash of wavy, raven hair disappearing behind my bedroom door. Impulsively, I rush over just as the door slams shut in my face. Rolling my tense neck and shoulders from the unpleasant encounter with the city harlot and masseuse, I relish in my amusement at Rae's constant temper, knocking loudly on *my* bedroom door.

"You can't stay locked away forever," I call out, and snicker when I hear something shatter against the other side. I have no sentimental belongings, so I'm not concerned about her destroying the room. It just gives me even more reason to punish her.

Something I would enjoy greatly… and know she would too.

"Your temper won't achieve anything, Rae," I say while continuing to chuckle at the sounds smashing against the door.

I take my chance in the break of items smashing and rip the door open, tearing through the entrance quickly. My feet freeze when I spot Rae on the other side of my massive bed with a bottle of brandy in her hand.

I was wrong; there is something valuable in here.

"*Don't* come near me," she spits out, and my muscles constrict with anticipation at the challenge and chase.

The hunt.

"I can assure you, that bottle of brandy in your hand will be much more enjoyable as a drink rather than decor over the wall," I tell her slowly, and her eyes flash dangerously as she bares her teeth, lifting the bottle higher. The woman is such a paradox, innocent and yet fierce. "I tell you what, Rae," I coax her, "what if we sit down and have a glass each and I promise I won't come near you or touch you. Unless you beg for it."

Her eyes flare with defiance again and I chuckle. "I will *never* beg for your touch," she seethes.

I raise an eyebrow, knowing otherwise, but shrug casually. "That's your prerogative. We can still enjoy a drink though— the brandy is the smoothest you'll ever taste. It has a somewhat numbing effect on a weary body."

Contemplation crosses her face as she tentatively lowers her arm, glancing curiously at the bottle in her grasp. Her bright blue eyes spear me as she nods once, and I inwardly celebrate the small victory. *Baby steps.*

I look around at the shattered glass scattered across the floor and chuckle at the irony. "Well, since you broke all the glasses, we will need to swig out of the bottle."

Rae shrugs as if she hasn't a care in the world and respect fills me at her nonchalant attitude. Any other woman would make a fuss and demand I order more glasses for them to drink from, in fear of not acting like a suitable woman. Though I assume they would not have smashed anything in the first place.

"Let's drink on the couch," I tell her, and her eyes dip to my large bed before widening with comprehension of what happens there. A wolfish grin spreads across my face at her blushing and I stride forward, taking advantage of her moment of incapacity to swiftly grasp the bottle in her hand. I lean in to whisper in her ear while running my knuckle down her soft cheek. "It won't be long until you're lying naked in this bed, little mouse."

A gasp leaves her lips, and she would have dropped the precious bottle if not for my tight grasp around it. It doesn't take long for her temper to eradicate her sudden lust and she pushes past me, storming towards the couch in my living room. An amused chuckle vibrates through my chest as I swiftly stalk after my prey, removing the mask from around my neck to throw it over the bench on my way.

"I don't want you anywhere near me," Rae spits as I approach the couch. "*Especially* if you have been gallivanting around the city, trying each woman. You have all those women at your disposal, why must you insist on bothering me?"

I flinch at her words and I momentarily regret my crass attitude towards the females of Segment One.

And the number of women I've fucked.

This is new for me. This relationship with Rae will be anything but casual, even though I keep telling myself she is only here to warm my bed.

I don't know what to say to appease her since I've never had to before, but I know I need to tread lightly.

I clear my throat. "I have had many partners in bed, yes," I tell Rae slowly, and her nose crinkles with disgust at me. *Bah.* I cannot change the past. "But I will never have another woman in my bed again. Only you. If you allow it."

Rae's eyes broaden at my declaration and her face blushes prettily as she looks away.

I hold out the bottle of brandy to her and she snatches it from my hand, taking a large swig, only to choke on the mouthful, spraying most of the liquid violently out.

"That's revolting!"

I laugh at her reaction and take the bottle from her, tipping it back to have a swig.

It's smooth and delicious.

"Do you not drink moonshine or anything similar?" I ask her curiously and her eye twitches.

"No. Us poor and struggling survivors cannot find the means to drink such unavailable liquid, particularly when it proves to hold no nutritional value." Her tone is deadpanned.

Ah, how insensitive of me. "I'm sorry, I didn't think."

Rae scoffs and rolls her eyes at me. "No, you *didn't* think, Xander," she reprimands, and my body tenses at the sound of my name on her lips. I want to hear her say it again. "That's the problem, you don't think. You didn't think about the consequences of taking me without my consent, you didn't think to let me say goodbye to my only friend in this world and you didn't think to educate me first before thrusting me into a society I don't belong to!"

Well, shit.

"Tell me what to do to make this better," I say sincerely, and her eyes brighten as she places the brandy on the low wooden table situated in front of the couch. She sits back to cross her arms and my eyes dip to the swell of her chest pushing up from the motion.

"Let. Me. Go." She tilts her chin up. "Give me my

independence."

I abruptly laugh at her request. "I will *never* let you go, little mouse."

Rage fills her face, reddening the pale skin, and she launches at me, her tiny fists flying in all directions as her petite frame mercilessly assaults my larger form.

"I hate that name and I hate you!" she yells, continuing to batter me with punches. Her efforts are futile, but I love the display of spirit and temper, so I welcome the solid punches, though her strikes hold no strength.

I let her vent her frustrations on me and after a few minutes she realises her fists aren't effective. Her assaults slow and then she crumples into a ball of defeat on the floor, her spirit deflating her like a leaking leather sack of water. I can't stand the sight of Rae miserable. I much prefer her filled with rage and fight.

Sliding off the couch, I sit cross legged and pull the little hellion into my lap as subdued sobs rack her body. Stroking her hair soothingly, I press a kiss to the top of her head.

"I need you in my life, Rae," I whisper into her soft hair. She tenses at my words. I don't know why I need to reassure her and make her feel better, nor can I fathom why I decide to speak honestly. I *never* bother myself with a woman's sentiments.

"You're the only woman who has enough spirit, intelligence, and passion to be my queen. All other women pale in comparison to you." My own truthful, startling words spear through my chest and I exhale roughly.

Rae's pixie-like face tilts up to look at me curiously, her beautiful eyes puffy and tinged red from her tears. "But someone who contains that much intelligence and spirit should not be controlled. Cannot be imprisoned. It will essentially oppress their essence."

I nod thoughtfully at her insight that once again proves her clever mind. "Well, tell me another way for this to work. Tell me how you can be in my life—in this city—without having to lock you up so you don't run away back to your meaningless life."

I know my words are harsh and Rae flinches.

"I could never be contained. I would not stay within the city walls if I had freedom. I would want to immerse myself amidst the survivors segregating on the outskirts of civilisations nearby. I know there are communities locked outside most Segments because Alayah told me about them."

I tense at the thought of her being vulnerable amongst the violent communities of neighbouring Segments, suddenly glad our city has none, and shake my head.

"I would never allow it. Those survivors are cast out for a reason. They're violent and a threat to peaceful residents. You would be walking into imminent danger if you were to immerse yourself within these communities."

Rae frowns as she absorbs the information. "They are only violent in order to survive."

It's charming that she only sees the good in everyone but can still remain wary of threats.

"Ah, sweet Rae, you are too forgiving towards strangers. People *always* have a choice."

"That's not true," she fires back, shaking her head. "I kill Breathers in order to survive. Everything I do is to survive. And none of it is a *choice*."

"Yes, but you don't steal or murder innocent humans for your own gain, do you?"

This causes her to soften and she shakes her head, finally

understanding my perspective.

"No, I don't." Her words are quiet and sombre. "But Hunters *you* use, steal and murder innocent humans for their own gain, and you allow *them* into the city."

Ah, her father and Alayah's mother.

My eyes travel to the pendant nestled between her breasts, its shape peeking out through the thin, deteriorating cloth.

I will need to acquire some clothes for her. I will give her *everything* she needs and more.

"Those Hunters are independent and were only employed *once* when desperately needed," I explain, defending myself. "For example, if our resources are dwindling and none of our citizens can acquire food on their hunts, we will implement their services, but only if we are in dire need and have no other options. The Hunters you detest so much only enter these walls when delivering me something. I cannot control their actions outside the walls because it's out of my jurisdiction."

Comprehensions fills Rae's crestfallen face, but she doesn't say anything more and slides off my lap. I instantly miss her heat and my heart clenches at the sadness filling her forlorn eyes. Her grief is palpable as she mourns the loss of her father, and I feel ill equipped to comfort her, so I offer the only thing I turn to when mourning the violent loss of my own mother. I pick the bottle of brandy up and hold it out—an offering of peace—and she tentatively takes it from my hand to tip her head back and take a mouthful. My eyes travel to her soft, pale, delicate neck and my pants tighten almost instantly.

Every part of her is so painfully beautiful; even the array of faded silver scars decorating her ivory skin and the less erotic anatomy such as her delicate nose.

Rae manages to drink a quarter of the bottle without spluttering and within a few moments I see the instant effect blanketing her eyes with a glassy glaze.

"Thish' feelsh' nice," she slurs, and I smile wickedly at her.

"Yes, it does. Fucking will feel nice too, but we will leave that for another night—when you're sober." I cringe at the automatic rude words falling from my mouth, internally reminding myself not to converse with Rae in such an approach.

A gasp escapes her lips at my crassness and her blue eyes go impossibly wide, albeit unfocussed.

"Oh."

I laugh darkly, loving this agreeable side peeking through her increasing inebriation. As pliable as Rae would be right now, I would never take advantage of her in this state, so I push to my feet and pull her with me. I slide my arms around her tiny waist when she sways unevenly, the brandy making her world spin, and I momentarily feel bad for subjecting her to the heady alcohol.

But she needs the escape.

Her father's death clearly weighs heavily on her chest still.

Directing her to my room, I pick her up and carry her over to the large bed, depositing her in the middle. Rae's dark hair splays around her, fanning against the deep green of my satiny sheets. Her snowy skin glows in contrast to the dark colour around her. The vision is breathtaking, and as I stand staring at this beautiful woman, I suddenly grasp how lucky I am to have discovered this gem.

Rae sends me a sleepy smile and her eyelids become heavy, flickering as she fights to keep them open. I strip down and make my way to the bath to wash off any grime from the day's journey then slip naked into the sheets beside her slight frame.

Rae's drunken state keeps her agreeable and she doesn't complain about my proximity to her—only muttering incoherent words, rolling over to sling a leg over me. I momentarily freeze at the unfamiliar gesture.

I don't keep women in bed after a fuck and I certainly don't cuddle them, but Rae's soft body, pliant and pushed up delightfully against mine, feels *right*. It's such a foreign feeling.

I somehow know tonight will be the best sleep I've ever had.

Rae's thigh shifts to brush against my groin and I clench my eyes shut.

Or the worst.

Inwardly groaning at the delectable feeling of her softness against me, I close my eyes to force myself asleep.

The next morning, I regretfully untangle myself from Rae's lean limbs with a moan as she accidentally brushes my arousal, and I stand up to look down at the peaceful expression resting on her face. My day now consists of copious amounts of staring ever since the raven-haired beauty appeared in my life.

Shaking my head from my idiocy, I make my way to the bathroom and splash my face with icy cold water. Anything to make the blood in my nether regions rush elsewhere.

Quickly dressing in my clean, black form-fitting pants and shirt—a nice change from the worn clothes of yesterday—I make my way down the flight of stairs and exit the building, making a beeline for my favourite person and seamstress. The clothes I wear are cleverly crafted by her own hands, and the memory of her spinning yarn on a wheel using wool from the animals we hunt still amazes me to this day.

Her shop is just down the dusty road, almost adjacent to my tower, and the little old lady peers at me over her wire-rimmed spectacles when I push through the glass door.

"My darling Xander," she beams. "To what do I owe the pleasure?"

This lady is the *only* person other than Lucas who gets away with calling me by my first name. Long, silver hair falls around her shoulders and down her waist, making her slight stature appear smaller. The pale wrinkles covering her delicate skin crease further with the smile spreading across her face at the sight of me.

Alma has been the Segment's seamstress long before I was born and has always treated me with motherly affection. As if I were her own son.

"Alma," I smile, striding over behind the counter to envelop her tiny and hunched frame in a firm hug.

No one has seen me show affection or emotion except Alma and Lucas.

And now Rae.

The sudden thought of Rae reminds me of my visit. "I will need several sets of both dresses and practical clothes. Pants and shirts," I tell Alma, and her eyebrows rise at my strange request. I recall Rae's attempt to swindle Lucas and me of our leathers back in the jungle. "And perhaps use the leather left over from my own gear to make braces for the forearms and a breastplate. If there is enough, also make a general vest for everyday use."

Alma tilts her head curiously and her milky, aged eyes asses me with amusement. "Now, dear, are these dresses and clothes for yourself?"

A laugh rips from deep within my chest at her dry humour and I wipe the stray tear from the corner of my eye. "Hilarious, Alma," I say and waggle my finger at her in a playful reprimand. "That's no way to speak to your Ruler."

Alma scoffs and rolls her once blue, now cloudy eyes at my teasing remark. I realise how similar Rae's characteristics are to her and my forehead puckers.

Odd.

"Though you will be pleased to know the dresses and clothes are not for me," I continue, pushing the strange thoughts aside, "they will be for a very slight woman."

Interest illuminates her antiquated wise eyes, and an expanding smile transforms her pasty, wrinkly face. "Well, well, well, Xander," she slyly begins, "this is a first. You have never requested clothes for any female. Tell me, is this female… important to you?"

I see no use in beating around the bush since Alma's the closest person I have to family — aside from Lucas. "She will be important to the whole city in various ways, but mainly she is to be queen." I won't give Alma a heart attack by telling her my plans to take Rae as a bed mate. Though declaring the words that Rae is to be queen sounds… right.

Alma's eyes widen with shock as she stares at me. "You have got to be pulling my leg," she says, her Irish lilt of the old world more evident through her elation.

I shake my head. "No, I'm dead serious. I'm to make her my wife, eventually." Each time I verbalise the words, the more I come to appreciate the sound of them.

Alma's eyes fill with overjoyed tears as she slowly hobbles closer to embrace me.

"I can see she makes you happy," she quietly says with a smile. "I demand to meet her soon."

A stupid smile spans the width of my scarred face as I return Alma's embrace and kiss the top of her silver head.

"I will bring her down as soon as she wakes."

I suddenly remember I'm to send a request out to the residents of the city, inviting them to the impending monthly meeting. "Fuck."

I will get one of my men to send the invites through the communications room.

My hand hovers over the communications device by my side as I contemplate sending the order to a guard now.

"Xander," Alma chides, breaking me from my own thoughts, "no cursing in my shop."

I chuckle and lean down to kiss Alma's cheek. "Sorry, Alma. I've got to go, but I will see you later."

I rub my cheek where Alma pinched it and my mind drifts to the meeting I need to organise as I make my way to the exit.

Once a month, citizens who have queries or needs, gather in a line at the City Hall appeal for a return of services or goods. I log each request and trade alongside the family name and place of residence to be executed over the following few days. Since currency is no longer valid—banks were raided and closed long before my time—most cities effectively run on trades of goods and services. For people within cities, they all contribute in some form, whether that's as a medical officer or simply as a street cleaner. In return, they all receive the refuge of residence within the walls and clean, running water as well as basic food to survive. If any extra is needed, they attend these monthly hall meetings to make the requests. Where extra services are needed—such as medical attention or maintenance on their residence, trades of their own services are made in overtime or by helping another citizen who has made a request. The Council members, who go through the list I create, effectively organise each appeal.

Fuck. Yet another thing to deal with.

I will just get Lucas to let the usual old ladies— the Council members—know. It takes a lot of organising. At least the old hags will get off my back once they hear I've found a queen who will produce my heirs. Even if it's just a lie for now, the gossip of Rae becoming queen will be useful for something.

Rubbing my hand over my face, I sigh wearily. Being a Ruler is not without its burdens.

Rule Thirteen: Keep Your Wits About You

17

Rae

THE POUNDING IN MY HEAD MAKES ME WINCE as I push up to a seated position in the large, luxurious bed. The room starts instantly spinning and it takes several moments for me to gain my bearings. I gasp at the realisation I'm in *Xander's* bed. Springing from the mattress frantically, my behind instantly hits the revolving floor with a thud.

Looking down, I sigh with relief at seeing my clothes intact, then instantly feel nausea rising in my throat, the acidic bile burning as it travels vertically. My head snaps up to see the opening to an adjoined tiled room, so I jump to my unsteady feet and rush to what I'm certain is the bathroom.

After I relieve the contents of my stomach into a white porcelain toilet, I remain on my knees and take deep breaths before glancing up to see a jug on the sink beside me. With a groan, I use the edge of the cold toilet to hoist myself up and I shuffle to the sink. Peering in the jug to see water, I gleefully grasp it and tilt it up so I can drink the cold, soothing liquid.

"Ah, much better." I wipe my mouth and place the jug back down with a clink.

Feeling entirely better after some hydration, though still with a pounding head, I make my way back to the bedroom. The sight of the large, mahogany bedframe and mattress covered in luxurious green material and plush pillows freezes me on the spot. My jaw drops at the reminder of how lavish the bed is. I've never slept in a proper bed before.

Xander.

My eyes narrow at the reminder of the insufferable man and I curse at my inability to recall the previous night's events through my hazy mind.

Last night I broke Rule Thirteen.

It is common sense as a survivor to stay alert to any threats lurking nearby.

Becoming intoxicated is the quickest way to lose one's wits and good sense, though it was nice forgetting the burdens of my responsibility to humankind.

And temporarily forgetting the violent death of Pa.

Shoulders sagging with sorrow, I shuffle out of the disconcerting bedroom and make my way to the couch, my aching muscles sighing with relief as I collapse into the plush padding. The lack of windows in the soulless space benefits my throbbing headache and I'm glad for the deficiency of light.

"Fresh air would probably benefit me right now," I muse with a sigh.

My eyes travel to the door and I jump to my feet at the sudden thought.

I wonder if I could just leave... Tentatively, I creep towards the symbol of my freedom and place my hand on the cold metal doorknob. I turn it slowly and hear a click as the latch unlocks. My brows rise.

Was he really stupid enough to leave me with the means to escape?

I grasp the handle and pull the heavy door towards me, needing to use both hands to move its heavy weight. My heart beats anxiously against my chest as I peer around the tiny gap, and a victorious smile expands across my face.

"Well. That was easy."

I slip through the narrow opening and shut the door behind me, spinning to make my sprint down the stairs, only to slam into the awful woman dubbed Nelinha from the night before. Her face morphs into disgust as she rights herself and peruses the length of me with distaste.

"You," she spits the word out, her lip curling. "He's only using you and then will discard you like the trash you are."

I laugh at her spiteful words, not caring the least, and she steps back slightly as her face transforms into shock at my outburst.

"You are welcome to have him because *I'm* not interested in being his whore." I deliver my statement with feigned cheer and push past her to skip down the stairs, not turning back to see the vicious sneer no doubt crossing her deceivingly beautiful face.

The smile that victoriously extends across my own as I near the looming door to freedom falters at the image of the beautiful woman in bed with Xander. Despising the rage of jealousy churning low in my stomach, I remind myself that I'm much better without a man—without *Xander*—dictating my way of life. The awful woman can keep him as far as I'm concerned. My smile grows once more as my hand reaches for the door to push it open and I instantly regret stepping out into the blaring sun.

"Ow!" I shield my sensitive eyes from the brightness and my

pounding head assails me again.

No time to whine, I reprimand myself. *Must run!*

My legs spring to action and I sprint in the direction I'm facing, not caring where it leads me—only wanting to get as far away from Xander's tower as I can.

Nelinha yells profanities from behind as she pursues me outside, accusing me of deceiving Xander into bed. I wince at the condemning stares of the onlookers in the street.

Oh well. It's not like I will see any of them again.

The thought has my feet screeching to a stop.

Wait, the plan.

I forgot about my plans to overthrow Xander and take over as queen. Or at least finding a way to share my Immunity. I *will* be seeing these people again. But I have already fled Xander's tower and have no means of finding a way back inside. I rack my mind for solutions and notice a small, brightly coloured shop across the street.

Maybe I will just pretend I'm browsing stores?

I could say I was not able to get back inside when Xander finds me.

Pushing back my shoulders, I cross the street confidently, ignoring the harsh words of Nelinha still echoing down the street, drawing the stares of civilians.

I look at the weird symbols above the brightly coloured shop and assume the jumble of letters state the name of its occupation.

Pa did not bother educating me with reading and writing and said my words would be more influential. A book or letter also was not going to save me in the wastelands.

I see materials and clothes in the display window as I near the yellow building and conclude the place is likely where people acquire their clothes. Just as I lift my hands to push the glass door open, it swings forward and I fall into a large wall of muscle, gasping at the familiar scent.

"Rae," Xander greets me bluntly, then pulls his lips into a tight line.

Instinctually, I attempt to spin around and run, only to have his large hands snake out and firmly grasp my shoulders.

"What are you doing outside?" his suspicious tone is hard.

"I was just getting some fresh air and wanted to have a look around," I reply with a stammer, my voice wavering when I meet his darkening and potent gaze, forcing me to look down as I wring my hands together. Sweat trickles down my spine, both from the harsh sun and anxiety.

"Xander, dear." I hear a frail voice cut in behind us and Xander's eyes soften at the strangely accented voice. "Is *this* the woman I am to make the clothes for?"

My head snaps back to Xander in question.

He's having clothes made for me?

Xander pulls me inside the shop and shuts the door behind us to block out the increasing heat, turning to present me to an extremely elderly lady. Her frail limbs are covered in wrinkly, papery skin and her fingers are gnarled like the branches of a twisted, dead tree. Beautiful hair falls around her shoulders and waist, the length of it like the silvery cascading current of a waterfall.

"Rae, this is Alma, the city's one and only seamstress," Xander says, his tone full of affection. I tilt my head curiously at the little old lady whose eyes widen with shock and... *recognition?* I've never seen the lady in my life, so I don't read into her reaction. My thoughts instead focus on Xander's demeanour towards her.

It is the first time I've seen Xander display such affection... as if Alma is his mother.

Or grandmother, considering her evident age.

Alma shuffles forward, her pale blue eyes twinkling with mischief, a toothless smile growing across her wrinkled face. My eyes widen as her arms reach out and she embraces me with surprising strength, crushing me as she laughs jubilantly.

Uh, is she mad?

I look over her head of thick silver hair to Xander, who has a rare grin across his usually arrogant face.

"Ah, little Rae," Alma says, her voice cracking as she steps back to scrutinise me, and I shift uncomfortably when she taps her chin thoughtfully. "You have such a special aura about you; you are just perfect for our dear Xander."

My eyes twitch at her words and I glare at Xander as the tips of my ears burn. A smug look crosses his face, and he shrugs casually at me, causing my nails to painfully stab into the palms of my clenched fists. I tightly keep my lips pressed together in attempt to refrain from saying something rude in front of the little old lady, but my temper prevails.

"Argh! You're such an arrogant, insufferable beast, Xander!"

I gasp at my own sudden outburst and slap a hand over my mouth as my widened eyes dart to Alma with concern. To my astonishment, she throws her head back and lets out a loud, melodic laugh while tears run down the crevices of her pallid face. I find it peculiar how different her attributes are from most people in the area. The humans I've seen, including Xander, are olive-skinned with dark and exotic features.

"Oh, dear Rae," she wheezes, "you are just what this pig-headed man needs!"

Xander glowers at me in displeasure and he crosses his large arms over his wide chest.

"I need to put Rae over my knee and give her a good smacking, is what I need," he growls, and I step closer to Alma in fright.

"Now, now, Xander," Alma says, "that is not how your dear mother, may she rest in peace, raised you to treat women."

Xander tenses at the mention of his mother and his jaw clenches as his eyes pierce me with a cold and calculating look. A chill runs up my spine at his sudden detachment from all emotion and I glance at Alma warily, only to have Xander's deep voice capture my attention again.

"Well, *Mother* isn't here anymore," he says, his voice dripping with cynicism, "so I will do as I please."

Fear swells low in my stomach as I look to Alma who clucks her disapproval.

"Well, either way, I will need dear Rae with me today so I can measure her up to fit all her clothes," Alma declares, and I exhale in relief.

"No."

My solace is short-lived at Xander's sharp and abrupt reply.

"Xander, do not defy me, young man, or I will take the wooden spoon to your behind like you're a small wean again!"

My mouth drops at Alma's reprimand and I glance at Xander to see how he will react to such disrespect. He sends me a dark look and scrubs a hand exasperatedly over his face.

"Fine. But don't let her leave. If she disappears then there will be consequences."

He storms through the front door without another word or glance backwards, and my mind spins at the tumultuous energy he leaves behind.

"Come now, dear," Alma says as if nothing just happened. "Let's get you cleaned up and looking like the queen you really are."

Her words wrench me back into reality and I frown at her with confusion.

"Your spirit and passion are what makes a good leader, dear." Alma chuckles at my bewildered look and I follow her as she makes her way back to a table covered in materials. I can hear her bones creaking as she slowly lowers herself into the rickety wooden chair. "Your lack of ego and vanity are also the fundaments of good leadership," she continues, and my mind sways to Xander.

I cringe, recollecting the glacial expression that fell over his face at the mention of his mother.

"Why was he so bitter about his mother?" I tentatively ask, curious to understand.

Alma sighs wearily and sorrow crosses her features as she looks up from her materials and equipment. "That is a story for Xander to share when he is ready, dear. But he may never want to, and you will need to be patient with him."

I nod, concern filling me as I study Alma, who clearly is more to Xander than just a seamstress.

My wavering plan to rid the Segment of him becomes more jaded with each heartening morsel I discover about him.

Not that I would have ever followed through with it.

"So, dear, he has requested leathers to be made for you too," Alma cuts into my troubling thoughts and my heart leaps cheerfully at her words.

"Really?" My palm rests over my mouth with pleasant shock.

Xander must have remembered my negotiating in the tree-hut

for leathers. How can he be so thoughtful and kind yet suddenly so cold and callous?

Ask Xander about his mother.

The more I think on it, the more certain I am that his troubling mood is connected to the death of his mother. Alma pulls me from my deep thoughts again as she stands and holds a long tape with markings along it around the girth of my arm and chest.

"What is that?" I ask her curiously and she looks up in surprise.

"It is a measuring tape, dear," she says slowly, her knowing gaze peering into the depths of my eyes. "Where do you come from and what is your story, girl?"

I tense at the sudden interrogation and she affectionately squeezes my shoulder in reassurance as she places the tape down. "Ah, I mean you no harm, dear," Alma tells me. "Come, let us have a cup of tea, with a dash of my brandy if you like."

I chuckle at her eccentricity and follow her to the back of the shop, instantly feeling more at ease by her grandmotherly nature. Alma hobbles through a door leading to her simple living quarters: an open plan living area, kitchen, and another small room that must contain the bathroom and bedroom. My eyes travel around to peer at the interesting ornaments and paintings decorating the space and I move to stand in front of one hanging ornament that appears somewhat familiar. I trace the intricate patterns, standing closer to inspect the smooth, wooden item.

"That is the Celtic Carolingian Cross," Alma's voice cuts through my deep reverie.

My hand lifts for the pendant around my neck as I study the patterns.

"It looks similar to my pendant," I muse, and Alma's stern voice cuts through my reverie.

"Show me your pendant, child."

I bite my lower lip, contemplating whether I should be revealing the most sacred part of my history to a strange elderly lady, but I remember the affection and trust that Xander exhibited towards her. Tentatively, I pull the brassy gold pendant from my neck and hand it to Alma who gasps sharply at seeing it.

"What's wrong?" I ask her apprehensively, concern rising in my chest.

Her pale blue eyes meet my own and I frown at the expression crossing her face as she attentively studies me.

"Did you find this somewhere?"

I shake my head, wondering if she is accusing me of stealing it.

"No, my Pa gave it to me before he was murde—before he died. It was my mother's."

Alma stares at me momentarily, her studious gaze filled with years of knowledge and wisdom.

"And who was your mother?" she asks eagerly, glancing back down at the knotted pendant in her hand.

"Well, she died giving birth to me," I tell her factually, still uncertain as to why she is asking so many questions. "So, I never knew her, though Pa said she looked like me. Her name was Riona."

Alma's eyes widen again, and she thrusts the chain and pendant back into my hand as she quickly shuffles to a shelf against the wall, wrenching various drawers open and closed while muttering to herself. "I knew you looked familiar."

Her mumblings astound me, and I do not think I've ever been this confused in my entire life. Alma exclaims upon retrieving her desired object and shuts the wooden drawer loudly before quickly hobbling back over to me. Stretching out her pale, wrinkly hand, she reveals a golden brooch. It is the exact symbol as my gold pendant. I gasp and my gaze darts up to Alma. "Why is it the same?"

Her excitable disposition calms as she nods, her own comprehension of the situation cumulative. "Come, lets chat over some tea. And brandy. We will definitely need brandy."

I follow her to the heavy wooden table near the kitchen and sit in an adjacent rickety seat, my mind racing with possibilities. Alma flutters about the kitchen, clanging pots and pans as she prepares the tea and sweets. Within moments, a steaming pot of brandied tea is placed on the table in front of me, alongside a plate of mouth-watering pale cookies.

Alma chuckles as she sees me eyeing them and pushes the plate towards me. "Have as many as you would like, dear."

Without hesitation my arm snakes out and I grasp a large cookie, shoving it in my mouth and simultaneously moaning as I bite down on the buttery sweet goodness.

My life will never be the same without these delicious things.

"This is the best thing I've ever eaten," I tell her with a full mouth.

Alma chuckles, though her face quickly falls serious as she pours the pot of hot tea into a cup for me. While pouring one for herself, she leisurely begins a story.

"There was a time, hundreds of years ago prior to humankind's downfall, where a particular country across the oceans was referred to as *Ireland*. The language predominantly used was Gaelic," Alma says wistfully as she transports back to the past and whispers, "Is sinne an fheadhainn a chaidh a thaghadh."

My eyes widen at the familiar words my Pa used to recite to

me over the years.

I thought he was just talking nonsense—muttering incoherent words mournfully, years after his love died.

"Pa used to say those words to me before sleep."

Alma blanches as she freezes at my words. "Then my conjectures are true."

I pause with a biscuit halfway to my mouth. "What conjectures? And what do the words mean?"

Alma pauses, studying me for a moment before continuing. "They mean *we are the chosen ones*. See your pendant?" she asks.

I nod. "Yes, the same as your gold one?"

Alma nods slowly. "It is the Celtic Trinity Knot. Thousands of years ago it symbolised eternal, spiritual life and being, though sometime later became common with the Christian religion as a symbol of The Father, The Son, the Holy Spirit." I look at her with a blank expression.

I have only heard snippets of the old religions that were rampant prior to The Vanquishing.

"Ah, never mind that though," Alma waves her hand in dismissal. "I forget your age—religion was still widespread for the first half of my life prior to this mess we are in now." My eyes widen at the realisation that Alma has lived in the old world, a civilisation lost to The Vanquishing.

That cannot be right, otherwise she would be hundreds of years old.

"How did you survive?" I ask intently, ignoring my bemusement.

"Ah, this brings us back to the pendant," Alma says, once again perplexing me. "You see, even though this ancient symbol has adopted many meanings over centuries—there is only one that is true."

My anticipation has me leaning on the edge of my chair, hanging on every thread of my patience as Alma pauses to take a long sip of her tea and a bite of cookie. I nearly fall over with relief as she chews and swallows her last bite to continue. "It is the symbol of Immunity—very much the original meaning of its first creation—eternal, spiritual life and being. There are other features it carries, but I will not overwhelm you."

My eyes widen at the gravity of Alma's news. "But my mother died, so how can it be eternal life?"

"Now child, this is where it becomes complicated and you must be open-minded," Alma says sternly, and I nod my head enthusiastically, keen to hear more. "Thousands of years ago, the eternal life was stated in a prophecy. Though, as it was in Gaelic, the meaning became lost in translation." She pauses and waits for me to absorb the information. "Now, I am not sure if you have been made aware seeing as your life outside the walls may have hindered any knowledge revealed over many years, but Breathers steal a particular... attribute from humans if we let them inhale our breath."

I gasp as the gravity of two memories hits me with full force. "Our soul? When I encountered Breathers twice, they had opened their terrifying mouths and I felt as if they were trying to suck my soul from me!"

Alma nods affirmatively and contemplation crosses her wise face. "Exactly. And it failed as you are Immune. The meaning of eternal life simply means our souls will never perish." Her information coincides with what Xander had mentioned.

My mind races with possibilities at the confirmation of my suspicions.

"And how did people thousands of years ago already know

what was to happen in order to produce the pendant—and the Immunity?"

"Ah, yes, this is where you will certainly need an open mind my dear," Alma explains.

RULE FOURTEEN:
KEEP AN OPEN MIND

18

Rae

I ALMOST LAUGH AT ALMA unknowingly quoting Rule Fourteen
for a second time.

When The Vanquishing occurred, strange events arose,
creatures of fiction became reality and people learnt very quickly
to keep an open mind to all possibilities in order to survive.

"I believe anything is possible, Alma," I tell her with
conviction, and she nods with approval.

"Good," she replies. "The Gaelic culture is very much a
spiritual and supernatural one. Premonitions and magic were
prevalent within communities of Celtic people. One tribe, *our*
ancestors…" Alma pauses and waits for realisation of her words
to dawn on me.

"We're related?" I exclaim, leaning back in wonderment.

Alma smiles tenderly and nods once and I tilt forward with
my forearms resting on the table. "Yes, but I will get to that in a
moment. Our ancestors' tribe had a seer among them. Her name
was Fedelm, the name meaning, '*to know; to see*'. Fedelm prophesied

The Vanquishing of humankind along with the monsters that sucked the spiritual life and essence from humans, feeding on their souls. Though not knowing the timeframe, Fedelm was terrified of her kin eternally perishing. So, she worked with other druids to fashion a spell of sorts, incorporating it into a drink that the family consumed and absorbed into their bloodstream — into their genetics — giving them the Immunity to pass down to each generation. The druids then created these Trinity Knots to symbolise each family's Immunity."

Stunned, I absorb the staggering knowledge of my heritage and sit back, waiting silently for Alma to continue as she takes another sip of brandy tea. I gulp a mouthful of my own, knowing I need it to take the edge off how heavy all this new information is. The tea is sweet and has a powerful kick to it as it runs down my throat. I relish the tranquil feeling that overcomes me as the warmth fills my stomach.

"Your mother's name has been marked on Fedelm's scribed generational family tree; Fedelm's prophetic abilities enabling her to identify each generation's offspring… though your own name does not match Riona's daughter's name. And there was mention of a son, but perhaps my memory has failed me. I am rather old, so I would not be surprised. Anyway, your mother and I are *distantly* related, which is why I thought you looked familiar."

"Wow." My heart bursts with elation at the knowledge I still have a family member left in this world — although Alma's *form* of relation confuses me so. I try not to dwell on the fact that I do not have a brother, though the idea of one is pleasing. "So, are you my grandmother?"

"Yes, wow is certainly the right word. It must be a sign that Xander found you and brought you to me. And like I say, I am only distantly related to your mother, though you may see me as a grandmother, if you like." Her eyes flicker away uneasily as if hiding something, but I'm too elated to think anything of it.

Tears fill my own and I nod. "I would like that. Oh, and my real name is Raine, but Pa always called me Rae since I was his ray of sunshine."

Alma's eyes widen at the mention of my birth name. "The chosen one, the queen!"

Confusion fills me at her outburst. "What?"

"The name Raine means queen, but there was a prophecy—a vision that a raven-haired girl would become queen, eventually leading the people to victory against the evil Vanquishing the world."

I frown at the fact, wondering if my father kept all these secrets from me. "Oh. Well, Mother named me Raine. Father did mention she *had a vision* before I was born but I thought he was muttering nonsense."

Alma's eyes brighten with impish glee. "Yes, of course, your mother was a Celtic seer. Sometimes the gift passes down through the generations, in this case from Fedelm."

My lips turn downward. "Well, the gift must have missed me."

Alma tuts at me in reprimand. "Now my dear, the gift of sight may sound wonderful, but it comes with many burdens. I imagine your mother even saw a vision of her death and had to bridle the secret as to not upset your father. He may have done something foolhardy at the knowledge he would lose his loved one to childbirth."

Understanding dawns on me and I nod in agreement. "Okay, well that makes sense."

"So, now that we have established we are kin," Alma continues, "let me explain the rest of our family's history."

I nod and anxiously wait for her to continue, taking another gulp of tea.

I'm addicted to the happy, floating feeling it provides. It is nicer and less severe than the uninhibited feeling from the bottle I shared with Xander last night.

I take another sip of tea, wondering if my speed and agility— and Alayah's strength—has anything to do with the supernatural accounts that Alma has spoken of.

"I can run for days at high speeds impossible to humankind," I suddenly blurt out, and she nods slowly.

"Yes, many people have adopted certain skills, passed through genetics and enhanced through decades of treatments."

I frown at the abhorred word and she chuckles. "Not all Ghasters created death or destruction—that is the name Segmented citizens refer to them by, as we have records in the library of certain treatments being *ghastly* tasting pills that had gruesome side effects. But in fact, many were created for the wellbeing of humans and instead of them causing deformities and disabilities as most did—some had the opposite effect—instilling abilities akin to superpowers to those who already carried the genetic components of enchantment—such as our family line. There would be similar families across the world. Essentially, the treatment acted as a chemical reaction but not in those with ordinary genetics."

Huh, that means Alayah most likely has an interesting family history.

My thoughts wander and concern fills me at the thought of innocent people who have no means to protect themselves against

Breathers.

"Do you think our own blood could be implemented in a cure or preventative way?" I ask Alma, and her expression becomes thoughtful as I cross my fingers under the table.

"Yes, I believe so. Xander has the resources and scientists with the abilities to create anything they want."

Jubilation fills me with new hope at the information I have absorbed. Any thoughts of fleeing the city or disposing of Xander vanish. For the time being.

I need him for the good of humankind.

Providing he is not overly insufferable.

"Now, dear, let us at least have you ready and adorned with one dress before the broody Ruler arrives to fetch you," Alma says as she slowly rises from her chair and cleans the table away.

My head is light when I stand up, though I feel positively relaxed as I float on a blissful cloud, following Alma into her store.

Alma fashions the most beautiful dress in a deep blue satin material, just in the nick of time. After being ushered into the bathroom, I strip down and soak in her rusting metal bathtub, scrubbing myself raw with a floral scented bar of the waxy substance that Alma labels soap. I quickly rinse and exit the tub, grabbing the fluffy, discoloured cloth she hands me. As I dry off with the soft length of material, Alma styles my damp clean hair, plaiting elegant twists along the side to allow half of its length to fall over my exposed shoulders and back in waves.

I slip into the silky material, relishing the feel of it against my soft, fresh skin, and allow Alma to lace the back up.

"Come look in the mirror, dear."

Following her into the front of the shop, I look in the full-length reflective surface she dubbed a mirror and gasp at the image before me. My hands smooth over the silken material caressing my sides and stomach.

I have only ever seen my reflection in water and never bothered myself with how I looked.

But as I absorb the beautifully fitted dress, hugging my slim waist and flowing seductively over the slender curve of my hips to kiss the wooden floorboards—my eyes tear up. The simple thin straps will ensure the material stays in place and I blush at the curve of my small but pert breasts overflowing from the feminine cut.

I look like a *queen.*

Spinning around, I fling myself at Alma who sniffles away her own tears of happiness and embraces me just as avidly.

"Thank you so much, Alma," I whisper with a quavering voice.

"It was my pleasure, dear," she whispers back, then, giving me another tight squeeze, releases me to stand back and admire her handiwork again. "I have your measurements now, so I will have the leathers and remaining items delivered by tomorrow afternoon, maybe even sooner if I can manage to snag one of the young women who sometimes help in the shop."

I nod just as the front door flings open and Xander comes striding through. He halts mid-step as his eyes find me standing in view, his jaw going slack and nostrils flaring. Alma inconspicuously floats back to her living quarters, giving us privacy.

I nervously bite my lip and peek up at him with uncertainty, his rich irises swirling with ferocious passion. My body heats with a blush as he unabashedly peruses the length of me, his searing regard becoming more intense with each passing moment.

"Do you like it?" I ask with an uncertain whisper, swallowing the lump in my throat as he moves towards me, his brawny legs rippling with each purposeful step.

"You're absolutely breathtaking."

I exhale with relief and softly smile at hearing the reverence behind his words as he stops in front of me. His hands clench beside him, twitching with the urge to have me in his grasp. We remain silently assessing each other and the air around us thickens with desire, my breathing becoming shallow. I inhale his spicy, male scent and become mesmerised under his dark powerful gaze, my balance wavering from both.

The tension becomes too unbearable for Xander and he swoops into my personal space, claiming my tingling lips in a passionate kiss. His hands slide over the silky dress, ravishing the arch of my back and slight curves of my hips underneath.

I moan as need builds between the juncture of my thighs, becoming slick with my body's reaction to this man's overpowering presence. My hands reach as far as they can go and run through his dark, short hair, caressing down and across the rippling muscles in his neck and shoulders, causing a growl to reverberate in his chest.

Xander breaks away from my lips and I whimper in protest as he rests his forehead on my own, breathing heavily, his eyes searching mine.

"Come with me," he commands, and I nod absentmindedly as he grasps my hand in his large, scarred one, pulling me urgently from the shop.

Through my haze of desire, I remember Alma and I yell quickly over my shoulder in hopes the little old lady—my only remaining kin—hears me. "Goodbye, Alma, thank you for everything!"

I hear her frail but mischievous voice carrying through the shop and smile. "Goodbye, dear Rae, come back soon!"

Xander does not slow his progress and we fly across the dusty street, my own slight legs barely keeping up with his long strides. He tugs me around and lifts me into his arms, considerately thinking of my healing feet.

Before long we reach the entrance of a looming building, though not the tower, and Xander places me down then punches in a code before pulling me hastily through the entrance.

My mouth gapes open as we climb a level of stairs, passing through towering shelves of books and archives until we reach a small wooden door at the top level.

Xander pulls a key from his belt—something so archaic compared to his coded security systems—and unlocks the door, pulling me through the entry with him before locking it behind me.

Nerves flutter in my stomach at being locked alone in a room with Xander, and I fidget with my hands as he strides to a large shelf and pulls a book from it.

My anxiety calms as he heads to a large plush couch and sits comfortably on it with his legs spread open in a masculine poise. My eyes drop to his crotch and my face heats at the wicked thoughts racing through my head.

What is wrong with me?

I need to focus on the issue at hand—creating a way for non-Immune humans to endure the wrath of Breathers.

"Sit." Xander's smooth yet commanding voice sends pleasant

shivers up my spine at his dominance, and my legs comply to his order, moving towards him on their own accord.

I sit on the opposite side of the couch and face him, his eyebrow raised in amusement at my blatant attempt to create space between us. He reaches over and his large hand clasps my exposed ankle, making me yelp as he drags me across the couch until I'm seated beside him.

"Much better," he states, and I shoot him my most withering glare.

"Don't manhandle me," I snap, and mirth fills his eyes as the corner of his lip tips up with delight.

"I will do as I please, Rae. You're in my kingdom now."

Bumps break across my skin at his words and I glance at the book in hopes of shifting his attention from me.

"What does the book contain?" I query, tilting my head sideways to see the cover.

The border is engraved with gold and the pattern is similar to that of my pendant.

Excitement fills me at the knowledge that this may be the book that holds all the truth and knowledge of my Immunity.

"Kiss me first."

My head jerks up to see Xander's resolute expression as his eyes dip to my lips, my tongue darting out to moisten them in response. He clenches his jaw and groans, lunging forward to claim my lips without hesitation. All thoughts of defiance flee my mind as the sensual feeling of his masculine lips brush across mine, then down my neck, his stubble raking across my sensitive skin delightfully.

"I need you," Xander rasps out between nibbling and sucking at the tender skin of my neck and collarbone.

I pant with mirrored need, my rational thoughts overridden by desire at the sensations sending shooting sparks of pleasure into the tips of my breasts and lower into the clenching wetness of my centre. I'm afraid I would agree to anything at this rate.

The people need you.

The sudden thought has me darting away from Xander, and I move to the far side of the couch, our heavy breathing slowly returning to normal.

Xander's eyes remain swirling with unequivocal voracity, though fixedly trained on me with curiosity at my sudden retreat.

"I have some important things to talk to you about," I explain, wiping my sweaty hands down my thighs.

Xander studies for me for a few moments and then a slight smirk tips one side of his mouth as he gestures for me to continue. "By all means. It's a rare treat for you to want to *talk* to me rather than rip my head off, mouse."

I clear my throat and blush. He speaks the truth.

"Firstly, stop calling me mouse," I chide, and he smirks, cocking his brow.

Not knowing how to broach the topic, I lurch directly into it. "I spoke to Alma, and she told me the history of my ancestors, which turns out are also her ancestors, including the meaning behind the pendant." I pause, and Xander nods encouragingly for me to continue. "With the help of your scientists, maybe we can recreate it for people who are not Immune."

Xander thoughtfully scratches his chin, a slight frown marring his handsome features. "As long as I know you are safe throughout the process, I completely agree."

My heart thumps erratically in my chest.

This could be it; this could be the chance humans need to survive.

It also does not escape me that this is the first time Xander and I have agreed on anything, conversing with civility.

Perhaps, I could be the queen by his side?

An image of me cooped up in the tower with guards on my every trail makes me flinch and I realise it could never be.

I belong in the wild, free as a bird.

I can contribute my genetics to the scientists' labs and then be on my merry way. Perhaps even travel to spread the news of the new treatment once it's created, providing it would be safe for me to do so.

Yes. That is the plan I will stick to.

The sooner we can achieve this, the sooner I can leave. The sooner I can return to Alayah.

19

XANDER

MY BLOOD FIZZLES WITH REMNANTS OF DESIRE as I study Rae, so beautifully adorned in the sensual, silk dress. Her eyes are somehow even more dazzling against the deep blue of the material, and I struggle to catch my breath. Power and intelligence radiates from her, though she probably doesn't realise it.

This woman was born *to be a fucking queen. Not just someone's lover.*

I shake my head at the unwelcome thought and continue to devour the breathtaking sight in front of me.

The visual of Rae almost brightens my sour mood, turned as soon as I ran into Nelinha outside my room. Again. The bitch was ranting on about Rae using and deceiving me—something about Rae pulling the wool over my eyes by spreading her legs. I inwardly scoff at the memory. Nelinha basically described herself.

My technicians are currently changing the codes to the entry of my building so the snake of a woman can't enter uninvited anymore.

Glancing up, I realise I've been staring into space, with Rae now curiously peering up at me.

"Is everything okay, Xander?" her soft voice reaches my ears and I close my eyes momentarily. I could listen to her beautiful voice all day.

"I'm fine. I just had to deal with a nuisance today," I say, and Rae's rosy lips bow into the shape of an 'o'.

Fuck, what is wrong with me? I just want to spend all day kissing her.

Women have *never* distracted me from my duties. Ever.

Rae sits silently, waiting for me to elaborate, and I hesitate on how much to reveal about my unpleasant encounter with Nelinha. "I changed the codes to my tower, so I will show you when we head over there. You will need to be able to access it when you like," I say, and Rae's eyes brighten. "Providing you don't attempt to run again."

I'm not stupid, I know she wasn't just trying to *get some fresh air* this morning.

"I promise I won't," Rae says enthusiastically. I love how forthcoming she is with her emotions. Her face exhibits everything she feels and thinks. Unlike most women, she doesn't put on a façade.

"Good. Nelinha won't bother us now that she won't be able to access my tower."

Rae's eyes flare at my statement and I turn rigid. "You already had a run in with her?"

Rae nods. "Yes, when I left this morning, I *physically* ran into her," she says, "and I think she really detests me."

I chuckle darkly. "Yes, well, you're a threat to Nelinha.

Particularly as I believe she thinks *she* should be my queen. I'm certain she wouldn't harm you though; she's just jealous."

Rae nods. "I'm not worried about her anyway. I'm more concerned about the welfare of humanity."

I smile widely at Rae and reach across the couch to grab her slender hands.

She was made to be queen, whether she believes it or not.

"You are a special kind of person, Rae," I tell her, and surprise flashes across her face at my endearment, blushing as she looks down shyly.

"Thank you, Xander."

"Now, I want you to have this book." Letting go of her soft hands, I pick up the leather-bound book I dropped in our brief moments of passion. "It has all the details and history of what I assume is your family, seeing as this book was passed down through Alma's family line and you are both related." My finger brushes against her hand as I pass it to her and

Rae's soft smile suddenly drops. Her face turns red with embarrassment as she clears her throat.

"Thank you, Xander, I will treasure it closely."

I study her evasive eyes as they refuse to meet my own and tilt her chin, forcing her to gaze up at me.

"What's wrong?" I ask her, my voice demanding, and she nibbles her lower lip nervously.

I almost forget I asked her something when seeing the plump flesh innocently teased between her teeth.

"I… cannot read." Her voice is so quiet and filled with shame that my chest clenches painfully.

I didn't want to upset her. I *never* want to upset her.

Taking the book, I place it on the floor before pulling her onto my lap and against my chest, my arms wrapping protectively around her as I inwardly scold myself for not being more thoughtful.

Of course she can't read; her upbringing was purely based on survival.

"I'm sorry, Rae," I say as I press a kiss against her soft, silky hair. "I will read it to you whenever you need." I'm too selfish to teach her. This way, when she needs me to read something, it gives me an excuse to be close to her.

I celebrate internally as I feel Rae's tense body melt into my own, her arms sliding around my neck.

"Thank you, Xander."

I squeeze my eyes shut at the consuming feeling welling inside my chest for this tenacious woman. I make a promise to myself to do everything in my power to ensure she is always happy.

Alayah.

The thought of Rae's friend pops into my head and I mentally note to have Lucas bring the feisty woman into the city for a visit. Rae will be over the moon at seeing her friend.

"Come, let's head home to eat and I can show you the new code," I tell her as we pull apart and stand, loving my new name for the cold, tall tower I reside in.

We make our way out through the vast library and I glance at Rae's expression of wonder as we walk towards the exit. I would tell her to visit here anytime, but don't in case it upsets her again.

As we cross the street, I look up at a little house and see Nelinha peering down from the top hazy window, a sneer crossing her features. It must be one of her *client's* houses.

I glower at her and indignation crosses her face as she disappears from the murky glass.

Within a few minutes, we arrive at the tower and I acknowledge my guards stationed out the front. They curtly respond, their curious eyes shifting to the beautifully attired Rae. I place my hand around her waist possessively to pull her against my side, staring them down menacingly. Both pairs of eyes widen and fill with fear as they quickly revert to their usual impassive state.

I will have a word to them later about keeping their appreciative glances to themselves.

I look down at Rae who curiously watches me with a cute tilt of her head.

"They were out of line," I explain, and her eyebrows rise with disbelief. "No one looks at *my* woman."

Rae's eyes widen and she glances back at the guards whose eyes dart everywhere but at her. A soft smile touches her lips, and her eyes sparkle as she looks back at me.

"You are such a caveman."

I chuckle at her insult and shrug, uncaring.

She hasn't seen my caveman yet.

I gesture towards the keypad by the entrance and she stands on her tiptoes to properly view it, her difference in height to me clear.

"Just key in these letters here then press the little hash symbol after," I say mischievously, enunciating each letter as I go. "It spells, little mouse." Her mouth drops at my new code.

Defiance rapidly fills Rae's features as she glares up at me, jolting back to jab her fists against her hips angrily. "I hate that nickname you frequently call me, and I had asked you to stop calling me it!"

I laugh at her anticipated temper. The guards' heads snap towards me in shock at my rare, sudden outburst. I generally never laugh, especially in public, and the only time I do laugh is when Lucas is with me. I shoot them a warning look and they immediately whip their heads away.

"Ah, but it was the first thought that entered my mind upon seeing you when we revealed your hiding place. So, I feel it is wholly fitting."

Rae scoffs, clearly unimpressed, and I lean down to whisper in her ear.

"I knew then that you were my little mouse, my prey, and I would eventually catch you and make you mine." Perhaps I'm exaggerating, but there is truth to my words.

A little gasp escapes her, and she crosses her arms over her chest, causing her slight breasts to spill over the blue silk. I reach out and trace my finger along the seam, against her creamy flesh, the little voice in the back of my head reminding me of our public position.

A blush climbs Rae's chest and I chuckle darkly.

"You can't help the way you feel about me, Rae." My tone is low, and I drag her through the entrance, away from prying eyes.

Her delicate chin tilts up defiantly and she sends me a withering glare, her eyes daggers. "My body does not know what is good for it, apparently."

I shoot her a feral grin and her irises flash with fleeting fear.

"Ah, Rae, your body hasn't *experienced* what's good for it yet."

I'm impatient to claim her as mine, to steal her innocence; but not yet. Something more profound is holding me back.

Not waiting for a reply, I swing Rae up into my arms, revelling her soft curves against me, and climb the steps, my long legs taking three at a time. We reach the door to my residence—our *home*—and place Rae down as I step through, venturing to the bedroom. Rae follows me in as I stride to the drawers and pull out my day's purchase, hiding it behind my back. This woman has me doing strange things. Like buying *gifts*.

"I've bought you some shoes. Well not bought but traded fur for them to be made," I tell her casually, and her face tilts up to mine, her expression hopeful.

"Really?"

Fuck.

The innocent hope and rapture shining brightly from her blue eyes could bring me to my knees. Bring *any* man to their knees.

I hold down the growl threatening to escape at the thought of any man being *near* her.

Rae is quickly becoming a priority in my life and I don't doubt that she will become my ruin very soon. I can no longer deny that I would do anything for this woman.

RULE FIFTEEN:
DON'T FALL
IN LOVE

20

Rae

I HAVE NEVER BEEN IN LOVE. I never knew any men *to* love. So, I'm quite unsure what it is.

But I'm certain what I'm feeling, as Xander hands me a pair of new leather shoes, *is* love.

I gape at the beautifully handcrafted pieces of art in my hands and look up at Xander with awe, my eyes filling with tears.

My Pa was always too poor—a struggling survivor—to ever give me anything. I always wore scraps of his old clothes and shoes were never a possibility. This is the first time someone has gifted me something apart from the dress, but I'm certain Xander relished it more than I did.

Xander's eyes are filled with such profuse emotion, I almost weep.

This cannot happen.

We cannot fall in love.

I refuse to break Rule Fifteen.

Don't. Fall. In. Love.

Pa always said falling in love was like tearing the heart from the safe cavity in one's chest and holding it in the air for everyone to see. For anyone to pierce it.

"What doesn't kill you won't *make you stronger, Rae, but it will certainly make you smarter."* My father's bitter words ricochet in my mind, the effect of losing my mother painfully clear in his tone. *"I wasn't strong enough to evade your mother's profound beauty, but* you're *smart enough to not fall in love."*

Love makes you vulnerable, as does the grief of losing a loved one. It overrides your common sense. Which is a highly dangerous thing to allow while surviving the lands of The Vanquished. Pa had said he learned the hard way. I do not *want* to have these feelings constricting my heart when I look at Xander, his own dark eyes reflecting an equivalent emotion. I take the shoes anyway.

"Thank you, Xander, they're beautiful" I whisper, sentiments thickening my voice.

Relief fills his eyes. "You're welcome, mouse."

I let the annoying nickname slide for now, too excited to try on my new acquisitions.

We sit in silence on the bed as I slip the perfect plush shoes over each foot and wrap the hanging rope attached to the tops downwards to close their sides. My silky dress parts to reveal my legs as I do so and I sense Xander's eyes trailing over them, causing tingles of awareness to briefly race over my skin like the diminutive limbs of little insects.

I gasp once securing each shoe, amazed that they are only slightly tight, and look up at Xander. "How do they fit so well?"

The dark brown leather hugs each foot and the woollen-lined interior caresses my worn-out extremities. They slide on easily and reach the middle of my shins, providing further protection to my vulnerable flesh. The soles have been crafted with a hardened rubber substance, affording further padding and protecting the underside of my feet.

"I guessed," he replies complacently, "though Alma was quite perceptive as well. They will be a little tight until the leather stretches and they will mould to the shape of your feet the longer you wear them."

My eyes do not waver from the beautiful items as I stare at them, my heart swelling ecstatically.

I've never worn shoes. Apart from the animal skin I tied to my feet that Alayah had given me, but they were not shoes. Not really.

Tears stream down my face, my own immense emotions confusing me, and Xander quickly pulls me onto his lap and into his arms as concern fills his chiselled face.

"Why are you upset? Do you not like them?"

I laugh and a snot bubble blows from my nose, but he does not seem to notice. "I've never worn shoes before."

A look of horror and understanding dawns on Xander's face and he grips me tighter.

"You will never be wanting for anything now, Rae," he says gruffly. "Whatever your heart desires or needs, just say and you will have it by the end of the day."

My tears subside as I gaze into Xander's fervid dark eyes, the shades of brown glinting with whirling emotions. My heart throbs again and a fluttering takes residence in my stomach, the unfamiliar feeling still disconcerting me. My throat forms a lump, so I nod in response.

I must not love him. I must not love him. I must not love him.

I repeat the mantra in my head until my heart forms a fortified wall around its perimeter in defence. These vulnerable feelings confirm that I cannot be Xander's queen, not when so much is at stake. Not when humankind's survival relies on me.

Even though I know all of this, I cannot help wanting to know the inner workings of this war-hardened man in front of me, so I blurt out my most prominent question. "Can you tell me about the death of your mother, Xander?"

My social skills and etiquette really need polishing.

Xander freezes at my abrupt question and his face hardens, making the sharp angles of his bone structure more severe. I swallow the nervous lump in my throat—he clearly does not want to talk about this. Ever.

"Please, Xander," I softly beg, "you already know so much about my desolate past."

Multiple expressions flash across his face; anger, grief, pain and resignation, yet he looks at me with a searing black gaze and stiffly nods. "Fine."

I can tell he is displeased about it, but I jump off his lap to throw my arms around his thick neck and kiss him softly on the cheek to show my appreciation.

Xander's eyes snap shut at the feel of my lips against his skin and he flinches, as if the sensation scalds him like the heat from a blazing inferno. I step away to create some space at his reaction, but his hand snakes out with lightning speed and grips my wrist firmly, pulling me back up against him as he crushes his mouth to mine in a possessive and demanding kiss.

I catch my breath and my balance wavers as he breaks away abruptly, pulling me onto the bed with him.

"If we are going to talk about this, you need to be near me," Xander commands.

I nod once. I would do anything to hear about the most integral part of his upbringing. This will be the key to why his suppressed aura is so darkened and why his moods shift so erratically. It will reveal why he attempts to cover the pain of his past with flirtatious and flippant behaviour.

Xander keeps his eyes fixed on a space in the corner of the room as his expression glazes over, transporting him to a moment rather forgotten.

"I was roughly ten and six in age. My father was becoming more brutal and unstable with each day that passed." His jaw clenches at the mention of his father and I feel the tension emanating from his large frame. "My father never loved my mother—she was just a vessel to bear his heirs. My father never loved *anyone*."

I nod in understanding. Rule Fifteen. His father was just trying to survive even if he did not realise it. He was doing what was best for the city. My heart still breaks for the young boy who did not experience a father's love, though.

"It was my fault that my mother died."

My brows slant downwards in confusion, his sudden confession vague. "How?"

"I liked this pretty girl... a commoner. Lucas's twin. He introduced us one day."

My heart drops at the underlying doom within Xander's words and I wait as he stares at the wall, his jaw and mouth becoming taut with rage.

"Lena. I thought I loved her, even though I only met her once. But she was so beautiful and sweet." Xander's eyes fill with a far-away expression and jealousy twists within my chest at the mention of another woman he loved. I push it down. It does not matter if he loved her since he is not mine to claim.

"One day, Lucas told me Lena wanted to meet one night, and I was surprised he was even allowing me near his sister. My father had already shaped me into a cruel and brutal young man through lashings and cruelty growing up. He once slaughtered a stray dog I had found and kept in my room to feed and revive. Made me watch the entire time and said love is only for the weak. So, I became hardened to compassion, love, and any other gentler emotions humans grow into. But Lucas saw through my toughened exterior."

"He is a good friend," I interrupt softly, and Xander nods, a strained smile tilting one corner of his lips.

"Yes. Especially after everything that happened."

I frown.

Do I really want to hear this?

I know whatever Xander reveals will be devastating, but it is the only bridge to understanding him better.

Xander does not prolong the inevitable any further but sighs wearily and continues talking. "My father found out that I was to visit Lena—he had eyes all over the city. He had guards bring me in that day, in front of my mother, and lashed me with a whip that had metal fragments incorporated into the ends."

My eyes widen at the cold-hearted nature of his father's punishment.

"After each whip, he declared I was not to *love* another. I was not to be *seen* with commoners. I wasn't allowed to see Lena that night. My mother watched the whole punishment with tears running down her already battered face. You see, my father beat submission into Mother *daily*. There was nothing she could do that would please him."

My eyes tear up at the horror both Xander's mother and

himself endured at the hands of someone who was supposed to *protect* and *love* them.

"I was locked in my room directly after the lashings, with no-one to tend to the wounds. Father said it would toughen me, mould me into a proper man. But my mother couldn't let her baby boy suffer the tyranny of my father anymore. I don't know why I even call him that, since he doesn't deserve the title."

As my chest constricts with compassion and horror at the awful upbringing, I realise that even though he had the physical comforts and luxuries none of us survivors ever had—he did not have the one thing we received from remaining family members. Love.

21

XANDER

I CAN'T STAND THE PITY FILLING RAE'S EYES, but I don't stop. I can't stop the words falling from my mouth. No one has ever heard the story. Lucas had an idea of what happened, since his sister was directly involved, and the city spread its rumours. But I never said a word.

Until now.

For Rae.

Because I would do anything for her. Including revealing the darkest part of my past; the part I had locked so deeply away in the recesses of my mind.

I grab her hand in a painful grip, using her physical presence as an anchor during this harrowing ordeal. But I don't look her in the eyes as I talk. No, I refuse to see any expression of disgust that might appear over her beautiful face at discovering the monster I really am.

"My mother came to me not long after I was locked away, bringing a bowl of salty water, cloths, and ointment to clean my torn back. I gritted my teeth as she cleaned the massacred skin, chunks of flesh falling to the ground as she did. I could hear her sobbing softly behind me while she did it—trying to stifle the sounds so she appeared strong for me. After she cleaned my back, she sat me on my bed and stood nervously in front of me, glancing to the door repeatedly—worrying her husband would come crashing through at any moment."

My heart pounds as I take a moment to breathe, calming the raging storm within me, and I can't help but glance up at Rae. Her soft blue eyes instantly ground me.

Mine.

I would destroy cities to make her mine.

The sudden thought gives me the strength to continue the tragedy.

"I will never forget the hope etched across her face as she turned to whisper to me, telling me to wait for an hour then go to Lena. I think she was hopeful I would find the love that her and my father never had. So, she said she would distract him. She pressed the key for my room into my hand and left. And I didn't stop her. I was too selfish *not* to take the opportunity."

A lump forms in my throat and I bow my head as my shoulders slump. Saying the words out loud after so many years exposes the guilt and shame I've locked deeply within my heart. But maybe if I accept it, I will be able to enter the ground residence without this remorse assailing me. It was the residence I grew up in, and I haven't stepped foot in it since I moved to this top floor. Which I did as soon as my father died.

Rae's soft hand against my cheek grounds me once again, bringing my face up to see her eyes filled with understanding, and I nod stiffly at her silent encouragement and continue the story.

"On the hour, I fled my room and made it to the barn Lucas said to meet Lena at. I waited for hours and she didn't come. Eventually, I made my way back to my room. My father was waiting with a severely broken Lena in his brutal grip. My mother was already in a bloody heap on the floor."

I stop at the sound of Rae's sharp gasp, mortification etched across her face, and offer a sad smile as her eyes fill with tears. Only Rae would feel the pain of others even if she hadn't experienced it.

Mine.

No one else will ever experience this beautiful side of her. Only me.

"What did he do?" Rae manages to choke out the question, terrified of hearing the answer but too curious to stop me now.

"He told me to slaughter Lena or he would finish my mother off."

My fists clench at the dark memory resurfacing, but movement of Rae shifting away, her face etched with horror, makes my heart race with anxiety.

No. I need to touch her.

I reach out and grasp Rae's ankle, sliding her back across the bed until she's seated in my lap.

My thumping heart instantaneously slows and my breathing returns to normal.

Much better.

"I would have saved them both if I was tougher, Rae," I choke out, my chin resting against the top of her head. A soft sob wrenches from deep within Rae's chest and my arms tighten around her, likely crushing her small frame. "My father was too strong and too fast; he had his guards beside him like the coward he was. There was no question to who I would choose. My mother was the only *real* love I ever experienced. So, I took the dagger from his hand and looked Lena in the face. Her eye was wide with fear, the other swollen shut from the beatings my father gave her. I remember looking down at my mother, who managed to lift her battered face and give the slightest shake of her head. Telling me not to sacrifice the life of an innocent for her own. I should have listened. But I drove the dagger deeply into the heart of the girl I could have *truly* loved, and her sudden scream of pain pierced the silence of the small room."

I stop talking again, letting the depths of what I had done sink in, and Rae's frame shudders uncontrollably as sobs wrench from her mouth.

"I'm so sorry, Xander!"

What? Why is she sorry for something she never witnessed? Sorry for the crime *I* committed?

Rae must see my confusion as she stares up at me with red eyes and a tear-streaked face.

"I'm sorry your father *tried* to make you a monster."

My jaw clenches at the name I was labelled for a long time after. The name that stuck after my father beat me mercilessly and scarred my face permanently.

"Xander," Rae's soft voice cuts through my downward spiral. "I'm not saying that you *are* a monster; because you're not. Through your gruff exterior is a caring man capable of loving."

If only she knew. There's no hope for my blackened heart.

It's unrealistic of me to even think this pure ray of sunshine could break through the cracks of my tarnished soul and save me. I press a kiss to her forehead and her eyes fall shut at the sensation. Keeping her head against my chest, I stare at the wall while I continue the most significant part of the tragedy. "After

I murdered Lena, my father laughed at me. There was so much venom in the sound that I remember feeling nauseous; although, that may have been from Lena's blood running down my arm and dripping off the dagger. Her death was all for nothing anyway. My father grabbed my mother—his *wife*—by her hair and scalped her in front of me. He screamed at me that this was her punishment for defying him, that this was an example to everyone, including me." My words weigh like heavy stones on my tongue and Rae's grief-stricken cries echo in my ears as I transport to the horrific memory, my vision glazed. "I remember the guards holding me back as I struggled to stop him, watching the excruciating pain fill her anguished face as her screams filled the room. There was so much blood. My selfishness was the death of my mother. The death of Lucas's twin."

My grip tightens around Rae and I hear the faint calls of her pain, begging me to stop.

I glance down at her oxygen deprived face as she struggles to breathe and throw her off my lap onto the bed, her body heaving when she takes large gulps of air into her lungs. My hands are shaking, and I look down to see and *feel* Lena's sticky, hot blood covering them again.

Must protect Rae.

"Get out." My words are quiet yet low, laced with unfeeling menace, but only concern fills Rae's face.

"No."

It shouldn't surprise me that even in my darkest, most frightening moments, she still dares to defy me. I feel her, the touch of her soft hands grounding me, bringing me back from the angst of my trauma.

"I'm right here with you, Xander," her sweet voice whispers

into my ear as she slides her arms around my neck, settling into my lap again. "You will not hurt me. I won't let you."

I pause at her last sentence, my forehead briefly creasing, but I don't bother to unfold what it means, my thoughts only focused on the feel of her slender, soft frame against my own and the gentle curve of her behind nestled in my lap. The violent need to promptly claim her overrides my compunction, clouding my mind until I lift her effortlessly to slam her down on the soft mattress.

"Mine," I growl at her, ignoring the fear that flashes in her soulful jewelled eyes.

Only thoughts of taking her in every possible way—mind, body and spirit—take residence in my mind and I start ripping my shirt off with one hand as I keep Rae's wrists pinned above her with the other.

"Xander, stop!"

Her pleas do nothing to bring me back from my unrelenting haze of need, brought on by the darkest memories of my past.

I just need to feel her innocence, and everything will be right again. I will feel my heart beating again. Her innocence will purify my tarnished heart.

I'm past the point of thinking straight; reality now becoming warped as my eyes glaze over with unyielding need. Unbuttoning my pants, I shove them down my thighs, revealing my swollen length that angrily protrudes to rest in between Rae's centre.

Fuck. Yes. Mine.

I roughly push her silk dress above her hips, baring her creamy flesh covered in a soft smattering of fine hair. Growling at the sight, I then grab the girth of my arousal and line it up at the entrance of her tightness.

"Please, Xander," Rae desperately begs, her plea sounding distant due to my ensnared state. "This isn't you. You are not a *monster.*"

My eyes snap up at the detested word that haunted me for so long, and the consuming daze fogging my vision slightly clears. Tears are flooding Rae's ivory cheeks and her brows are creased with a mixture of concern and horror. Her shifty eyes reflect remnants of fading fear.

My heart drops as I look down at us and then at the hand gripping my erection, about to *violate* the one person I hope to love again in this world. An anguished bellow tears from my mouth.

I am *a monster.*

Darting off the bed, I pull my pants back up, roughly tucking myself back in, punishing myself with the self-inflicted pain that I deserve.

Rae studies me vigilantly, wiping the salty moisture from her face, then pushes herself up and slowly slides off the edge of the bed, hesitantly making her way over to me.

My entire body is coiled with the need to fuck, to kill—to release the *tension* building within; yet Rae's steps don't waver, and she reaches me swiftly. I look down at her, my hardened glare meaning to warn her away, but she steps closer until her hand caresses the hard muscles of my stomach. My body clenches even more.

Her bright crystal eyes filled with remnants of tears watch me curiously, though cautiously, as she slides her palms and fingers over each ridge, over each scar—trailing up my heaving chest, tickling the dark smattering of hair.

I clench my fists to control my urge of grabbing her again and squeeze my eyes shut, snapping them open at the feel of her soft lips pressing a kiss to my heart.

"You have so much pain welled up inside of you, Xander," Rae whispers. "Let me take control. Let me take it away."

My entire body burns with desire at the meaning of her words and my jaw grinds as I look down at her determined, sweet face. I can't believe she would be willing to do this for me after what I almost did to her. If I take her to bed, there is no saying what will happen.

What I will do.

I don't have the strength to resist this maddening feeling flaming within my chest as it makes its way lower into my abdomen.

I also don't have the strength to resist her touch, and I nod once.

Rae's eyes widen in surprise, as if she didn't expect me to agree.

Too late now to back down, little mouse.

A look of determination and resolve takes place, and she lifts her chin as if attempting to be brave.

I chuckle darkly. "Bravery won't do a thing for you here, mouse."

Her unfaltering, confident smile ignites sparks deeply within my core as anticipation feels my groin, and I choke on my breath. The darkness blanketing my mood slowly lifts as her red-rimmed eyes twinkle with innocence and mischief.

"Arrogance won't do a thing for *you* here, big bad wolf." Her words waver with a lack of confidence in her seduction, only serving to make her appear demure.

A predatory smile expands across my face. I'm enjoying the game she's playing, and I stalk forward, backing her up towards the bed. My hands itch to imprint and brand the soft white of her behind. Rae squeals at my sudden advance and darts to the other side of the bed, her face flushing with anticipation. "Xander, *I'm* in control, remember?"

"You *think* you're in control, *Rae*."

Her eyes widen as I lunge across the bed and snag her in my grasp, pulling her beneath me once again, her shoes still donned. Without hesitation, my lips crash against hers in a groan and I ravish her. Little whimpers of delight escape Rae as I claim her lips in a bruising manner, taking the opportunity of her opening mouth to slide my tongue in to sensually dance with hers. My hardened length presses painfully against my pants and I grind it against her own hot centre, her hips rolling wantonly with need in return.

Pressing kisses against her jaw and down her delicate neck, I roughly pull her breast from the dress and take her hardened tip in my mouth and bite. A gasp of euphoric shock leaves her mouth and I smirk, repeating the action to elicit another gasp. My tongue soothes and licks after each bite and her mewls become persistent and begging. I become lost to the world as Rae's cries fill the air, preventing me from hearing the unrelenting pounding at the door until Rae's firm grasp on my shoulder urges me up.

"This better be fucking important," I fume, hearing the heavy fist clanging against the metal. Springing off the bed, I stride angrily out the bedroom towards the entrance to rip the door open. Lucas stands tensely with his clenched fist mid-air, his face grim and gas mask hanging around his neck.

Anxiety swiftly replaces my arousal. He would never interrupt unless there was something urgent.

"The gate has been breached."

It takes me a moment to fathom his statement, but I still need confirmation. "What?"

"Breathers have been sighted within the walls." Lucas has never been one to say words unnecessarily. "We need your orders."

I scrub my hand furiously over my face and glance towards the bedroom where Rae waits, then back at Lucas who pointedly looks to my naked torso.

Clothes.

"Let me grab my shirt and I will come with you," I tell him gruffly and half sprint back to the bedroom, groaning at the sight of Rae splayed across my bed with her tits gloriously on display.

"I'm needed on the front," I urgently tell her while grabbing a shirt and pulling it quickly over my head. "We have Breathers breaching the gate, so you need to stay here. Do not leave under any circumstance, do you understand?"

Trepidation fills Rae's face, and she nods in affirmation as concern clouds her blue orbs. "Please be careful, Xander." Her shaking hands pull the covers up to hide her nakedness.

I grimace and nod, leaning over to kiss her vigorously before grabbing my gas mask and retreating down the stairs with Lucas.

The only way Breathers could have made it through the gate is if someone opened it for them.

If anyone loses their lives today, it will be the guards on duty.

Following Lucas closely, I shout orders to the guards who have joined us. "Take a hundred men and scour the city for Breathers. Kill on site. Kill anyone who has been in contact with them."

Lucas whips his head back to me, concern filling his face at my brutal orders.

The city needs protecting. This is the only way, otherwise the city falls.

"Sound the alarm for citizens to implement the drills of a breach if they haven't already!" I yell to another guard who nods affirmatively and rushes away.

Lucas and I make haste towards the guard tower at the gate. We can hear isolated screams of people and the blood curdling screeches of Breathers as they wreak havoc through the streets. My men need to neutralise the situation immediately.

I pick up my pace and run ahead of Lucas who chuckles drily at the break in protocol—I always need someone in front of me and placed behind for protection. But there is a lot more at stake here than my life.

As we reach the gate tower, I look up to see the guard peering through the open window and I scowl at seeing his guilty, fearful expression.

Lucas quickly keys in the code and I burst through the door with him closely following behind. Taking the stairs three at a time, I make it to the top in a matter of seconds and knock loudly on the locked door to the control room.

"The Ruler demands you open this door *now!*" Lucas shouts, his voice threatening.

We hear rustling and hushed voices behind the door, until finally it opens to reveal the apprehensive faces of two young guards.

"Who the fuck opened the gate and let Breathers in?" I roar at them and they visibly shrink at my burning wrath. Neither of them replies, and they only look at each other, silently communicating.

I see red.

My fist slams into the closest guard and the sound of a crack splits through the air, his broken nose immediately gushing blood from the impact as he crumples to the ground.

"One last chance before I execute you *and* your family," I grind out between clenched teeth. The threat towards their family briskly brings them to their senses and the guard still standing blanches.

Ah, good, he must have some loved ones.

"T-t-t-the masseuse offered us f-f-free services for a year if we let her up and did what she asked," the young guard stammers, his face becoming paler by the second.

He must sense what's in store for him.

Lucas tenses beside me at the mention of Nelinha and my jaw clenches as I take a deep breath. I glance at Lucas who has the same question reflected in his eyes.

Why is she doing this?

My mind flicks back to the way she sneered at Rae and an ominous feeling crawls up my spine.

"Rae," I tell Lucas, and his eyes widen as comprehension dawns.

We need to get to her *now.*

I glance back at the two quivering guards and pull my sword out, Lucas copying my movement. With one nod at Lucas, we raise our sharpened, gleaming swords as I glare at the traitors before us.

"You are both guilty of treason and have been sentenced to death effective immediately."

All blood drains from their faces and their eyes fill with dread. Their whines and pleas for mercy fall on deaf ears and they reach their arms in front of them in defence.

Both our swords come swinging down, slicing clean through their necks and decapitating them with one swift motion. Their concurrently severed arms that were raised in the attempt to protect themselves, also fall to the ground. The noise is subdued in comparison to the thumps of two heavy heads.

The intoxicating scent of death fills the air as I look down at the traitors' heads rolling to a stop at our feet—the expression of horror, wide mouths open in a silent scream, frozen on their pitiful faces. The satisfactory moment is fleeting, and I turn abruptly to Lucas and nod at him. "Nelinha is next."

That treacherous bitch just signed her death warrant.

Rule Sixteen:
Don't Leave Your
Back Vulnerable

22

RAE

FULLY CLOTHED AGAIN, I tiptoe to the edge of the staircase and stare down as fear settles heavily in my stomach. My well-trained ears twitch at the muffled screams of horrified people outside on the streets, following the terrifying screech of Breathers. My hands itch to reach for my sword and run into the chaos to help the citizens of Segment One. Xander's order is the only thing stopping me.

A queen would do as she pleases. A queen would fight for the lives of her people.

Squaring my shoulders, I run back in the entrance to our home—*wait, what? Our home?* I shake my head to rid myself of the sentimental feelings and spot my sword lying on the kitchen bench. Sprinting over, I grab it, sliding it halfway from its sheath to check it. Seeing its dinged blade in dire need of sharpening, I groan and slam it back in then sling the holster over my chest and shoulder. There is no time to sharpen it on a rock right now and I remind myself to do so as soon as this is over.

A sharp blade is imperative for survival.

At the slightest creak, I swing around and am unexpectedly assaulted by a black blur. Pain shoots through my temple, causing me to crumple to the ground instantaneously as darkness envelops me.

My head throbs as I groan and my eyes flutter open, falling on the face of the one woman I despise. An ugly sneer crosses her face as she stands in front of me, looking down with hateful eyes. "You're awake."

I roll my eyes at her stupidly obvious remark and my back stiffens when noticing the hideous man beside her, staring hungrily at me with beady eyes.

My temple throbs and I feel something hot running down the side of my face and dripping onto my chest, so I glance down to see a smattering of blood, making my nostrils flare angrily.

Scanning the surroundings, I notice we are in an unfamiliar room, surrounded by moss-covered stones. We appear to be deep underground.

Nelinha's venomous voice pulls my attention to her and my mind races for ways of escape. She thanks the beastly man for helping and tells him to leave, which he does reluctantly, but not without sparing me one last leer. My entire being shudders, but I freeze as my assailant's focus turns to me.

"You're such a filthy bitch, spreading your legs for *my* man. How dare you!"

The last sentence is followed by a hard backhand to my face, snapping my head back with the force. Stars dance in front of my eyes, and if I did not hate the woman so much, I would be impressed by her strength.

Her angry green eyes narrow at my impassive reaction and she huffs, spinning on her ridiculously tall shoes to pace the room. The click of her heels on the stone grates my nerves and enhances the pounding in my head.

What is the sense of wearing such impractical footwear?

"You're in the way. You are distracting Xander from who he really needs to have his sights set on," Nelinha mutters as she paces. She appears to be carrying a conversation with herself. *Her mind is unstable.*

"He's the father..."

I pay no attention to her nonsensical words, keeping quiet while I survey the room and the door. A glint of silver beckons and I spot my sword in the corner. Wriggling my hands, I realise they are bound tightly behind me, resting around the chair I'm tied to. My legs are not tied... a slight relief.

Nelinha's threatening words cut into my concentration, filling my stomach with fear.

"He must like your face too much since there is not much else going for you," Nelinha says as she turns toward me and looks at my diminutive breasts with a curl of her lip. I gulp when noticing the sharp dagger that she is wielding.

"Perhaps we can fix that issue."

Her smile turns vicious as she nears me, and my heart palpitates erratically.

Nelinha's hand snakes out and roughly grabs a fistful of my long hair, triumphantly smiling as she hacks away at the ends, leaving it to fall unevenly around my shoulders.

Oh, she has only decided to spoil my hair.

I remain expressionless as she makes quick work, the black waist-length waves falling in long chunks around our feet. My lack of reaction only serves to agitate her, and she cuts the last remaining fistful violently before stepping back to admire her handiwork.

My mouth runs without a further thought to consequences. "Xander will still love me without long hair because he loves me for *me*, not what I *look* like. I'm not a cold-hearted snake, nor have I slept with the entire city... so I can see why he chose *me*."

I'm making it all up, but I smile widely at the woman in front of me, feeling a fleeting triumph at the rage that crosses her face. A vein pulses visibly in her forehead and my smile drops at the murderous look filling her eyes.

Shit.

That was not my most intelligent choice of words and I should know better than to run my mouth. My only defence is my untied legs if she comes at me.

Which she does.

Her dagger is raised in the air, arm shaking as she lunges at me, her eyes wide with fury.

I wait until the last moment and kick one leg up between her thighs, glad to have my new boots. Nelinha's cries of pain fills the room, reverberating off the stone walls as she falls to the ground grasping her crotch. Without delay, I bring my leg up when she falls to her knees in front of me, smashing the heel of my foot to her face with as much force as I can muster, breaking her nose instantly.

The force of my kick repels her backwards and I do not hesitate to use the opportunity of her downfall to spring into action. I stand with the chair tied to my arms and look down at Nelinha who is rapidly recovering, starting to crawl on her knees towards her dagger. Blood streams from her nose, leaving a sticky, crimson trail. A smile teases my lips at the vision.

I run towards her with the chair behind me and as I reach her crawling body, I turn and jump so the chair is facing down. The momentum and weight of my action has me falling directly on top of Nelinha and she cries out in pain as the chair shatters beneath me, crushing her from the impact. My bonds come free as the chair's frame falls apart and I rush towards my sword in the corner of the room, rapidly tying it around my hip.

I need to help the people vulnerable to the Breathers' attack.

Without a backwards glance, I rush towards the door, thanking the heavens that it is not locked as I yank it open. Rule Sixteen niggles at the corner of my mind but I ignore it, my only focus being the city streets and protecting the innocent.

I run down the cold, damp corridor and reach a set of stone stairs leading up. My chest thumps intermittently as I ascend the stairs carefully, ensuring I do not slip to my death on the slimy steps.

Nelinha's voice carries down the hallway and I internally kick myself for not finishing her off. I've never killed a human before. I don't know if I could have followed through.

"You bitch! You will die!"

Perhaps I should have.

I grimace at her vicious threats promising much excruciating pain and reach a heavy door. Using all my strength, I push through it and turn to glimpse Nelinha painfully limping up the bottom of the stairs, her murderous snarl aimed at me. Without a moment's thought, I slam the heavy door shut and pull the convenient bolt down, locking the crazed woman within the dungeon. Her furious yelling and pounding carries through the other side and I step back, hoping the door will keep her contained.

I could not physically kill her, but perhaps she can starve to death. Staring at the door, I contemplate what to do when I hear the familiar sound of a high-pitched, discordant screech. Distant screams of civilians cause me to brace and I hear the wail of an alarm echo across the eerie night. Turning around, I only see a darkening, dusty street, but cannot pinpoint my location. Fear snakes through my veins and travels up my spine as the fine hairs on the nape of my neck prickle with foreboding awareness. Taking a few tentative steps into the street I instantly freeze at the familiar sensation of invisible claws gripping around my soul.

A Breather is nearby.

My hand goes to the exposed pendant around my neck and my eyes adjust to the fading daylight, searching for any mutated forms in the shadows. The breath leaves me when I see a terrifying figure in the distance darting behind the corner of a building.

Raising my sword, I slowly make my way towards it.

I may be Immune to their breath but I'm certainly not Immune to having my head ripped off.

Bumps line the surface of my skin as I close the distance, and a shiver racks my body at the sudden chill in the air.

My slinky silk dress is not suitable for this and I silently curse Nelinha for putting me in this precarious situation.

Sweat forms in the palms of my hands and trepidation creeps up my spine as I press my back against the wall.

The last of the sun dips below the horizon and a blanket of darkness falls upon the city, creating the perfect hunting ground for the now overrun Segment.

My ears strain for any sounds to alert me of Breathers but I'm greeted with silence, and I grind my teeth together.

All rules of survival whirl around in my mind as I consciously tick them off.

Listen to my instincts. Check. My instincts are screaming there are multitudes of Breathers lurking in the shadows.

Keep my wits about me. Check. Obviously, I'm on high alert.

Be aware of my surroundings. Check. I never realised this rule is pretty much the same as the previous one, but I suppose we cannot have one without the other.

Don't leave my back vulnerable. Check. I'm pressed flat against the cold, hard wall behind me; so, unless a Breather can morph through the wall, my back is covered.

Kill or be killed.

Well, I failed that rule when I did not pierce Nelinha's heart with my sword.

But I will not neglect the rule if a Breather encounters me. So, check.

Position is power. Ah. I need to find a better position. One that puts me at an advantage. But I cannot do that without exposing my back.

I chew my lower lip and flinch at the sound of another screech nearby. It spurs me to immediate action; I'm a sitting duck if I wait in one position. Taking a deep and calming breath—I can ignore the rule of not breathing since I'm Immune—I push off the wall and stealthily make my way down the street in the hope it leads me to Xander's tower.

Staying close to the cover of buildings, I follow street after street until my frustration rises at my lack of directional sense. I eventually pass Alma's brightly painted yellow shop, glowing in the rising moon, and internally celebrate at the small victory.

The tower is nigh.

Quickly checking my left and right for any stalking Breathers, I dart across the road to see the large, familiar building looming in the distance. My heart plummets at the disproportionate shadows lurking at the entrance of the tower and I freeze on the spot. Their milky skin glows in the rising moonlight.

Blast. What do I do now?

My momentary standstill becomes my first mistake and I feel the terrifying Breath of Death lightly blow against the back of my head, the malignant exhale wafting the loose strands of hair and tickling my scalp. The pungent, acidic smell ignites a bout of bile, the burning fluid rapidly rising in my throat, and I internally reprimand myself as I swallow it down.

Don't. Leave. Your. Back. Vulnerable.

I slowly turn around and crane my neck to face a colossal, heinously malformed Breather and my heart plummets into my stomach.

This is not ideal.

The familiar feeling of fear snakes its way up my spine as I absorb the terrifying image in front of me.

The Breather's sunken black eyes perforate me with their burning amber pupils, and its chalky skin glows eerily in the dark night. It towers over me by at least a metre with its gangly, disproportionate limbs gnarled and twisting into long blades. My breath hitches and I'm frozen to the spot as its mouth opens wider than its own hairless head, the popping sound of its unhinging mandible causing nausea to climb my throat. Striated mounds of sickly flesh grasp the jaw to its skull as the black gaping hole reveals an abyss of razor-sharp teeth, dripping with blood and remnants of its last meal.

A human meal.

I have concluded from what Alma has taught me and from my own experiences, that when Breathers are hungry for souls, they suck the life from humans. When they are hungry for physical sustenance, they tear a human's head off.

Please be the first.

In my immobile state of fear, I suddenly remember the effect my breath has on the monsters so I inhale as softly as I can, and then with as much force as my lungs can expel, exhale heavily towards the creature.

It throws its head back at an unnatural angle and releases a bloodcurdling, inharmonious scream that pierces my eardrums. Instinctively, I cover my ear with my free hand and raise my sword in my other. I realise how foolish I am to try and save my hearing when my very existence is in jeopardy so I end up grasping the metal handle of my sword with both hands and swing up with as much strength as I can. Since the blade has not been sharpened in some time, it catches between spinal vertebrae and muscles. The blade lodging results in jarring my arms painfully and my teeth clench while I struggle to maintain a grip on the hilt as the Breather flails and screeches, dropping to its knees.

The artery from its jugular spurts black blood, and it sprays over the front of me, burning any exposed skin. Agony fills me and I scream alongside the screeching monster with the efforts of pushing the sword through its neck, my eyes wide and crazed. Hacking violently to cut through tendons and bone, vomit threatens to eject at hearing the popping and cracking sounds. The sword finally cuts through, the suddenly freeing motion pitching me forward, and I stumble before finding my balance. Its head hurtles to the ground with a muffled thud and its writhing body crumples to the dirt.

My chest heaves with adrenaline and I sigh with exhausted relief at my victory, turning back towards the tower to see the horde of Breathers that were loitering there have now vanished. *Shit.*

The Breather that I slaughtered must have alerted them to my presence when it screamed. Now they have scattered to begin their strategic hunt of me.

Use your speed.

The only thing that could save me right now is my forgotten ability.

So, I sprint.

With the sword in one hand, my legs move faster than lightning, a rapid blur of moving limbs to the human eye. I reach the keypad of Xander's tower and struggle to remember the keys he had shown me to press. The metallic smell of death permeates the air and urgency makes me whimper as my fingers hover over the incomprehensible symbols. A screeching Breather in the distance spurs my decisions.

Hesitantly jabbing the sequence Xander had demonstrated, I nearly cry with happiness at my timely stroke of luck when the door clicks as it unlocks. I hastily push inside, dry heaving as my feet squelch through the human remains on the outside of the entrance.

Those poor guards.

Once behind the safety of the locked door, I peer outside and study the eerily quiet street, my heart sinking upon seeing vague silhouettes of human remains scattered across its surface. The remaining citizens must be hiding in their homes.

A few shadows dart past the entrance, causing me to jump

back with fright at the flash of pallid, white skin. I whip around to sprint up the stairs.

Please be home, Xander.

I need to touch him and know he is alive.

The living area is swathed in darkness and I feel around the wall for the strange switch Xander showed me for when I needed light. I'm still unused to the bizarre luxury, but mightily thankful for it in this instance of terror.

The place is too quiet and still for Xander to be here, but I cautiously walk in anyway.

"Xander?" I call out his name, hopeful, but receive no reply and desperation flares my temper. "Blast it!"

Making my way to the bathroom, I wipe the thick, black blood off my sword with a cloth and glance up in the mirror, startled at the reflection of my shoulder length, scruffy hair. The rough style only enhances the full pout of my rosy lips and large, almond shaped eyes. I shrug to myself. Looks have never been my priority and never will be.

As I glance down at my sword, checking over to ensure all the blood has been cleaned off, my ears instinctually twitch when I hear the slightest sound of shuffling in the living room, the ability to hear so far away only possible from years of honing my senses for survival. My instincts switch to highly alert and I calm my breathing to better focus. The light in the bedroom flickers off and my eyes dart up to the mirror again to see swift movement of something in the shadows behind. I whip around with my sword raised and ready, but I'm not quick enough, and something hard comes crashing down on my head. My world rapidly fades to black—but not before I see the glinting malice of Nelinha's green eyes. The final thought I think before I crumple is, *how did she escape and break into the tower?*

23

XANDER

THE ISOLATED SOUNDS of our laboured breath under the gas masks unsettles me. The streets are usually bustling and full of life at this time of the evening, but everyone has locked themselves safely away.

Besides those who perished to the Breathers.

My jaw clenches at the thought. Once again, the blood of innocent people tarnishes my hands. Just because I failed to see the threat Nelinha posed.

Shit! Fuck!

All that matters now is getting back to the tower to make sure Rae has returned. One of the guards at the tower radioed in saying she wasn't in her residence when they checked.

We scoured the entire city for her, fighting off Breathers during the hunt, but after hours of searching, both Lucas and I came up empty-handed.

My heart clenches at the thought of not finding Rae in time. Of finding her delicate, porcelain skin stained with blood. The image spurs my legs to sprint faster and harder and Lucas increases his speed to keep up with me.

We both remain silent as we sprint through the sinister stillness, keeping our eyes trained on the deserted, dark streets as we progress.

The silhouette of the tower finally comes into view and my heart plummets at the sight of bodies and large shadows scattered over the ground around the entrance. We pass a Breather sprawled across the ground as we near the tower and a ray of hope flitters within my chest at its decapitated head. With how much of a warrior Rae is, maybe this is her slaughter?

Please be alive my little mouse.

Lucas quickly darts forward and punches in the code to my tower as I stand guard behind him, softly whistling when I see a flash of white, though loud enough for him to hear the sound under my mask. He immediately halts his progress and draws his sword, turning to join me as I unsheathe my own. Another flash of white whizzes past and a strange sensation of evil prickles my skin.

Thank fuck we have masks on.

We wait silently, our backs against the door and wall, when a large mass of milky white skin unexpectedly emerges and lunges for Lucas, its twisted long limbs reaching out to grab him. I reflexively swing my sword down and slice its head clean from its shoulders, a wicked smile spreading across my face. Thick, black blood sprays over Lucas and me, the pungent stench nauseating. Satisfaction fills me at the clean decapitation, and I puff my chest out, pulling my shoulders back proudly. But the triumph quickly dissipates, replaced with a dread that weighs heavily on my chest. My pride deflates and shoulders drop at the comprehension dawning; the Breather was watching us from the shadows. I recall seeing a fallen guard with his mask smashed in, his eyes blank beneath the bloodied mess.

They're getting smarter. They understand the masks prevent them from stealing our breath.

Knowing there are more lurking in the shadows, waiting to strike, I make the decision to hastily enter the building. We can't stay out here all night. I need to find Rae.

Signalling at Lucas to watch my back, I whirl around and punch in the code as quick as I can and the door beeps as it unlocks.

Relief fills me as I swing it open and step through, turning to gesture Lucas in when unexpectedly, another flash of white comes hurdling towards me. I slam the door shut on it, locking Lucas outside.

Fuck.

My heart pounds desperately in my chest as I watch him effortlessly slay the Breather, and I swing the door open and yell at him, the urgent order muffled under my mask. "Get inside, now!"

He briefly scans the surroundings for any more threats then darts in through the door just as another Breather comes flying out of thin air. We can't close the door quick enough and it barges through, knocking me over. Thankfully, the heavy door automatically shuts behind the odious creature and any threats of further breaches have been eliminated.

I spring to my feet, ready for the Breather to attack, but it vanishes as fast as it appeared.

My head whips to Lucas whose gaze darts to the shadows, just as confused by its disappearance.

We look up the stairway to catch the flash of pasty, mutated flesh at the top and my heart plummets. Rae's in danger if she's in there and unarmed.

Without hesitation, both Lucas and I readjust our masks, tightening them painfully as we sprint up the stairs, our long strides taking four steps at a time. My pulse beats erratically in my neck, matching the thumping of my heart, and adrenaline torpedoes through my veins. Rae *must* be okay.

We reach the top of the stairs within seconds and I tense at the view of the open door leading into a dark abyss.

"Fuck," I hiss, the sound barely audible through the mask over my mouth. Lucas nods in agreement as we stealthily move to each side of the entrance, glancing in to see any signs of life.

My ears strain to hear anything and I shake my head in frustration at the silence that greets me. As carefully as I can, I reach a hand inside of the doorway, feeling around for the light switch.

My chest lightens as my fingers slide over the cold, plastic protrusion and immediately switch it on. Glancing at Lucas, he nods his relief and gestures for me to stay behind him as he enters.

I would rather burst in there and tear everything apart looking for Rae, but I contain my impulses—my body coiled and tense as I wait for the imminent attack.

Lucas enters slowly and his head darts around to scope the room for any signs of movement, he looks back at me with a shake of his head. He goes to walk farther in when a chilling scream pierces the air. My blood freezes and I look to Lucas with wide eyes, sprinting to action when the unmistakable screech of a Breather bursts my eardrums.

Blood rushes to my ears as I rip into my bedroom, and my stomach drops at the copious amounts of blood splattered over the wall, spraying from out of the bathroom.

I'm too late.

The large, pale Breather stands in the corner with its back to me, fixated on whoever it has trapped.

Please don't let it be Rae's blood.

It's in this moment that I realise; Rae is my everything—if she's still alive—and she *will* be my queen.

Nothing less.

I love her.

I don't care if it is too soon; this overwhelming, all-consuming feeling gripping my chest could only be love.

The thought of losing Rae tears a new, gaping chasm in my heart—the heart that I didn't realise was slowly healing from the impact of her beautiful soul.

Suddenly, the Breather's head flings back on a ninety-degree angle, its horrifying face now directed at us upside-down. Its mouth unhinges as it lets out a spinechilling, grating screech, and I take the moment of its immobilisation to dart forward with my sword raised in the air, slicing down with the speed of light to decapitate its twisted face. Blood spurts from the Breather's neck, spraying the radius around it with black slime before the body drops to the floor... revealing a bloodied and bruised Rae, tied to a chair.

"Fuck!"

I dart forward, ripping my mask down as Lucas makes his way around the perimeter, checking the wardrobes and shadows before making his way into the attached bathroom.

"Mouse," I croak with a whisper as I kneel in front of her. "Tell me you're okay, please?"

My eyes roam her delicate white skin, checking that the

smattering of blood isn't her own, and I frown at the rough, shorter lengths of her black bangs. Now isn't the time to ask about why she cut her hair. She is still beautiful as ever.

"I'm fine," Rae rasps, her swollen lip splitting to ooze blood as she speaks. Dried blood cakes the side of her face and a swelling lump protrudes from her temple.

My chest squeezes at her bravery and I inwardly punish myself for leaving her when she needed my protection. I quickly pull out my dagger and cut the rope binding her ankles and wrists and she collapses into me with relief, her shaking arms sliding around my neck in a grateful embrace. My own arms shake, and I swallow down the lump in my throat.

Fuck! I must *love her.*

There is no other explanation for this disorder ailing me.

The words die in my mouth and I can't bring myself to say them just yet. It really is too soon, so maybe it is just the adrenaline and dramatic past few days generating irrational emotions. There is no time to ponder that now, though.

Pressing my face into the crook of her neck I kiss her gently then tip back her head and softly press a kiss to her forehead. I pull back, frowning at the swelling on her temple.

"Nelinha," Rae whispers, her hand going to her bruised throat, and I whip my head around to check the venomous bitch isn't behind me.

"Did she do this?" My tone is deadly, and my blood burns at the fear pooling in Rae's eyes. I can feel the vein in my forehead bulging as it pulses erratically.

"Yes."

Nelinha must have secretly watched the entrance of the tower until someone entered the code, then stored the information away for an opportune time.

Lucas's voice breaks through my haze of anger as he calls from the bathroom. "Xander, you need to see this."

I stand up with Rae nestled in my arms and stride to the bed to place her gently down, lying her bloodied form across the soft mattress. "I promise I will be back to help clean you and dress your wounds." At her slight nod, I whip around and stride to the bathroom, but the sight brings me to an abrupt stop at the entrance. "Fuck."

Lucas looks up from his kneeling position beside a massacred Nelinha, and I cough at the metallic stench emanating from her remains. The visual of intestines spilling crudely from a deep gash in her abdomen onto the stained red floor doesn't bother me—I have seen plenty of human entrails throughout my violent life. I have even been the cause of such gruesome outcomes.

No, the blood doesn't bother me at all.

What has my breath caught in my throat and my heart clenching with fear is the empty, soulless eyes staring back at me from Nelinha's decapitated head. The flesh around her exposed neck is roughly torn and bloodied; indicating the extremity was ripped from the shoulders rather than bitten or sliced. Her face is gaunt, as if the life were sucked from her.

I have never seen the effects of the Breath of Death before. Breathers generally just feed on the flesh of humans most of the time.

Both Lucas and I stare at the once green eyes of Nelinha and shudder simultaneously.

Her eyes have been drowned in midnight ink, darker than the pitch-black, lifeless depths of an ocean.

My brows pinch at the rapidly changing colour of her skin;

the olive hue now turning into a milky white, and Lucas jumps back, his face darting to me. "What the fuck is happening?"

I shake my head, not tearing my eyes from Nelinha's face. "I don't know, I've never encountered this before."

"It took her soul. The body is changing to that of a Breather's... we are lucky she is decapitated."

I turn at the sound of Rae's weak voice coming from the bed and a chill runs up my spine at her words. Rae manages to push herself up to a seated position and I refrain from demanding she lay back down.

"Nelinha was too busy torturing me to see the Breather creep up behind her, and when she turned around, she took a breath to scream."

My body tenses at the thought of that bitch hurting my Rae.

Rae continues reiterating the event in a whisper. "I saw the essence—her *soul* leaving her body as the Breather unhinged its jaw to inhale, then it dragged her convulsing body into the bathroom, though I don't know why. Maybe to feed more? Either way, her soul must not have been satisfying enough if it proceeded to tear her head off in retaliation, then come after me."

We all remain silent, deliberating the ominous events. Losing your soul would be worse than death itself, so Nelinha is better off in this incapacitated state than as a Breather.

Lucas's voice brings me out of my grim state. "Shit, Xander. We better figure out how to solve this mess otherwise we will have a city full of people in the same boat as Nelinha. What's the plan now, man?"

"The city is still overrun by Breathers, isn't it?"

Lucas nods with a defeated expression. "We were losing too many guards, so I gave the radio order to retreat into hiding with the citizens."

"We're going to have to call Segment Two," I say with a glower. Their Ruler is a fuckhead.

In all my years as a Ruler, I have never had to call on the tyrannous man.

I met him once when I first came into ruling, at my father's and mother's funeral.

He's only slightly older than me but much taller and leanly built. He may not be a physical threat, but where he lacks brawn, he makes up for in an intelligence used malevolently for his own gain.

Kasim.

Both his parents were warriors from the Old Nigeria. Their surviving forefathers migrated overseas decades after the fallout, and ventured across land, settling on this continent to escape the constant threats of predators in their own land.

If people think *I'm* a brutal Ruler, then they should try living under Kasim's dictatorship.

Irritatingly, we are somewhat similar in the fact that neither of us have a wife or heirs yet.

"Shit, that man is so full of himself," Lucas spits at the mention of Kasim and I nod grimly.

I turn back to Rae who has fallen asleep from exhaustion and her body's need to heal. I frown at the thought of Kasim seeing her. He's overly competitive and will no doubt want something that's *mine*. Kasim isn't blind either, so he'll see how beautiful Rae is, both internally and physically.

"He will want her for himself," Lucas steals the words from my very lips as he quietly states my own subsequent inferences slowly, glancing in the direction of Rae's motionless body.

I clench my jaw. "I was just thinking that."

"What will you do?"

"I need to make her mine before he gets here."

Lucas nods affirmatively. "My thoughts as well. I will go to the communications room down the hall to call Segment Two and request assistance. I suggest you wake your woman and let her know your plans."

I slap his back in appreciation as he moves past me and disappears out of the bedroom. My eyes travel back to Rae's sleeping form in my bed and I run a hand over my face.

There will be an argument about my demands. The little mouse won't like me telling her what to do, particularly since it's to become my wife—my queen. And right *now*.

24

RAE

I DART UP FROM MY HEAVY SLUMBER at the soft fluttering of knuckles brushing against my cheek, coming face to face with Xander. Even through the pounding in my head and throbbing cheek, my stomach clenches at his proximity and subtle, spicy scent. A smile tips one corner of his lips, causing a dimple to appear, and his eyes travel to the top of my head. My hand flies up to play with the ends of my shorter, shoulder length hair and I wince at his curious expression.

"Nelinha wanted to make me less pretty so you weren't interested anymore. She started with my hair, though I don't know why she left it at this length. I'm not sure what else she had planned, or if she was just going to kill me."

Xander narrows his eyes. "I wouldn't mind reviving her and replaying the torment she suffered at the Breather's hands," he says, his tone hard. He looks to me with a softer expression. "And nothing could detract from your beauty."

I blush and shyly smile, only to gasp in pain at the throbbing sensation in my cheek and lip. My hand drops to gingerly press the swelling flesh of my mouth, and I hiss at the sting, reflexively ripping it away.

I must look a fright.

Xander growls and I look up at him as fury darkens his burning gaze. "I *really* wish she was still alive so she could suffer some more."

I should feel afraid of his ominous words and deadly tone but my heart leaps at his protective conduct.

"It's okay, she is dead now and that's the main thing," I tell him softly while reaching my hand out to caress his stubbled jawline.

The anger vanishes from his eyes at my touch, only to be replaced by apprehension as his expression becomes serious. "I need to talk to you about something. You won't like it."

My hand drops and I instantly become guarded at his words. "What is it?"

Xander clears his throat and slides off the bed to crouch between my knees. "You need to become my wife now. You need to be titled as queen."

It takes a moment for the reality of Xander's demand to sink in and once it does, I scramble away from him and point an accusing finger at his face. "You will not tell me what to do. I will not have you dictating my life!"

A severe pain shoots through my temple at the sudden movement, causing me to wince, but I remain steadfast and refrain from cradling my head.

A smirk crosses Xander's face and the brown of his eyes darkens in challenge. "I find it amusing that you *think* you have a choice, mouse."

My ire rises at his audacity and I scoff in protest. "You couldn't force me to agree. I would just run away or stab you."

Xander's cheek tics as he grinds his teeth and stands abruptly, his threatening stance towering over me. My forehead wrinkles and the question of *why* he needs this so badly crosses my mind. "Why do we need to do this *now*—why not wait?"

I can see Xander consider his answer carefully before speaking. "The city has been overrun by Breathers, so we have requested the help of Segment Two to eliminate the threats."

Rolling my eyes, I gesture for him to continue. "I fail to see why that has anything to do with us marrying. Please elaborate."

The corner of Xander's mouth twitches at my attitude before he continues. "The Ruler of Segment Two will see your beauty and demand that you be *his* wife. And provide him heirs."

My eyes bug in disbelief at Xander's words. "You cannot be serious! That is so… archaic. Firstly, I would say no *if* he demanded that. Secondly, he doesn't even need to see me."

Xander looks at me, deep in thought, and he nods slowly. "You're right, he doesn't need to see you. *If* you promised to not leave my room until Kasim and his guards leave, then I won't force you to marry me. Yet."

A guffaw escapes me at his barbaric ultimatum. "In the interest of my own wellbeing, I will not leave the room, because I know how rare women are, and seeing an unpaired one will cause issues. My choice has nothing to do with your ultimatum."

Xander scowls at me, causing the scars to stretch over his eyebrow and cheekbone. "Fine."

His gaze drops to my bloodied dress—its once beautiful material torn and ruined—then peruses my battered skin as he frowns. "Let's get you cleaned up first so I can check to make sure you don't have any serious wounds. That lump on your temple looks bad, so we will take you to the infirmary for the doctor to check that you don't have a concussion or any other serious complications."

My hand travels to the throbbing egg on the side of my forehead and I wince. "I assumed that it looked bad since it feels it. I'm pretty sure Nelinha thumped me twice in the same spot... But I will not bother with the infirmary. I have survived my entire life without a doctor, so I won't start relying on one now."

Slipping out of bed, Xander moves to the side and helps me limp to the bathroom, but I ignore his grunts of disapproval. My stomach revolts at the violent sight of Nelinha and the thick odour permeating the small space, but I turn to Xander assertively anyway. "I would rather wash myself without prying eyes. Once I'm clean and in fresh clothes, you can check if I have any other cuts." I'm lying through my teeth but just need some time to myself. It would not be the first time I have had to check my body for serious wounds.

Xander nods stiffly, unhappy to be leaving my side, but he quickly cleans the blood from the floor as best he can, compiling the soiled cloth with Nelinha's remains once complete. He gathers the pile up, giving the area one last wipe with a clean cloth before stalking from the room, closing the bathroom door behind him with his foot. There is only a smeared patch of blood and some insignificant lumps of flesh remaining—his cleaning efforts surprisingly efficient—but he still leaves me with the lingering, bitter stench of death. My face crumples with distaste and I instantly groan when pain shoots through my injured cheek and temple, reminding me not to pull any expressions.

Breathe, Rae.

Inhaling and exhaling deeply a few times, it does not take long for serenity to fall upon the small room. A sigh of relief escapes me, my shoulders dropping to finally relax. Xander can be so intoxicating, it is as if he sucks the air out from around me.

I start to peel off the tattered dress, wincing at my aching muscles and bruised flesh where Nelinha struck me repeatedly. Stopping my progress, I pause to take a breath and start again, managing to slide the dress down to my legs where I can kick it off. Bending over painfully, I place the rubber disk into the drain of the yellowing, porcelain tub with a moan of protest at the excruciating task. I then turn on the running water connected to the overhanging shower head, flinching at the iciness of the water.

It appears to be gradually getting colder each night.

The water reflects the temperature outside… it is simply freezing. My brows furrow at the strange, erratic change in weather becoming more prevalent. The days are unbearably hot, but the nights are dropping to the point of almost freezing.

I look down at the filling tub and tentatively place my toe in, only to rip it back with a quiet gasp. Most cities have no hot water like Pre-Vanquished civilisations did but I'm still extremely grateful for having any kind of running water.

Holding my breath, I step in under the flowing showerhead and squeal at the sudden frigidness cascading over my battered skin. My outburst causes Xander to come barging in, his lethal eyes darting around to find an assailant. I wrap my arms around me automatically to cover my nakedness and when he realises there is no threat, his gaze pins my wet body. Immediately, his expression morphs into one of burning desire, consequently heating my icy skin.

"It's just cold," I whisper, "but you can leave now. Thank you for checking on me."

Xander's eye twitches as he struggles internally—not wanting to leave me—but eventually he exhales roughly and spins around to stride from the room, firmly shutting the door behind him.

The water becomes tolerable after a few moments and I completely immerse myself under the unrelenting spray, running my hands over the soiled skin to remove as much blood as possible. Grabbing the soap resembling Alayah and Alma's bar—though this one smells spicy like Xander—I lather myself up and furiously scrub my skin raw. My open cuts sting but I hold my breath and keep my lips tightly pressed together to stop me from screaming out again as I thoroughly wash the grime from my body. My previous waist-length hair was much heavier when soaked with water, so it's the strangest sensation washing the now shorter strands. It *is* much less effort though, and I smile at the positive outcome.

Once I've rinsed remnants of soap from my clean body and hair, I turn the running water off then step out, grabbing a soft, fluffy cloth as I move. Making quick work of drying myself, I wrap the cloth around me and make my way back into the bedroom where Xander sits on the bed, waiting. His body is rigid, and I swallow the lump in my throat at the penetrative look in his darkened gaze, freezing me instantly on the spot.

His voice is gruff when he speaks. "Alma made the rest of your clothes for you, with the help of her assistant, and delivered them to Lucas before shit hit the fan. He delivered them here while you were in the bath."

I smile weakly. "Thank you."

Xander grunts and gets up to pull a selection of clothes from a drawer. A flurry of anticipation grows within my stomach.

Leathers.

He really got me leathers!

I cannot believe this tough, brutal Ruler went out of his way to have something I've *dreamed* about, made just for me!

Holding back a squeal, I take the pile of clothes Xander hands me and smile widely at him. "I really appreciate this, thank you again, Xander."

"You're welcome, *Raine.*"

I freeze with a gulp, and my stomach plummets. He does not sound happy.

"*Why* have you not told me your *real* name, mouse?"

My brows pull down slightly. He must have visited Alma while I was in the bath. "I did. I've been called *Rae* my entire life by my father. *Raine* is the name my mother gave me before she passed away, but my father refused to use it."

Xander visibly relaxes at my explanation and dips his head once in acknowledgement.

"Now, will you let me check over you? We should take you to the infirmary, just so the doctor can check your head."

He is being annoying, stubborn, and persistent about this.

I roll my eyes. "I never needed a doctor before, for any wounds. Pa always tended to me if there were serious gashes, but otherwise my body heals rather quickly. So, you do not need to examine me or accompany me to the infirmary."

His eyes partially shutter with suspicion as he crosses his arms stubbornly, so I quickly add, "I also perused myself for any wounds, using the mirror, and there are only shallow cuts."

He stares at me momentarily before grunting and walking from the room without another word, allowing me to get dressed.

I roll my eyes, the increasingly repetitive action making my head throb worse.

His moods can be so temperamental sometimes. It is as if he is at constant war with a darkness inside of him. I frown at the troubling thought but push it aside for now, not wanting to tarnish the excitement of receiving such a precious gift.

My heart leaps when I look down at the clothes and leathers in my hands and a joyous smile extends the width my face, though instantly sends biting pain shooting through my cheek, split lip, and forehead.

"Ow," I hiss as tears fill my eyes from the smarting throb. Pushing the discomfort aside, my enthusiasm too tremendous, I gaze back down.

Perhaps I could become accustomed to this.

The cloth around me drops to the floor and I impatiently spread the items out across the bed to see what I need to dress in first. My eyes dart to the light shirt that goes under the leather vest and I grab it, quickly slipping it over my head. Looking down, I smile again at the slim fit—perfect measurements—and send silent thanks to Alma. I have never had clothes that fit me or were made for me before. My Pa always gave me his old clothes when he acquired new ones. Sometimes, we would go *years* without obtaining new garments. So, I never cared about the fit or how something looked on me, but from a practical perspective, loose clothes hinder my ability to defend myself properly, and they get in the way of general duties.

As I pull the leather vest over the shirt and slide the slim pants on, I look down and almost weep. It is the appropriate attire of a capable warrior.

The material brushes against my scrapes and bruises but the happiness that fills me overrides the niggling pains. I'm overcome with appreciation at Xander's thoughtfulness and run out to where he is sitting on the large, plush seats. He barely has time to look up before I sling my arms around his neck and kiss him on the cheek.

"Thank you so much for these, Xander." I step away from him and his searing gaze peruses the length of me as a self-satisfied smirk tilts the corner of his mouth, puckering his facial scars.

"You look stunning," he says, his voice low and husky.

I cannot help but beam and fall into the space beside him.

"When I met Alayah, I envied her leathers and she had promised we would get some for me." My voice turns sad at the reminder of my new friend, and concern fills me at the thought of her out there alone with the Breathers.

"After this attack of Breathers blows over, I am sending Lucas to fetch Alayah so she can visit you," Xander says softly and slightly turns on the seat to face me. He lifts his arm and runs his hand through my hair, his fingers exploring the new length.

I'm suddenly glad Nelinha didn't shear my hair close to my head like I thought she was going to. My heart expands with emotion at Xander's gentle touch and I close my eyes as feelings threaten to overflow at his constant thoughtful actions and words.

I did not even have to say how much I missed Alayah and he makes the decision to bring her in. Just for me. *Though he would not have had to if he did not steal you from her in the first place.*

I quickly quell the rational thoughts, only wanting to enjoy the present moment. We remain silent as Xander explores the feel of my hair and I keep my eyes closed, beginning to feel sleepy from his massaging strokes. The serenity is broken as Lucas bangs on the front door, yelling to be let in.

"Fuck," Xander growls and immediately jumps up to stalk over and wrench the door open. His position of Ruler slips back into place and the tender display of affection and emotion vanishes instantaneously. Lucas strides in past Xander and pauses as his eyes land on my clean, new garb. A sincere smile graces his usually playful face as he peruses me platonically. "You look good, Rae."

Xander mumbles threateningly behind him and Lucas chuckles as he turns to his friend. "I mean that in an amicable way, Xander. No need to get all territorial."

I roll my eyes at Xander. "Yes, Xander, I'm not even your wife yet."

Xander freezes at my words and my own eyes widen at the use of *yet*. As if I am speaking like we *will* be getting bound. It was a mistaken slip of my tongue. I did not mean to say it nor give him any hope.

Lucas ignores the exchange and does not delay in divulging his news. "Segment Two has agreed to assist us, so Kasim and a small portion of his army will arrive in two days by truck. The second wave of his convoy will be on foot since they don't have enough vehicles. They will be handy if we need more men in a few weeks or so—otherwise they will turn around before they even reach us if Kasim's first group defeats the Breathers."

Xander nods grimly. "Then we will need to hold down the fort for two days. Send out a widespread message from the communication room to let the residents know to remain locked in their homes until we sound the alarm again."

"Will do. Kasim and a select few of his highest ranking

men have also requested sanctuary here in your residence until his convoy has conquered the Breathers." Lucas delivers the statement warily and with good reason.

Xander clenches his fists and looks to me as his jaw ticks before he mentally solves the issue. "There is your spare residence on the floor below; since we have three in this tower, he can have that one and you can stay in the third residence below. That way we are either side of him and can keep an eye on them."

Lucas agrees and walks back out of the entrance, shutting the door behind him.

"Where does Lucas usually stay?" I ask Xander, curious as to how the guards live.

Xander narrows his eyes at me, clearly displeased with my interest in his friend's living arrangement. "He has his own residence down the street when he isn't on duty. Otherwise, he can stay in the dwelling below where Kasim and his men will be staying. Most of the time, he still prefers his home and will choose to stay there. Tell me, why do you ask?"

"I'm just curious as to what lives your men lead—particularly ones with families or wives."

"They live normal lives of any occupational hands, with regular shifts and hours of work, including time off. The night shift guards are the same as well."

I nod and bite my lip thoughtfully, wondering what his scientists do all day. "What do your lab people do to occupy themselves all day, then?"

"They are constantly trying to find a cure for Breathers or at least a way to defend ourselves effectively from them. They also tirelessly create antibiotics for disease and sickness."

"Should you take me there soon so they can work on my

genetics?"

Xander stares at me for a few moments before answering. "Yes, but I will be there while they do. I'd like to oversee everything that happens."

Well, that is a little overbearing, but I will not complain after all he has done for me.

"When will the experiments start?" I ask Xander and he winces.

"As soon as it's safe to go outside again."

The next few days in Xander's home drag painfully. I have never been so cooped up before and it is starting to drive me slightly senseless. The time locked away has given me a chance to reflect on what my ambitions are now that I know the history of my kin. Xander has been reading me the book from the library, in the hopes that either of us pick up something crucial from its records.

So far, we have nothing to help us for when the scientists start their work on my genetics, but we still have at least half of the book to go through.

Still, I'm appreciating learning about the history of my Celtic hereditary and the fascinating events that have happened throughout the generations.

Xander is reading me an amazing story of my kin from a · hundred years ago when Lucas bursts through the door without knocking. Both Xander and I look up in surprise at the intrusion, instantaneously becoming rigid upon seeing Lucas's demeanour, suggesting a valid reason for breaking protocol.

"They're here."

My eyes widen and I jump up, darting to the bedroom to hide. Xander has been sleeping on the couch for the time I've been here so the bed unfortunately no longer smells like him. I will need to get him to roll around in the sheets to leave his scent if I'm to be cooped up here for however long it takes Kasim's men to clear out the Breathers.

Xander comes striding in through the bedroom door and shoots me a warning look. "Do not leave this bedroom under any circumstance until I come and get you." I nod ardently and his shoulders relax slightly but only marginally. This Ruler's arrival is burdening him.

"Good. Kasim will meet with me privately in the living area so it's imperative that you don't make a *sound*. Not even a sneeze, do you understand?"

I nod again, my movements becoming robotic, and Xander crosses his arms, his eyes peering at me suspiciously through half-lidded slits.

"Don't try anything stupid or I will take you over my knee and smack you." He spins around and storms out without another word as heat pools between my legs. I clench my thighs together to relieve the now regular feeling.

I never thought in my life that I would want a man intimately, but Xander has awoken something that was locked away deep within. I wonder if that was partially my Pa's doing. Perhaps he kept me away from men my whole life for a reason.

I ponder over everything Alma told me about the prophecy. Pa knew. Perhaps he did not want any men distracting me from my true purpose in life, though if this was the case, then his deceit of my abilities and history would fail to make sense. Maybe he could not find the right time to tell me and was just doing his best to prepare and equip me.

For what though?

I silently question his reasons, but deep down I know the answer.

He was preparing me to be a queen.

To be the world's beacon of light in its increasing darkness.

25

XANDER

CLENCHING MY FISTS AGAINST MY SIDE, I try to remain calm as I stand at the top of the staircase, waiting for Kasim. My sword remains sheathed but reassuringly tied around my hips. He is the last person I want in my home, especially when a certain woman is there. I don't trust Kasim as far as I could throw him.

Since he's taller than me, I wouldn't be able to throw him far at all.

There's not much I can do, though, since my city needs his assistance. There are too many lives at stake, so I'll swallow my pride.

My body tenses when I see Lucas open the door to let a tall, dark man through. He looks up, pulling his gas mask down to smile; an expression that doesn't suit the wicked, sinister character that we all know him to be. It's not a genuine smile.

The corner of my eye twitches and I attempt a smile in return, knowing it will appear strained. It doesn't faze the man. He climbs the steps three at a time, his long, lean legs not faltering as he nears me within a few moments. He might not be bulky, but he is slender and agile. The hundred steps usually take people a few minutes, give or take, to reach the top.

But not Kasim.

I hate feeling threatened.

The fucker has a silent dominance exploited through shady, underhand dealings and brutal commands to avoid sullying his hands. There is palpable corruption and deceit radiating from every pore. My legs remain shoulder-width apart, my stance formidable as I pull myself to the tallest height.

"Xander," Kasim says with the hint of an African accent as he reaches the top. "So good to see you again."

Doubt it.

I keep my thoughts to myself and clasp his outstretched hands in the traditional Ruler greeting, bowing my forehead to touch his.

We step apart and I greet him back. "Likewise, Kasim. I trust you encountered no issues on the journey here?" It is testing my absolute willpower to remain civilised.

Kasim laughs, the deep sound reverberating off the walls as we walk through the entrance of my home. "We slaughtered a few hordes of Breathers on the way here, but nothing we could not handle. Tell me, are you still living as an unattached?"

My spine stiffens at the sudden change of topic, particularly a sensitive one that involves Rae. "Yes."

There's no way I would clue him into the presence of another woman here—wife or not.

Kasim nods thoughtfully and turns to study the room. "Ah, yes, I can see there is no woman living here."

His underlying insult annoys me, and I grind my jaw to refrain from snapping. It bothers me I hadn't thought to make the place more feminine for Rae, but somehow, I doubt she would care since she's mostly dwelled in caves. Still, I promise myself to add some decorations just for her.

"So," I say, and he reverts his attention back to me. "What is your plan of attack?"

Kasim looks behind him, making himself at home on my lounging seat, sitting back in a casual manner that infuriates me. The man comes into someone else's home and doesn't show any respect, which is typical of his arrogance.

"Well, Xander," Kasim begins, crossing his legs and linking his hands together in his lap, "my men will begin scouring the streets at night in line formation; one line facing forwards and the line behind facing the opposite direction, stepping backwards in synchronisation. They move as two lines in one formation. Each street will have two lines of my men."

My temper bristles at Kasim's condescending tone but I force a smile and agree with his plan. "Great. When do they start?"

"Ah," Kasim says nonchalantly and lifts a hand to study his nails. "We will start when I have received something in return for our services."

I remain standing above him and cross my arms defensively, my tone deadpanned. "What do you want?"

A diabolical spark glints in Kasim's dark eyes and he smiles, his white teeth flashing in contrast to his dark skin. I'm immediately on guard at the rapacious look transforming his face.

"Well, what do you have to offer?"

I don't hesitate to reply. "Food, water, and medical supplies is all we have."

Kasim picks at non-existent lint on his lavish, silky pants, seemingly uninterested in my answer, and my lips clamp tightly together. It takes all my effort not to scowl at the fucker.

"We have all the food, water, and medical supplies needed at Segment Two. What else do you have?"

I grit my teeth, suddenly realising what he's asking for. Women.

That's not how we run, here in Segment One. We don't trade women. Ever.

"We don't have any unpaired women." My tone is low and threatening but it doesn't seem to deter him, and he stands to his feet to step inside my personal space.

"Well then, I guess my men and I will be on our way."

Kasim turns and starts walking to the entrance when I hear something drop in my bedroom. My eyes briefly close in controlled frustration and I tense as Kasim stops and cocks his head to the side, as if tuning in to listen. He slowly turns around and his eyes narrow suspiciously at the door to my bedroom. My body coils with tension as he slowly walks towards it.

Fuck!

Kasim looks back at me as he points to the door in question. "You don't mind if I… check to make sure there are no threats in this room, do you?"

I clench my fists and gesture for him to go ahead, hoping that Rae has had the sense to hide. "By all means."

A vicious smile crosses Kasim's face and he turns back to swing open the door, stepping fully into the room. I stride in behind him and inwardly breathe a sigh of relief at the empty space.

With each moment Kasim lingers and his perceptive eyes

study each nook of the room, my heart beats faster. The longer he's in here, the more chance he has of discovering Rae.

I quickly rack my mind for solutions to remove him as quickly as possible without making him suspicious. "Well, it looks like no assailants are waiting for me in my bedroom," I say casually and gesture Kasim back out of the bedroom. "Thank you."

He cocks his head slightly as if listening for any sounds, but then to my relief nods curtly, leisurely turning to walk back out of the room. From out of my peripheral, I see slight movement under my bed and silently curse.

Fuck, Rae, stay still!

But it's too late, as the tiny movement is adequate in capturing the peripheral of Kasim's attention also. He whirls around and quickly crouches to strike; his long arm snaking out to grab Rae's ankle.

My muscles tense in preparation for the imminent fight I will have with Kasim as he drags the screaming little mouse out from under my bed. Kasim's gaze brightens with lust and elation at his sought-after discovery and Rae stares back up at him with her bright, fearful eyes. My heart clenches with dread at her seeming even more innocent with her new, shorter hairstyle.

Kasim will discern the innocence also.

Rae's chest heaves with apprehension and anxiety at being exposed and she remains frozen, lying on her back with her arms defensively bent in front of her chest and face.

"Well, well, well," Kasim says slowly, punctuating each word. He looks to me and I tense at the gleam in his eyes, relating only too well to the emotions swirling in their depths. "Looks like we found a pretty little assailant that needs to be reprimanded appropriately."

Rae's wide eyes dart to mine, her forehead puckered with worry as she silently pleads for me to do something.

This puts me in an extremely difficult position. I automatically prepare the words I will say in defence of Rae to keep her safely within my grasp, but I know Kasim won't assist us in eradicating the Breathers. Now that he has his sights set on Rae, *nothing* will distract him from his unyielding need to take her back to Segment Two.

Kasim smiles at me knowingly, the expression anything but friendly, and strides from the room silently to sit back on the couch. I glare at Rae; whose regretful expression drops to the ground at my feet.

Good.

I hope she knows the shitstorm she's just created.

"Follow me out there and *do not* say a word. Let me do the talking," I whisper furiously. She nods jaggedly.

I don't bother helping her up and stride angrily from the room to join Kasim with Rae trailing hesitantly behind.

Supressing the growl within my chest at the lecherous and greedy expression on Kasim's face as he studies Rae's bruising complexion, I wait for him to talk. I'll let him think he has the upper hand.

"You lied," Kasim begins casually, his lewd gaze never leaving Rae.

My hands itch to gouge out his eyes.

"I did not." My words are low and authoritative, and Kasim's face turns to me, his eyebrow raised in doubtful question. "You asked for *unpaired* women. This woman is to be bound to Lucas, my second in command."

Rae's wide eyes dart to me with confusion. I couldn't say she was bound to me as I already told Kasim I had no woman.

He remains silent as he studies me closely, his eyes calculative, then moves his focus back to Rae. His silence is unnerving, but I remain outwardly impassive to ensure he doesn't see my uneasiness.

"So," he begins slowly, "is she or is she not already paired with your man?"

My eye twitches. I can't lie. Rae doesn't have the small mark of a paired woman on her wrist, which Kasim can clearly see.

I take a deep breath, knowing my answer will seal her fate. I can't refuse Kasim. It would cause a war between the two Segments.

Fuck.

Kasim will take her from me, and I will grudgingly let him. I need him to free my city of Breathers even though every fibre of my being tells me to run a sword through his chest, without a care to the consequences.

Clenching my teeth angrily, I tamper down the urge to follow through, the increasing need to keep Rae within my grasp fighting for dominance over common sense.

But I will come for Rae. And I *will* kill him for taking her. Though logically I know both actions would likely start a war.

I need to appear casual, as if I have no interest in her.

"The girl is not yet officially paired with Lucas; she has been waiting here while he readies the home for her arrival."

A foreboding smile grows across Kasim's face as his eyes spark with victory. "In *your* bedroom? Well, I'm sure your man will not mind the trade for keeping his Ruler's city safe from Breathers."

Rae gasps at the insinuation and stares at me with horror falling over her expression. "No," she whispers with disbelief.

Kasim thankfully doesn't hear her protest, so I force myself to nod in agreement, the simple movement going against my screaming instincts. "He would be honoured to sacrifice Rae for the good of the city. And she is only staying here with me as you are in the residence below where she was staying originally." I congratulate myself for the quick lie to cover up my tracks. My impulses still scream at me to slay the man, but I force out the words through clenched teeth as I turn to Rae, who remains frozen in horror. "Go fetch your belongings and be ready to leave within a few days."

My words snap her from her frozen state and fury burns in her flashing eyes as her expression morphs into defiance and disbelief. "No! You can both go stab yourselves!"

My eyes widen at her retort and I glance at Kasim whose perverse smile somehow stretches wider. "I like her already."

Rae has just painted a *larger* target on herself.

I'm about to grab her by the arm and drag her to my room to pack when she whirls around and whizzes past us, out the door and down the tower's stairs.

"Fuck," I growl. I forget her ability of speed sometimes.

Kasim belts out a laugh, looking at me with challenge sparking his dark eyes. "Don't you just love a good chase?" He pulls up his mask and I keep my lips tightly shut so I don't drily laugh at his disadvantage. He will never catch the fast mouse unless he traps her.

My body remains rigidly wired with contained anger, but I follow Kasim out the entrance and down the stairs in the direction Rae went, not bothering with my own mask. His few personal guards follow us for protection, but I couldn't care less about my own safety right now. Deep down, I hope she manages to evade Kasim and that he won't get his grimy hands on her. Unfortunately, he is highly intelligent and even more dedicated when he has his sights set on something.

My heart pounds at the other threats that will await Rae out in the open.

Without her sword.

I don't know what's worse. A Breather hunting Rae. Or Kasim.

RULE SEVENTEEN:
WHEN IN DOUBT;
HIDE

26

RAE

MY HEART POUNDS FURIOUSLY AGAINST MY CHEST as I fling Alma's shop door open and sprint to the back in hopes of finding her. I briefly glance behind to check the men are not following me and nearly bowl over Alma herself.

"Rae, dear, whatever is wrong?" Alma asks as she grasps my shoulders to steady me.

Forcing myself to take deep breaths and calm my erratic heartbeat, I glance behind me again and gesture Alma towards her residence at the back of the shop. "We need to hide first."

Alma does not query my demand and we hastily make our way into her quaint home. I hate feeling cowardly but Rule Seventeen is valid in situations such as these.

When in doubt; hide.

There is no possibility to escape the city since it is on lockdown with Breathers lurking in the shadows until they fancy a meal. So, I'm hoping the tall, lean and dark man named Kasim tires of searching for me and agrees to a trade for something else for his men's services. I need to stay in the city anyway so I can begin the important tasks of research and experiments.

For the sake of humankind.

So even if I could escape the city, I would not.

Alma ushers me to the kitchen table to take a seat and she goes back out the front to lock the shop door, then locks the residential door behind her as she shuffles through. Remaining silent, she bustles around the kitchen, placing a pot of water on the fire to boil tea before taking a seat across from me.

"So, dear child, what has you in such a frazzle?" Alma watches me attentively with her wise gaze and I lean forward, keeping my voice low on the odd chance that someone passing by might somehow hear through the back of Alma's residence. I know I'm being paranoid.

"Xander just agreed to trade me for the services of Segment Two's army." My tone is hushed but bitter.

Alma's eyes widen in horror. "Surely our Xander would not do such a thing! He has never dabbled in the trade of humans like most other Segments!"

I nod my head miserably. "Well, he is now, and it seems that the Ruler of Segment Two has his sights set on me."

Alma scrunches her face and taps the table, deep in thought. "Perhaps Xander has a good plan and knows what he's doing. He has never been one to make foolish decisions."

I laugh bitterly. "Well, trading a *human being* without their consent seems pretty foolish to me."

Alma remains silent as she concentrates on a solution for the ordeal, only to have her countenance fall with defeat.

"Ah, dear Rae, I believe fate has chosen your path already and there is no sense in fighting it," she begins slowly, and I tense at her insinuation. "It may be best to go along with whatever Xander's plan is now."

My jaw drops. "Are you being serious, Alma?"

She nods, her expression grave. "I know Kasim is a man who is very adamant when he has his sights set on something. Or someone, in your case. It may be our city's only hope in eradicating the Breathers. Kasim will not give the order unless he gets what he desires. Perhaps something great will come of this—though it will not appear that way now."

I shake my head in disbelief.

Why is Alma supporting this barbaric plan?

"But what about the lab work using my genetics? Will we just forget about that? What about the good of humankind?" The questions rattle from my mouth at highspeed, my tone laced with desperation.

Sympathy fills Alma's wise eyes, and she smiles softly at me, coming around to pat me on the shoulder. "Segment Two also has their own lab, dear." Concern promptly worries her brows as she adds, "But you will need to be careful around Kasim. Protect yourself as much as you can, dear. He is not a trustworthy man."

She hobbles off to the kitchen before I can loudly protest and ask why she is content for me to surrender to someone she knows is not decent.

My mind whirls at my impending fate, the reality of my situation closing in like a horde of Breathers hunting their prey. This cannot be happening. I barely trust Xander, who I've only spent five days with, let alone an intimidating stranger. My eyes close as I slowly come to accept what needs to happen, and Alma brings over the boiled tea to pour me some.

"This better have brandy," I tell her flatly and she laughs.

"Of course, dear."

Alma has barely poured a cup for me before I grasp it and gulp the hot tea down, not caring that the liquid scorches my throat. I'm desperate to feel *anything* to overcome the numbness settling over me. It is hard to think that I would sacrifice my freedom for people who I once thought were just the greedy, rich, and powerful residing within the safe walls of a city.

My time here has opened my eyes.

The people are just everyday survivors that happened to pull the long straw and now reside behind the safe walls of the city. There is also an underlying pull, tugging deep within my soul, urging me to help against my own survival instincts.

I just hope the citizens of Segment Two are the same humble people as here.

The brandy relaxes my tense muscles and I begin to float happily on a cloud.

I can do this.

I *will* do this.

Standing up and lifting my chin bravely, I walk to Alma and embrace her tightly. "Thank you for everything, Alma. I will miss you so much. It hurts to have just found family only to be ripped from them so soon."

Alma's eyes soften as she looks up at me. "Our paths are destined to cross again, child. Do not lose hope. Your journey takes you where you need to be."

Against my own will, my eyes water and I choke back a sob.

I'm really doing this. Giving up my freedom *willingly.* Something that goes against my nature and way of life.

Alma lets me go and I straighten and shoot her a watery smile. "Well, until our paths cross again, Alma. Stay safe."

"You too, dear."

Forcing my legs to move, I turn without another word and stride toward the front of the shop, stopping abruptly at what I see through the glass. Kasim and Xander are impatiently waiting on the other side of the front door, both pairs of arms crossed over their chests and a gas mask hanging around Kasim's neck.

Xander obviously knew to find me here.

I resist the urge to escape again, walking tentatively to the glass door and unlocking it, remaining frozen with my hand on the handle. Surrendering is the hardest thing for me to do. My whole life has revolved around surviving and maintaining my freedom.

Pulling back my shoulders, I stand tall and push my way through the shop entrance. Both Kasim's arms twitch, readying to lunge for me if I attempt to escape again, but I walk over to them and lift my chin, meeting each man with a steely gaze. "Fine. I will go, but I'm doing it for the sake of the city. And I refuse to be submissive or mindless."

Kasim's eyes flash with delight and the promise of something darker. I become uncomfortable under his gaze, so I direct my focus towards Xander. A scowl shadows his face as he stares at me and I roll my eyes. "You agreed to it, Xander, I don't know why you're so grumpy."

Kasim chuckles and I briefly glance at him, noting the amusement in his coal-black eyes.

Xander tenses and his jaw grinds in frustration. "I'm doing what's best for my city. It doesn't mean I like it."

My eyes widen at his slip. Kasim is obviously supposed to think I'm bound to Lucas, but the way Xander is acting suggests otherwise. I take the opportunity of Kasim and Xander staring each other down to study the dark Ruler of Segment Two. I have never seen skin so beautiful. Like it is a mixture between charcoal and the deep, rich soil found in the jungle. Pa used to tell stories of African tribes and his descriptions of their attributes perfectly match Kasim.

I'm just taken aback with how beautiful he is.

The fine line of his jaw is clean shaven, and his head is also void of any hair. His tall frame may not be rippling with strength like Xander or Lucas, but rather his lean muscles suggest agility. I can feel my face heating as my eyes look to his full, thick lips and the wide nose above them. I turn even redder when I meet Kasim's own ebony eyes, but my spine stiffens at the hard amusement swirling in their inky abyss. The amusement does not reach his mouth and feels empty. I frown at the soulless glint of malice buried deep below the callous mirth. If I had not experienced the horrors of evil Hunters, then it would be easy to miss the hidden darkness in Kasim's eyes. But I don't and it turns my blood cold at the uncertainty of my future with someone who is so beautiful but appears to have something sinister lying deep within. Perhaps I'm just being paranoid.

My life of survival has shaped me to view the world warily, so naturally I look for the worst in everything to ensure I do not underestimate any potential threats.

Listen to your instincts.

They are screaming for me to run again. I quash the feelings, knowing any attempts at escape would be futile, then force myself to accept the situation. Continuing to scan Kasim, my apparent husband-to-be, I reassure myself that it could be worse.

Xander's chest emits a low warning sound and I tense as I realise both men have caught me unabashedly studying Kasim.

I have gone a life without the company and interaction of men and now I have *two* showing interest, though one is unwanted. It perturbs me that Kasim is clearly a man to be wary of, yet my body reacts to him as if it has no concerns for my safety.

Inwardly kicking myself at my lack of awareness, I take note, ensuring I do not fall to the whims of such physical inclinations in the presence of men again.

No. I must focus on the important task at hand. Saving a city, then saving humankind.

I really hope Alma is right about the laboratory and scientists at Segment Two.

Xander's gruff voice pulls me from my musings and I meet his hard stare. "We need to get you back to the tower. It's not safe out here, even during the day."

I nod and begin walking to the large building, not bothering to wait for the two men and their surrounding guards.

Keeping my spine straight and shoulders back, I maintain the outward appearance of bravery when really, my insides are churning with apprehension.

We make it to the tower without any encounters with Breathers and Xander angrily punches in the code to let us all through.

My body tenses at the feeling of Kasim's large hand splayed against my lower back as he ushers me through the door. I hate people touching me without my consent but Kasim's touch leaves a chill racing up my spine. Xander notices the contact and rage fills his eyes as he sends Kasim a deathly look. Kasim either does not see or simply does not care as his hand remains pressed against me. I step aside to break the contact and quickly walk ahead, climbing the stairs as hastily as I can to avoid any more physical interaction with *either* man.

As we near the floor that Kasim and his men are to be staying in, Kasim stops and looks at me. "Since you're mine now, you can stay with me until we leave."

My wide eyes dart to Xander, who attempts to keep his clenched fists by his side, his jaw twitching discontentedly. Crippling alarm crawls up my spine as he looks at me, his chocolate orbs darkening as they turn hard. The floor feels as if it is falling out beneath me when Xander gives me one stiff nod of his head and turns to bound up the remaining stairs.

He just left me with a man. A stranger.

Thoughts of Alayah cross my mind and my heart plummets at the realisation I probably will not get the chance to see her again.

You are doing this for the sake of humanity, I remind myself, clenching my eyes tightly shut to keep the tears at bay. I jerk when a vice-like hand clasps my own and my eyes snap open to see Kasim, his own eyes deceivingly docile. "I will not hurt you. I promise."

My lips remain tightly pressed in a straight line as I nod, refusing to stare into his deceptively gentle gaze. I'm afraid of what malevolence I might see in the expanse of his ink-black irises.

Kasim pulls me along the hall and pushes me through the door leading to our temporary living space. I stop to absorb our surroundings. The place is an exact replica to Xander's quarters, though on a smaller scale.

"You must be hungry," Kasim's assertive voice breaks through my musings.

Nodding, I quietly reply, "Yes, I am."

He immediately clicks his fingers at the one guard by the door, who nods in acknowledgement and leaves the room in search of food. I fidget under Kasim's stare as he studies me, and I stand awkwardly, realising it is just the two of us in the residence. I frown and look up at him in question. "Where are all your men? Aren't they staying here with us?"

Kasim flashes a humourless smile, his dark eyes twinkling in contrast to the whiteness of his perfect teeth.

White, straight teeth are a rarity in the Vanquished world.

Ah, rich and powerful.

The wealthy, influential humans have the means and resources to acquire whatever they want and need—such as dental services and toothpaste. It makes sense since Xander's teeth are also perfectly white and straight. I'm lucky mine are as well and surmise that it originates from decent genetics.

"Well, since you are now with me, the men have been ordered to start eradicating the infestation of Breathers. That was the deal, was it not?"

I wince at the reminder of my value as merchandise rather than a human being. "Of course."

Kasim makes his way over to me and I watch him distrustfully, wariness becoming more prominent the longer I'm in his presence. He offers his hand, and I tilt my head at the contrast of the pale underside of his palm compared to the darkness of his skin. I've never seen something so beguiling. And inviting.

My curiosity at how his hand feels outweighs my common sense and I place my own hand in his—almost baulking at how his large hand engulfs my own tiny one. The warmth surprises me and as I feel the soft pads of his fingers and palms, an involuntary shiver races up my arm. The sensations compel me to walk mechanically as Kasim leads me to the lounging seat and I sink into the plush chair beside him. His proximity and warmth pressed against me sends tingles into my extremities and I frown at the odd reaction.

Is it normal for females to have this reaction with every man?

The thought bothers me at the unearthing of a female's biological responses, and I loathe to think that would be why a lot of women did not survive The Vanquishing.

I hope I'm not alone and it isn't just my body being traitorous.

Kasim chuckles beside me, the deep sound reverberating against my ribs, and I glance up at his fascinated expression, the lighter shades of ebony flecks glinting in his coal-black eyes.

"You're always deep in thought. I can see the intelligence flashing through those beautiful eyes of yours."

A blush heats my cheek as I look down, and his fingertips tilt my chin up gently again. "So shy, there's no need to be. Xander did not even tell me your name. Would you please share it with me? My name is Kasim, though you already know this."

I blurt out my birth name. My other name is only for Xander, Alma, Alayah, and Lucas. "Raine."

His eyes momentarily widen in surprise before becoming thoughtful. "Ah, how fitting for you. This name means *queen*." His eyes rake my body before darting up to meet mine again. "You look like a queen too. You *will* be a queen."

It infuriates me that these two men keep saying this, but more so that I even *want* to be a queen. Well, I just do not want to be *their* queens and certainly not Kasim's queen.

"And *you* should jump off a cliff." My vehement tone reflects the contempt festering inside me.

A shocked expression falls across Kasim's face before he throws his head back and belts out a loud, smooth laugh. My eyes narrow at him. I was not trying to be funny.

As his laughter subsides, he directs his focus back on me and his hand snakes out to play with a strand of my shoulder-length hair, the ends of it tickling my chin. I hold my breath at his touch. I'm unable to trust him.

"Your hair is so soft," he says gently, "the length suits your pretty, round face."

I clear my throat with discomfort at his attention and pull back, forcing his hand to drop from my hair.

Kasim smiles at my retreat, unfazed that I'm not returning any affection, and he stands to stretch just as his man comes through the entrance with a handful of food.

My eyes remain trained on Kasim's extended torso as his shirt lifts, mesmerised by the sheer strength and agility displayed within his toned, lean muscles.

He may not be as broad as Xander, but he still clearly contains a power and strength that could easily squeeze the life from a human.

Suspicion crinkles my eyes, obscuring my view as I peer at him through narrowed slits.

That's right. Do not trust him.

Kasim claps once at the arrival of food and smiles at me, though once again, I notice the expression is void of mirth. "Let's eat!"

The contrast of his positive demeanour, however ostensible, to his threatening presence gives me whiplash every time he smiles. Something sinister lies behind the expression, though I cannot quite place my finger on it.

I push up regretfully from the cosy seating and follow him to the bench where his guard places the food and retreats to stand at the front door. My growling stomach distracts me momentarily from the circumspection that fills me, instigated by being left alone with Kasim.

We settle down in odd, tall seats without backs at the bench, and my mouth waters at the array of brightly coloured fruit and cuts of dried meat.

Kasim surprises me as he prepares a plate of food for me first. I take it graciously. "Thank you."

He pauses and looks at me curiously. "You're welcome, Raine." The use of my birth name feels odd, but I keep my face impassive. "It is strange but refreshing that you have refined manners yet such a terrible temper," Kasim adds with a finger stroking his smooth chin.

I smile sweetly at him before replying sardonically. "Well, when people deserve my manners, then they are afforded with them."

Kasim chuckles, his eyes glinting as he bites into a juicy piece of yellow fruit. The reminder that this man is to be my husband causes a cold chill to wash over me, contrasting the strange attraction battling for control. My body slightly tremors but I tamper both conflictions deeply down. There is no sense dwelling on the inevitable.

Juice dribbles down his chin and drips onto the exposed vee of his toned chest and my eyes drop with fascination as I watch the yellow juice run down his dark skin.

"Find something interesting, Raine?"

My eyes dart up to his amused ones and my cheeks are suffused with heat.

He stops eating and places the piece of fruit down as he shifts on his seat to reach over and run a sticky finger gently down my flaming cheek, the intrusive action causing me to flinch. "Ah, so soft, just as I expected," he murmurs and sits back. "Tell me, what makes you blush so furiously?"

I choke on the piece of fruit I had started eating and sputter before composing myself, wiping off the trail of juice he left on my face. I stare at him silently, unsure of what I'm supposed to say.

I was staring at your chest, and was fascinated by the contrasting colour of the juice running over your smooth skin? And then you caught me staring?

He chuckles at my flummoxed expression and leans forward as if about to whisper a secret. I reflexively lean towards him as he softly speaks. "Either way, I love how your delicate, white skin turns a pretty shade of pink. All I can think about is different ways to make your skin turn that colour."

I may not have much experience with men, but I pick up on his implication and my eyes widen as I jolt back on my seat with a gasp, gripping the edge of the bench tightly. By now my entire face and chest must be as red as blood and Kasim's expression becomes thoughtful as he studies my innocent reaction mingled with fear. A look of realisation dawns on him and a new baleful glint sparks within his gaze. "You're not unbroken, are you?"

My eyes widen. I cannot determine what his intent is, and my spine stiffens as fear suffuses me again. I keep my lips tightly pressed together and glance towards the exit.

Maybe I should run back to Xander and forget saving the city.

Except most of the Breathers would have been eradicated by now.

The sudden thought gives me an idea.

I can play along until I'm able to escape.

As adamant as I am on having my genetics used for the greater good, I would rather do it in this city, under the ruling of a man I already know. I know Xander's motives and he has never forced himself on me. Well, he did, but he was under some trance and stopped before going too far. The thought causes me to frown. I'm slowly coming to realise that it is not an excuse.

My lips press together into a tight line. Who knows what Kasim is capable of?

I defiantly raise my chin and give him a cold look. "No, I am *not* unbroken."

His sinister smile indicates he believes otherwise, and I swallow the lump in my throat.

The portentous display of his pearly teeth indicate my impending peril.

Rule Eighteen:
My New Rule

27

RAE

ACH NIGHT, I BARELY SLEEP A WINK, which has nothing to do with my insistence on taking the couch, leaving the tall man to an appropriately sized bed. My troubling sleeps are due to the countless thoughts that assail me throughout the night and I'm sure to have no lower lip left if I were to look at the mirror on the bathroom wall—in the bathroom where the largest of my troubling thoughts currently is.

Kasim.

My knit together into a frown as I toss and turn on the lounge seat that is too soft. I have always slept on the ground and even after sleeping on Alayah's and Xander's mattresses, I'm still unused to the luxury.

Alayah.

My other troubling thought.

I am determined to see her even if Kasim breaks his promise. He did not even blink before agreeing to my visiting her prior to our journey for Segment Two. I need to make sure she is unharmed despite the influx of Breathers in the area. Even though she is almost a day's journey from the city, Breathers move fast and cover vast amounts of ground.

Breathers.

My last and most troubling thought. Kasim's lack of support in my endeavour for creating an Immunity or even a cure to turn Breathers back into humans, has cast a dark cloud over this whole ordeal.

I huff my annoyance at remembering Kasim's response when I told him of my Immunity and asked if I could use his scientists to run tests on my genetics in the hopes of finding a cure.

"Raine, I know you believe there's a chance at redemption, but there is not. I forbid you from spreading false hope over the city. It will cause unrest and eventually uprisings."

Xander inherently sold me—and essentially my freedom—but I thought I could deal with being traded like livestock *if* I were still able to make a difference in the declining human population. And now *that* has been ripped from me like a baby being torn from its mother's hands by a ravenous Breather.

I spend the remainder of my last night in Segment One running through solutions for my dire position when daylight begins to stream through the tiny window on the wall. Thankfully, my lack of sleep was not entirely unproductive, as through my perturbing thoughts I kept fixating on the only feasible solution for this whole situation.

Kill Kasim.

He may be a deceivingly handsome man, but those midnight

black eyes only reflect cold and calculating menace. I'm not ignorant. I can see through his pretence, and though it disconcerts me that I cannot decipher his long-term plan, I will not feel any remorse driving a blade through his hardened heart. Especially when so much is at stake. *Especially* when he will hinder the progress in finding an Immunity.

I can do it. After all, I had planned to eliminate Xander before I started falling for him.

No.

That does not matter anymore, not since he almost violated me and *sold* me to a seemingly heartless Ruler. I scowl at a corner of the room, feeling as if men are nothing but selfish and greedy sacks of flesh.

The sound of the bedroom door scraping open pulls me from my dark thoughts and Kasim walks through the living area, his torso naked and glistening from bathing. Rivulets of beaded moisture sluice over the granite ridges of his lean muscle into the material wrapped around his tapered waist. I swallow the lump in my throat, forcing myself to look away, for I do not trust my traitorous body to behave. My disloyal eyes keep darting back to steal glances of his toned chest and abdomen as he walks towards me.

It bothers me that I can detest a man so much, yet my body reacts immediately to anything remotely intimate.

Everything is just a sensory overload.

I miss the uncomplicated days of surviving as a hermit outside city walls.

"Bathe yourself before we leave," Kasim demands, and my temper bristles at his order. He must detect this as he explains in a gentle tone, "We will be travelling a few days without spare water to wash and the journey will be hot and dusty."

I cannot argue with his reasoning, so I reluctantly get up and stretch my stiff back. As I reach my arms above my head, Kasim's gaze roams my body. I notice the change of his countenance— immediately stopping mid-stretch to drop my arms and push past, making my way into the bathroom. There is something about him that I cannot quite identify. It is darker, more dangerous than the lechery I have witnessed in his eyes.

I will need to stay completely alert around this man.

The water is heavenly, though glacial, and I rapidly wash all the important areas, drying off as quickly as I can. I don't trust Kasim, so I hastily clothe myself then walk back out to see that he is not even in the room. Briefly frowning at the empty space, the sound of muffled conversation behind the closed door at the entry piques my interest. My curiosity trumps common sense and I sneak towards the door to press my ear against it, hearing Kasim's hushed voice talking to one of his men. My eyes narrow when I hear my name and I press my ear harder against the surface of the cold metal to hear better.

"Take ten men and leave now. We won't be far behind."

He must just be sending men to scour the place before we make our way through. For my safety.

Satisfied that nothing minacious was being conspired, I step back just in time for Kasim to open the door, abruptly pausing at the sight of me nearby. His pronounced brows pull down, as does the displeased line of his full lips.

"Raine, how much did you hear?"

I frown at the accusatory question.

Why is he being so defensive?

"Nothing. Just that you are sending men ahead of us. I assume to make sure the area is safe for us when we travel?"

Kasim's shoulders relax and he nods once. "Yes. Your safety is my main priority. Come, we must leave for Segment Two while the sun is rising to give us the advantage of daylight."

Panic at the thought of leaving Alma, Xander, Lucas and Alayah claws at my throat, instantly eradicating any scepticism provoked by Kasim's odd behaviour.

"Can I say goodbye to my grandmother and Xander? And Lucas?" I ask him urgently, realising I ought to have said Lucas's name first as he is supposedly my betrothed. Thankfully Kasim does not notice my error. He hesitates and I clench my fists, ready to fight for the chance to say goodbye, but he reluctantly nods his head, gesturing for me to exit the door.

Not allowing him time to change his mind, I rush from the residence and up the stairs. Betrayal cuts me but I'm still eager to see Xander's familiar scarred face. I smile politely at the guard situated at the door, my impatience increasing. He nods and moves aside, and I knock urgently, hoping Xander will be awake and home. I'm seething he bartered me even if it was for the good of the Segment, but he is the only man I've been intimate with. I feel as if I'm leaving part of my heart here with him, so I *need* closure before Kasim takes me.

I may never see Xander again.

Relief embraces me as the door is wrenched open and Xander stands in the entrance, his large frame taking up the space. He blinks once at my unexpected presence and peers downstairs where Kasim is waiting patiently. My stomach flutters when his beautiful, expressive chocolate eyes flick back to mine and a strained smile tips his tempting lips at their corners. "Little mouse."

Tears fill my eyes at his infuriating nickname for me.

I may not hear it ever again.

I'm still angry at him for almost violating me—more so for forcing me into the hands of another man, another life—but I cannot help my intoxicating feelings for him.

Anger fills Xander's face as he sees tears spill down my cheeks and he curses, pulling me inside before shooting a dark look at Kasim, who is occupied with one of his guards.

"Rae, has he hurt you?" Xander asks as he shuts the door behind me, and I shake my head.

"No, but I do not think he would hesitate in doing so. He also refuses to let me work on the Immunity with my genetics."

Exasperation crosses Xander's face and he rubs his hand roughly over his jaw before grabbing me suddenly and pulling me against his firm, warm body.

"I'm so sorry, mouse," he whispers, his voice breaking. "If I had a choice, I wouldn't ever let you go."

I choke back a sob at his sincere words and the soft press of his lips to my forehead.

"Don't let me go then," I whisper back, desperation clinging to my tone.

Xander sighs in defeat. "It's too late, Rae," he rasps, "it would start a war between the two Segments if I went back on the deal now."

I already assumed this, but I had to try.

My arms tighten around Xander's waist and I look up at him through blurry eyes. "Please kiss me goodbye." I can barely whisper my despondent request but Xander still hears and his pupils dilate as his gaze drops to my lips. Pain flashes across the scarred planes of his face and he nods once—the only warning I receive before he plunges down and captures my mouth in a greedy, impassioned kiss. I moan and whimper against him as his large hands roam my back and come to rest with his fingers tangled in my hair at the nape of my neck.

His kiss slows from burning desire to a tender, sensual loving of my lips, and tears leak from the corner of my eyes.

In this moment, I realise without a doubt, I have broken Pa's crucial rule.

Rule Fifteen.

Don't. Fall. In. Love.

Even though Xander nearly forced himself on me and stole my innocence. Even though he is trading me for the safety of his city; I still love him.

The realisation shakes me to my core, and I break from Xander's kiss with a gasp, my hand pressed to my open mouth in shock. My watery eyes stare into his own softening ones and a muffled sob tears from behind my hand. Understanding crosses Xander's face and he smiles sadly, pulling me back against him in a firm embrace to whisper in my ear, "I love you too, Rae."

I cannot return the words. Not when I'm about to leave. It would make it too difficult. So, I just break away from Xander's safe arms, nod my head and look away as silent sobs shudder through me.

"I'll come for you, Rae."

Xander's promise fills me with hope and my shattering heart grasps to it like a lifeline as if I were sinking and his words were a vine being cast out over the waters that were swallowing me.

A loud knock startles me and I step farther away from Xander, knowing Kasim is behind the door—most likely growing suspicious. Xander presses a soft kiss to my lips as he passes by to open the door, whispering in my ear one last time. "Don't forget my promise." He continues past and calmly swings the door open, revealing the irritated Ruler of Segment Two.

"We need to make a move," Kasim says coolly as he glances inquisitively between Xander and me. My cheeks warm and my eyes drop to the floor, hiding the turmoil of emotions bound to be swirling in their morose pits.

Without saying a word, I brush past Xander, purposely grasping for one last touch of him, then walk out the door... and his life.

Kasim's dexterous footsteps follow as he places a hand on my lower back possessively. I can feel Xander's gaze burning into me and glance back to see fury morphing his handsome face at Kasim's touch.

Sadness is sure to reflect in my eyes as I send a last thin smile to him and mouth three words, just out of Kasim's sight. *I love you.*

Xander's eyes soften and his hands clench beside him—clearly refraining from chasing after us and seizing me back. He mouths the three little words in return, and I choke back my sob, whipping my head around so Kasim does not become suspicious.

Kasim leads me quickly out of the building, his numerous men surrounding us, and I see Alma's shop as we make our way down the dusty road.

"Stop!" I yell, and everyone freezes, turning to look at me. I look pleadingly to Kasim. "Please, I need to say goodbye to Alma."

My heart drops at the cold expression freezing over his face and I think he's about to say no when Alma's hoarse voice breaks through the mass of men. "I'm right here, dear."

Relief fills me and I burst into tears at the sight of my only kin pushing past all the brawny guards. I fling myself at her and sob against her shoulder as she embraces me fervently. "Now, now, dear," she coos, "you be strong and remember that this life will take you where you need to be—no matter how dreary the path seems."

"Thank you, Alma, for everything. I love you and will always think of you." My words are muffled with my mouth pressed into the thick, silver mop of hair on Alma's head, but she hears, nonetheless.

"I love you too, Rae," she whispers, and I feel Kasim tense beside me at the mention of my preferred name that I purposely kept from him. He pries me from her arms and gruffly shouts orders to the men before turning his wrathful eyes on me. "We are leaving. Now."

I send one last weak smile to Alma, whose hand touches her chest, and I nod at the indication to my pendant. A reminder to focus on what is important. To focus on my purpose. To not lose hope. If only I could convince myself that *love* is not part of my *purpose.* But I know that is what my love for Xander and my love for Alma has gifted me.

I decide in that moment to insert a rule of my own, even though it contradicts Pa's reiterated one.

Love gives purpose.

The convoy moves out with Kasim and me at the centre of his substantial militia. The gate closes behind the last of them, its heavy thud and clank a final goodbye to this chapter of my life. I need to be brave now. I cannot concentrate on what could have been anymore. I need to forget Xander and look ahead, regardless of his promises to retrieve me.

But I could never forget my first love, however fleeting it may have been.

Hours pass as we continue into the thick of the jungle, the extreme humidity stifling the air around us. I begin recognising certain trees and realise that Alayah's hut is nearby, so I turn eagerly to Kasim. "This is where my friend lives," I tell him, and he nods impassively. "Am I able to say goodbye to her?" I see something flash through his jet-black eyes but do not think anything of it—only focusing on his impending answer.

"Yes. Make it quick," his voice is muffled under the respirator mask covering his mouth and nose.

Finally, something positive is happening for me, and I point in the direction of her home. He nods and briefly lifts his mask and shouts directions at the men, causing the convoy to steer towards Alayah's tree-hut.

Jubilation at the prospect of seeing my new friend bubbles up within me, and I spot the tree fifty metres ahead of us. My heart splinters at being ripped from my new life at Segment One with Alma and Xander, but at least I will have some closure with Alayah.

As we close in, the vile smell of death assaults my nose and I dry heave, tugging my shirt out of the leather vest and up over my nose. I glance at Kasim warily, who appears unphased by the insulting stench. I frown at his expressionless reaction.

How can he not be affected by the smell?

Perhaps the mask assists in stifling the odour, and I suddenly wish I had not informed him of my Immunity so that he spared a mask for me.

We reach the clearing at the foot of Alayah's tree and the smell becomes intolerable, making my eyes burn and water. The large number of guards crowding the base of the tree block my access, so I look to Kasim and speak with a muffled voice through my shirt. "Are they going to move so I can go up?"

Kasim nods once and shouts a brisk order, causing the men to part into two groups. My eyes drop to the soaked ground they had been standing before, and foreboding spiders scurry up my spine. The wet ground is tinged with a deep, discolouring red. With blood. *No...* Unease fills me at seeing what I feel deeply within my soul is not animal blood. Frantically pacing the surroundings, I start looking for the source of it and notice tracks indicating something has been dragged into the bush. My heart pounds erratically as I tentatively follow it, unable to clamp down the dread rising in my throat, taking the form of acidic bile. I look back to Kasim who is whispering to one of his guards and he glances at me briefly, the emotionless, bitter eyes shaking me to the core.

The change of his friendly demeanour—even if it were in pretence—to this cold and calculating man has my equilibrium askew. My hands shake as I move large leaves to make my way through the thick foliage, and the stench becomes more rancid. A smell of death like none I've smelt before hits me, verifying my original assumptions that it is not the flesh of an animal producing the offending smell. I take another step and my new leather shoes squelch, sliding in something mushy. I look down and my heart stops. My skin turns cold.

Intestines.

The breath in my chest becomes ragged as my eyes follow the trail of innards to a bloodied lump a few metres ahead of me and I scream at the massacred sight. "No!"

My knees buckle and I drop with a mournful cry as tears flood my cheeks and I gasp for air. Alayah's brutalised body lies in front of me, her abdomen slashed and torn—leaving her internal organs splayed out in a violent array of pale colours and dark red. Disbelief fills me.

Alayah's too strong for a Breather to get to her.

My sobs become harsh gasps for air, and I sit back on my haunches, wailing as I stare at the horror etched across Alayah's final expression. Her mouth gapes wide in a silent scream and her eyes are blank and unmoving. Lifeless, but not soulless. At least the Breather did not steal her soul.

Time blurs into non-existent minutes as I remain in the coagulating bloody puddle on my knees, sobbing and crying mournfully until Kasim pulls me up.

"We need to move now, *Rae*," Kasim says, his voice cold, and I flinch at the use of my veiled name. "There may be more Breathers in the area."

The mention of the detested monsters urges my movements and I glance back one more time at Alayah's remains, tears silently cascading down my face at the helpless sight. My fists clench tightly, wishing the Breather that maimed her was still nearby so I could inflict the same pain upon it.

Kasim's tight grip digs into my arms, sure to leave a bruise, but I'm numb to any pain and follow the convoy of guards—blank to the world and with no sense of reality.

Even through my lifetime of loss and desolation, I'm still not prepared to deal with the amount of loss I've experience in this one day.

28

XANDER

CLEANER CLIMBING THE STAIRS distracts me from my rage, and he nods at me as he walks past, heading into my residence with a bucket full of soapy water. I silently thank Lucas for his foresight in requesting the cleaner when he left, considering the remaining odorous mess in my bathroom and bedroom.

My gaze quickly flickers back down the stairs and it takes all my restraint not to punch the wall as Rae disappears from my sight, my rage exacerbated by Kasim's hand on her back. If anything happens to her, it will be on my head. Choosing the Segment's wellbeing over Rae was the hardest decision I've ever made. I knew if the city were overrun, I could lose her to Breathers, raiders, or Kasim's probable war, so at least now I have a chance to go after her and bring her back to a *safe* city.

I give in to the erupting anger. "Fuck!" The wall echoes and the thin sheets of metal crumples beneath my fist as my restraint unexpectedly snaps. I pretend the impressive indentation in the

327

wall is Kasim's face and slight satisfaction appeases me.

Lucas walks up the stairs just as I remove my bloodied fist, and his grim face perturbs me. I sigh. "What now?" My tone is bland, as nothing else could trump the loss of the one person I love in this world.

Lucas clears his throat and pain clouds his eyes. His voice is strained as he manages to relay the grim news. "The scouts we had spying on Kasim's convoy spotted them near Alayah's tree-hut." I don't like the tone of his voice but nod for him to continue. "They scoured the place after the convoy moved on and found the remains of Alayah. Brutally murdered."

I frown. "Murdered? By a Breather?" My disbelief is evident, and Lucas shakes his head grimly.

"I thought the same. Alayah was too adept, too capable to let a Breather—"

Hearing the grief in Lucas's tone as his voice breaks, I grasp his shoulder and pull him in for a quick embrace, something neither of us have done since his twin's brutal death.

"I'm sorry, man. I know you fancied her."

A strangled sound tears from Lucas's throat and his green, sorrowful eyes meet mine. "I could have loved her, Xander."

My heart breaks for my only friend. He must have visited her off-shift, meaning he travelled through the nights to see her for the few days.

That explains the dark circles under his eyes.

"We will have a proper burial for her," I tell him ardently and he nods, the movements stiff. "Come in for some brandy. I think we both could use a few glasses."

Lucas doesn't pause, following me into my residence, over to the kitchen where I pull out two glasses and the brandy from under the bench.

The amber liquid has barely been poured before Lucas snatches the glass to tip it back in two gulps. I instantaneously follow suit and relish the liquid burn down the back of my throat.

Pouring us both another glass, I gesture for us to sit in the lounge and we make our way over with the bottle. We glance towards the bedroom when hearing the cleaner scuffling about and I look back at Lucas. "Thanks for requesting him."

Lucas dips his head in acknowledgement and we both fall solemn.

"We need to get Rae back," I tell him quietly, feeling bad for putting this on him so soon after his loss, though he takes it better than I expect and nods in agreeance.

"I know." Lucas looks up at me with understanding reflecting in his eyes. "You love her."

I chuckle darkly. "Yes. It must be odd to see after all this time." I become sombre at the reminder of his sister. My last love, or at least what I thought was love. It pales in comparison to what I feel for Rae.

Lucas senses my direction of thought and pats me firmly on the shoulder. "It's in the past," he reassures me in a quiet voice.

We sit in silence, reflecting the tribulations we've both endured at the hands of a violent man. After a few solemn moments, Lucas leans forward with a sigh. "Anyway, back to your suicidal mission. How on earth will we take Rae back without starting a war? You handed her over just so you avoided one in the first place."

I nod slowly. "We could make it appear as if Rae has run away. Escaped. We need to be shadows in the night, unseen and undetected so Kasim doesn't suspect it was us."

Lucas becomes thoughtful and scratches the stubble on his

chin slowly. "Yes, that's a good plan but highly improbable he wouldn't suspect us. Worth a shot, I guess. We should set up camp outside the walls for a few days and study possible ways of stealthily infiltrating Segment Two. The rest will be improvised; it's been too long since we last visited the place."

I nod grimly. "It will be risky. We need to move as quickly as we can to minimise any chance of being seen. We will take a drone and map the city before we enter it, so we have the upper hand."

Lucas falls silent again, leaning back against the lounge as he absorbs the information and goes over semantics in his head.

A thought flickers in his eyes. "Why don't we hire someone to kidnap her *before* they reach the city walls? That way, we don't have to worry about infiltrating the city, finding Rae, *then* getting her out. They also won't suspect it has anything to do with us if it's just a group of filthy Hunters."

We both grimace at the mention of Hunters, displeased we will need their services once again.

I take a moment to sort through all the possible outcomes in my head and slowly sip my brandy, savouring the heat and dulling sensation it provides.

"It would make it less risky," I start slowly. "We would need to ensure the Hunters attack from the opposite direction otherwise Kasim will know we sent them." My eyes narrow at the reminder of what we learnt about the Hunters who brutally murdered Alayah's mother nine years prior. "We need to make sure we trust them with Rae."

Lucas nods his agreeance. "I can send the request out now to see what Hunters are looking for jobs. It's best we get them sorted out sooner rather than later, as they have a vast amount of ground to make up if they are to move in front of Kasim's convoy."

I nod at Lucas. "Thank you. Report back when we have a bite."

Lucas downs the rest of his brandy in one mouthful and pats me on the shoulder as he gets up from the seat and stalks from the room. The cleaner walks from the bedroom holding his soiled supplies with a grim expression. "Your space is all clean now, Ruler," he tells me, and I send him a strained smile.

"Thank you."

He quickly scurries out and shuts the door behind him, leaving me to my own darkening thoughts. I look towards the empty bedroom and around my quiet space, sighing drearily.

I'm already missing the noise and passion Rae usually fills it with—missing her defiance.

"Fuck. I have to pull my head out of my arse," I mumble to myself. "A whole city counting on me."

Looking at the clock on the wall, I realise I'm late for an impromptu meeting and hastily push up from my lounge.

"Shit."

The residents with urgent queries and requests that couldn't wait until the next monthly meeting will be waiting on me at the City Hall and once again, I've let them down by focusing on a woman.

That woman will be their queen, though.

I throw back the rest of my brandy and grimace at the slight buzz, the haze of alcohol blurring the room.

Lucas and I probably shouldn't have had that many glasses.

We always need to keep our heads on straight in case any issues arise.

Throwing the glass in the sink, I stride to the bathroom and wash my face with cold water under the running tap. The frigid liquid momentarily provides a reprieve from the spinning and I quickly dry my face and stride back out, leaving my peaceful yet lonely dwelling to descend the stairs and enter the dirty street outside. The guards have cleaned up the remains of Breathers slaughtered by Kasim's men and I inhale deeply. The air still has a slight stench to it but at least it's not overbearing.

I break into an easy jog and make my way down the dusty, hot street to the City Hall, arriving at a large, low-set building made from thick, reinforced metal. The hall is the designated refuge for all citizens if shit were to ever hit the fan.

A large line of murmuring people spills from the entrance out on to the street and I flinch.

Fuck.

It's going to be a long day.

The noise increases as the citizens see me moving past them and I greet them collectively while making my way to the entrance.

No point in apologising for being late since I'm doing them a favour.

One of my most trusted guards waits for me, a speck against an opposite wall of the large space, and I break into a jog to reach him.

The guard nods in greeting as I approach him, and I slap him on the shoulder.

"Thanks for holding the fort down. What's the schedule for today?"

The guard grimaces and glances down the endless line leading up to the large mahogany desk I'm to sit at, then looks back at me. "Well, you have over a hundred citizens to speak to. It will take up the day."

"That's okay. They must all have questions either about the breach of the city wall or Rae's absence." Word of the woman I had chosen to make queen spread like wildfire, and I presume the guards on duty at the tower must have told their families about her.

My guard nods in agreement as I turn to study the line of people and scratch my stubbled chin in thought.

I need to segregate these people into categories to move through the line quickly.

Turning back to my guard, I explain my plan. "Get three of your men and tell them to go along the line. We are going to break the people into three groups; one for those who have questions about the recent breach and Breathers; one for those who have deceased to tend to; and lastly, one for all other general queries."

The guard's eyes light up at the brilliant idea and he runs to the entrance to organise three more guards, leaving four heavily armed guards to remain around me.

I watch as the massive line slowly breaks apart and the people trickle into formation behind the three guards. A smile twitches at the corner of my mouth. As much as I love hunting and fighting, there is something satisfying about solving problems. But my brows pinch at the thought of hunting. It was what led me to Rae in the first place. A sharp pang stabs through my chest and I rub it to relieve the pain.

I lean against the table and watch as three perfect lines form in front of me; one larger than the other two.

The guard approaches me once again and I nod. "Good work. I might stand up on the chair and address the citizens first."

I make my way around the desk and step onto the sturdy chair, then face the mass of people to address them in a booming voice. "Good morning, citizens of Segment One. Thank you for coming today. As you can see, I have broken you all into three groups." I point at the longest line. "I will make my way down this line first, but if the question called out is the same one as yours and you are satisfied with the answer, please voluntarily leave to save us all time. If I get asked the same question twice... there will be ramifications."

The people in line nervously murmur.

Good.

I remain standing on the chair and point at the old man hunched at the front. "Your question first."

He hesitates before asking in a strained voice, "Why was there a breach? How did the Breathers get in?"

I knew this would be the main question and I answer loudly to inform all present. My hard glower meets the eyes of each citizen as I scan the lines. "We had a traitor in our midst who bribed the guards to open the gate. All parties involved have been executed, so there is no need to worry about further threats."

I ensured to add the execution element as an underlying warning to everyone—a promise that no treason will go unanswered. The line begins to disintegrate as half the citizens walk off towards the exit. A sense of achievement rises in my chest.

Thank fuck they all had the same question.

I point to the next man still standing in the line, who looks apprehensive as he asks his question. "What happened to the lovely Rae? We all heard she was to be *your* queen and now there are rumours the Ruler of Segment Two has her."

I tense at the underlying disrespect in his tone but remain impassive as I answer. "It is a temporary situation that I am working on to quickly rectify. Rae sacrificed herself as a trade so all of you could live in peace without Breathers infesting the streets."

The crowd of people murmur appreciatively, and someone calls out that they want Rae back, instigating a collective cry of agreeance from the remaining citizens. My smile is strained as I address the chattering mob with a stern tone.

"We *will* retrieve Rae and you *will* have your queen. But you need to be patient."

A collective cheer goes up and pride fills me at how Rae has already won the hearts of the citizens.

The remaining line of people have trivial questions; predominantly by citizens who had the fortunate chance of not encountering the monsters. Questions such as the appearance of Breathers. I answer all enquiries and within half an hour, the first line has dwindled rapidly, until no one remains.

Older folk in the two outstanding lines have begun sitting on the floor to rest their weary bones and I look out to the sea of faces to address everyone collectively again. "For those who are older than sixty or have chronic pain, please make your way to the front of the lines in chronological order, oldest first."

Relief instantaneously fills the fatigued and pained faces of the elderly and they collectively make their way to the front of the line as the healthy and youthful shuffle back to make room.

See, I can be a fair Ruler.

Satisfied with the orderly change, I step down from the chair and take a seat at the table, pulling up the graphite pencil and paper.

The next few hours consist of citizens requesting extra food or medical supplies, trading their services or goods in return. As usual, I log each request and trade alongside the family name and place of residence to be executed over the next few days. Once I effectively address each citizen's needs, the paper is then handed over to one of my men who will deliver it to the Council members. I don't hear much from the members unless it's to badger me about producing an heir; an issue that will be rectified as soon as Rae's back in my grasp. Either way, I'm glad the Council is satisfied with every other aspect of how I run the city.

Hours quickly disappear and I eventually reach the last citizen, who, thankfully, was an easy request for extra food. My shoulders ache and I roll my head to crack the pressure building in my neck, then stand to stretch out my stiff limbs.

Thank fuck that's over.

The crowd of people finally vanish, leaving just a collective of guards, when Lucas comes rushing in. I stiffen at his grave expression. He doesn't bring good news.

"What's the outcome?" I ask as he reaches me.

He shakes his head grimly. "There are no Hunters willing to go against Kasim and his convoy."

My jaw clenches at the thought of Kasim having Rae in his grasp and I furiously scrub my hand over my face. "Fuck."

I rapidly assess options and scenarios in my mind, which only leaves me with one alternative. "We're going to save Rae ourselves."

Lucas shoots me a deadly smile, his green eyes darkening with the exhilaration of possibly spilling blood. I don't blame him.

He will need an outlet after the death of Alayah.

"So, what's the plan?" Lucas asks keenly.

"We need to gather intel first. Send out some men to scour the area surrounding Segment Two and report back with everything they notice; how many guards are outside the wall if any; how many in the watch tower at the gate; how often the gate opens and who comes and goes."

"It will be a long process," Lucas states grimly, and I nod, my face solemn.

"I just hope Rae can hold up against any of Kasim's advances before we reach her. We will need to take the trucks we have to reach her quicker."

Lucas chuckles and slaps my back. "After the defiance I've witnessed in that woman, I think she's perfectly capable of looking after herself."

My hands clench against my side. "But, if Kasim *does* touch her, we take him out, no questions asked."

Lucas nods in understanding, a gleam entering his eyes. "It would be my pleasure."

We might die on this treacherous mission, and it might start a war if Kasim finds out we were behind rescuing Rae—which is likely—but I would destroy the earth to keep my queen safe.

Perhaps we need to eliminate him while we are there. At least it could prevent the imminent battle of Segments seeing as he is the only man with the authority to start one, unless his successor decides to instigate any warfare... though I don't see why since the odds are in our favour. Kasim has no heirs to take revenge.

29

RAE

WE HAVE BEEN ROVING THROUGH a vast, forlorn wasteland for two days and my eyes are gritty from the constant dust and debris that batters us. Irritation suffuses me at the quick pace of the vehicles' speed across the unforgiving terrain, only meaning that whatever my fate is, it will transpire quicker than expected. There will be less time to plot Kasim's death.

The thick stench of stale blood fills the interior of the truck from my soiled pants and shoes, making my stomach violently churn. Even the lowered glass windows do not offer any reprieve. The constant reminder of my massacred friend assails me, and the inner side of my cheek has ulcered from constantly chewing on it to prevent me from wailing each time the bloodied image of her spears my mind.

My eyes sting with unshed tears and I look out the opening from the passenger seat I'm tied into, grimacing at the blurry, barren land whizzing past. My own speed matches that of this truck, yet I nonetheless feel unsafe from lack of control.

Working vehicles are rare unless derived from Segments, and the lack of diesel does not help their case, though I've been told that Rulers with enough resources have engineered their own synthetic fuel. Kasim clearly has an abundance of resources since he appears to have enough fuel for the vast number of trucks transporting half his army. We already passed the rest of his men who were travelling by foot, and Kasim slowed down to tell the leader of the group that they could all turn around and head back to Segment One. There must not have been enough trucks to transport everyone.

Kasim drives the one we are in, giving me the chance to take note of the direction we take and mentally catalogue landmarks— which is difficult seeing as there are not many. Due to a large amount of the Amazon and surroundings having perished after the fallout over the centuries, endless, cracked ground now appears to the predominant landscape. The fissures and cracks transfusing the lifeless earth resemble the webbing black veins of Breathers. Other smaller forests and jungles must have perished completely.

Deep sorrow grips me at the reminder of my friend and I bite my inner cheek to prevent myself from sobbing, staring out the window while my eyes prickle with tears.

The continuous dead land extends as far as the eye can see, and only various skeletons of trees and animals remain scattered across its harsh environment. But each one will be of assistance in ensuring I can make my way back to Segment One. My speed and endurance will prove most useful.

"We will need to fuel up soon, so you can have a break and relieve yourself," Kasim says, breaking through my contemplations. Every time he talks, I tense, wondering if he is irritated or insulted by my undisclosed use of the name familiars calls me. It is not as if I had done anything wrong considering I provided my *real* name but concern still fills me at wondering if he will be an unreasonable man who would find trivial excuses to execute punishment. The malice I have occasionally witnessed glinting in his gaze causes me to believe this theory and my shoulders slump in the seat, fear making the palms of my hands slick with sweat at the mere notion.

"It will also give us an opportunity to discuss your dishonesty and further discipline."

His words make me stiffen and my hands clench tightly together. It is as if he read my thoughts.

I say nothing in return but nod slowly—my hands remaining tightly linked together in my lap to stop them from shaking with panic—and keep my gaze trained on the horizon. A large ridge of rock formations catches my eyes and I take note of it as a landmark.

We travel for some time until we pass through an abandoned settlement where Kasim slowly drives through the streets. It is hard not to gape at the crumbling, stone shells of each building as we make our way through, and a shiver runs through me at the image of desolation and destruction. My heart aches for the souls of the poor people who would have either died slowly from disease or perished at the brutality of Breathers.

Or Hunters.

The vehicle comes to a stop when we emerge from the other side of the deserted, skeletal settlement, and Kasim pulls the filtration mask up as he jumps out of the truck, waiting for the groups of guards to arrive. Two trucks pull in beside us not long after and the remaining convoy of vehicles continue past us. Kasim strides over to the parked trucks, curtly giving them orders through the doors. I hear their muffled voices but cannot make out any words. Kasim looks back at me, his dark, cold eyes puncturing, and my mouth turns dry as a shiver runs up my spine. Either he is extremely upset I did not tell him my proper name, or his true cold-hearted character is being revealed. I'm hoping it's not the latter, though my optimism is likely fanciful as, right now, my instincts are telling me to escape.

He strides back towards our vehicle, his baleful expression a menacing sight, and my frame turns rigid as he comes to my side then yanks the heavy metal door open. He stands silently, assessing me with his dark eyes, my own recoiling reflection peering back at me in their surfaces. I swallow the dryness in my throat then hold my breath, preparing to defend myself if needed.

"Come," Kasim orders, his voice low, and he pulls down his gas mask. "A group of my men will scout the area for any threats while we acquire some privacy to... discuss things."

The hairs on the back of my neck stand to attention and I take my time untying the seat's safety fastenings, delaying the imminent discussion with Kasim.

After pretending to struggle with the tight knots for a few minutes, I scoot to the edge of the high vehicle and reluctantly take Kasim's outstretched hand as he helps me down.

Maybe if I play along as the helpless damsel, it will work to my advantage. He might underestimate me.

We both remain silent as we walk towards a shaded tree and I look up at the odd sight of greenery amongst the wastelands.

"There's still underground reservoirs left from the previous settlement, so plants have a fighting chance here," Kasim breaks through my musings and I look at him. He seems *too* calm and it unsettles me, so I just nod in response.

He steps forward, taking me by the hand and tugging me down to sit at the base of the tree with him. I refrain from flinching at the contact.

"Now, I want you to explain why you lied about your name," Kasim says, his voice quiet, yet not without threatening undertones.

The familiar feeling of defiance wells up inside my chest, but I tamper it down, knowing it will not benefit my strategy. Kasim has already seen my fiery attitude at Xander's tower when they originally bartered my body as a trade, but hopefully he will soon brush that off as a defence mechanism.

"I didn't lie to you," I tell him with my chin held high, meeting his gaze without wavering. "My birth name *is* Raine but the name my *family* calls me is Rae."

Kasim falls silent as he absorbs the information. I've noticed in the past few days that he is not fickle with his words and his silence is unnerving. I know it means he is orchestrating something within the turning cogs of his mind, silently ensuring his words will be effective at manipulating me to be playing a key part in what I assume is an ulterior motive. He would be classically handsome if it were not for the cold, manipulative depths reflecting in those stark onyx eyes.

"Well, if your *family* is to call you Rae, then I will too," Kasim states as his expression hardens, spiking my nerves. "Since you will be my wife in *every* sense, it only seems fitting." His hand moves to rest on my upper thigh and the possessive, lewd gesture causes me to flinch. He squeezes almost painfully before moving up, closer to the junction of my legs, and the taste of blood fills my mouth from clamping down on my tongue.

I look away and tightly squeeze my thighs together to prevent his hands from wandering any farther, but he chuckles darkly. "There is no point trying to avert the impending consummation from happening. You would enjoy it much more if you are willing. Though, we will not be doing that yet. Not until I have you in the comfort of my bedchamber."

My eyes snap to him and I crush down any hope of all the misguided notions that Xander will be the one to share my innocence. But I'm doing this for humankind and there is a bigger purpose to all of this. Pulling my shoulders back, I repeatedly chant the reminders in my head and eventually my heart becomes hardened to any perceptions of love and happy-ever-afters. My lack of bedroom experience means nothing in the grand scheme of things and there are no happy endings in The Vanquished world. My years of desolation and survival should have taught me that, but I've let my softened feelings towards Xander contradict the essential ways of survival.

Kasim lets me up after he is finished subjecting me to his disconcerting presence, the shade from the tree causing his already sinister features to become more ominous.

"You can relieve yourself behind the tree. Don't take long or I'll come and drag you back to the truck with your pants around your ankles." His order is clipped, and I shiver at the innuendo behind it.

Darkness is closing in and Breathers will be out in force, so we need to be on the move before the orange sun dips below the dusty horizon.

As discreetly as I can, I hide behind the tree to relieve my bladder before rushing back to the vehicle, hoisting myself up into the passenger seat. I don't want him touching me, but I know he will eventually. It will not stop me from attempting to delay the inevitable.

Kasim chuckles darkly at my hasty return to the truck and addresses me, his tone thick with amusement. "You might have enjoyed it, Rae. Next time, give me the chance."

I know without a doubt that I would not care for his touch, but I remain silent as I look sidelong at Kasim who is already fastened in his seat. Realising he is waiting with the engine running, I quickly tie myself in just as he takes off.

"We aren't too far from the city walls now," Kasim says without taking his eyes from the dusty land we are speeding across. "Once we arrive, I will have my... maid... take you to our chambers to freshen up. There is a tub to bathe in and there will be fresh clothes. Isabella can then deliver you to the dining room for dinner. I expect you to eat with me at every meal."

I refrain from rolling my eyes at his already dictating methods, managing to paste an artificial smile across my face as and nod my head. "Yes, Kasim."

I can be the doting, obedient wife when it suits me.

We travel the remainder of our journey in silence and finally, after an excruciating amount of time, I glimpse a massive city encircled within a colossal, fortified wall. The Segment is larger than Xander's, though I grimace at the abrupt rumination flickering through the recesses of my mind. How many skulls has the foundation been built on? From the hints of malevolence in Kasim, I would say hundreds if not thousands.

Discoloured walls of metal, wood and stone—similar to Segment One—loom over us as we rapidly close the distance to the city, and I swallow the lump forming in my throat at the faint outlines of decaying corpses hanging precariously from the walls.

I hope they are just Breather remains.

Kasim must see me staring at the corpses and his frame shakes with subdued laughter before he enlightens me. "The executions of prisoners and rebels are made public and displayed as an example to all who reside here, and all who visit. Sometimes we hang the humans alive, so their screams and pleas of mercy are heard throughout the night. They eventually die of starvation, or when vultures tear the flesh from their weakened bodies."

I gasp at his inauspicious words and fear prickles my skin at his threatening tone. He only utters a hollow laugh and stares at me with an expression void of empathy, those eyes glinting wickedly. His portentous expression forces me to look away.

"I am not a complete tyrant, Rae," Kasim declares and I turn back to him, disbelief etched across my face.

"And how could you say that when I've just witnessed the most inhumane and ruthless form of punishment?"

We follow the leading trucks through the large metal gate and he eventually looks to me, breaking the suspense. "It's important to keep the people in line, living in fear so they do as they are ordered."

I scoff at his preposterous excuse. "Firstly, that is utterly archaic, and secondly, Xander does not rule as brutally as you and his citizens love and respect him." I pause at the thought of Nelinha, then add, "For the most part anyway. Not everyone will be loyal but that reflects their own character, not the Ruler's ability to gain respect. You clearly just enjoy these brutal deaths."

Kasim regards me, his lids briefly constricting. I tense at my slip of mentioning Xander, particularly such a personal statement.

"You seem to be closely acquainted to the Ruler of Segment

One, Rae," he says suspiciously and turns to watch the road as he continues driving. "Tell me, what is your exact relationship with Xander?"

I swallow the lump in my throat as I rack my mind for trivial answers. "My kin, Alma, has been a seamstress in his family for as long as he has been alive, so naturally I have been a part of the family by extension." I'm hoping my answer keeps Kasim satisfied.

It would not surprise me if he planned to hurt or even murder Xander if he had an inkling of our actual relationship. After everything I have witnessed, I'm certain Kasim would be a ruthless and jealous man. Thankfully, he does not know I'm a survivor only recently residing within the Segment's wall. That knowledge would certainly contradict my response.

I breathe a sigh of relief as my answer appeases Kasim and he nods, keeping his eyes trained on the road as the trucks following behind us begin breaking off to take alternate roads. Using the silence, I absorb the sights around us, my brows bumping together at the comparison between this Segment and Segment Two. The roads here have been covered with a hard, dark substance, creating a smooth and dustless road. I glance up at the buildings and my frown deepens. All the homes and buildings are in worse condition than the structures at Segment One.

We near the centre of the city and I cross my arms over my chest, my forehead remaining furrowed. A massive tower emerges before us, with glints of gold ostentatiously decorating its sharp edges. Entirely unnecessary, just like the two large statues either side of its entry. From my father's descriptions of apex predators, the beastly statues appear to be lions.

My heart drops, knowing this building is Kasim's, and it takes me but a moment to construe a theory from all I have witnessed so far. He must hoard everything for himself and take precious resources from the citizens. The comprehension hits me like a ton of stone.

The stories Pa had told me of the greedy and powerful tyrants ruling every Segment with their privileged citizens basking in gluttony, is partially untrue. It seems that each city just consists of people who are struggling to live day to day—true survivors like those residing outside the walls, though with more of an advantage. But my father was on the right track in saying that Rulers are greedy and ruthless, though I wish he were alive so I could tell him it does not apply to each one of them. Guilt steals my breath from the reminder of leaving him to his death and I glance at Kasim to distract myself. My eyes narrow and I glance away. He is one of the Rulers I had been warned of growing up... but the truth does not apply to Xander as he does not profit from the struggling people of his city—though, Alma did mention that his father ruled exactly like Kasim does. I shiver at the reminder of Xander's father. How could a man murder two innocent women? And so brutally. One of those women was his wife!

Somewhere farther inland lives another awful Ruler. He was the one who must have been informed by travelling Hunters of my existence. The group had likely spotted me passing through some land with Pa and knew they could trade me. Either way, the Ruler sent Hunters back out to retrieve me for his harem of women; effectively sentencing Pa to death.

My remorseful musings abruptly vanish when Kasim parks the truck at the front entrance to the tower and gestures for me to move, his hand a knife slicing through the air. "Get out and head into the tower. I'll be right behind you."

I slide out of the high truck and make my way tentatively towards the obnoxiously decorated entrance. The two guards on either side of the large metal door leer at me, and dread slides over the surface of my skin at the lecherous expression morphing their faces into a crude sneer. Xander's guards never looked at me like that. They only looked at me with appreciation, not lewd and hungry expressions.

One guard punches a code into the pad and the door clicks open, allowing Kasim to place his hand on my lower back and firmly push me through. My eyes widen at the interior and I refrain from shaking my head in disappointment at his greed and exorbitance.

White marbled tiles line the floor, and gold statues are placed methodically throughout the vast space. Large paintings of exotic animals hang precariously on the expansive walls. A thick, deep red rug runs from the entrance all the way up the large winding stairway, and I cannot help the scoff that escapes me.

Kasim's hand drops from my lower back and snakes out to painfully grip my arm, stopping me from walking any farther. I grimace and turn to face him, quickly resuming my weak, submissive facade in hopes to mollify him. My heart pounds in my chest as I watch his gaze harden, becoming cold and menacing.

"I will not tolerate any disrespect from you, otherwise there will be serious ramifications."

I bow my head submissively. "Yes, Kasim."

The acquiescent gesture apparently pleases him, and a frosty smile slowly grows across his face. "Brilliant. Now come this way. Isabella will show you to your room and prepare you for dinner."

I obediently walk with him, his hand still a bruising grip around my arm, when a beautifully exotic woman suddenly shuffles over, making me wonder where she unexpectedly emerged from.

Her shoulders hunch forward with fear, the cowering demeanour indicating she will not be a threat to my wellbeing. When she looks up at me, my heart breaks. The beautiful olive skin of her cheek is swollen and yellowed, and a large purple splotch is forming across the side of her face. One of her almond shaped brown eyes is also blackened and swollen shut on the same side. Kasim must beat her.

Yet the dreadful man seems unphased by her dishevelled appearance and gestures coolly at Isabella to take me upstairs. "Fix her up."

He then turns to stride away without another word.

Isabella keeps her head bowed as she quickly shuffles away, whispering to me in a strained voice. "Follow me, please."

Not wanting to land her in any more strife than she has already been in, I follow her up the winding stairs to an excessively large wooden door with gilded handles.

This time I do not refrain from rolling my eyes.

Following Isabella through the monstrosity, I gasp at the extensive room and catalogue the large bed covered in deep red and gold blankets and pillows. This must be Kasim's room.

I spin around to take in the rest of the space and conclude the interior is decorated in the same fashion as the entrance below.

Isabella's voice pulls me from my contemplations, and I turn to her as she speaks, her strained voice hoarse. "The bathroom is through here," she says, pointing to the open door, leading to another room. "Kasim has ordered for you to bathe and dress in the clothes provided. I have hung them behind the door." Her eyes drop to my bloodstained pants and shoes then slightly widen at understanding what the thick, dried substance is. "I will clean your clothes and shoes."

I nod at Isabella slowly and study her momentarily. Her thick, dark wavy hair hangs to her waist and her slender figure suggests lack of sustenance. My chest constricts at the abuse this woman must endure at the hands of Kasim.

Isabella shifts uncomfortably under my scrutiny and I inwardly chastise myself for blatantly staring. Clearing my throat, I step closer, only resulting in her tensing as she visibly withdraws and hunches over defensively.

Her reaction reinforces my plan to eliminate the man who has caused her such grief.

"Thank you, Isabella. I'm Rae, and if there is anything *you* need, please let me know."

Isabella's head whips up at my cryptic offer and her full lips pull into a tight line. I gasp at seeing the bruising around her neck, the discoloured hand and fingerprints.

Her hoarse voice is evidently caused by Kasim's hands around her neck.

Isabella rasps, "I am perfectly fine. I have everything I need. Please wash up and press the buzzer by the bedside table once you are done, and I will escort you down to dinner."

Before I can reply, she spins on her toes and scurries away, leaving me baffled at her abrupt reaction that only indicates fear. I assume she is terrified of doing anything remotely wrong, in fear of painful repercussions.

Shoulders slumping and sighing at a failed connection to a possible ally or friend, I make my way into the large bathroom, adorned with gold trimmings and white, marbled tiles. The visual triggers me to roll my eyes again. The beginnings of a headache from all the eye rolling niggles the sides of my forehead.

The grimy layers flake off me when I strip down, and compacted bumps line my skin at the sudden drop in temperature. I frown at the erratic weather, its capricious moods much like a human's, but I push my concerns aside to concentrate on the task at hand.

Turning towards the tub to run the water, I gasp when I realise there are *two* taps. I twist both taps on and steam begins to rise, fogging up the reflective surfaces in the room. My jaw drops. Hot water. I have had a rare bucket of boiled water to spot-bathe myself before, but never heated running water that I can *soak* in.

How has Kasim even managed to engineer this?

I suppose his endless supply of resources and power goes a long way. Right now, I'm incapable of caring *how* he managed to get hot water running, since my aching and stiff muscles desperately need rehabilitation.

Once the tub has filled up, I carefully step in and sink blissfully into the hot water. My muscles sigh with relief as I close my eyes, letting the euphoric sensation soak deeply into my bones, and I take the peaceful moment to articulate a plan of attack. Kasim needs to die. Not just for my sake; but for the sake of Segment Two and for Isabella.

Thoughts whirl around in my head at possible scenarios where I could successfully defeat him, and I bite my lower lip at the notion of who would take his place as Ruler.

"I can worry about that later," I mutter.

The utmost importance is that Kasim *must* die, even if my stomach drops at the sheer thought of slaying someone.

"No. He deserves it," I reassure myself vehemently.

30

RAE

THE HOT WATER MUST HAVE LULLED ME TO SLEEP and a knock
to the bedroom door startles me awake. I dart up quickly
to rinse the remaining soap from my clean, wrinkly skin.
My fingers have shrivelled, and I realise I've likely been in the
bath for an extensive period of time.

Mindfully, yet as hastily as I can, I step out of the cold water
and spot a large fluffy cloth hanging on a rack, grabbing it to
dry myself. Remembering Isabella's instructions to change into
the new clothes provided for me, I push the bathroom door half-
closed to find a beautiful satin dress hanging behind. Of course,
the deep, blood red is the same colour as everything else within
Kasim's tower.

The knocking persists, prompting me to snap from my
musings, and I quickly slip the dress over my head, staring down
at its snug fit. My nose wrinkles in distaste at how the built-in
cups push my breasts up, displaying them in an overtly obscene
configuration. The pink areolas surrounding my nipples are

almost visible.

Great. More leering looks from more men is the last thing I want.

The knocking becomes more demanding and I rush out of the bathroom to the front door. "Coming!"

I swing the heavy wood open to reveal an anxious Isabella. Her wide, uninjured eye darts over my attire and she visibly relaxes. "Thank goodness you are ready," she whispers, her voice still strained. "Kasim is becoming impatient as he waits for you in the dining room."

I look at the material wrapped elegantly around her neck and my stomach plummets at sighting the finger-like bruises peeking above it. The direction of my stare perturbs Isabella and her hand subconsciously hovers over the scarf before she promptly drops it. Whirling around, she turns to start brusquely walking away without another word.

"How often does Kasim beat and strangle you?" I call out and hastily follow her.

My question startles her, and she abruptly stops then spins back to face me, the sudden motion causing me to run straight into her.

"You can't ask questions here, otherwise you will experience the same fate." Her eyes are wide and filled with fear as they dart around to make sure no one is listening. "We must hurry to the dining room," Isabella continues and turns to keep moving, but my hand darts out to gently stop her.

"Isabella," I whisper, "I have survived outside city walls my entire life, so I can look after myself. But please, let me help you. I have conquered worse monsters than Kasim before."

Isabella gasps and her eyes widen at my unbelievable admission. "Really?"

Hope flickers across her face before quickly disappearing as a guarded expression takes its place. "Now isn't the time and place to discuss this. Kasim is waiting and most likely growing more furious by the minute."

I nod in agreement, letting the topic drop for now as I hastily follow Isabella to a large dining room down the end of the dark hallway.

Kasim's hardened gaze immobilises me as I enter through the doorway and dismay settles low in my abdomen like the thick sludge from a marsh, at the violence I now discern in the expanse of his dark eyes. I can only hope my ability of speed will assist me when it comes to wiping the earth of this monster. I must not let my conscience hinder me.

"Rae," his deep voice booms, echoing off the large walls. "You are extremely late. This is your first and final warning."

I refrain from snapping back with a smart retort, almost stating that he did not actually give me an exact timeframe to be ready by. Biting my tongue firmly until the hint of blood fills my mouth, I simply nod my head. Once the brief urge to retaliate passes, I then release the bruised appendage and reply through clenched teeth. "Yes, Kasim."

He gestures for me to take the seat across from him and I take the opportunity to admire but simultaneously detest the large sepia dining table we are to eat at. The length of it seems excessive considering it is only Kasim that eats here.

As I take a seat, an aged man hobbles out, wheeling a metal serving cart with two large, gold plates of hot steaming food. I can go days without food, but the delicious aromas instigate the growling in my stomach, my mouth watering.

Temporarily wondering if the people of Segment Two are

supplied with enough food to eat or if Kasim hoards it for himself and his men, my appetite begins to rapidly vanish. That is, until the plate is placed before me and the decadent smells of roasted meat and vegetables assail my senses, then all thoughts of the people's suffering dissipate.

I look to Kasim who nods for me to start, and I ignore the unfamiliar silver utensils beside my plate to dig in with my fingers. The tender and juicy meat is almost between my teeth when his curt and reprimanding voice freezes my hands' progress.

"You are to use the cutlery provided. You are to start acting as a queen would."

A queen.

The only motive preventing me from snapping back in defiance and stabbing said utensils through Kasim's hand. Whether I'm queen of this Segment or Xander's queen, I must not risk the outcome of my plan with my temper.

Slowly placing the meat back onto the plate, I study the way Kasim holds the trident utensil in one hand with the knifelike instrument in the other, then carefully imitate the grasp. Xander never bothered eating with such things and only used his fingers, so this is the first time I've attempted to eat like a *proper lady* within the walled societies.

Clasping both cold items tightly in either hand, I painstakingly use the pronged utensil to stab a piece of meat and smile triumphantly when successfully lifting the decadent morsel, then placing it between my lips. My face scrunches at the metallic taste fused with the delicious meat and I look up to freeze at Kasim's curious expression.

"You have never used a fork and knife before?" he asks with amazement, and I shake my head. He chuckles in disbelief. "I'm amazed your *betrothed,* Lucas, did not provide you with such items since he clearly had the means to."

I freeze at the allusion of my upbringing within city walls and force the meat down my throat, smiling sweetly at him. My hesitation in answering affords me the opportunity to quickly weave a lie to cover my tracks.

"My family was poor, so we did not have such luxuries growing up. Even though I am *betrothed* to Lucas, I have not lived under his roof."

My eye twitches at the foreign feeling of lying but I manage to keep an impassive face. My entire life has been spent predominantly in my Pa's presence, so there never had been the need to lie. We were always completely open and honest with each other.

Or so I thought.

Pa failed to mention many things to me.

Shaking my head to remove the downcast thoughts, I resume concentrating on implementing the *fork* and knife as I continue eating, still wincing at the awful metallic taste.

"Is the food not up to your standard?" Kasim asks coldly, and I look up at him mid-chew.

"I'm unused to the taste of metal with my food."

Understanding dawns on his face and he nods, then silently recommences eating.

The remainder of our meal is thankfully without conversation and the elderly man suffering from fusing joints, comes to take our empty plates once we have finished. My stomach hurts at the amount of food it is clearly not accustomed to, but I tell myself the extra reserves will be beneficial in preparation for whatever may transpire.

Kasim stands, offering his hand to me, and I stare down at it. The familiar sensation of disquiet scurries over the expanse of my skin.

What is he going to do with me now?

"I won't bite," he states, amused by my hesitance. His tone darkens as he adds, "Yet."

I swallow deeply, nibbling my lower lip in uncertainty at the crude insinuation behind his statement, but take the outstretched hand, nevertheless. Standing, I move behind the chair to slowly walk with him. An anxious sheen of sweat covers my skin and I take a deep breath to calm the increasing nerves.

"You look beautiful in that dress," Kasim remarks, breaking the silence as we make our way back to the bedroom.

I hope he does not expect me to open my legs for him.

I clear my throat nervously. "Thank you."

We reach the end of the hallway and he opens the large wooden door to his bedroom and ushers me through. "Ladies first."

I walk though hesitantly and stiffen at the touch of his large hand splayed low on my exposed back. Kasim chose the dress with easy access in mind.

"Your skin is so pale and soft." His low, suggestive voice sends shivers racing across my skin.

My eyes frantically dart around the room and I grind my teeth apprehensively.

It will be happening tonight.

The reprehensible affair is impervious.

I jerk away, causing Kasim's hand to fall from the skin on my lower back, and my mind races for solutions to avoid any intimacy with him. Turning to him, I cross my arms protectively over my chest at the sadistic lust swirling in his eyes and take a step back, only to have him take one forward.

Clearing my throat nervously, I blurt out the only viable excuse that might hinder his sickening plans with me for the night. "I'm exhausted after our journey. Could I please have a night's rest?" My tone is purposefully submissive and convincing enough that Kasim reluctantly nods and gestures to the bed.

I just hope he does not track down Isabella to fulfil his *needs* instead.

"You may get undressed and rest for tonight. I will have a bath and join you soon."

I nod with relief and rush to the bed, turning to wait for Kasim; ensuring he disappears into the bathroom before slowly removing my dress. The delicate straps have just fallen over my shoulders when he walks back to the bathroom's entrance and brusquely speaks, causing me to jump. "This night is the only night you have reprieve, *Rae*. I expect you to tend to any *womanly* duties from now on. Starting from tomorrow morning."

I nod and swallow the lump forming in my throat as he disappears behind the door once again. My plan to destroy him will need to happen sooner rather than later.

Morning gradually breaks and bright, golden rays of the sun beam through the large window in the bedroom, streaming across the bed. The night was restless and sleep was unattainable.

I sigh, rolling over to face a sleeping Kasim before cringing at the view of his handsome, restful face. My eyes roam his dark, smooth skin and trail over the sharp planes of his pronounced cheekbones and jawline, finally resting on his thick, inviting lips. Shaking my head to rid myself of any sensual thoughts, I remind myself of the icy, wicked gleam in his eyes when he is conscious. He would be a breathtakingly beautiful man if it were not for his violent and cruel nature.

His deep state of sleep gives me an idea; the best time to strike would be when he is vulnerable. My mind races with different possibilities and I conclude that slitting his throat while he sleeps would be most efficacious. It is a cowardly move but holds the most chance of success. I need to grasp *any* opportunity presented and the least innocuous time, the only time he hasn't an array of guards surrounding him, is when in bed.

A loud, wide yawn cracks my jaw, causing my eyes to water—I did not sleep during the night. It was disturbing having a naked man lying beside my own nude body, particularly when I do not trust that man.

Kasim's eyes drift open at the sound of my yawn and I'm momentarily mesmerised by the sleepy and placid state of his expression. He looks almost docile; not cold and calculating.

As he pushes up, the sheet falls from his naked, toned torso and my eyes drop down to the discoloured, puckered scars smattered across his dark skin. I tug the falling sheet back up to my neck when his eyes darken with desire. The protective movement causes his almost approachable gaze to revert into his characteristic callous stare and the instant change dazes me. Kasim's ebony eyes hungrily ravish my curves underneath the thin sheet and I freeze with fear at remembering his promise from last night. My breath grows erratic and my gaze darts around the room for an escape, even though I already know there is not one.

"You won't be able to hide yourself from me anymore, Rae,"

he growls and tears the material from my hands, ripping it off my body. The sudden movement has me gasping and darting out of the bed in the vain attempts to cover myself. He slides off the bed and stalks towards me, his eyes darkening with carnal intent. His advance has me backing up against the wall; caged like a trapped animal ready for slaughter.

"You had a night's rest like you requested, which I so kindly allowed."

My eyes widen and dread crawls up my spine as Kasim lashes out, his relentless grip crushing my wrist as he drags me back to the bed. The instinctual need to survive burns within my veins as I struggle against his strength in the attempt to break free. Alas, my efforts are futile and a scream tears from my throat as he violently flings me onto the bed, the sheer force knocking my teeth together, causing me to clamp down on my tongue and draw blood.

There is simply no way I can escape from this and tears fill the corner of my eyes as I lie helplessly on my back while Kasim climbs on top of me, his weight pressing down and leaving me breathless. I swallow down the bile that rises at the feeling of his arousal jabbing against my thighs and close my eyes to visualise Xander.

Just as Kasim lines himself up crudely at my exposed, clenched centre, a soft knocking interrupts him and he cranes his neck to protest. "This better be important, otherwise I will splay and gut you myself!" he snaps loudly, and I flinch when his spit sprays my face.

I choke out a sob of relief, my gaze drifting to the ceiling as he pushes up from me and stalks to the door to wrench it open, not caring in the least that the both of us are still naked.

Isabella's eyes widen as they dart to my vulnerable state

and tear-stained cheeks, then to Kasim whose chest is heaving angrily at the disruption. Utilising his distraction, I quickly jump up to slip my skimpy red dress back on, the struggle made more difficult by my shaking hands.

"What is so important that you must defy any orders to not disturb me?" Kasim snaps at Isabella, his voice low and threatening.

Isabella looks down to whisper in reply, her voice still strained. "There has been a breach of the walls."

Palpable fear is evident in her posture as she nervously waits for Kasim's reaction.

His deadly silence is unnerving, and Isabella cowers in preparation for him to strike her.

The glimpse of her recoiling in petrified submission only serves to ignite my fury and I stiffen my spine in anger, boldness boiling in my blood. Kasim *will* die today.

Isabella's eyes dart behind his wide frame to look at me and I tilt my head at the expression crossing her face. Kasim simultaneously turns, missing her silent communication as he fixes me with a hardened glare.

"Do not leave this room. I will be back to finish *this*."

I flinch at the implications of his words and he roughly pushes past Isabella to stride down the stairs while yelling orders at his nearby men.

"You have no idea how much I appreciate the timing of your interruption," I walk to Isabella and she nods with a small, sad smile. My eyes dip to the cleaned boots hanging limply by her side and joyous tears fill my eyes as she hands them to me. I lean over to jam them on my feet and wrap the ties around the circumference of them quickly.

"There *is* a breach though, so it worked in your favour," she says as I finish with the shoes and straighten to tilt my head at her. Her words have me hopefully curious.

"Do you know anything about the breach?"

Isabella nods and a subdued light enters her eyes. "Two men apparently. I saw one. He was tall, with dark hair and bright green eyes." I gasp at the description of Lucas.

"They came for me," I whisper, and a rare, soft smile graces Isabella's face.

"I know a way out," she whispers, looking behind her nervously. My heart pounds with rhapsody at the prospect of freedom, but something holds me back from following her.

"Wait," I tell her, and she frowns, confused by my hesitance. "I need to kill Kasim first."

Isabella's eyes widen with fear and she shakes her head.

"It's impossible," she rasps, "he has too many guards and is too strong."

I smile mischievously at her. "Perhaps, but I have speed and agility against his size. If I let him take me to bed again, his guards will not be present. I can strike *then*."

Isabella shakes her head sadly. "You cannot risk being... violated by him. He has vicious tendencies in bed that could kill you."

I frown at the inflection in her strained voice, knowing her words come from firsthand experience. Anger bursts through me like wildfire at the injustice against this sweet and vulnerable woman, and I clench my fists. "Well then," I say, my voice deadly calm, "Kasim *has* to die today. At *any* cost."

Another flicker of hope flares in Isabella's eyes and she nods bravely, displaying a moment of strength in her broken state. "We can use the secret passages to our advantage."

My eyes bulge at her statement and my jaw gapes. "Secret passages?"

Isabella nods and gestures me to follow her, and I take after her with a run as she addresses me over her shoulder. I inwardly rejoice at the strengthening of her voice, which must be slowly healing.

"Not even Kasim knows of them since he massacred the architect's family. I was close with the architect's daughter, and he told me about them before I was old enough for Kasim to enslave me."

I stare at her in disbelief. "Why haven't you used them to your own advantage?"

Isabella sighs and turns to me as we slow our pace in order to converse. "I'm terrified if Kasim catches me using them he will either hurt me badly or just kill me. I'm not as brave as you."

I reach out to hold her hand and she stops to face me, the both of us quickly glancing around to check no one is nearby.

My words are soft, and I'm hopeful what I say will encourage Isabella. "I grew up with no choice but to survive in unforgiving environments. I'm not brave, just adaptable—it has become habit. Bravery is making a conscious decision to act even in the face of fear. *You* are being brave by helping me now, as you're risking your life by making this *choice*."

A soft smile touches Isabella's lips and her eyes become watery. "Thank you, Rae."

I return the smile and squeeze her hand affectionately before dropping it. "Now, whatever happens, please promise that you will go with the men who came for me, back to Segment One. You will be safe there and have your own, independent life."

Isabella nods as grateful tears roll down her bruised face, when suddenly, we hear male voices below the stairs. My heart thumps erratically and Isabella's eyes widen with fear as she grabs my hand to pull me hurriedly along the hallway. "Quick, we mustn't let them see us," she whispers.

We race through the extensive hallways until we reach a tiny alcove nestled beside a statue. I watch with fascination as Isabella glides her hand over the seemingly normal wall before finding a spot and pushing on it. A small laugh escapes me at hearing a click and the wall opens to reveal a dark passageway. I quickly slap a hand over my mouth to prevent any further noises of delight alerting the men nearby. Isabella crouches to squeeze through the small opening and I follow her as we crawl in. The door automatically clicks shut behind me and I take a deep breath to calm my claustrophobia, inhaling the musty and stagnant air.

Isabella pauses to turn back to me, and I accidentally bump into her, straining my eyes to see the shape of her in the darkness.

"Follow me," she whispers.

We continue down the dimly lit passageway quietly on our hands and knees until light begins to illuminate the widening tunnel. Isabella stands up to brush her hands together and I mimic her—grateful we are not in the confined space anymore.

Following her farther into the winding passages, we make various turns until encountering a small room of sorts.

"Wow," I whisper as we enter the quaint space, pressing my face against the peering holes situated inconspicuously in the wall.

Isabella softly chuckles and I turn, whispering to her quietly, "I'm so glad to have met you, even under the dire circumstances."

Isabella smiles softly in return. My heart breaks and tears fill my eyes at the reminder of Alayah. "I recently lost my only friend and discovered her brutally killed in the jungle."

Isabella's eyes fill with sympathy and compassion before broadening with recollection.

"I heard Kasim's men complain that they were ordered to murder a woman who lived in the jungle," she gasps. "Your name was mentioned."

Memories of the day Kasim took me to meet Alayah flicker through my mind and certain aspects start to unfold.

That morning I heard him talking to his guard in hushed voices behind the door...

He must have been ordering the men to head out before us to slaughter Alayah.

But why?

My eyes narrow with supressed rage. *Why* Kasim did it, no longer matters. Scorching fury replaces my grief and niggling conscience, so I square my shoulders to meet Isabella's sympathetic gaze.

"Kasim will be dying a slow, painful death. Even if it means I risk my own life."

31

XANDER

SWEAT BEADS ALONG MY FOREHEAD as Lucas and I stealthily dart through the shadows of buildings. We spent the last few hours assessing the outside walls and then made our move beneath the cover of night, using the underground reservoirs to infiltrate the Segment. The scorching sun has risen now, so without the camouflage of darkness, we're visible, but the city should be large enough that we are not suspicious.

We will be once we attempt to infiltrate the tower, though.

I'm hoping the guards don't find the truck we sped here in. If they destroy it, then we have no way of getting safely back to Segment One. Either way, we will remain in the shadows to err on the side of caution.

Thank fuck the engineers had a miniature drone in stock so that we were able to map out the grid of the city.

Movement in the street ahead has Lucas and me abruptly flinging our bodies out of sight, and I press my back flat against a building's wall. Lucas swiftly slides the pack of gadgets off his back to do the same.

Fuck.

Even though we are but needles in a haystack, we still look different to most of the citizens beginning to bustle about, and I look down at our midnight black clothes to grimace.

"Shit, we stand out like a sore thumb," I hiss to Lucas.

Worry shadows his face. "Someone has probably alerted the guards of two men getting around in dark clothes."

Most people seem to be wearing brown or discoloured linen, some even wearing colourful adornments showering their necks and wrists, the jewellery indicating the wealthy residents.

I glance at Lucas who silently signals the plan of attack, gesturing he will run across to the little alleyway first before I follow. I curtly nod in agreement.

Lucas slips the pack over his shoulders then darts out with agility and speed as I keep my gaze trained on the streets that are buzzing with increasing activity. A rush of breath leaves my chest in relief as he makes it across with no one becoming suspicious. He then peers around a corner wall he's against to check my blind spots and turns to gesture at me affirmatively. Quickly giving my surroundings one last survey, I launch into action, sprinting across to disappear into the concealment of the alleyway with him.

"We need to make it to Kasim's tower quickly," I tell Lucas, my face grimly taut. We know what Kasim is capable of.

"Agreed."

Systematically darting through the dingy alleyways of Segment Two, we manage to make it to the city centre where Kasim's excessive tower looms before us. Both Lucas and I wait in the shadows of the alley and peer around the corner to study the entrance of the tower.

"Fuck," I utter under my breath

"There's two guards at the door and a coded lock," Lucas whispers. "How will we get in?"

I study our options and peruse the walls on either side of the tower.

"There's most likely a fire escape at the back of the tower," I whisper, and Lucas nods in agreement.

I silently beg I am right. Otherwise, we will be forced to take a violent approach at breaching the tower.

Lucas turns to make his way back down the dark alley and I follow him through the winding, debris-filled path until we end up on the opposite side of the city centre, facing the back of the tower. I don't use any resources for accumulating my own luxuries like Kasim does, but I invest in the best technology and security instead. The safety of my city comes first, not my comfort and pleasures.

Not that added security stops conniving bitches from manipulating guards in opening the gates, though.

My nostrils flare at the reminder and fury reignites at the betrayal. Pushing those thoughts aside and squinting my eyes, I scan the back of the building and notice a protrusion from the surface of its wall, the length of it starting from the ground level.

"There," I tell Lucas and point to my findings. "The fire exit has been camouflaged to deter anyone from attempting to break in."

"Not us," Lucas's frame shudders as he quietly laughs at his own humour. "Well, now we just need to figure out how to get in without anyone noticing,"

I rub my hand roughly over my face as the exhaustion sets in, then push my fingers against one side of my temple to relieve the throbbing headache. We haven't slept in the past twenty-four hours.

"We will need to *casually* stand by the building one at a time, so we don't draw attention," I tell Lucas quietly. My eyes travel to the black pack secured on his back, filled with various gadgets. "Do you have the silent detonator?"

Lucas pulls out the square contraption from behind him and holds it up in reply. "It will alert the security that we are in the tower though."

I nod, grimacing. "That's okay, we just need to be quick. They are likely already looking for us if any citizen spotted us and thought we looked out of place, so hopefully the bulk of his men are on the streets rather than in the tower."

"Don't forget Kasim needs to die as well," Lucas says grimly. "Otherwise, this will definitely start a war between cities, since he would have been alerted to a breach by two men of our description."

"Fuck, I know."

It would be much easier if love wasn't involved, but with or without loving Rae, she's still the only chance at redeeming humanity.

"Do you want me to go first?" I ask Lucas, and he shakes his head, a widening, crazed smile morphing his face.

"Nah, man, I want to be the one to blow shit up."

I chuckle as he sprints to the tower, backing up against the wall near the fire exit while I astutely glance around to watch for guards or citizens that might alert someone of our presence.

Lucas feels around the protruded section of the wall until he pauses at what must be the locking mechanism of the concealed door. He sticks the detonator directly over it then glances over.

I nod and his eyes light up with charged excitement, instantly reaching into his pocket to press the detonator. A muffled pop sounds as smoke curls up from the explosive.

Relief fills me and I exhale a sharp breath as the fire door instantly cracks open. Checking our surroundings one more time, my long legs lurch into action, pounding the hard pavement of the tarred ground, carrying me towards Lucas. I dart inside as he opens the door quickly, following me in once removing the detonator from the outside.

It takes a while for my eyes to adjust to the dark, concreted stairwell and Lucas pulls a solar-powered light from his backpack to switch on. The damp smell tickles my nostrils, causing them to twitch, so I sharply blow air out of my nasal passages to prevent the developing sneeze.

Knowing the security breach would have already alerted Kasim's guards, I gesture at Lucas to make his way up, following him as our long legs take three steps at a time.

We quickly reach the first level and are greeted with a large metal door. Lucas looks back at me with a gleam in his eye and holds the detonator up in question. "It has three detonations left; can I use it again?"

I chuckle at his penchant for blowing shit up and shrug. "Sure, why not."

Making quick work, Lucas sticks the detonator over the locking mechanism and stands back to press the activator in his pocket. The stifled cracking sound echoing through the space has him smiling like a mad man, and smoke curls up from the device as the door clicks open once again. Lucas removes the detonator and peers through the cracked door to check for any unsuspecting guards. He moves back to glance at me and carefully shuts the door to whisper, "It's our lucky day; all the guards must be out on the streets looking for us."

I frown at Kasim's unwise tactic and shake my head. "It seems odd that he hasn't kept any guards in his tower though."

Lucas's eyes widen with realisation. "Of course, half the convoy of guards are on foot still, from when they left our Segment. He must be temporarily short on men."

"Well, that's lucky for us."

We peer around the ajar door and take the opportune time to sprint out across the large foyer. We head straight for the stairway and I scoff at the excessiveness of the interior as we race upwards. The exorbitant amount of superfluous décor explains the poor state of the citizens' homes. Kasim must hoard all resources and goods for himself.

Selfish dick.

Lucas suddenly stops, signalling frantically for me to crouch low, and my adrenaline spikes at the sounds of two voices growing louder.

Well, it seems Kasim has kept some of his lackeys here.

Both of us unsheathe the deadly daggers from our leg holsters while we remain crouched at the top step behind the corner of a wall. Then we wait.

I see Lucas's muscles tense and take the cue as we both strike forward to grab the unsuspecting men, slitting their throats with ease. Vibrant blood spurts in violent ribboning streams as we hit the main arteries with precision, though it doesn't take long for the torrent to slow to a thick, pulsing dribble. Lucas's green eyes gleam with bloodthirst at our first kill when he turns to me, his high cheekbones protruding with a demented smile. I shake my head in mock disapproval, even though I'm feeling the exact same thrill.

There is too much blood spilled over the pristine white floors to attempt hiding the lifeless men. Briefly glancing down at the stark contrast of deep red staining the pearly floor, I smile with satisfaction at the thought of Kasim finding the scene. He seems like a man who is pedantic about keeping his possessions unsoiled.

We don't delay and keep pressing forward, knowing that more men could arrive at any moment. Lucas gestures the all-clear, and we stealthily sprint down a long hallway, brandishing our bloodied daggers—ready to strike again.

Before long, we reach the end of the hallway and come to a large wooden door. I grab the gold handles and crack it open, cautiously peering around to discover an empty dining room. Lucas follows closely behind as I slink inside, shutting the door behind us, then we take the moment to reassess our situation.

"This place is pretty massive and there are lower levels we still need to search," Lucas says.

I rub my face. "Yeah, I know. The longer we're here, the more chance we have of being caught, so we better keep moving."

Lucas nods and takes the lead as we sprint back out and down the hallway to the massive door we passed. I turn to keep watch behind us as Lucas slowly cracks the door and looks in, softly hooting at me to indicate the all-clear. Spinning around, I tread on his heels as we sneak through and click the door shut behind us.

I let out a low whistle and Lucas shakes his head as he circles the room. "Is he compensating for something?"

I chuckle at Lucas's crude comment and nod. "I would say so."

The enormous bed is framed with thick, dark wood and

adorned with luxurious trimmings of deep red and gold. "Kasim would have had to trade medical supplies or expensive blades to acquire such material," Lucas says in disgust.

My expression turns grim. "Or he slaughtered a few people and stole it. So, we should get a move on before anything happens to Rae."

Moving through the opening leading to a massive bathroom, I ignore the inordinate display of power; focused only on finding the raven-haired beauty that consumes my heart and soul. I let out a dry chuckle and shake my head in disbelief. Who knew I was capable of such feelings—me, the monster?

"Clear," Lucas says, and we hastily retreat from the bathroom and out the bedroom door.

"Fuck, where is he keeping her?" I mutter, dragging my hand harshly through my hair.

It crosses my mind as we sprint through the hall, past the bloodied men and down to the level below, that Rae may have already escaped. A smirk tugs at my lips. I wouldn't be surprised. My little mouse doesn't like to be caged, as I have learnt from personal experience.

The second level appears to be one entire room, as we only see one door when we glance up and down the hallway. Lucas tries the door and swears. "Shit, it's locked."

"How many detonations do you have left?"

"Two."

I nod at him. "Use it."

Lucas smiles widely and repeats the same process again, quickly peering behind the breached door. His back stiffens. "Holy shit."

Highly curious as to what has him frozen in surprise, I push him through and close the door behind us. The mass of technology and weaponry in front of us has me whistling again.

"Why didn't Kasim use *these* to help with the Breathers at our Segment?" Lucas asks, his tone impressed.

The large room holds various desks with monitoring screens systematically placed throughout, and in the centre, a massive podium holds a large cylindrical looking weapon.

"That looks powerful enough to blow through any Segment's wall," I grit out through my tightened jaw.

Lucas walks up to the large blaster and inspects it closely.

"Shit, where did he get this?"

I grimace. "I would say he has engineers. They most likely designed and fabricated it themselves. Just like we have engineers who design and create our technology."

Glancing around the space, I notice smaller versions of the blaster displayed in bulk on the wall and hiss, my hands curling into fists. "Fuck, he's creating weaponry to establish an army."

Not many civilisations brandish firing weapons anymore due to the unsustainable need for ammunition.

Lucas scratches his chin, his expression concerned. "Do you think he's planning an attack on our Segment?"

My eye twitches and I don't hesitate to answer. "Yes." Without a doubt.

Our momentary distraction from the shock of seeing the weapons prevents us from hearing the men creeping through the door and we freeze at their loud, threatening voices.

"Put your hands behind your head and slowly turn around! No sudden movements or we'll shoot!"

Lucas and I look at each other in concern as we place our hands behind our heads and turn, both of our expressions mirroring the same thoughts.

We're fucked.

And they have guns, so we're doubly fucked.

As soon as we find Rae and make it back to Segment One—I'm investing in guns. Since no other Segments had been using them, there was no threat of being at a disadvantage. This changes everything now.

I study the two men in front of us and weigh up our chances, grimacing as my eyes rest on the small blasters in their hands, the exact replica of the ones from the wall.

Kasim mustn't have wanted me seeing them when he visited my Segment.

His men only used the traditional blades that every other Segment uses—likely acquiring them from being handed down over generations just as we did—to wipe out the Breathers that plagued my streets.

The guards move closer, one in front with his gun trained on us as the other walks behind, yanking our arms back to place metal cuffs on our wrists one at a time.

Shit. This isn't good. We're losing precious time to find Rae.

I can only hope she's already escaped.

The guard behind roughly shoves us forward. "Start walking. No sudden movements or I'll blow your brains out."

We begrudgingly follow the first guard out the door and down the stairwell to reach the ground floor where Kasim waits for us. My entire body tenses at his smug expression as he tuts, addressing us with a smooth, condescending tone. "Tsk, tsk, tsk, Xander. You have overstayed your welcome here and, unfortunately for you, stuck your nose where it does not belong. I do not appreciate you spilling blood in my clean hallways, either.

Pity you didn't create any heirs for your city—it will be easy to overthrow with you gone."

I clench my jaw at the threat of tyranny on my Segment, then glance to Lucas as his face falls grim.

Kasim chuckles at our silence. "Nothing to say? Well, I'd rather not listen to your annoying voice anyway." He gestures at the guards. "Take them to the chambers below. Make sure they experience the whole array of toys we have down there but keep them alive." Kasim turns to us with a sadistic smile and adds, "I want the honour of ending their lives."

One guard nods before grabbing us each roughly by the napes of our necks and pushing us forward. His bruising grip is tight as he leads us to the far side of the tower's foyer.

I spy a discreet door, hidden on the underside of the stairs just as the guard with the gun trained on us punches in a code. The door clicks open and he pushes it wider, revealing the perilous descent of a dark, concreted stairway leading deep underground.

The guard behind us lifts his hands from our necks to turn on a light before pushing me slightly. "Start walking single file."

I step through the entrance first and carefully start making my way down, Lucas closely behind. The damp, rotting smell assails my nostrils and I choke back a cough at the stench.

Minutes pass until we eventually reach the bottom, the opening stretching into the space of a dark, ominous room. I can smell death emanating from the hard, cold floors and my muscles contract, readying myself for whatever pain is to be inflicted on us.

A dim light is switched on, barely illuminating the various metal tables stained in dark reddish-brown, and I grimace at the four straps meant for arms and legs that bolt into the tables. My eyes dart to the walls and my stomach pitches violently, filling with lead at the assortment of bloodied, sharp contraptions and devices meant to torture a victim.

Lucas glances at me with steely resolve and I nod at him. We've endured worse, but that won't stop us from taking these two fuckers out as soon as they remove our handcuffs. The dumb shits didn't even think to check our bodies for concealed blades. The handcuffs won't hinder us at all.

My adrenaline spikes and my muscles tense in preparation of reaching for my ankle and the concealed blade.

One guard moves towards me—the blaster trained at my head—and pulls a knife from the strap around his thigh with his spare hand, his intentions unknown. The sharp blade is threatening, and my instincts spur me to reach for my own dagger. Unfortunately, I am at a disadvantage with my hands cuffed behind me, making the movement awkwardly jagged. The guard instantly lunges forward at my sudden movement, driving his dagger into my side.

I roar as it pierces through my flesh and searing pain courses through me, forcing me to drop to my knees. Lucas moves swiftly to my side and crouches but the second guard snaps at him, and we hear the gun whir as it loads, ready to fire. "Stop! Move away from him, or I'll blow your brains out."

I nod at Lucas to do as the fucker says and he sends me an apologetic look. We must comply for now until there is an opportune moment.

Blood *will* be spilled—but no more of ours.

RULE NINETEEN:
DON'T HESITATE

32

RAE

MY HAND CLASPS OVER MY MOUTH to stifle a horrified gasp as I peer through the looking holes in the secret room where Isabella and I are. Just as I was about to call out to Xander and Lucas, thoroughly excited that they found us, two of Kasim's lackeys came through the door behind them, training outlandish yet deadly blasters on their backs. My eyes dart to Isabella with desperation and I whisper, "Xander and Lucas have just been caught. Do you know where they would be taking them?" Isabella nods and goes to peer through the holes in the wall, in the hopes of catching a glimpse of the two men who have come to rescue me. "I would say the torture chambers. Kasim will generate any excuse to use them."

My face blanches, my blood turning cold as consternation slithers the length of my spine at the mention of torture. Tears fill my eyes at the thought of Xander and Lucas being subjected to such horrors on my behalf.

"Do these tunnels lead to the torture chambers?" I ask shakily.

Isabella nods enthusiastically. "Yes. The architect was adamant on creating the tunnels to the advantage of other innocent civilians. Since he designed the building under Kasim's orders, he knew there was a torture chamber, so he ensured the tunnels started from there."

Tangible relief lightens my tightening chest at the positive news, and I steel my shoulders. "Good. All we need to do is find some weapons since Kasim took my sword." As soon as the words leave my mouth, I whirl back around to look through the wall.

Just as I thought!

Turning back to Isabella, I gesture back at the wall. "And does this lead into *that* room?"

"Yes, follow me."

I follow her around another corner and the passage becomes increasingly smaller until we are both on our hands and knees. A thick layer of dust coats the floor, our movements disturbing it to billow up and tickle my nose. Wiping my nose with the back of my arm, I succeed in stifling the impending sneeze.

Isabella stops and presses against the far wall, then a click echoes in the small space as light floods the darkened tunnel. An exuberant smile makes my cheeks hurt as we emerge into the very room Xander and Lucas were captured in, and I greedily eye the wall displaying numerous amounts of blasters. The thrilling buzz of energy hums through my veins at the prospect of holding such an item. I have never seen a gun in my life. I stride over to inspect the gadgets up close and narrow my eyes at the obvious triggers and buttons. I'm surprised by the femininity of such a deadly item and chuckle to myself.

I suppose I'm feminine but also deadly, so the blaster is somewhat fitting.

The small, white metal weapon is rounded at one side with slight indents to show where the hand grasps it, then tapers into a slightly pointed cone. Chewing my lip nervously, I hesitantly pick one from its display and turn it around to examine each side, becoming accustomed to the unexpected weight and cold feel of it in my hand.

"I've seen Kasim's guards use them if you would like me to show you," Isabella whispers as she glances over her shoulder at the door.

My eyebrows shoot up and I judiciously hand her the deadly weapon, watching closely as she points at each mechanism.

"I see the guards press this little button on the side before firing, and this lever underneath is where your index finger sits to fire."

I smile, relieved at the simplicity of the weapon, and grasp onto it as Isabella hands it back. "Thanks."

Looking back at the secret door that we emerged from, I glance at Isabella and gesture for us to leave. "Let's go rescue the damsels in distress."

We both snicker at my joke, but our moods grow sombre again at the seriousness of the situation. Isabella grabs another blaster from the wall before we make our way to the secret door and back through the tunnels. I follow closely behind as she leads me back the way we came, intermittently crawling when needed until eventually each section becomes larger and we can walk.

Some time passes as we start making our way through new quarters of the secret tunnels and before long, Isabella turns to me, placing a finger to her lip in a silent mandate to be quiet. I instantly hear the muffled sounds of Xander roaring in pain and a guard yelling behind the thick walls. I go to rush forward, but Isabella puts her hand up to halt me and shakes her head in warning. The dim light spilling through the cracks is just enough to illuminate her as she holds up the blaster, silently communicating for me to have mine ready as well. I nod and press the little button on the side, hearing a soft click as the metal vibrates slightly in my hand, its whirring matching the thrum of adrenaline ferociously pumping through my veins.

Through the dim light, I see Isabella hold up her clenched fist and flash three fingers at me and I nod in understanding.

On the count of three.

My frame shakes with anticipation and I bounce on my toes, ready to make the attack, as Isabella moves closer to the secret door and looks back at me. The outline of her fist is faintly visible in the air as she puts one finger up, then the second, and on the third she violently pushes through the hatch.

We instantaneously burst out with our blasters trained on the two unsuspecting guards. They whirl around but are not bestowed the chance to even train their weapons on us before our index fingers pull the triggers and a loud woosh echoes throughout the room, the sound reverberating off the concrete walls. A ball of energy-like matter blurs through the air and forcefully hits each of their chests with our surprisingly accurate aims. A brief, horrified expression of surprise and shock fills the guards' faces as they struggle for breath and fall to the ground, writhing as they grasp their chests. Shock morphs into agony while blood pours from the gaping hole in their bodies, their hands failing to cover the deep wounds. Barely a minute elapse before the life fades from their eyes and their bodies stop twitching altogether.

Slowly lowering my arm, my hand holding the gun tremors with the gravity of *killing* a human. Sliding it into the hem of my pants then looking to Isabella, I shoot her a weak smile at seeing her paling face. "We were lucky with our shots."

She nods, but her eyes remain trained on the deep red puddle pooling on the grimy and already bloodstained floor—remnants of flesh from the guards' chests scattered amongst it.

My head snaps up to gaze at Xander, whose busted lips tip into a strained smile and admiration fills his deep brown eyes, making the rich colour shimmer brilliantly.

"Am I glad to see your beautiful face, mouse."

The overwhelming need to hold, to *touch* him, fills me with urgency and I rush over at the sound of his raspy, pained voice. All prior thoughts of his betrayals—selling me and almost violating me—vanish as he leans down to kiss me on the forehead with his arms remaining behind him. My hands desperately wander over his body to check for injuries, only to jerk back when my fingers feel hot liquid as they reach under his ribs. Pulling away, I look down to see deep red dripping from my hands, and my mouth turns dry as dread washes over me.

"Don't worry about that, beautiful," Xander rasps, clearly in pain, and my eyes dart up to see his own filled with heady love, even with a grimace over his face. "We're both lucky you reached us before the two fuckwits strapped us to those tables... though as you can see, one of the fuckers still stabbed me."

Sliding my arms around him, careful not to bump the knife wound in his side, I embrace him tightly with my face pressed against his granite chest.

"I love you, Xander."

I look back up and his eyes soften as he cranes his neck down to kiss me softly before pulling back.

"I love you too, mouse."

The sound of a throat clearing has me reluctantly stepping back from Xander, and I glance over to Lucas whose eyebrow is cocked in question. "Do I receive a greeting like that?"

I laugh at the low rumble of protest in Xander's chest then turn to Isabella, who is shyly standing in the shadows.

"Isabella, come meet Xander and Lucas, and then it would serve us well to leave this place."

Isabella steps into the dim light and I hear Lucas's sharp intake of breath, so I turn to him. "This is Isabella. She had been enslaved by Kasim but helped me escape. We will bring her back with us." I glance at Xander who nods, and relief fills me at his approval. "It's the least we can do," Lucas tells her softly.

Isabella's eyes drop to the floor as she whispers, "Thank you."

"Now, let's get these handcuffs off somehow," Xander orders, twisting around to briefly show us, and I look to Isabella.

"Do you happen to know how to do that?"

Isabella smiles softly and nods as she walks behind Xander to key in a code, pressing various symbols on the small screen built within the flat surface of the cuffs. We all sigh in relief at the sound of a locking mechanism robotically droning, then clicking as the cuffs unclasp and fall to the ground with a clank.

"So, do we have to squeeze back through that tiny entrance you both just came through?" Lucas asks with a grimace after Isabella removes his cuffs and he rubs his raw wrists. "I'm not a fan of small spaces."

I roll my eyes at him. "Well, you can stay here if you want."

Xander chuckles at my sarcastic comment. "He'll be fine."

I nod at Isabella who turns to lead us back, but Xander's deep voice cuts through and stops us mid-step.

"We can't leave until Kasim is dead."

I turn back to see his face has tightened with fury and a nerve in his jaw is pulsing angrily. "We believe he plans to attack our city with all the weaponry he's accumulated, and he will do it sooner now that I've taken you back."

"I agree," Lucas says, and I scrunch my face in concentration as my mind whirls with possible plans of attack.

"We could wait here and ambush him when he comes down to finish Lucas and me off," Xander suggests, and I blench at the implication of his words, horror filling me at the thought of nearly losing him.

Isabella nods in agreement at the plan, and I look down at the dead guards then bend down to pry the blasters from their stiff fingers, handing one each to Xander and Lucas.

"Well, *one* of us is at least bound to hit him." My tone is light yet strained, and everyone snickers at my hollow positivity in the dire situation.

Xander steps towards me, pulling me into a quick hug, and I melt against his solid frame as his large hands affectionately roam my back.

"Now, now, kids, keep it in your pants," Lucas jokes, and I step back, looking at him with a heated face despite the smile tugging at my lips.

The sound of a heavy door opening echoes down the long, concrete stairway and we all simultaneously fall silent, tensing at the imminent conflict. My eyes dart around the room and I swiftly hide behind the wall that borders the stairs, indicating for Isabella to join me. Once in position we quickly brandish the blasters, clicking the buttons to release the safety and load them, with Lucas and Xander imitating our movements.

Should we keep him alive, so he dies slowly? I inwardly query, but the unsettling feeling generated from my conscience niggles at the corner of my mind, urging me to be humane regardless of Kasim's crimes.

My internal battle of ethics swiftly dissipates when the footsteps become increasingly louder as they descend the stairway. Relief fills me at the sound of only one pair and I smile at Xander, who winks in return. My heart flutters at the simple yet effective gesture, and I bite my lip as a blush heats my cheeks.

Xander's gaze is ripped from mine at the sound of the person nearing the last step and we concurrently lift our blasters.

"Well, well, well," Kasim's voice booms out from behind the wall Isabella and I are hidden against. The sound of his hands slowly clapping bounce off the damp, hard surfaces of the ghastly room and I calm my breathing, positioning my stance to jump out at any moment.

"You men should come work for me if you managed to take down two of my most trained soldiers *and* escape from your coded handcuffs."

Xander scoffs as he keeps the blaster trained on Kasim. "No thanks. Can't work for someone if they're dead anyway."

I hold back my laugh at his sarcastic comment and tense as Kasim walks into view from the last step. Isabella and I train our blasters on his back.

Kasim holds his hands out in surrender and continues talking to Xander and Lucas, oblivious of the two weapons aimed behind him. "Surely, there is something you want that we could negotiate over."

A bloodthirsty smile extends across Xander's face and concern fills me at the crazed expression as he speaks in a low voice. "I only want you to suffer slowly and die a painful death."

Kasim's muscles strain, and my temple where Nelinha thumped me suddenly begins throbbing. I clamp my lips together tightly to avoid calling out in pain. Without any further warning, my vision abruptly turns white as an image of Xander, lying *dead* on a cracked ground, flashes into view before instantly dissipating. My brows pull down, furrowing deeply at the troubling image, though my heart palpitates with the occurrence indicative of a new coveted ability.

That has never happened before.

The vision seems unlikely anyway since there are four of us against one, but I don't take any chances and clear my throat to pull Kasim's attention away from Xander. I will analyse the strange vision and its meaning later.

Kasim spins around, his hand reaching for the small blaster holstered to his side, but he wavers upon seeing both Isabella and me aiming our weapons at him.

He seethes at Isabella, his eyes murderous while he hisses at her, "You stupid whore. You will suffer greatly for this betrayal."

I chuckle at his empty threat and his burning black gaze turns on me as I tut. "Oh, Kasim. Isabella will not suffer at all since you will be in various pieces across this room." It is an empty threat, but I still want him to fear for his life.

I glance over his shoulder at Lucas. "Take his blaster and put him in cuffs, please."

Lucas shoots me a wild smile. "With pleasure."

Once he removes the threat and cuffs Kasim, I walk towards the detestable man slowly, his furious glare attempting to warn me away. Ignoring it, I walk around to kick the back of his knees in, the action proving effective as he crumples to the floor with a grunt.

My eyes travel to the wall where an array of sharp devices hang, and I look back down at Kasim with a wide smile. "Well, how about we give you a dose of your own medicine?"

Satisfaction fills me as a fragment of fear enters Kasim's eyes for the first time since meeting him. I walk over to the wall and inspect the stained contraptions, wrinkling my nose at the rotten flesh clinging to the serrated edges. The shiny equipment does not tickle my fancy, and my eyes rest on the traditional curved blade of a large dagger. I recognise the Pre-Vanquished artefact from a drawing Pa had shown me when teaching me the diverse kinds of blades found in the world.

"Knowledge is power and knowing what weapons you could be up against is beneficial to your defence," Pa would say.

I reach for the bloodied Jambiya dagger and study the ancient markings on the golden handle appreciatively, deciding to keep it permanently. Walking back over to Kasim, I kneel to show him the blade. Recognition flashes in his eyes and I smile at him. "Ironic that I chose this weapon of your probable ancestors, isn't it?"

I glance up at Xander, whose eyebrows are creased with a concerned frown. I tilt my head at him. "What?"

He shakes his head slightly. "I think we should tie him to the table so there's no chance of him hurting you."

I stand up at his suggestion, knowing he is right. Amidst my increasing need to hurt Kasim in return for all the suffering he has inflicted, my common sense escaped me.

The brief interval allows my burning vengeance to clear, and the haze of boiling anger rapidly vanishes, my heart in turn weighing heavily at the realisation of what I was about to do. My shoulders slump and my conscience tugs forcefully at me, begging me to do the right thing.

I'm better than this. I would be just as bad as Kasim if I purposefully inflicted pain on him.

Frozen on my feet, my eyes trail down to the dagger in my hand with disgust, and I scowl. The indistinct activities of Xander and Lucas yanking the struggling Kasim up and removing his handcuffs to throw him on the metal table, nudge me back to the present.

No matter how evil someone is, I am not sanctioned to determine their punishment, nor to implement it.

Sighing in defeat, I feel everyone's eyes on me as I stride back to the wall and pull down a large, heavy sword. Placing the dagger back in its scabbard and clipping it around my waist, I turn to a confused group of people. Xander looks at me questioningly and I look at the ground, ashamed. "I don't feel right torturing him. It would make me as bad as Kasim himself."

Understanding dawns on Xander's face and his eyes soften with affection. "You're so beautiful and pure, Rae. Too good for a monster like me."

Kasim hisses at hearing Xander's declaration and I realise he still thinks I was Lucas's betrothed. "I knew you were lying about her," he seethes.

Ignoring Kasim's outburst I smile sweetly at Xander. "No, you're just what I need, Xander. I'm not too good for *anyone*; we are all human with different stories that shape us. No path makes us more superior than another."

Xander strides over and crushes a chaste kiss to my lips, then a softer one to my nose, silently conveying his adoration for me. My sentiments with Xander appear to be torture enough for Kasim and he groans.

I glance at Isabella to see how she is faring and notice her lips quivering, displaying the contained, silent rage directed at Kasim.

Her eyes have not left him.

It is in that moment that I realise, this should be her retribution for everything Kasim has made her endure. The rape, the brutal beatings and general suffering.

"Isabella," I softly call her name, and her eyes reluctantly leave the man. I pull back from Xander's warm embrace and hold up the sword in offering. Isabella walks over and reluctantly grasps the hilt, her knuckles turning a stark white as angry tears fill her eyes.

"It is your right to end his life for your own closure," I tell her quietly, and she nods jerkily.

Lucas's eyes widen at the change of direction and we all wait, the air thick with anticipation as Isabella slowly walks toward the table where Kasim is tied down.

Fire ignites her gaze as she looks down at him with disgust and spits on him. Panic enters Kasim's eyes, knowing the sword is in the hands of the female he has brutalized and tormented for so long. He knows his death will be painful and imminent.

Isabella hesitates as she raises the sword above Kasim, and I realise she probably has not killed someone in this style before, if at all.

I quickly walk over to stand beside her trembling frame, reassuringly placing my hand on her shoulder as she turns to me. The arm holding the sword drops.

In my years of survival, there has been one rule that has kept me alive; a rule that I learned the hard way. The time I encountered a predator — a staunch beast with large fangs that the old civilisations called a canine. A moment of hesitation gave it an advantage, and it leaped into action while I was frozen in fear. When it lunged for me, my throat its target, I thankfully snapped from my rigid state and managed to drive my sword into its chest as it knocked me to the ground. But my moment of hesitation could have resulted in a torn jugular.

"There is a rule I implemented in my years of survival that may help you," I tell Isabella quietly, and she looks up at me hopefully. "Don't hesitate."

Resolve hardens her expression and she nods abruptly. Pleased she understands, I back away from the table as she takes a deep breath and raises the sword with two hands above her head. Kasim begins struggling against his bindings, but Isabella does not linger and forcefully brings the sword down with swift precision over his neck, slicing cleanly through. A chilling crunch of severed spine, then an ensuing gurgle fills the room, the sound of air leaving his lungs, subsequently meeting the blood as it pulses out. The strands of sinew keeping his head attached finally tears, causing it to roll from the metal table and fall to the dirty ground with a thud. We all watch as death swiftly takes residence in his dark eyes.

Isabella remains frozen in position, shocked by the image of so much violence, and a tremor racks her body as the reality of what she has done overwhelms her. The sword gripped tightly in her hand drops with a clang on the hard ground and her knees buckle. I lurch into action, darting for her, but Lucas beats me and manages to sweep her up before she hits the floor. Concern fills his face as he gazes down at Isabella, sobs racking her small and bruised frame. His brows furrow at the sight of her discoloured bruises smattering the side of her battered face, and he looks to me for explanation.

The dimly lit room had concealed the violence Isabella endured at Kasim's hands, and Lucas is only just perceiving the evidence upon his closer inspection.

I shake my head at him to indicate now is not the time nor place, inwardly telling myself that it is her story to share with him and not mine.

The room is filled with solemn silence as we look down at Kasim's head resting in a puddle of dark red blood blossoming like a macabre rose. We are each filled with our own personal, weighty deliberations.

A victorious smile suddenly spans the width of my face.

"Oh my," I whisper, and everyone looks up at me curiously. "There is hope for Segment Two now."

33

XANDER

I'M SO FUCKING HAPPY TO SEE MY LITTLE MOUSE and I swear to myself I will never let anyone take her from me again. Rae's soulful eyes pierce my chest, the intensity of her gaze gripping my heart so forcefully it leaves me breathless. It will be a long time before she can ever forgive me for what I've done and had almost done to her prior, and I would go back in time to change my decisions if I could.

My gaze dips at the movement of Rae's lips as she speaks, the innocent motion of her lush, crimson pillows mesmerising me.

Snapping myself back to the present, I smile at her hopeful words, pride filling me with her display of strength and leadership, but then a frown suddenly morphs my face at an unexpected, troubling thought.

"Who will be Ruler?" I ask as my eyes travel over everyone. "Kasim doesn't have any heirs that I know of to take his place."

Rae nibbles her lip thoughtfully and my body tenses at the innocent gesture. It's one of her habits that tends to drive me crazy; yet she is completely oblivious of the effect it has on me.

She peeks at Isabella, whose gaze drops to the ground, apparently uncomfortable with the amount of attention on her. I study the beautiful, exotic woman and anger curls in my stomach at the sight of her swollen eye and bruised face. Kasim didn't deserve such a quick and honourable death.

Glancing at Rae's beautiful face again, I feel my chest squeeze and groin tighten, and I realise that while Isabella would be described as beautiful, she does nothing to stir my interest.

My eyes travel to Lucas as he watches Isabella with concern *and* curiosity, though his face is still shadowed with grief. I smile to myself. His attention is roused. It would be a balm for his broken heart at the loss of Alayah, to concentrate on this woman.

"I think Isabella is most suitable as Ruler."

Rae's proclamation stuns us unexpectedly and we all gape at her, waiting for her to explain. Her eyes sparkle with eagerness and zeal as she meets each of our regards with steely determination.

"Think about it," she begins, gesturing to the increasingly apprehensive female. "Isabella has been living in this tower and witnessing politics and strategies of how it has been run for *years*. On top of her knowledge, she is intelligent, kind, and full of spirit... well, when a man is not oppressing her."

We look at Isabella, who gawps at Rae as if she has grown a second head. "I simply cannot. I'm a *woman* and the people would likely be disinclined to accept a woman as their Ruler."

Rae's eyes brighten. "So, if that is the only thing standing in your way, we can *prove* you are just as capable as a man."

"I thought she was coming back to Segment One with us?" Lucas asks hopefully, and Isabella glances at him, a blush staining her fine cheekbones.

"Rae," I interject softly, and she looks at me. "We can't force someone into something they don't want to do."

Her eyes darken at my statement, fury igniting and flashing in their depths as they replace the waning merriment. Clenching my jaw, I inwardly kick myself for my choice of words and prepare for her angry assault.

"Well, *I* was forced into something I didn't want to do, wasn't I?" Rae's words drip with venom and I frown, unsure how to go about fixing this.

Do I tread lightly?

I've never had to ask for forgiveness before or apologise.

Pushing the confusion aside, I decide to just declare what is weighing heavily on me.

"I will be forever sorry for what I put you through, Rae. I had no excuse and would take it back if I could." My words are profoundly sincere, and her eyes soften slightly. "I hope one day you can forgive me and learn to trust me again."

Rae's eyes tear away, churning chaotically as they drop to the ground. I ache to pull her against me but refrain, knowing she needs space. Her head slowly rises again, those crystal orbs cutting through my chest, and I press my knuckles into the aching over my heart.

"Thank you for saying that Xander. I do forgive you, as I know you were doing what you thought was best for the city," she says softly, and I inwardly rejoice. "But it will be a long time before I can learn to trust you again."

My shoulders drop and I nod in understanding at her implicit matter of when I had nearly raped her. "I will wait as long as I need to, mouse."

I almost cry with relief when Rae tentatively hugs me, and I wince at the pain in my side.

Lucas pipes up at seeing my pain. "Shit, we need to get you to an infirmary before we do anything else."

Rae gasps, pulling away to peer up at me with wide, remorseful eyes.

"Are you going to be okay?"

"Yeah, I'll be fine. I just need to get the cut sterilised and sealed."

I look to Isabella, who has regained her composure, and lift my chin at her. "Could you show us to the infirmary?"

Her dark brown hair bounces around her face as she nods and walks to the stairs quickly, only to have Lucas interject and halt her progress. "Wait, how will we go about being in public? The guards are bound to find Kasim down here and probably issue an arrest warrant on us all."

Isabella smiles at him before plucking Kasim's head up by the hair, unflinching as she holds it up. "If you carry this is out and claim you have usurped the role of Ruler, they have to abide your instructions. Kasim overthrew the Council, murdering its members, so we don't have to worry about going through the trial."

I chuckle at the grim expression settling over Lucas's face as he takes hold of the still dripping head. I'm impressed both women haven't fainted from the gruesome appearance of it.

Lucas hesitates and looks to me, seeking approval of the plan, and I gesture for him to lead the way. We all ascend the stairs quickly as we follow Lucas, avoiding the drips of blood that trails behind, and make it to the top where we are greeted with the heavy metal door. I turn to Isabella with a raised brow and she nods at my silent request, making her way past us all to key in the code to unlock it. The mechanism produces a heavy grating sound of metal against metal, clanking as it whirs and unlocks, then clicks open. The final sound is symbolic of our freedom.

We all collectively take a deep breath in preparation to deal with whatever is on the other side, and Lucas pushes through, ensuring Kasim's head is in view of any men lurking.

One guard across the foyer sees us emerging and urgently shouts to his partner on the other side. "Hey! The prisoners escaped!"

We all tense as he runs over while yelling in his communication device. His eyes travel to Lucas's hand and widen as he sees his Ruler's decapitated head, abruptly halting his progress. The second guard pulls his blaster out and trains it on us as more men rush in, freezing upon seeing what Lucas is holding. Isabella steps on her toes and whispers into Lucas's ear, and he nods at whatever she's directed him to do. He steps forward once a large group of guards have gathered and holds the head up, addressing the men in a loud, demanding voice. "I have defeated Kasim and hereby appoint myself as the new Ruler, providing no unknown heirs have been produced."

A collective buzz arises as the guards turn to each other with either confusion or dispute, murmuring and scratching their heads. Some glance nervously at Lucas while they weigh him up during their hushed exchanges.

I guess they haven't experienced this before.

Others raise their voices, arguing that they are best suited as successor. Thankfully, they are quickly shut down by the majority. Lucas will need to keep an eye on those opposing guards and other citizens who do not agree with his or Isabella's succession as Ruler... if they succeed in making it that far.

The men finally come to their conclusion after a few painstaking minutes and one guard steps forward to address Lucas.

"Ruler," his voice wavers with uncertainty and he bows slightly. "May I have permission to speak?"

Well, this is a good sign, I privately muse.

Lucas nods, gesturing for him to continue, and I hold back a chuckle at the sparkling amusement in his green eyes, instigated by the guard's mannerisms. It appears Kasim ruled over the guards in an archaic approach, forcing everyone to bow before his presence each time.

The guard clears his throat and speaks in a loud, clear voice. "We, as a majority, collectively accept you as new Ruler, *regardless* of any unknown heirs, and are at your disposal."

A few men yell their protests but are reprimanded efficiently by their surrounding comrades.

Neither Lucas nor I can hold back our laugh when the guard before us bows. It's ridiculous. The bowing guard suddenly uprights himself, startled by our outburst, and Lucas wipes tears from his eyes then addresses the alarmed man as murmurs arise within the small crowd again.

"You never have to bow again under my leadership. I may be Ruler, but you are all my equals who will help me in protecting this Segment."

A new respect enters the guard's eyes and I scan the others, the majority similarly having deference visible within their gazes. Scratching the back of my head, I wonder how Isabella will now take the public role as Ruler, as *queen,* if the men have already established their loyalties with Lucas.

A slight frown pulls down Lucas's eyebrows and he shoots me a troubled look with the same question reflecting in his eyes.

Pushing my concern aside, I lean down and whisper into Rae's ear. There is only one priority in my foremind.

"We will leave Lucas and Isabella here for the time being so I can get you home."

The breath leaves my chest as she looks up at me with a bright smile, the mention of *home* causing her eyes to shine.

"I would love that."

Rae's words leave me feeling complete and I almost cry out with the immense elation that fills me.

"We should go straight to the lab so your scientists can start running tests on my blood," Rae adds, her tone now serious.

Of course, I will only want her for myself when we return, but I slowly nod my head to appease her.

Turning to Lucas, I gesture towards him and Isabella. "You two will need to stay alert. If the city finds out their Ruler has died prior to discovering your succession, there will be unrest. I would suggest sending out a collective message as soon as possible to all citizens and guards, informing them. Perhaps also be on the lookout for opposing people who may want to remove you."

Lucas nods his agreement and looks to Isabella. "Is it okay with you that I'm staying?"

Isabella looks at the ground to whisper shyly, "Yes, I would prefer you to stay since I'm an unbound female with no protection of Kasim anymore." She adds even more quietly, "Not that I was protected from him."

Lucas stares at Isabella, clenching his jaw angrily at hearing her admission, but she misunderstands the direction of his fury and visibly shrinks under his wrath. Noticing her adverse reaction under his fuming demeanour, he quickly softens to reassure her quietly, "I would never hurt you or any woman."

Isabella nods reticently, her distrust of any man still prevalent, but accepts Lucas's sincere words.

Rae walks over and hugs Isabella tightly. Both women are awkward with the display of affection and my heart aches at the lack of physical touch they must have experienced throughout their lives. They pull apart, still holding hands, and Rae smiles sadly at Isabella, who imitates the expression.

"I wish I didn't have to leave you, but hopefully we will see each other one day soon," Rae says mournfully, the grief of losing Alayah still visibly raw.

I look up as Lucas addresses the guards still gathered. "Men, you can head back to your usual duties, though I will need two of you to stay behind. One to lead Rae and Xander to the infirmary, then one to retrieve supplies for their journey home."

The guards comply, all dispersing efficiently bar one, who stands quietly at the exit as he waits to lead us to the infirmary.

Rae sighs sadly and quickly hugs Isabella one more time. "Thank you for helping me, Isabella. I owe you more than you could ever know."

Isabella smiles softly as they break apart. "It was my pleasure, and you owe me nothing. We both helped each other."

Lucas and I nod farewell to each other, a silent exchange of comradery that reflects our extensive friendship. Rae and I follow the guard from the tower, and we pass another guard who is packing supplies for us into Kasim's truck.

"Please don't forget my sword and attire from the main bedroom," Rae kindly says as we pass him, and he nods curtly in reply.

We quickly reach the small infirmary stationed directly across the road from the tower and walk inside to greet the aging man hunched over the front desk.

"I've been sent here to attain medical attention," I tell him, hoping the guards spread the word of Lucas's new role. The old man looks to the guard beside us, who nods in confirmation at my statement and then leaves us to return to his duties. The deep wound in my side has insistently been throbbing, making me painfully aware of its presence, and relief fills me as the old man gestures for us to follow him.

"I'm the doctor," he tells me over his shoulder as he leads us through the back.

The white room reeks of sterilisation and the caustic chemical scent tickles my nose.

Well, at least I won't get an infection here.

I follow the doctor farther into the room and lie on the examination bed. Thanks to my many battle wounds and injuries, I know the procedure well.

"My name is Clarence," the doctor says.

"I'm Xander, and this is Rae."

Clarence's eyes widen at our names and his head snaps up as he pauses in lifting my shirt. His face is filled with incredulity. "You're the Ruler of Segment One?"

I nod and smile at Rae. "And Rae here is the soon-to-be queen."

The doctor peers curiously at Rae, who casts me a furious look, and I realise my error too late.

"I mean… she will be the queen *if she chooses.*"

Rae nods in approval of my delicately re-worded statement and the doctor chuckles.

"You are a smart man. So how do you know our apparent new Ruler, who allows you access to his medical resources so freely?"

"Lucas is my second in command. We were in some torture

chamber to be executed by your now dead leader, Kasim," I say and then gesture to Rae. "This one caught the eye of Kasim, and he had already brought her here. So, when she found out that I was to be executed, Kasim's slave managed to save us. He was decapitated by his own sword."

Clarence's eyes bug at the bizarre story before he smiles brightly, flagrantly producing more wrinkles.

"Well, either way, the citizens will be thankful. Kasim was a tyrannical leader that ruled through bloodshed and fear. Most of the city has been living in poverty because of his greed."

I nod, relieved that the city will take to the new leadership with positivity.

Clarence fills my exposed wound with a stinging solution to sterilise it and I wince. He gives me a leather strap to bite down on as he prepares to sew the wound up. My muscles tense as the needle pierces through my skin.

Fuck.

I look to the beautiful warrior standing anxiously beside the bed and smile through the leather strap at the concern on her face. Clarence senses Rae's concern and addresses her while his eyes remain focused on the task at hand. "He'll be fine. I'm assuming this is the least amount of pain he's ever experienced."

The doctor glances at me for confirmation and I grimly nod at him. He's a smart man and probably noticed my other thick scars peeking out from underneath my shirt. And he couldn't have missed the scars on my face.

Clarence efficiently sews the wound in a puckered, yet neat line, and I pull my shirt down then hand the leather strap back to him.

"Thank you for working on me, Doctor," I tell him, and he

smiles widely at me.

"It was my pleasure, and I wish you both safe travels home."

We leave the infirmary and make our way back to the tower where the guard is waiting for us at Kasim's truck.

After saying farewell to Lucas and Isabella one last time, I lift Rae into the passenger side, relishing the feel of her feminine curves under my hands, then jog around to clamber into the driver's side. We fasten ourselves to the seats and I grimace at the thought of driving in Kasim's truck. Lucas will probably have his new guards retrieve the truck that we originally came in and hid on the outskirts of the walls, to use it in place of this one.

"Where is your mask?" Rae suddenly chimes through my musings, her tone alarmed.

I shrug, glancing at the back seat. "Somewhere back there. Don't worry, I won't need it since you're Immune and I have a sharp sword."

"Xander!" Rae reprimands me unhappily and I smirk at her before returning my gaze to the path ahead of the truck as I drive. "I love that you worry about me, mouse."

She scoffs and twists in her seat to look behind us, watching as we eventually leave the outskirts of the city walls.

A relieved sigh escapes her when the Segment finally becomes a speck on the horizon, and she turns back to the front.

Little does she know of the deviant thoughts I'm having.

I finally have her all to myself.

I keep my eyes trained on the vast, barren landscape ahead as I drive and sense Rae staring at me. Casting her a sideways glance, I see desire etched across her face and smirk.

"What are you thinking, mouse?" I ask her and she blushes, quickly turning to gaze out the window beside her.

I chuckle at her innocent reaction and place my hand over hers to give them a gentle squeeze. "Don't hide from me. I will never judge you for your feelings or thoughts."

Rae's eyes reluctantly meet mine and she bites her lower lip, eliciting a groan from deep within my chest.

"If you keep doing that, I will pull over and ravish you here in the truck."

A little gasp escapes her, and her jaw drops before she snaps it shut and crosses her arms over her chest. My gaze dips to the cleavage spilling over the top of the deep red silk, and the blood in my body rushes south.

"You wouldn't dare touch me," Rae warns, her tone defiant. "I'm still angry at you for forcing me into that situation."

I chuckle at her fiery attitude and glance at her with a strained smile.

"I know, Rae. Words will never be enough to show how sorry I am."

Surprise crosses her face at my unexpected reply, and she softens slightly.

"Thank you, Xander."

Comfortable silence surrounds us and eventually Rae drifts to sleep, lulled by the thrum of the large engine and exhaustion of the past few days. I take the opportunity of silence to plan a way to ensure Rae becomes my queen.

I will not accept any other outcome.

RULE TWENTY:
SAVE YOURSELF FIRST

34

RAE

A SUDDEN JOLT WAKES ME ABRUPTLY from my much-needed sleep and I swiftly straighten to look around as I slowly gain my bearings. Xander glances at me and I relax, realising we must have only driven over a bump. The sun is slowly dipping below the horizon, creating a magnificent display of pink and orange pastels across the hazy sky. Silhouettes dart quickly in the distance and I squint to focus on the disconcerting movements. My heart thumps erratically.

"Breathers," Xander grunts, his tone low as he flicks on the truck lights.

I grimace. "Can we outdrive them?" I'm concerned for our safety, particularly Xander's due to his deep knife wound.

"I hope so. Unless they're extremely hungry."

I keep my eyes trained on the distant figures and bite my lower lip. "It's odd that Kasim's trucks didn't encounter any on the journey to Segment Two. Perhaps the movement from his convoy has made them more active in the area?"

"I would say you're right," Xander replies grimly as he glances down at the dashboard. "Fuck."

My concern spikes at his outburst and I grip the seat tightly. "What?"

Xander glances over and grinds his jaw before replying. "We need to refuel."

"Blast." I bite my lip as I run through possible solutions in my head and exclaim as I think of one. "Oh, I know what to do!"

Xander looks at me guardedly. "It better not involve anything that compromises your safety."

Biting my lip again, he growls, and I instantly release the flesh from my teeth as he speaks in a guttural voice, "Now isn't the best time to unknowingly seduce me, mouse."

"Sorry," I say, and heat rises in my cheeks. "Anyway, my plan is that you keep driving and I can run alongside and fuel up."

Xander shoots me an incredulous look. "You've got to be shitting me. That's a hard no!"

I roll my eyes at his overprotectiveness. "You know how fast I can run. I will be fine."

Xander shakes his head. "Still a hard no. How about you take the wheel and I'll just get in the back to hang out the window?"

Hesitant to reply, I look out the window and see the now dark horizon with flashes of pale flesh darting into view randomly. Bumps instantly prickle the surface of my arms, causing the fine hairs to stand on end.

"They're close now. You would have to be really quick."

Xander nods and unties his fastenings with one hand, the other remaining on the steering wheel. He bends down to pull a latch and glances at me to explain. "Releasing the covering of the fuel cap."

Once I have untied my own, I lean over to firmly grip the metal wheel and wait for Xander to climb over into the back before I slide sideways in his place. The truck slows down from him removing his foot from the accelerator, and I whirl around to glance at him.

"Which pedal am I pressing down on again?"

I've never driven before but have an idea from watching Kasim when he originally drove me along this stretch of land.

"Keep the pedal on your right pressed down. If you need to stop or slow, gently press the pedal on your left."

I press my foot down on the right pedal to feel the truck suddenly lurch forward, rapidly regaining its full speed. The thrum of the engine vibrates the steering wheel, tickling my hands as I grip it tightly with the efforts of keeping the heavy vehicle from veering sideways. Glancing in the reflective glass hanging from the roof in front of me, I see Xander leaning over the backseat compartment and grabbing a metal container. I keep my eyes trained on the blurred ground in front of us, making sure not to hit any large stones or holes. Xander hangs precariously out the back window to lean over and waveringly unscrew the exposed fuel cap. My eyes keep darting to the side mirror as I nervously watch him. Each little bump causes him to jolt and the loud clang of the fuel cannister against the truck startles me, keeping me on edge with my spine ramrod straight. The tightening of my grip around the wheel has my knuckles turning a striking white and my jaw hurts from clenching it too tightly.

Forcing my gaze back ahead of us, I squint through the truck's beams of light and my eyes widen at the looming figures gaining speed.

"Xander, could you please come back inside... we have

company ahead."

Xander quickly screws the fuel cap on and begins to edge his torso back inside when a sudden flash of white appears in front of the truck. The unexpected appearance startles me, and I wrench the steering wheel sideways. My heart pounds furiously, threatening to escape my chest as the sudden action has the truck jerking abruptly.

I hear a woosh followed by a grunt and then an unsettling lull fills the truck.

Keeping my eyes peeled ahead, I call out to Xander to make sure he is okay.

"Xander, are you alright?"

Silence greets me and I quickly glimpse back. My heart drops at the empty seat.

"Shit!"

Xander must have fallen out. Slamming on the breaks, my torso flings forward and my forehead smashes into the hard wheel, momentarily dazing me with the impact; I had not fastened myself in during the swap over.

With no time to recover from my blurred vision, I jump out of the vehicle, ensuring to grab my sword from the back seat. I sprint as fast as I can, covering a few hundred meters in seconds when I spot the abhorrent spine of a large pale figure crouching over a still life form. My chest constricts when the gravity of the situation dawns on me and I dart forward without hesitation, brandishing my sword above my head. With all the strength I can muster, my arms forcefully swing the blade down across the pasty, twisted skin of the Breather's back. It throws its head back with a shrill scream and I tense at the distant replies of multiple others.

Jumping into action, I dart forward again, but the Breather

whips up to loom over me and unhinge its jaw. The amber glow in its black eyes spear cold arrows through my soul, though I do not recoil. Deeply inhaling as much air as I can, I move directly in front of the mutated monster and stand on my toes, tilting my head up to its terrifying face. The acidic, icy stench of its breath makes me shudder and I release a battle cry, allowing the breath in my burning lungs to finally expel. My scream echoes through the eerie wasteland and the Breather throws its head back unnaturally as it issues a bloodcurdling scream of agony. I lunge, sword angled as I use all my strength to slice sideways, partially decapitating the horrifying mass of pallid flesh. With a few violent sawing motions, I hack its head from its shoulders then limply drop my shaking arms. My breathing is heavy from adrenaline fused with the exertion of my movements, and I glance down at Xander's still form. A wail tears from deep within my chest at his pale face and wide, open eyes.

They are completely black.

I gasp for breath, choking on my own despair when suddenly, increasing vibrations on the ground beneath my leather boots snap me to reality.

There is no time for sentiments right now, Rae.

Do not hesitate.

Swallowing down the fear in my throat, I steady my breathing and remain in a defensive posture with my sword raised and ready, standing protectively in front of Xander's limp body.

The first burst of white forewarns me of the Breathers' presence, and I tense as the familiar prickle of evil crawls over my flesh once again. Swinging around frantically to catch sight of them, I am shaken to the core and frozen on the spot when a monstrously sized Breather hurtles towards me. Its pasty, sinewy flesh grotesquely hangs from its deformed limbs, flapping in the air as it runs at me, the erratic undulating indicative of its speed.

I hold my chin up, brandishing my sword higher as I scream, "Come and get me, fucker!"

Rage ignites my blood, and I clench my jaw at the fury I feel towards its kind for sucking the soul from the man I love.

It moves within range and lunges for me—the jagged rows of teeth displayed horrifically in its unhinged jaw—but I do not falter, and exhale deeply just as its mouth hovers petrifyingly close to my face. The vile stench of evil and rot cause my eyes to sting and water, but I continue exhaling into the gaping chasm of death. Just as expected, the Breather violently recoils to throw its head back and scream dissonantly.

Gritting my teeth, I swiftly bring my sword down with as much force as I can muster to vertically slice its head in half. Its mangled body drops to the ground with a loud thud just as the claws of something behind me curls around my waist and lifts me from the *ground*. The action has me dropping my sword as I gasp for air and it tightens its hold, the sharp hooks digging into my sides, puncturing my soft flesh. I scream in anguish as it turns me around and the sound dies in my throat at the creature before me.

A massive, deformed, animal-turned-monster. Its large, furless body slightly replicates Pa's description of a bear, but there is no room to conclude its species as soul-gripping fear clutches my chest, its talons squeezing in an unforgiving manner.

Animals are prone to the Breath of Death as well.

I whimper when the deformed beast unhinges its jaw and displays rows of mutated teeth. Its black eyes remain trained on me as it attempts to inhale. Instincts kick in and I exhale, hoping my breath will have the same effect. Thankfully, it throws its head back, but I recoil with horror when it roars. My ears bleed at the deafening sounds of two tones projecting from the monster's mouth, the high pitch that of a demonic screech and the deep pitch a thunderous roar.

It drops me roughly to the ground and I silently rejoice before scrambling forward and grabbing my sword. Without any moment to spare, I lunge forward and leap into the air, the world around me slowing to a sluggish pace. As I reach the towering height of the creature, I simultaneously swing my sword to slice its jugular, the vile vapours of pungent blood making my eyes sting. It screeches, dropping to its knees and holding mangled claws to the large gash across its neck, so I strike again, aiming for the same target. Its mutated paws drop to the ground as my sword manages to slash through them, the gurgles from its lungs filling with blood shaking me to my core.

"Just die already!" I scream at it. A human would be lying in their own blood by now.

Once again, I swing, managing to cut through its neck until my blade catches on its spine, the sinewy ligaments and bones stopping my progress. I begin sawing, and the breached nervous system causes it to spasm, but I vigorously maintain my efforts. Adrenaline provokes my frantic movements until finally, the sword cuts through air and satisfaction fills me at the heavy thud of the large extremity hitting the ground.

The thick, mutated body remains upright, resting on mounds of flesh, stubby knees or contorted limbs—I cannot tell—and grimace at the sight of the headless atrocity. With a hard kick to its bloodied chest, I force it to fall over and yell victoriously, sharply pumping my fist in the air.

Sweat pours down my back in torrents despite the chill of the frigid night, and I look down at the inconveniently long dress constantly getting in the way. I frantically check the coast is clear, pleased that there are no flashes of white. *Yet.*

Bending over, I rip the dress to free my legs and use the scrap to wipe the black blood off my face and chest as I run over to Xander, who has begun twitching.

The change is taking hold of his soul.

"No!" I wail in agony and drop to my knees as I clasp Xander's white face. The sounds of his jaws breaking as it unhinges turns my blood cold and I fervently shake my head.

"No, no, no, you cannot change!"

Grasping the last thread of hope, I climb over to straddle him and lean forward with desperation as I cover his gaping mouth with my own, exhaling all the oxygen in my lungs. His head and arms begin thrashing and flailing beneath me, bruising me, but I somehow manage to weigh him down. I tightly grip his face to begin desperately kissing his mouth that has thankfully stopped widening under my breath.

There is nothing more I can do.

The ground rumbles with vibrations, and my face snaps up to see more pale figures looming on the horizon. Tears roll down my face in a scorching trail and I become frantic, knowing I will need to leave without him if I want to survive. My eyes desperately search Xander's blackened orbs and my heart plunges as I realise there is no hope for him now.

What was I thinking? My breath will not turn him back.

It would be a great kindness to put him out of his misery, but I could never do such a thing.

The horde of Breathers are nearing, and the vibrations of the stampede becomes thunderous. Tears continue to run down my dirt-caked face, and I look down, gazing at Xander one last time.

"I'm sorry, my love," I sob, "but I have to go. If I survive this, I will come back and search for you."

But I know my efforts would be to no avail and that the words are an empty promise made to an empty shell of a man.

A wail rips from the depths of my chest and I eventually force myself to stand. Pressing my lips tightly shut to prevent any more noise, I mournfully gaze down at his twitching life form. It is time to leave. Otherwise, he might turn completely and attack me. I would not be capable of fighting the man I love.

Loved. He is no longer a man now.

Looking up to see the mass of Breathers closing in, I quickly glance down at Xander one last time.

"I love you, Xander."

I launch into a sprint, swiftly bending down to grab my sword as I head towards the truck with startling speed, not glancing back once. Losing the mass of Breathers with ease and numbly jumping into the truck as I reach it—throwing my sword onto the passenger seat—my lip quivers with brewing woeful cries.

Turning the key, I copy what I had seen Kasim and Xander do and the engine rumbles to life. Instantaneously, I hit the accelerator, causing the wheels to spin before gaining traction and lurching forward. The glow of bleached aberrations in the rear-view mirror gradually disappears as tears drench my shirt, my cries becoming more rampant the farther away from Xander I drive. My throat burns raw as it becomes hoarse, my wailing eventually subsiding to incoherent mumbles and intermittent sobs.

I begin reciting Rule Twenty repeatedly. The rule that drove me away, leaving Xander to perish.

Save yourself first.

I ponder the rule and wonder why Pa had it so far down the list.

It seems much more important than other rules.

Perhaps, because we had each other, he could not even fathom saving himself first; protecting his daughter was his priority.

The notion causes my eyes to burn, and disgust at leaving Xander behind assails me. He should have been *my* priority—I would have been his. I'm certain I was, if his prior actions have been any indication.

Logically, there would not have been any way for me to help Xander if my head were ripped off; but I still cannot help the all-consuming chasm of guilt swiftly replacing the shame of abandoning my father all that time ago. Only this time, the guilt is tearing my heart in two.

I will never forgive myself for this.

It feels as if I have essentially ripped a part of my soul out and left that behind with him.

Another violent sob tears from my mouth, and the barren wasteland in front of me rapidly becomes a blur through my hot tears.

Months ago, this decision would not have affected me whatsoever. *Now* I know why Pa always reinforced Rule Fifteen of not falling in love and why it was *before* this rule. The grief of losing someone we love clouds our mind and affects our ability to survive. The grief is all-devouring and wholly harrowing.

I slap myself to snap me out of my haze of sorrow, the motion fleetingly flinging my face sideways, then lift my chin in determination.

I *must* reach Segment One.

I *will* survive.

The truck manages to drive all night and I rub my gritty eyes then chuckle drily, the bittersweet success of Xander filling the massive fuel tank before falling out not lost on me.

Thank you, Xander.

I remove my foot from the accelerator to slow the truck's progress as the massive jungle looms before me, and I sigh with relief at the familiar area. Sadness suddenly grips my heart at the reminder of Alayah, and I swallow back the tears to lift my chin with resolve.

No more tears, Rae.

The deep orange sun peeks over the large trees as it slowly ascends, imbuing the sky with its colourful array of pastel pinks, reds, and oranges, and I smile softly at the beautiful sight. The sign of a new dawn.

A new beginning.

The truck rolls to a complete stop at the jungle's edge and I bite my lip at whether to make my way around it in the truck to reach Segment One or go through it by foot.

"Mm... I'm much safer inside the vehicle," I quietly muse to myself.

Making the wise decision to keep driving, I jump out of the tall vehicle and release a jaw cracking yawn while stretching my arms high above me. Then heading to the back door to grab the last heavy canister of fuel, I make my way around and unscrew the exposed cap, noticing the open cover. Xander did not have time to close it before he fell out and my shoulders droop at the reminder of his loss.

"Head up, keep moving," I order myself and steel my spine as I hoist the canister up.

Wrinkling my nose at the choking fumes emanating while tipping the lip of the canister in, I cough to catch my breath.

With burning, watering eyes by the time the last drops of fuel trickle into the tank, I screw the caps back on both fuel tank and canister, close the covering, then run back around to the driver side. Hoisting myself up into the truck, I throw the canister in the back, but just as I turn the metal key in the ignition, the loud, familiar sound of a macaw has me jumping back out.

Frantically spinning around with my face to the sky, I spot the familiar colours of red, yellow and blue. The sight has my knees buckling and I instantly detect Alayah's presence. Tears roll down my face once again and I smile up at the majestic, feathered animal as it spirals lower towards where I kneel. It comes to rest on some foliage in front of me, and I cry out with incredulity as the dark, familiar eyes peer into my soul.

"Alayah?" I whisper with disbelief and the macaw squawks loudly in response.

I choke back a sob and crawl closer, never taking my eyes from her. "I'm so sorry for the violence that happened to you. I hope you can forgive me for causing it."

The macaw squawks loudly again and I gasp in incredulity when she, ever so slightly, nods her feathered head once. Hot tears spill over and I smile, peace filling me at the closure I've just miraculously experienced. I then watch in awe as the macaw—Alayah—squawks loudly again in farewell and flies away. My mouth parts with amazement as I watch until the beautiful bright feathers disappear, then push myself to standing.

A happy daze covers me as I walk back to the truck and hoist myself in, fastening the ties across my body. I turn the key once again and the engine splutters, roaring to life. Accelerating, I jerk the steering wheel to swerve the vehicle around and begin traveling along the edge of the greenery.

My memory of landmarks from the original journey with Kasim has me heading towards the peaks of three small mountains where the main source of the river flows from. The journey around the mountain's perimeter swiftly passes by, with the other side revealing the continuous length of water, and I continue driving alongside its edge.

A few hours slip away before I see the massive city walls looming before me and anxiety rises at the thought of how to inform everyone of Xander's death. Through my apprehension, it also does not escape my notice that the truck must have been driving at its fastest speed the entire trip seeing as it took much less time to make the journey here than when Kasim took me away.

My anxiety suddenly spikes when the vehicle rolls up to the wall and I slowly drive alongside it until I reach the entrance. Gently pressing the brake, I come to a slow stop in front of the rusted, heavy iron gate.

Sticking my head out the lowered window, I reluctantly wave up at the watch tower and the guards whistle down in greeting as they recognise me. Relief fills me when they wave me through as the gate slowly rolls up.

Pushing my foot lightly on the accelerator, I crawl through the gate and to the other side where the familiar sights of dirt roads and homely buildings greet me. Thoughts of seeing Alma lift my spirits a smidgeon, knowing I can seek comfort in her frail arms.

I follow the roads to her brightly painted shopfront and the vivid colour mockingly blares at me, taunting my melancholy mood with its joyous pretence.

The last kin I have left in this world comes rushing out at the sound of the truck pulling up and I take the key from its ignition and untie my fastenings, instantly jumping down without a second to lose. Not even bothering to close the door, I rush towards Alma on numb legs and we embrace in a tight hug, her arms my only consolation after the events of last night.

"My dear Rae," Alma croaks, her voice thick with emotion. "I'm so happy you've returned unharmed."

I sob at her words and she pulls away from me, holding my shoulders at arm's length while glancing at the empty truck. Concern shadows her face, and she looks back at me. "Where is our boy, Xander?"

Tears stream down my cheeks as I attempt to choke back my cries. Alma hushes me, pulling me into a hug, but not before I see pain flash in her milky eyes.

I'm not the only one who has lost a loved one.

"Let us have some tea inside, dear, and you can tell me everything."

Alma leads my shaking frame inside and locks the shop door behind her, placing the *closed* sign up before taking a hold of me again. I numbly walk through the shop and enter her personal quarters. Collapsing in the kitchen chair when Alma releases me, I watch her resignedly as she moves and places the pot on the stove to boil.

In the corner of my mind, through the stifling grief, I inwardly hope Alma pours a whole lot of that numbing brandy in the tea.

My cries subside to occasional hiccoughs, my lungs erratically spasming by the time Alma has brewed the potent tea and placed it in front of me. I close my eyes and gratefully take a sip, almost smiling at the familiar numbing taste of brandy before placing the cup down. I take a deep breath and open my eyes to gaze into Alma's own tear-filled ones. I reach for her hand to offer my support, all the while grasping them as my own lifeline.

"Thank you for the tea, Alma," I whisper, my voice raw from the screaming and crying emitted over the past twenty-four hours.

"You are welcome, dear," Alma replies, her own voice shaky. "We both needed it, so I made the tea stronger than usual."

I squeeze her hand and offer a sad smile, bracing myself to tell her the bad news that I'm sure she already knows.

"Xander's gone, Alma," I manage to say, my voice wavering with tears, and Alma nods slowly.

"I know, dear, I could feel it in here," she says, pulling a hand from my tight grip and placing it over her heart.

A tear runs down her wrinkly cheek and she smiles sadly at me. "Everything happens as it is meant to, even if we feel like it should not."

I snort, shaking my head, and reply with a quiet voice, "No, Alma, it was my fault. I could have prevented it."

I swallow the lump of tears and Alma tuts at me.

"Oh, dear Rae, you have much to learn. If you think back to the story of our ancestors and the Seers who had visions, you will understand the ways of destiny and fate. You see, for some time, if a Seer had a vision and warned people of the prophecy, those people would attempt to change the outcome. They quickly learned how futile their attempts were to warp fate; because no matter what actions or decisions they chose... what the Seer had seen would always come to fruition."

My face scrunches at the idea we are unable to control our fate, and I send a weak smile at Alma for reassuring me Xander's demise was not my fault. My face crumples again and my throat goes dry at the mention of visions, remembering my own one at Segment Two. I look up at Alma with wide eyes and clap my hand over my mouth.

Alma tilts her head curiously at me. "What is it, dear?"

I drop my hand to the table. "I think I'm a Seer."

35

RAE

LMA STUDIES ME RAPTLY FOR A FEW MOMENTS, her eyes travelling to the fading bruise on my temple where Nelinha had previously struck me, and a strained smile hesitantly fills her face.

"Well, dear, this is both great and ill-timed news," she says to me slowly.

Concern fills me at her reaction. "What do you mean ill-timed?"

Alma carefully contemplates her answer before replying. "The ability is an amazing gift to have, but only if you are able to control it. As you probably discovered, it can happen at the most inopportune times." Her eyes travel to my temple again. "I would surmise the knock to the head you had received probably has something to do with awakening the ability. Either way, that is why it is ill-timed. We need to prepare you and the city for your claim as Ruler and we cannot afford for you to have visions in public."

I sigh wearily and groan as I lean on the table with my elbows, pressing the balls of my fists into my eyes when remembering that Xander has no heirs to take over. Shifting my fists so that I am resting my forehead in them, I stare intently at the wall while musing.

"But wouldn't the Council choose a successor from their own ranks?"

"Ah, you see, dear, even though you were not married to Xander and have only been here a week or so, whispers of your unyielding nature of a warrior and your Immunity has spread over the city, and many people already admire and respect you," Alma replies strongly, and I lean back to watch her with interest as she continues explaining. "The Council would be foolish if they overlooked you as a potential queen. I will visit them tomorrow and inform them of what has transpired, suggesting my case. Since I am well known and respected amongst those ladies—the highest Council member being a dear friend—I am confident they will agree with me."

I pause and digest her words.

This is good, Rae—this is what you originally wanted, right? Control and power to enable your involvement in the lab. This is how you can save humanity.

Confusion plagues me and I tap my fingers rhythmically on the surface of the table, staring at the beaten wood as my forehead creases. Why are the visions only coming to effect now? Why have I not had them before? Perhaps it is as Alma said and the knock to my head instigated them.

The feel of Alma's reassuring pat on my shoulder has me lifting my head, and I look at her doubtfully.

"Firstly, are the citizens even going to accept a female as their

Ruler?" I ask uncertainly. "And secondly, I do not know any particulars of how Xander rules this place. Like, where do we get all the food and water from? How are the trades services set up? I'm extremely ill-equipped."

"One thing at a time, dear," Alma coos and stands to put the tea away. "Don't forget how long I have been serving Xander's family for. I will help you with everything. We will start by showing you the greenhouses."

My eyes widen and my mouth gapes open. "You have greenhouses?"

Alma chuckles. "Yes, dear, how else would we eat, apart from the meat our city's men hunt and bring back? Though, the scientists have manufactured a chemical formula that the soil is treated with first, to counteract any traces of lingering radiation from the fallout. Not that there is much, seeing as it has been centuries since the original nuclear assault. It is just a precaution. Quite ingenious of them, really. I am baffled as to how they manage such clever and seemingly impossible feats."

"I assumed you traded goods and services with other cities for most of the food."

Alma shakes her head. "Not anymore. We became self-sufficient when Kasim took over as Ruler at Segment Two. It is better to rely on ourselves. The journey to other Segments is much too dangerous as well—you have experienced this yourself."

Nodding slowly in understanding, I get up to help Alma with the dishes and she ushers me away.

"You better go clean up before I take you anywhere. We need to get the citizens familiar with seeing you publicly—but not before you have a bath and change that ratty dress."

I look down at the bloodied, grimy dress and grimace.

"Good thinking. My sword and clothes are in the truck."

I follow Alma to her bathroom, and she hands me a clean cloth to dry with.

"I will retrieve your clothes, but you will not be wearing them since I also thought to make you some more attire with the help of my assistant—so I will clean your old pair of clothes first and you can wear the new items."

I look down at the dress again and quickly call to Alma before she disappears.

"Can you please bring me a pair of pants and shirt, not a dress?"

Alma shoots me a disapproving expression but nods curtly before scurrying away.

I remove my boots then strip down, throwing the dirty dress on the floor before hopping into the tub to turn on the water. Flinching at the cold water, I take a deep breath and sink down, placing the plug in the drain as I go. Alma shuffles back in with all my clothes and a pair of furry looking items and I glance at her in question.

Her face becomes grim and she replies with concern, "The nights appear to be dropping rapidly in temperature here, which is unusual."

I think back to my drive here and nod slowly. "Yes, I noticed that. I think it is becoming colder everywhere since Segment Two was similar."

Alma looks down at my skimpy dress piled on the floor and raises a brow. "How on earth did you manage in that scrappy piece of material, child?"

My face becomes solemn. "Kasim forced me to wear it. Also, lots of adrenaline... fighting Breathers would keep anyone warm."

"I'm sorry you had to go through all of that dear."

"I'm fine," I reply, and then frown at the memory of the animal-turned-Breather. Looking at Alma, I bite my lip before cautiously wording my next sentence. "So, do some of the citizens leave the city walls to hunt for food with the guards?"

"Yes, we have a rotating roster for the hunting families who bring in enough for us to trade vegetables with."

My mouth waters at the idea of a juicy cut of meat and my stomach growls, reminding me I have not eaten in a while. Alma looks at my naked stomach, clearly hearing the sound, and chuckles. "I will get you some food, but first—why the question about the hunters?"

My brows pull down at the horrifying memory of the massive beast. "My Pa used to describe animals to me and sometimes would show me drawings of foreign ones. Knowledge is power," I say, and Alma nods in agreement. "But there was a horde of Breathers that attacked us, and one was not previously human. I'm fairly certain it was a bear-turned-Breather if I'm remembering my father's descriptions of the beasts correctly."

Alma's eyes widen. "That would have likely been a Spectacled Bear since they were the only species of bear on this continent— though if it is as monstrous as you are implying, perhaps the mutations have affected its size. Everyone thought the fallout had wiped them out since they were rare." Her face crumples with fear. "So, you are suggesting animals are now turning as well?"

I bite my lip and narrow my eyes as I think over the possibilities before slowly nodding. "I believe so." Turning to Alma, I grit my teeth. "If animals are now changing, that means something within the genetics of Breathers has mutated or evolved."

Alma shakes her head and tightly grips my dirty dress as she places the clean clothes on a bench. "This does not bode well for the city's hunters. We must spread the news that they will need to take extra precautions."

"Yes," I agree.

"Good, you need rest though, so leave that to me. On my way home, I will tell one of the night guards to inform all hunting groups first thing in the morning. They do not leave to hunt until midday."

Alma taps a gnarled finger to her chin, cloudy eyes glazed before they snap to mine. "I will need to show you how the communications room works so you can send messages out to citizens."

My eyes bug. "Communications room? Xander... never mentioned one."

Alma deflates at the reminder of him while collecting the boots and dress, and my face falls as I instantly fill with a seizing grief.

"There will be much Xander hasn't shown you. But do not forget your pain will heal in time as well, dear." Her last sentence appears to be a reassurance for herself as well, though she does not give me a chance to reply, quickly leaving the room to dispose of my grimy dress and prepare food for us.

I take a deep breath before sinking fully into the water, submerging my face while keeping my eyes open to look at the obscured, rippling surface with fascination.

Water is the life of everything.

Suddenly parched, I rise and take a deep gulp of air then lean over to turn the flowing water on. Cupping my hands, I drink greedily from the source and turn the tap off again. Spotting the bar of soap, I grab it from the little rack and quickly scrub every inch of skin. Lathering it through my hair, it occurs to me how much easier it is to clean with its now shoulder-length strands. I smile at the bitter-sweet outcome of the now deceased Nelinha, who was responsible for hacking it off.

Thank you for making my life easier, Nelinha.

Jumping out of the bath, I remove the plug and watch as the mixture of dirt and black blood is sucked down the drain, then grab the cloth to dry myself.

Contentment fills me as I slip into the familiar comfort of pants and a shirt, and I almost squeal at the new leathers hidden beneath the pile, quickly grasping a vest and sliding my hands through the arm holes. Once it is securely fastened over my linen shirt and around my torso, I follow the scent of hot, savoury food, making my way into the kitchen where Alma turns at hearing my entrance. She nods approvingly at my clean state, though she frowns at my damp hair. "I will trim your hair to tidy the uneven strands."

I drily laugh and walk over to hug Alma, becoming used to the physical affection.

"Not that I care much about my appearance but... thank you."

Alma tuts and I realise I have begun to enjoy her bizarre, motherly mannerisms. "Appearances are important now that you will be Ruler. Not as important as *how* you rule, but it still plays an important role in how the citizens will perceive you."

"That makes sense," I say, eyeing the plates of food Alma sets on the table and placing a hand against my loudly protesting stomach. Even through my grief, the need for sustenance cannot be ignored.

"Now, sit down and eat, dear, you will need your energy for the days to come."

After a hearty meal and copious amounts of water, my stomach feels full to bursting and I force Alma to remain seated while I clear the table and clean the dishes. "Thank you for the meal, Alma."

"Any time, dear."

Once the dishes have been cleaned and put away, I contentedly sit on the stool and wait as Alma fetches a little cutting tool that she dubs scissors. The soothing feeling of her fingers gently running through and tugging my hair as she snips away causes my eyes to droop from lack of slumber. My head repeatedly drops when I begin nodding off to sleep and jerking back up as I battle to stay awake, but thankfully, Alma finishes up and steps away to admire her handy work.

"Much better. Now, you better catch up on rest and *only* wake when you have had enough sleep."

The exhaustion from the last few days weighs too heavily for me to argue, so I blearily nod my head and follow Alma to her room, where she ushers me into her bed.

My face barely hits the soft mattress before darkness blankets my world.

By the time I wake, the sun has dipped, and night has claimed the now quiet city.

I can hear Alma bustling around in her shop through the dividing wall and I sit up to stretch my sore muscles. The empty, silent room allows the sorrow of missing Xander to fill my heart once again and I rapidly blink back the hot tears filling my eyes. I refuse to cry anymore. There is no point dwelling on what has already passed.

Jumping from the bed, I notice my sword on the little table across the room and smile at Alma's thoughtfulness.

I stride over to strap the holster around my waist and make my way into the back of the shop where Alma is hunched over a table and working on some lovely indigo fabric.

Walking up to her and sliding my fingers over the silky material, I smile at Alma.

"This is beautiful."

Alma stops her work and pulls the glasses off her face to look at me with a cheeky grin. "Well, I'm glad you like it, dear, since you will wear it to the City Hall meeting in a few weeks' time."

My nerves turn to jitter at the news. "What happens at a city hall meeting?"

"Citizens in need of supplies or services—or have general queries—gather there once a month, sometimes less, depending on the urgency, to see Xander. With everything happening of late, the meetings are more frequent, and we only just had one recently. Either way, I thought it would be a good time to reveal you officially as their new Ruler, providing the Council members agree with me tomorrow."

Nerves flutter low in my abdomen. "Are you sure that is a good idea?"

Alma chuckles and stands to give me a brief hug before sitting back down. "They will be sad Xander is no longer here, but I know they will take to you quickly. They already adore you from hearing about your sacrifice to rid this city of Breathers. Even though you are female, there had been much chatter already when Xander bought you in to be his queen. Citizens have already dubbed you as a fierce and stubborn warrior, from the gossip that has spread of your tenacity."

I relax at the delivery of positive news. "Well, that is considerably encouraging. How about the guards' loyalty? Will they be happy to start following my orders?"

Alma nods slowly. "Yes, I believe they will. Xander only spoke highly of you to his closest guards. His devotion to you will ensure their loyalty."

A sigh of relief escapes me, and I nod, looking outside at the dark, empty streets. Alma begins speaking and I look back to her. "It will be handy to have a second in command appointed by your side as well. You will feel better with the extra protection and guidance." Alma frowns as she realises something. "Lucas was Xander's, so will now be yours—but where is Lucas, dear?" Concern fills her face and I inwardly kick myself for not filling her in on everything that has happened.

"Oh! I completely forgot to tell you everything that happened back at Segment Two."

Alma pats me. "It's okay, dear, you were overcome with the loss of Xander."

"Thanks," I tell her as she pulls across a little stool for me to sit on.

"Well, I befriended Kasim's slave or maid—I am usure of her label. Isabella. The only reason I escaped was because of her. Anyway, Kasim had captured Lucas and Xander and held them in his dungeon to execute them, but Isabella showed me some secret tunnels that led us in there. We managed to eliminate the two guards holding Xander and Lucas and free them before Kasim came down to finish them off." I pause for a breath and Alma watches me intently, leaning forward in her seat with enthralled curiosity etched across her face. "With the four of us against him, we managed to capture him and tie him down. I gave the sword to Isabella and she decapitated him. Lucas and Isabella are now running Segment Two. So, I'm not even sure when—or *if*—Lucas is coming back. Oh, and Kasim left a whole room of engineered weapons behind. I have a few in the truck."

Alma silently absorbs the copious information I rattled off and concern fills her eyes as she looks at me. "Guns and firing weapons were constantly the downfall of countries back in the day. There was so much death. Hopefully, there will be no need to use them unless in defence."

I gasp at the meaning behind her words and exclaim, "I would never go to war if that is what you are implying!"

Alma chuckles at my outburst and pats my hand. "Good, dear. Now back to Lucas. Since he is no longer available for service, perhaps I should appoint you another second in command?"

My heart clenches at the idea of another man living so closely to me but I reluctantly nod, and relief fills Alma's eyes as her shoulders relax. "Good. I will have some suitable options for you by the end of the day." She grows weary, weighing her next words before hesitantly saying, "And now we need to plan how to ease you into the public role of a Ruler. Perhaps we will need to convince the citizens first that Xander is otherwise engaged at Segment Two. The news of his death may cause an uprising from certain citizens and possibly encourage other Segments to attack us if they thought the male Ruler had fallen. We will tell them soon, but maybe not quite yet. I am positive the majority will be ecstatic, seeing as they already worship you, but I like to remain vigilant. There will always be those wanting to claim the position for themselves."

My eyes become suspiciously itchy, only hearing her words

of Xander's death, and I rub at them to prevent any tears leaking out. Alma sighs and grasps my hands tightly, and I'm surprised by the strength. "I know it is painful now, dear Rae, but time will heal your bruised heart. It will heal both of our hearts, though we will never forget Xander's precious memory."

Smiling sadly at her, I nod and squeeze her hands back. "Thank you, Alma. I suspect your pain is deeper than my own since you have raised Xander from a little boy."

Alma tears up and shakes her head. "No, Rae. Because I loved him as a son—the pain I feel is acute—but your pain will feel as if you lost a part of your soul. That is what loving a man is like. Sharing a part of yourself." Extreme sadness fills her distant eyes and I deduce Alma must be sharing this wisdom from her own experience. I remain silent to let her work through her pain and let my own thoughts wander to my next trials as a new Ruler. As *queen.*

I'm not afforded much time to contemplate as Alma abruptly stands, snapping from her longstanding grief and pulling me to my feet. "Come, we must see to the tower and city as it will be your permanent home."

Alma grabs a lantern, retrieves my boots and furs, then hands them to me. I quickly don the warm fur coat and have barely just slipped my foot in each boot when she pulls me from the shop. The chill air is bitter, and I pull the warm furs tightly around me. I smile gratefully at Alma as she nods in acknowledgement. Locking the door behind her, we hastily make our way down the dusty street towards the looming shadow of Xander's tower.

My tower.

I push the rising dejection down and we greet the familiar guards at the door who nod in reply and move to the side to let me punch in the code. The letters are still incomprehensible, but I remember the sequence and each of their attributes.

L-I-T-T-L-E-M-O-U-S-E#

The reminder of Xander's pet name for me finally pushes me to succumb to the sadness and I glumly shuffle through the entrance with my feet dragging as Alma trails behind me. Turning to her, I smile sadly.

"If you ever need to get in here, the code is Xander's pet name for me. Little Mouse."

Alma returns her own crestfallen smile and replies, "Thank you, dear. I will be sure to bother you as much as possible now."

Her playful tone lightens my mode and I throw my head back to laugh, causing Alma's eyes to brighten at my reaction.

"Ah, I would encourage your company, Alma. You could never bother me."

We make our way up the stairs and eventually come to the top floor where two guards are waiting. They brighten at the company of two familiar women and look behind us to see if Xander is closely following. Alma turns to me and winks as she looks to the main guard.

"If you are looking for Xander, he has been held up at Segment Two and has asked for Rae to run things for the time being."

I manage to keep my face impassive at Alma's blatant lie, but inwardly sigh with relief when the guards do not bat an eye, only nodding in acceptance. I silently commend Alma's quick thinking.

"Now, could you kindly take us to the communications room so we may contact Segment Two to let them know Rae is safely home?"

The guards nod at Alma and we follow them downstairs to the second level and down the hall to a room filled with various devices and satellites. Alma turns and beams at me. "This is the communications room I was talking about."

I nod and bite my lip nervously, wondering if I should inform Lucas that his closest friend and Ruler was caught by a Breather. Alma must sense my dilemma and ushers the guards out of the room, gently shutting the door behind them.

"We need to contact Lucas and tell him," Alma says quietly, and I look up at her, nodding miserably.

Clearly versed in using the equipment, Alma fiddles with the controls on a black wall and gives me a headset. I hear static noise rise and fall until a man's voice comes through to my ears, startling me. "Segment Two here, over."

I look at Alma in amazement—experiencing the ability to hear someone without them being in the same space for the first time—and she encourages me to reply, whispering, "Talk to him and ask for Lucas."

I clear my throat awkwardly and begin speaking. "Uh, Segment One here. Is Lucas or Isabella close by for us to speak to? This is Rae."

I hear the guard chattering to his team member and then address me after receiving a reply. "Yes, he is in the tower next door, so someone will fetch him for you now."

Static fills my ears again for several minutes and I wring my hands nervously before the communication device clicks back on and Lucas's voice reaches my ears. "Rae, so glad you made it back safely; is Xander there with you? I wanted to ask him if I could stay here with Isabella for a little while longer."

I choke back a sob and clear my throat to speak in a strained voice. "That is actually why I asked to speak to you Lucas," I say hoarsely, tears already forming in my eyes. "Xander did not make it back with me. It is all my fault."

I cannot hold back the sob that erupts from me as Lucas momentarily falls silent while he absorbs the horrible news. My sobs are the only sounds heard over the line until he speaks, his voice pinched.

"What do you mean, *he didn't make it back*?! Is he stuck somewhere? Do I need to leave and pick him up?" Lucas rattles questions off hopefully, clearly in denial about his closest friend's demise.

Alma takes the headset upon seeing my hysteria preventing me from talking rationally.

"Lucas dear, it's Alma here," she says gently, and I hear Lucas cry out upon hearing her voice.

"Rae is too upset to talk, but what she is trying to say is that Breathers got a hold of Xander when he was attempting to fuel the truck. Rae fought off as many as she could, but she would not have survived if she stayed."

I have never heard a man cry before and the sound that echoes from the headset on Alma's silver head shakes me to the core. Becoming oblivious to the room surrounding me, I sink to the floor and let the muted grief pour out of me.

Alma must finish her quiet conversation with Lucas as she turns the communications off and leans over to pat my head. "It is done now, child."

Alma's words do everything but comfort me, and I wail even more while she sinks painfully to the floor beside me, her joints cracking as she goes. I cling on to her when she wraps slender arms around me in consolation. "There, there, dear. Let it all out. Tomorrow will be a new day."

I drench Alma's shoulders with my remaining tears for

perhaps an hour—there is no way to tell—until my cries subside and I exhale a shaky breath. Looking at Alma with gratitude, I give her a watery smile. "Thank you, Alma. I needed that."

"Everyone should allow their grief to pour out, otherwise it tears a deep chasm in their hearts."

I nod slowly at her wise words and silently remind myself to never hold back my tears again.

Providing I'm not in public.

Alma continues talking on a more serious note and I listen closely. "Now, Lucas—bless his poor heart—has given us three candidates who he believes would be the most suitable as your second in command. They are men he trusts with his life and he knows they all have good hearts; I know one of them personally, though I have not seen him in quite some time. Anyway, Lucas has put in a call to their portable communication devices from the Segment Two communications room, and they will meet us in the foyer below in an hour."

I push down the nerves at meeting unfamiliar men and having to choose one to ultimately live in my shadow. "I will do it, but it does not mean I'm comfortable with any man being so close to me daily. Or ever."

Alma chuckles and pushes to her feet slowly, her joints cracking again. I dart up to help and she nods gratefully at me. "Thank you dear. And I understand how you feel, particularly since you were raised without any interaction with other men and made to believe they were all dangerous." Alma's expression becomes wistful as she gazes out the small window. "But there are most certainly good and honourable men in this world."

My thoughts are directed to Xander once again and I exhale sadly. "I know. Xander was one."

Somewhat.

I promptly feel remorseful for holding the negative thought now that he has succumbed to death's icy grasp.

Alma nods. "Yes. And he knew my husband, who was also honourable."

Sympathy fills me at her confession, and I pull her into a quick hug and whisper, "I'm sorry for your pain, Alma."

Alma waves at me in dismissal. "Ah, pish. It has been over fifteen years since he passed away, so I no longer feel the excruciating pain. Only loneliness now."

"That is still poignant, Alma," I tell her, and she looks at me and nods.

"Yes, it is, which is why I need you to promise me you won't close yourself off to people. Make friends and, when your heart is healed, fall in love again."

I laugh, though the sound is without humour. "I will not fall in love again. But I will continue to make friends if that appeases you."

Alma narrows her eyes at me and pokes me in the shoulder. "Love will smack you in the face without any warning, so we will see about that. Now, I'm feeling partial to some tea and cake, so let us head up to Xander's residence. I stocked the cupboards with a heap of sweets when I was up there last."

Not arguing at the mention of the tasty, sweet food Alma introduced me to when I first arrived in Segment One, I quickly follow her upstairs.

36

RAE

I SINK INTO THE FAMILIAR COUCH AND INHALE DEEPLY, relishing the scent of Xander still permeating the air of his home. The apartment is silent bar the occasional clang of Alma preparing the tea and cakes, and I jump up to help, needing a distraction from the constant reminder of *him*. Alma passes me the brandy to pour into the tea and I gladly grasp the glass bottle, pouring a generous amount in, astutely aware of the effect it will have.

To relax me and calm my whirling mind.

A wistful smile teases my mouth at the comforting glugging sound and I reluctantly stop pouring after a few moments.

Alma chuckles knowingly and she nods with approval when I glance up at her. "Yes, we both could use another large dose of that."

We sit down and eat the delicious dark cake that Alma says is *chocolate* flavoured and I moan with each bite of the moist and fluffy food. I thought we were going to eat the cookies I tried when I first met Alma but this cake is a hundred times better, even though its rich colour reminds me of Xander's expressive eyes.

An hour passes quickly as we finish the last of the tea and I giggle at the idea of attempting to see anyone in our tipsy state.

I may have poured too *much brandy in the tea.*

Alma grimaces before chuckling herself. "I think we should have waited to consume the tea *after* we met the men Lucas sent, dear."

I shrug without a care in the world—embracing the mellow effects of the tea taking hold of me—and get up on unsteady legs. "Oh well. At least it has calmed my nerves."

Alma leads the way downstairs and I follow on wobbly legs. We make it three quarters of the way down and I look up, stumbling at what I see. Swallowing the lump in my throat, I survey the three men standing rigidly in a line at the centre of the lobby.

Only one captures my attention.

The largest man in the middle. His scintillating, emerald eyes carefully assess me as I farther descend the stairs and I am powerless in tearing my gaze away from him. There is a restrained aura that surrounds him, and I immediately go on alert; my survival instincts kicking in. Knowledge is power, but his shrouded demeanour and expression are entirely unnerving. People only mask their true character when hiding something.

His face is expressionless except when a fleeting frown tugs his eyebrows, faltering my progress, and I almost faceplant as I stumble slightly on one concrete step. Regaining my composure, I continue while keeping my eyes glued to him. His hair is light brown but has a tinge of auburn from the light above, creating an array of burnt coppery shades throughout the thick strands.

Alma and I reach the bottom step, stopping metres away from the men, but my gaze remains fastened to the massive man in the middle. He stands with his legs shoulder width apart and arms firmly crossed over his chest.

Goodness, and I thought Xander *was pure muscle.*

This guard has arms and a chest twice the size—perhaps indicative of more labour-intensive work.

As I approach the men tentatively, my mouth parts. On closer inspection, *his* eyes are much like green moss, with flecks of natural gold and browns commonly found in a forest floor. Rusty flakes speckle the irises, their dappled pattern positively unique. As disconcerting as his penetrating gaze is, I have never seen such entrancing eyes.

His alluring, yet sternly set lips form a solemn slash amidst the chestnut growth dusting his chin and jaw. High cheekbones shape his face into a deadly visage, each line of his face sharper than a blade. His deadpanned expression gives me the sense that he does not smile much, yet he does not seem temperamental, not like Xander, who was like a fuse ready to blow.

Gah, no more thoughts of Xander!

I quell the sharp pain in my chest, rubbing it while surmising that this man is only serious given the circumstances. Scanning the rest of his face, the corners of my lips tilt down, once again noticing the burgeoning beard. A mixture of honeyed brown and auburn growth covers his face—the facial hair another reminder of Xander even if his own stubble was stark black and much more course in appearance.

A quiet sigh escapes me; the similarity instantly filling me with sadness again.

I will miss the feel of Xander's rough face.

Alma clears her throat, shaking me from my grief and forcing me to focus on the men before me. It takes all my willpower not to single out the middle one. I feel his assessing eyes following me as I stand in front of another man and smile sweetly. This man falters at my feminine wiles and I tilt my head curiously.

Well, not him then.

His eyes lack the intelligence found in the other malachite gaze anyway. I internally reprimand myself for the sudden thought.

Do not think about his eyes like that!

Walking past the auburn-haired man again, my skin prickles but I refrain from looking sideways at him as I stand in front of the other guard. His eyes are black, and on close inspection his appearance and cocky demeanour reminds me *too* much of Xander, so I instantly dismiss him.

I do not need a daily distraction while I'm trying to rule.

Sighing, I reluctantly step in front of the middle guard again, not feeling overly positive about the cognizant sensation plaguing me from his presence or his lack of expression. It is easy to push the strange feelings down since they are not necessarily negative, though his aura is still unambiguously disconcerting.

Once again, my focus is pulled back to reality and I scrutinise the brawny male. I know by his stance that he is powerful enough to protect me, and by his careful gaze—intelligent enough to assist and advise when needed.

There is just something wavering at the shores of my awareness, tickling my senses, that bothers me. Yet the more I attempt to grasp it, the faster it fades away. Perhaps ignorance is bliss and it is just the unknown being bothersome.

The man's calculating look evaluates me, and I narrow my eyes at him in defence. *I'm* the one who should be assessing *him*. Not the other way around.

Lifting my chin, I address him in my strongest voice. "What is your name?"

His shoulders pull back at the sound of my voice but otherwise he replies with no indication of being affected. "Gideon."

His deep, gritty voice sends a chill racing up my spine. At least his tone is not smooth or honeyed like Xander's.

That is only one positive aspect.

"How fitting," I say dryly, the effects of tea still thrumming through my blood. I'm unsure if the name *is* fitting so my words are null, but I have no other sardonic retorts and would like to see him react or show *any* kind of emotion. Through the haze of my mind, my theory is that he can be provoked with infuriating jibes or simply a snarky attitude. But it appears my attempts are in vain seeing as he stands there impassively without indication of any irritation.

Alma coughs in warning and ushers the other two guards away, sensing my final decision. Briefly, she looks up at Gideon affectionately before leaving. "Good to see you again, dear. At least now I will be seeing you regularly." My balance teeters with shock when she winks at him. "You will not have a choice."

"Sorry, Alma. I have been... preoccupied. It is good to see you again." Gideon's voice softens somewhat as he addresses her, though it is still rough like gravel.

So, Gideon is the man Alma mentioned she knew.

Alma shuffles away and my gaze follows her decrepit frame until she disappears up the stairs. I then return my focus on the large, rugged man in front of me.

I suppose I should be nice since he will be with me every day.

He has not replied to my snarky comment—does not deign to speak at all; only watching me fixedly with those compelling eyes. My boldness wavers and I clear my throat awkwardly.

I realise I will be edgy with any man I encounter since I was raised to believe they would all inflict harm on me, but this man's silence is unnerving seeing as I became used to Xander's smug remarks and loud nature.

My shoulders droop and I sigh defeatedly. Peering back up at him, it does not bypass my notice that his eyes never leave mine, though they do not hold violence. The supposition is somewhat reassuring.

Cringing at my lack of social etiquette, I decide to make amends.

"I'm sorry for my attitude and manners. I'm... unused to men. Can we start again?" I hold my hand out in a truce and Gideon glances down, a crease marring the middle of his brows slightly before he nods sharply. He takes my hand to shake once. Its warmth envelops my own dainty one and I feel the roughened skin of his palm, the callouses causing bumps to break out over the surface of my skin. I snatch my hand away at the strange reaction to the physical contact.

Clearing my throat, I look back up at him. "If you had not already presumed, since the others have left, I have chosen you." Tilting my head again at seeing his intelligent eyes I give him a strained smile, "Though I suspect you already knew that *before* they walked away, since nothing appears to evade you."

I cringe at my babbling mouth, an indication of my rising nerves, but his face remains impassive as he curtly nods. It is in this moment that I realise he must not talk much.

Or express emotions.

With his lack of social skills and my inexperience with men, every day with him is going to be slightly painful.

Biting my lip, I contemplate what to do next and conclude standing in front of Gideon's assessing gaze is becoming discomfiting. I gesture up the stairs and turn on wavering feet to ascend them, addressing Gideon over my shoulder. "I will show you to your living quarters."

The sudden movement has me swaying as my head spins, and I clasp the railing to steady myself before continuing. Sensing Gideon's judgmental eyes drilling into my back, I halt to whirl around. My position on the stairs above him brings us face to face, and I narrow my eyes at the disapproval that briefly flashes through his mossy green orbs before reverting to their usual indifference.

"I know what you are thinking," I tell him sternly, and the slightest flare of curiosity flashes through his eyes before he resumes blankly staring at me, infuriating my temper more. "You're thinking I should not be drunk." I don't pause to let him respond. "Well, to ensure you are aware—I just lost the man I love, and in the worst way possible! So... if I need a drink to deal with the excruciating pain in my chest, then I will bloody well do so!" I snap my mouth shut and take a deep breath, attempting to calm my erratic breathing. Gideon slowly blinks in surprise at me.

I guess no one knows I loved Xander.

I instantly freeze at realising Gideon does not know what *really* happened to Xander... and I just blurted it out.

No more tea for me.

"I understand," Gideon suddenly says, and my eyes widen at hearing his gravelly voice. "Lucas told me everything that *really* happened to Xander. He knew you would choose me."

I bite my lip and silently thank Lucas for his foresight before slightly cocking my head and studying Gideon. He states the words factually and without arrogance, which pleases me. Though my stomach drops at the undercurrent of condemnation in his tone. He must blame me for Xander's demise.

Well, he is right, so I will not try to prove to him otherwise.

Satisfied that we have addressed the elephant in the room— my inebriated state—I spin around and continue my unsteady journey upwards with Gideon closely behind.

We make our way to the second floor and I lead Gideon to his new residence, gesturing him through the door. "This is where you will be living. I believe this is where Lucas occasionally resided when he was not in his own house. But you can live here indefinitely if you prefer."

Gideon silently assesses the space as we walk through, and his studious eyes scan every dark corner for threats. We head towards the bedroom and I pause at the door, my eyes falling on the large bed which causes me to blush and look away. I have a slight idea of what goes on in beds now.

I suspect Gideon watching me and look up to meet his curious gaze, brows raised, when his expression quickly turns impassive once again. He nods once.

"This is fine, thank you."

The words are dismissive—a subtle request for me to leave— so I awkwardly smile, then clear my throat.

"Oh, okay. Perfect. Uh, I will see you in the morning for your first shift."

Not waiting for his reply, I spin around and rush from the residence, exhaling with relief as the door shuts behind me. My entire body relaxes, indicating I must have been tensing the entire time I was in Gideon's proximity.

"He's here to protect and help you; not hurt you," I mumble with my forehead against the door, reassuring myself before turning and swiftly making my way upstairs.

Smiling at the guards on post at the entrance of Xander's—*my*—residence, I make my way through to see Alma bustling around in the kitchen again.

"Thank you for your help, Alma," I tell her, sinking into the couch, closing my eyes as I sprawl out.

Alma chuckles. "That is okay. I'm glad you chose Gideon—I have known him since he was a boy. Xander, Gideon, and Lucas used to secretly play together growing up—when Xander's father was occupied, anyway." She adds more quietly, "But just so you know, Gideon and Xander did not remain friends for long. Xander's father saw him with Gideon once, early on in their stages of friendship, and threatened unspeakable acts against the boy. His status was much lower than Lucas, who was a stable hand at the time. Poor Gideon only ever came to visit me after that, keeping to himself to avoid trouble."

My eyes snap open at the information, the pain of losing Xander still raw, but I quell the feeling and sit up to look at Alma curiously. "Really? I wonder if that is why I'm getting a hostile vibe from him? Xander was his childhood friend."

Alma nods and says prudently, "Not to cause you more worry, dear, but there may be people who will think you killed Xander to take his place, even if they were not his childhood friends."

I tense and recall my old plan to assassinate Xander, grimacing on how close Alma's words are to the truth.

"Not to worry, Rae. They will grow to love and respect you. Gideon included."

I nod my head doubtfully and my stomach growls, surprising me. Alma hears it from across the room and laughs. "I have nearly finished making some dinner."

"I only just ate this morning and then had cake before! How on earth am I hungry again?"

Alma frowns at my question. "Dear child, in this city, you will eat regularly. Please promise you will have each meal like every other citizen here?"

I shake my head. "I do not need to. I have survived on one meal a day—if that—so would burst if I started eating more."

Alma tuts at me with disapproval and brings a plate of food, sitting beside me with her own. "Well, at least eat this since the tea would have worked up an appetite."

My mouth waters at the delicious array of food and I dig in to shovel every little morsel down.

Alma finishes her plate not long after and takes the dishes to the sink. It is utterly strange having someone look after me, but I'm growing to appreciate it and assume this is what it would have felt like having a mother.

Alma comes back over and sits beside me, twisting so we are facing each other.

"Now, dear, before you go to bed—and you will start going to bed at night—we need to discuss your Seer abilities and what the next step is for the experiments on your genetics."

"Yes, I was just thinking about that."

Alma studies a corner of the room before looking back at me.

"I do not have any prophetic abilities myself, but my mother did. So, I have enough knowledge to mentor you in harnessing and controlling them."

I sigh with relief at the news. "Thank goodness! I was worried my visions would become out of control. I have only had one—and it was at an inopportune time—so I would hate for it to happen regularly like that."

Alma pats my shoulder. "Yes, and if you have a vision that does not come to fruition at the time you *think* it should, then it probably means a similar situation will happen in the future, though not always as we perceive it. You should begin sensing things as well, though I cannot tell you what they would be seeing as I am not familiar with such ethereal matters—you will be the only one to ascertain the sensations."

"Ah, that makes sense." Perhaps that is what this baffling feeling around Gideon is, even if it is not a vision.

Alma nods in appreciation at my quick learning but reassuringly pats my knee. "You will grow accustomed to the visions. Tomorrow we can take you to the labs if you like. Lucas has already called the head scientist to let him know you have full access, and your blood will need to be drawn for tests. But I am unsure if he let the man know what he is testing. He has also been told you are *filling* in for Xander."

I look up at the ceiling and take a breath, knowing I will eventually need to be able to hear Xander's name and not spiral into a cloud of grief. Alma's gentle hand on my shoulder pulls me to reality and I send her a strained smile.

"It will take time to heal, dear. Just let the process of grief happen naturally. Now, this old hag is ready to hit the hay, so I suggest you catch up on some rest as well. The next few days will be tiring."

I nod and walk Alma to the door. "Why don't you stay here for the night, Alma? I know the streets are safe now, but it is dark out there. I think I saw a spare mattress under the bed."

I'm still becoming accustomed to the idea of luxuries like a *second* mattress, but I will not complain.

Alma considers my suggestion briefly before shaking her head. "No, I will be alright dear. The short walk will be beneficial after all that cake, tea, and dinner."

I laugh as she rubs her non-existent stomach as if it is protruding from her slim frame.

Alma leaves and I stand by the door, watching her disappear down the stairs until she exits the tower's entrance. Exhaustion causes my eyes to droop heavily and my mouth opens into a jaw-cracking yawn. Wincing at the sound, I shut the door with a click then make my way to the bedroom. Standing in the entrance, I cross my arms and narrow my eyes at the large bed, still fragrant from the scent of Xander.

Great.

Sighing with exasperation but too tired to care in the moment, I strip down to the simple underwear Alma kindly made for me then slide into the sheets. My breath hitches at the icy temperature, the cold caress of silken material against my skin verging on the point of painful. I vigorously rub my arms and legs around to warm the bed, and once satisfied with the result, I relax and become limp.

My muscles sigh in relief at the reprieve of lying down, yet my mind screams in protest at the inescapable reminder of Xander. As my eyes begin to flicker shut, the briefest white flash of a vision assails me before I fall into a deep slumber, though I'm far too exhausted to grasp its meaning. A distant image of a pale, soulless man haunts my dreams for the entirety of the night.

37

GIDEON

THE SMOOTH AMBER LIQUID burns its way down my throat as I tip back the glass. Brandy will help me sleep tonight so I'm fully rested and alert tomorrow—for my first day on the job.

It will be strange filling in for Lucas, and I still do not completely trust the small, raven-haired woman who is to be the new Ruler.

I am also none too happy about my custodian duties.

Rubbing my face roughly, I stand up with a loud sigh and take my empty glass to the sink to rinse it, then stand with my fingers pinching the bridge of my nose.

"For the good of the city," I remind myself, quoting Lucas's words when he contacted me. He understood my hesitance once he explained who I would be second in command to. Not just any woman, but an *outsider* who knows nothing of the semantics of running a city. In the entire history of The Vanquishing, there has never been a female Ruler.

I shake my head, unsure what to think about the ocean-eyed beauty who already had Xander wrapped around her finger.

Look where that got him.

Leaning over and gripping the edge of the bench tightly, I clench my jaw in frustration at the entire situation. There is something strange about that woman and I cannot quite establish what the main element is to be causing this thought. Until I can ascertain what it is, I consider her a potential threat. Lucas assured me to trust her, but he was not the one who left Xander's body in the wastelands. Rae was.

Tilting my head sharply to one side, a loud crack releases the tension tightening my neck and I exhale with relief, repeating the movement for the opposite side.

I'm going to go crazy within the city walls.

Maybe I can convince Rae to come hunting with me and my usual party.

A dry, abrupt laugh escapes me, and I shake my head at the notion. My job is to protect and guide her. Not lead her into danger.

My men, as well as those who participate in the hunts, all voiced their complaints and concerns when I revealed I would not be leading the hunting rallies anymore. They were irritated that one of the guards—the one who was not chosen by Rae for second—was allocated to be their new hunting leader.

"Lucky bastard," I murmur to myself.

All citizens that hunt for Segment One are allocated to a guard for extra protection and guidance. It has been my job ever since Xander's father died.

"Well, it was my job," I grumble and push off the bench, making my way to the bedroom.

I strip down completely and slide into the sheets, only to toss and turn.

The bed's too bloody soft.

Most people would kill for a soft place to sleep but I have only ever slept on the ground. Except when I was with *her.*

The thought causes me to roll over and pinch the bridge of my nose until I force the bitter memories down and resume tossing and turning to find a comfortable position.

After being restless for a few minutes, I huff in annoyance then jerk up from the bed, dragging the sheets to the cold, hard ground. Rolling onto my back, I instantly fall asleep.

The sound of shuffling footsteps outside the residence's door has me bolting up with my dagger clutched tightly in my hand. It stays under my pillow when I sleep, and I keep my hand resting on it all night.

The muffled noise continues, and I narrow my eyes at the darkened entrance across the living space. I have kept the bedroom door open for this reason; the view is clear from this room out to the entrance, enabling me to establish if there are any threats at the residence's entrance.

Like in this instance.

Moving stealthily, I creep out of the bedroom and to the door, hiding beside it with my dagger raised. My entire frame bunches with tension as the handle slightly moves, and I become deathly still as the door shifts inward. The heavy metal begins opening towards me, allowing the panel to hide my presence until I can ambush the trespasser. A pleased smile grows across my face. Maybe a fight will help my restlessness and frustration. Nevertheless, anyone who *sneaks* into someone's home is always a threat. Not that this is *my* home.

My eyes move to the crack under the door as I watch the shadow move farther in, and my muscles coil in preparation to lunge for the assailant whose profile is about to emerge into view.

Just one more step...

The figure enters the room and I charge forward, taking the person down with me, their face pressed to the ground. A loud, feminine shriek has me darting up in shock as Rae rolls to her back and looks up at me with fear etched across her face. Her eyes dip down my body and widen at what they see; then a flash of something unfamiliar instantly replaces the fear.

The silky, alabaster skin over her cheeks and exposed décolletage flushes a pretty shade of red in the moonlight streaming through the small window.

I look down, realising I'm naked, and an unfamiliar smile tugs at the corner of my lips.

Perhaps I can scare her out of the Segment and far away. Nakedness does not bother me; it is just flesh covering the bones, blood, and organs. But it seems to bother our new Ruler.

Rae's eyes dart away from me and she awkwardly stares at the ceiling. "Can you please put some clothes on?" Her voice then turns vehement with a hint of defiance, "And why did you attack me?"

I stare at her silently for a moment, enjoying her discomfort. Eventually I speak in a casual tone, my voice rough from its lack of use. "I will put some clothes on when you explain why you are breaking into my residence at an unreasonable hour of the morning."

It is still dark outside, indicating the city will be fast asleep for another hour at least.

Rae keeps her eyes trained on the ceiling and I take the opportunity to rake my gaze down her, approving the practical attire she is wearing.

At least she appears to have common sense and does not prance around in those ridiculous dresses most women love to wear.

My eyes shift to her pink face as she clears her throat to reply awkwardly, "Alma mentioned I could let myself in if I ever needed anything. I did not realise you would still be asleep. And naked." The last word is whispered.

My hand rises to squeeze the nape of my neck at the mention of Alma, who essentially forced Lucas, Xander, and me under her motherly wings when we were younger.

Some things never change, I think, remembering back to her meddling ways. It appears she is still meddling, though her intentions are unclear.

"Firstly, it is rude to just barge into anyone's home without knocking," I quietly but curtly say.

Rae peers up at me, her baffled expression indicating she did not know any better. Her eyes instantly widen once realising I'm still naked, and she whips her head back to look at the ceiling.

Brief amusement fills me at her heating face, though the amusement is quickly replaced by curiosity at her reaction to my reprimand.

"Why are you seemingly confused? And what is so urgent that you need to bother me at this time of the morning?"

Humiliation flashes across Rae's face as she continues staring at the ceiling, remaining flat on her back. Her pretty mouth opens then snaps shut again, so I patiently wait for her to organise the seemingly chaotic thoughts in her mind.

She eventually clears her throat. "I have lived most of my life outside of civilisation so never learned such social etiquettes." Silence fills the air before she adds with a whisper, "I lived in caves most of my life."

Her answer intrigues me. I knew she was an outsider—not local to Segment One—but I assumed she came from another settlement. I wait silently for her to continue as my mind comprehends living such a life. The life of a survivor.

"I'm sorry for letting myself in," Rae says quietly, and she meets my eyes without wavering. I can see she is trying her hardest to keep them from straying downwards, which amuses me. Every woman I have ever encountered have usually been so forward in their interest, even though I ignore them since I prefer my solitary life. Nothing will ever tempt me to settle down with a woman again. I shiver involuntarily at the thought.

Never again.

Rae stares at me expectantly and I realise she is waiting for me to reply.

"I understand... you did not know any better. Just do not do it again. Now, *why* did you let yourself in to see me?"

Rae sighs and looks away, nibbling her lower lip. It appears to be a regular habit which causes me to tauten every time. Her bright, aquatic eyes meet mine and the sorrow reflected in them almost floors me. I have had my own share of grief in my eight and thirty years and have seen plenty of other civilians grieve—but the depth of pain and trauma I see in her eyes is unlike anything I've witnessed before. They are *haunted*.

My muscles rigidify as her eyes become suspiciously glassy and I look at the exit, wondering if I should make my escape. I'm inept in handling a crying person let alone a woman.

"I desperately needed company and did not want to wake Alma," Rae whispers, and I look back at her, concern filling me at the hopelessness etched across her face.

I stare at her silently, assessing the truth of her words, and conclude that no one could fake that much sorrow.

What have I gotten myself into? This is the reason women are not Rulers.

I squeeze the bridge of my nose with two fingers before reluctantly convincing myself to help her.

"I will put some clothes on and then pour you a drink."

As I stalk from the living area into the bedroom, I feel her burning gaze infiltrating my bare back and glance over my shoulder to see her ogling the length of my naked body. Her lidded eyes meet mine and she gasps at realising I caught her unabashedly staring. Strange satisfaction fills me at the ordeal, and a smile teases the corner of my lips at her flushing, mortified face.

Striding into the bedroom, I efficiently pull on pants and a shirt, each of my movements swift and not bothering with any warm clothing, knowing the cold will keep me alert. By the time I have dressed and made my way out, Rae has composed herself and is sitting on the couch awkwardly. Her eyes shift haphazardly and land everywhere but on me, so I stride over to stand in front of her. I'm tempted to ask why my nakedness bothers her but feel it would be crossing the professional boundary into personal territory.

I do not do personal. Not with anyone. Not anymore.

Alma is the closest person to family I have ever had, though I know I've been a recluse, and I cannot remember the last time

I visited her for some cake. Sudden amusement fills me at her underlying reprimand for the very same thing the previous night.

Xander and Lucas were friends as children and still are, but I kept to myself as we got older even after Xander's father died.

"Would you like a brandy?" I ask, forcing her to look at me. Relief fills Rae's eyes at my now attired state, and I bite back a dry laugh.

The reaction is... interesting.

"Yes, please."

Walking over to the bench, I lean down and grab the bottle filled with the coveted amber liquid, and additionally pull out two glasses. Holding the cups together between my fingers, I pour a lick of brandy into each. Rae joins me at the bench, and I hold a cup out to her, slightly amused at her eager grab as she snatches it greedily from me. I stare at her and she looks up with a sheepish expression.

"Thank you, Gideon."

I roll my shoulders back, perturbed by how much I like the sound of my name on her lips, but quickly suppress the odd feeling.

No time for that nonsense.

Clearing my throat, I reply, "You're welcome," before tipping my own brandy back.

Once Rae swallows the last of her brandy, I gesture for her to sit on the couch, now knowing she just desires company.

Buggered if I know what to do or say though.

What classifies as company?

I figure I'll just sit silently and let her steer the conversation. My eyes twitch at the thought of casual conversation with *anyone* but I inwardly sigh, knowing Rae and I need to become comfortable with each other if we are to spend copious amounts of time together.

Rae sits as far away from me as she can—which suits me fine—and I carefully study her intricate facial expressions which she probably does not even realise are flashing across her lovely face.

I spent my entire life assessing people's body language and can successfully ascertain what a person's motives are, just by the twitch of a nose.

We sit silently for a few moments until Rae shifts uncomfortably under my assessing gaze.

"Why are you so quiet and impassive all the time?" Her question surprises me, and I'm pleased she is able to determine a person's nature within a short amount of time. This will be a helpful attribute as Ruler.

I still do not welcome the personal question, though, and uncomfortably rub the back of my neck. "I prefer to watch people rather than engage in trivial conversation."

Rae narrows her eyes at me, defiance sparking within their depths as she crosses her arms over her chest. I realise too late that she has misconstrued my answer as an insult towards her character, and quickly chime in to amend my error.

"I do not mean it in the way you are thinking."

This seems to appease Rae and she softens slightly, uncrossing her arms. "It's okay. I only engage in *trivial conversation* now because I had been by myself for approximately three years prior to Xander bringing me here. I enjoy being able to talk to another human. Although their unfamiliarity is uncomfortable at first."

Comprehension unfolds at the pieces of the puzzle coming together and I realise there is more complexity and history to this woman than I had previously considered. Shaking my head from the sentient thoughts, I study Rae as an array of emotions flash across her face.

Deciding to remain silent, I wait for her to continue talking, but she becomes uncomfortable under my calculating stare. I shift slightly on the couch, bringing one leg up casually to face her, and she does the same. Rae sighs and her gaze falls to the floor as sadness suddenly transforms her demeanour, causing me recoil at the unpredictable change.

I sharply suck air in through my teeth before addressing her quietly against my own nature. "Are you okay?"

Rae clears her throat and looks up at me with a slight watery sheen to her bright, cerulean eyes.

"I'm okay," she replies quietly. Her shoulders slump. "Well, not really. I miss Xander. I have never mourned anyone in my life—except when Pa died, but not even to this extent—as there has been no one else to lose. I'm sad and am incapable of managing this feeling."

I'm left astounded at her confession and am unsure how to respond, so I remain silent and watch Rae meaningfully as she sorts through her conflicting emotions. Her admission makes me realise she could not have murdered Xander to take his position as Ruler like I originally speculated.

Rae's eyes swirl like a violent storm as she gazes off into the distance. The unfamiliar emotion of empathy clenches my chest and I lean forward on my elbows and scratch my chin.

It is just a one-off occurrence, I convince myself as my brows pull inwards.

"Why are you frowning?" Rae asks, and my expression deepens as I look at her. She quietly laughs and points to my forehead. "You are doing it again. You rarely display any facial expression, but when you do, it is always a frown."

Her truthful insight irritates me, and I lean back to cross my arms over my chest. Rae's eyes dip briefly down and pink tinges her cheeks at whatever she observes. Her reaction has my arms loosening, and she clears her throat awkwardly.

"I did not mean that in a negative manner. I was just curious as to what goes on inside your mind that causes you to appear so distressed. I'm only concerned, that is all." Her hypnotizing eyes dart back up.

I slightly relax and unfold my arms at her explanation, then carefully evaluate her. Everything she says astounds me, making her even more of a mystery. This somewhat pleases me, but only slightly, and my original objections and view of her is slowly morphing favourably. There appears to now be hope for the new Ruler of Segment One.

38

RAE

WARMTH SUFFUSES MY CHEEKS and I shift uncomfortably under Gideon's assessing gaze.

Gah! Why does he have to watch me like that?!

I go to clear my throat awkwardly again but stop myself midway, realising the action and sound is becoming habit around Gideon.

"Well, if you can ask me why I frown all the time, then I can ask you why you blush all the time," Gideon calmly says with subdued irritation, though his voice is still gravelly. I cannot work out if it is like that naturally or just from disuse.

His words suddenly sink in and my eyes widen with mortification. I would rather sever my own tongue before telling him why my face turns annoyingly red. It never used to, but since being exposed to Xander and the eye-opening experiences of intimacy, it is suddenly a regular occurrence—like he awoke something deeply seeded inside of me that had been hibernating my entire life.

My eyes drop to the floor with embarrassment and I mumble in reply, knowing my face is stained red again. "That is fine, I no longer need to know why you frown, anyway."

A quiet chuckle has me flicking my head up in surprise at the pleasant, though rough, sound. I had not heard his laugh or seen any indication of amusement until now.

Gideon's own surprise at his rare display of humour is also evident as his mouth swiftly returns to an expressionless line and he looks away to clear his throat.

I twist my hands and look up at Gideon, overcome with the need to address a more serious matter. "Will you take me to the lab later today?"

He immediately shifts forward to lean on his elbows at the request and regards me with suspicion. "Why do you need to go to the lab?"

I bite my lip in contemplation and calculate how much I can disclose. Gideon's speckled, emerald gaze drops to my lips and I immediately stop nibbling them, once again feeling heat rise to my cheeks at the familiar sign of desire clouding his eyes.

Perhaps I can use the distraction to my benefit in the future?

Men seemed to be easily swayed and distracted.

I stiffen my shoulders and take my lower lip between my teeth again to gauge Gideon's reaction, inwardly celebrating as his frame becomes rigid and his gaze evasive.

I take the opportunity to brush over the reply with a superficial answer, hoping he is somehow too distracted.

"I figured as the new Ruler I should become familiar with all aspects of the city."

Gideon blinks, snapping from his discomfort and studiously staring at me, his caginess once again taking place.

Blast, he is too intelligent to fool.

At least he will be a good guard.

"I can take you there at first light," Gideon replies slowly, "but only if you tell me the *real* reason you require to visit the lab."

His stern, unrelenting stare makes me swallow and I break the intensity of his gaze by looking away.

"Has Lucas told you anything?"

Gideon stiffens and his lips tighten.

Oh. Clearly not.

His low, threatening voice confirms my suspicions.

"And what *exactly* might he have told me?"

My hands twist in the crook of my lap and I keep my eyes downcast, unsure on how to solve this dilemma without revealing too much.

"Rae, if we are to work with each other daily—and *closely*—we both need to be open and honest with each other."

I peer up at him from under my lashes and hesitantly nod, knowing his reasoning makes perfect sense, then remind myself that Gideon was selected by Lucas and approved by Alma.

Surely, he would be trustworthy and have good intentions if I told him?

Deciding to take the chance and reveal everything, I tilt my head at him questioningly. "Can I have another drink first?"

Gideon raises an eyebrow in amusement at my odd request. "You are the only woman I've ever met to drink so much brandy."

I tilt my chin up at him stubbornly. "Well, that just goes to show you have not met a woman like me before."

Gideon chuckles, the sound foreign to both our ears, and he gets up to casually make his way over to the bench, glancing behind as he does. "You are correct in your assumption. I definitely have not met a woman like you before."

Feeling pleasantly relaxed after another drink, I adjust my position on the couch to face Gideon once again and take a deep breath. His eyes search my face as he patiently waits for me to speak.

"I'm related to Alma by blood," I begin, and surprise flashes in his eyes at the new piece of information. "I only found out when I was brought here by Xander. Anyway, Alma told me about my heritage and how my abilities and genetics have been around for centuries. So… because of my ancestors, I seem to have an Immunity to Breathers."

I deliver the last statement bluntly and Gideon stares at me dumbfounded.

"You are actually Immune."

I nod, ignoring his tone of disbelief. "If you do not believe me, ask Alma."

I wait in suspense as several emotions cross Gideon's face before it turns impassive again. He brusquely dips his chin in acceptance.

We both remain silent as Gideon studies me before glancing away. It is as if my appearance makes him uncomfortable.

Unable to wait any longer, I break the silence. "So, *will* you take me to the lab today?"

Gideon briefly closes his eyes and takes a deep breath before looking at me cautiously. "Yes. But we will drop into Alma's first so she can verify what you have told me."

I stare at him with disbelief as frustration blooms like a field of flowers after a bout of torrential rain. I cross my arms with a huff over my chest. "You still don't believe me?"

"I like to be a hundred per cent certain of everything."

I stubbornly tilt my chin. "Perhaps you are not suitable as my second in command if you are incapable of even trusting me. Besides, if I request to go somewhere, you cannot deny me."

Gideon pinches the bridge of his nose and tightly shuts his eyes, then drops his hand to abruptly stand, towering over me as he stares down with indignation.

The sudden change of attitude has my mind whirling and I stand up as well, not wanting him to think he can intimidate me. Secretly, I celebrate his display of emotion, regardless of how troubling it is.

I poke my finger at his chest and ignore the marble I feel there as I accentuate each of my words with a jab. "You. Don't. Scare. Me."

Gideon narrows his green eyes at each poke and his muscles harden with tension, but I ignore any warning bells ringing in the back of my head. I continue reprimanding him. "In fact," I seethe, jabbing his chest again, "you think you are entirely mysterious with your impassive attitude! But I have you figured out!"

I gasp as Gideon's hand snakes out and imprisons the one assaulting his chest as he quietly, but threateningly replies. "Is that so? And what exactly have you figured out, *little mouse*?"

He knows the code to get into the tower just as every guard does.

My ears ring and the room surrounding me becomes a blur, the mocking tone used to quote Xander's pet name triggering the tempestuous feelings torpedoing through me. Angry tears fill my eyes and I choke back a sob at Gideon's spite—bringing up the man I lost. I spin on my toes to rush from the residence and feel tangible relief when there is no indication of him pursuing me.

Without realising the direction I have taken, I end up in front of Alma's colourful shop. My tear-stained face has the early risers of Segment One casting me curious stares, but I ignore each one.

Alma is up early and milling about in her shop before opening, but she spots me through the glass, instantly rushing to let me in, concern shadowing her wrinkled face.

"Dear child, whatever is the matter?" she asks gently, ushering me to the back of the residence.

I'm oblivious to the world around me as I stare blankly, and before I know it, I'm sitting in Alma's kitchen at the table with a concentrated brew of tea beneath my nose. Alma sits on an adjacent seat and watches me with sharp eyes before leaning forward.

"Now, dear, tell me what is bothering you."

I pick my tea up with shaky hands and sip the hot, soothing liquid. The brandy instantly subdues my distress and I inhale deeply to reply, "I do not think Gideon is the right choice. He cannot be my second in command and I told him he might not be suitable."

Alma's eyes alight with curiosity at my concession and she raises her eyebrows. "Oh? And why is that?"

My eyes drop to the floor and I mumble, "Because he's a dick."

Alma tuts. "Rae, you should not use this language now you are to be a Ruler."

I refrain from rolling my eyes. It hardly seems like an issue during this day and age, but I do not want to upset Alma since she has done so much for me. "Sorry, Alma, I'll make sure I keep my colourful language private. Now, can we replace Gideon with one of the other men who were an option?"

Alma slowly shakes her head. "No, dear, I'm afraid that would be unfair on everyone, as those men have been allocated to hunting parties already. And you still have not told me *why* you are so adamant on replacing him."

I sigh, realising Alma will not let this go. "He is just so… insufferable!"

Abruptly standing, I start pacing the room to rant my frustrations. "He thinks he's so tough and mysterious! But really, he's just a coward who hides behind his silence as he judges everyone else!"

Defeated, I slump down onto the floor and look to Alma with a melancholy visage.

"He called me Xander's pet name. But not in a nice way. He really detests me, Alma, and it will be impossible to live with him shadowing me if he is going to treat me with such disdain."

Alma sighs and weighs her words carefully. "Gideon is a good man, Rae. The best you will find. But he does have his issues with women and does not trust them easily."

I frown and look up at Alma in question. "But *why* doesn't he trust women?"

Alma taps her finger on the table, ascertaining how much to reveal. "It is for Gideon to tell you when he is ready to open up. But I will leave you with a little piece of his history, so you understand him better and perhaps feel more compassionate towards his conduct."

I lean off the wall in suspense of the information I'm about to receive. "He was hurt very badly by a woman he loved dearly—the details are not for me to recount—but now Gideon is distrusting of women. Particularly ones he is… attracted to."

I throw my head back as an incredulous laugh bursts from me at Alma's preposterous insinuation.

"He definitely does not have any inclination towards me, Alma. You can tell the bulky oaf despises me from a mile away."

Alma chuckles and her eyes twinkle at me. "Ah, dear Rae, you do not know the ways of men and how they think, as you were not raised with them. I can see the way he looked at you, the glimpses of attraction. Although, I can see from your point of view that his mistrust was certainly more dominant."

I frown, concern filling me. "Well, he definitely needs to be replaced if he will be distracted so easily. Particularly if he will not trust me… I'm to be his Ruler for goodness sake!"

Deep down, I know I'm grasping for any trivial excuse. The terrifying thought of anyone trying to replace Xander grips me tightly.

Yes, Gideon is extremely attractive in his own rugged, subdued way, and he is the second man in my life that my traitorous body *really* reacts to. But *no one* will ever be able to fill the gaping hole in my heart that Xander left. Regardless of how many times I deny it.

I leave Alma's shop feeling slightly better.

I guess just being able to talk to someone makes everything seem less overwhelming.

Alma convinces me to give Gideon a chance and I chuckle at her devious ways. I'm extremely stubborn but it appears Alma is more so.

It must run in the family.

As I step onto the street and start walking in the direction of the lab—I made Alma tell me where it is—a little girl no older than four catches my attention.

Her grubby little hands rub large, tear-filled eyes as she cries and looks around frantically. The sun has risen enough for light to flood the streets and citizens rush about, ignoring the distressed girl. My heart constricts at the sight and I rush over, concern filling me for her wellbeing. Dropping to my knees, I crouch in front of her, careful not to intimidate the little thing.

"Hi there, sweetie," I coo. Her cries turn into jagged breaths and sobs at hearing my gentle voice. I brush a strand of wild, unruly hair behind her ear and her eyes widen at the affection. "My name is Rae, what's yours?"

The little girl looks around, her brows creased, then looks back at me with large, brown doe eyes as stray tears leak down her filthy, chubby cheeks. My chest constricts at how familiar she looks, but I brush the feeling aside and reassure myself her olive complexion and dark hair is a common trait in this Segment. I shoot a kind smile at the little girl who is studying me dubiously, assessing whether I'm a threat or not. Her rosy, little lips open as she finally whispers to me. "Lee-lee."

Relief fills me and I nod earnestly. "That's a very pretty name, Lily."

Her eyes brighten at my compliment and she shyly looks away before her current dilemma upsets her again. Lily's chin quivers and her eyes fill with renewed tears. I gently grab her hands and squeeze them reassuringly.

"Hey, Lily, is there something I can help you find? I'm great at finding treasures, so surely I can find what you have lost?"

I assume she has lost her parents, but I make sure to word my sentence in an exciting way that seems appealing to little kids. The method is exclusively a supposition since I'm lacking in experience with children.

I loved finding trinkets as a child, so surely, she will too.

Lily's chubby cheeks protrude as a hopeful smile crosses her petite face and I exhale relief. "Treasure?"

I nod ardently and lean forward to whisper as if I'm telling a secret. "Yes, lots of pretty, sparkly things that shine. We might even discover some when we can find your parents."

Lily's chin quivers again as her lips pull down and she wails, "I can't find my mummy!"

My heart clenches at the fear in her voice and I pull her into a hug, ignoring the strange stares of people walking around us. "We will find your mummy, Lily," I say into her hair and she pulls away to look at me, hope etched across her face.

"You find my mummy like you find treasure?"

I smile at how adorable she is, her speech not quite developed, and bop her playfully on the nose. "Exactly. Now do you remember where you live?"

A frown crosses Lily's face as her nose crinkles in confusion, and she shakes her head before wailing, "Mummy didn't come home, so I looked for her!"

I quickly pull Lily into a hug and she clings on to me. Biting my lower lip with uncertainty, I decide to spend however long it will take to look for Lily's house and her mother.

I stand up, lifting Lily with me as I go, glancing in each direction with the little bundle clinging onto me. Spinning on my heels, I freeze at seeing the familiar large frame standing against the wall adjacent to us.

Gideon.

He is standing in the shadows, but I can make out his bright, mossy eyes that penetrate straight through me, though I cannot decipher the unusual emotion whirling in their depths. I'm used to only seeing disdain and mistrust.

Releasing an exasperated sigh, irritation rapidly fills me; knowing I will need his help to find Lily's home and mother. There was no mention of a father, so I'm assuming Lily does not have one. It is common for children to have no father as a lot of them perish on dangerous hunting missions.

With a huff, I cross the street to him, and he pulls his shoulders back, straightening his spine as I approach.

"What are you doing hiding in the shadows, Gideon?"

He affixes me with his unwavering gaze, then his eyes flick to Lily, softening at the sight of the little girl with her face shyly plastered into my neck. I tilt my head curiously at Gideon's reaction to her but wait silently.

"I'm doing my job and watching over you." His voice is hushed but much deeper and more gravelly than usual as he answers, sending shivers racing up my spine.

Oh. That makes sense.

I awkwardly shift on my feet and prop Lily up on my hip as she slides down slightly, and Gideon's eyes fall to her again.

"What is the story with the little one?"

I look down at the little cherub who is rapidly falling asleep as I bounce her gently on my side. "Lily cannot find her mother, who apparently never arrived home, and I'm thinking she has no father at all, seeing as he would have probably stopped the girl leaving home. Unless she snuck out, I suppose. Either way, the little cutie decided to leave in search of her ma."

"You are a natural with children."

The random compliment has me snapping my head up to stare at Gideon in surprise. My mouth gapes open and I shut it when his eyes fall there and darken to a deep turquoise, resembling the tumultuous waves of an ocean illuminated by the sun. It is the same expression he had when I first discovered him watching me from across the street.

Now that I can see his face on closer inspection, I surmise it is a mixture of desire and something else I cannot quite determine. Heat rises over my chest, warming my face, and I drop my eyes to break the intense connection between us.

Alma was right.

I look down at Lily as a smokescreen of my cowardice and clear my throat before looking back up at Gideon. His face has returned to its typical impassive countenance.

"Does the city library have any way of searching records for the addresses of citizens within the Segment?"

Gideon nods abruptly before his eyes travel to the sleeping girl again. "Only if you have their name though."

I contemplatively chew my lower lip and rack my mind for ideas, glancing up to see Gideon briefly staring at my mouth before looking away—his stony expression quickly taking place.

An idea suddenly pops into my mind, and I exclaim quietly, "What if we ask Lily what her mother looks like? Surely someone will know her by description, and we can put out a transmission to all citizens. The transmission can describe both Lily and her mother. Either her mother will come forward or someone that knows the mother and daughter will let us know."

Gideon looks at me with respect in his eyes, and I silently celebrate the small victory. "That is a valid idea."

I gently rouse Lily—her need for a nap obvious—by placing a soft kiss to her forehead. "Lily, honey, can you wake up please?"

Lily looks up at me sleepily and sees Gideon—her eyes widening at the large, strange man. Fear fills her eyes and I quickly rush to reassure her. "This is Gideon, a close friend who also searches for treasure. He is very kind."

Lily softens at the mention of treasure but remains wary of Gideon's presence, and I recognise the look of mistrust. The little girl likely does not have many male influences in her life, which unquestionably indicates no father.

Pleased that she has calmed, I gently place her on the ground and crouch to her level.

"Sweetie, can you tell me what your mother looks like?"

Lily glances at Gideon and I gently grab her chin to tilt her face back to me. "Ignore him, he looks like a big, scary oaf, but he's really a nice man."

Gideon clears his throat at my marginally insulting comment, but Lily giggles and I glance up with a cheeky smile at him. The smile freezes on my face at the expression he sears me with and I quickly look back at Lily. I'm unsure how to deal with the mixed display of desire and something more profound in his entrancing jade eyes.

"So, Lily, what colour are your mother's eyes?"

Lily scrunches her face in concentration and then exclaims as she remembers. "Green!"

Gideon stiffens beside me and I glance up at the frown pinching his brows.

I ignore him, looking back to Lily to speak with an encouraging tone, "Well done, sweetie! Now, what colour is her hair?"

"Black."

Now it is my turn to stiffen. I hate the reminder of Nelinha but as I study Lily, my eyes widen impossibly. It is as clear as the untainted water of a crystal lake now; the sweet girl does uncannily share the same physical traits as the woman who tried to murder me.

39

RAE

B Y GIDEON'S REACTION TO LILY'S DESCRIPTION OF HER MOTHER, I conclude that he either *knows* Nelinha or at least knows *of* her. My shoulders drop, the sinking feeling in my stomach weighing heavy as boulders, and I glance up at Gideon, wondering if he knows Nelinha is dead. Another troubling thought suddenly plagues me; *how* did this little child survive on her own without a mother or father for that long? Nausea threatens to rise at the mere idea of this little girl starving to death.

Though if Nelinha had left her alone to see clients regularly, it would force the tiny thing to be self-sufficient.

Anger immediately suppresses the nausea, and I narrow my eyes at the possibility of Nelinha's questionable parenting.

"Maybe it is just coincidence that her mother looks like the town *masseuse*," I suggest weakly, knowing Lily's physical likeness to Nelinha is irrefutable evidence. Gideon scrubs a hand roughly over his chin and he glances down at the little bairn who is watching us both curiously.

"The library will have a record of any children Nelinha has had. *If* she had any. No one has mentioned anything of that vile woman producing offspring but the resemblances Lily and Nelinha share are too noticeable to ignore."

I stand and press a hand to my stomach at the nausea that has suddenly taken hold of me, and I lean against the cool stone wall, closing my eyes. A large, warm hand gently grasping my shoulder has me tensing, and I open my eyes to see Gideon peering down at me in concern. "Are you alright?"

My heart flutters at the display of concern and I weakly smile at him. "Yes, I will be fine. Let us head to the library. The sooner we can solve this, the better it will be for Lily."

I look down when Lily's hand slides into mine and I instantly forget all prior concerns. My heart plummets for the little, innocent human that has yet to experience heartbreak and grief.

Gideon and I walk either side of Lily, her hands holding each of ours, and she swings them playfully as if nothing is wrong in the world. I look over at Gideon, who fixes me with a gaze full of such deep emotion, my breath hitches.

I need to find out what happened in his past that made him the man he is today.

There are too many unanswered questions and *knowledge is power*. Not knowing matters has always made me extremely uncomfortable.

We make it to the large wooden door of the library and Gideon keys in the code, letting go of Lily to push it open before gesturing us through. Lily lets out a happy squeal, running to the first tall bookshelf. She pulls out a book, pure delight etched across her sweet little face. A smile extends across my own as she settles on the ground and chatters happily to herself as she turns each page, pointing at the colourful pictures.

A sudden unfamiliar pang hits my chest and I rub at it, frowning at Lily. The strangest feeling begins unfurling deeply in my womb again. My hand rests on my stomach, the peculiar sensation unsettling me, and I look at Gideon who is watching me explicitly.

He shuts the door and locks it behind him, then takes two long strides to stand directly in front of me. I inwardly curse at the butterflies fluttering violently in my abdomen due to his proximity but cannot tear my eyes away from his probing gaze. My lips part as he lifts a hand to brush back an unruly strand of hair and I close my eyes at the physical touch, hoping he cannot hear my heart thumping erratically against my chest.

Why am I feeling like this? I still love Xander.

The uncertainty exasperates me, and I step away from Gideon, the reminder of Xander wrenching me out of the foolish haze. My sudden retreat seemingly snaps Gideon from his strange behaviour as well, and his face turns to granite once again.

My eyes dip to his enticing lips as he speaks, and I only partially hear what he is saying.

"Rae, did you hear what I said?" Gideon's low voice snaps me from my hypnosis, and I blink up at him, my face warming with embarrassment.

I attempt to recall the few words I heard and remember the mention of Lily and archives.

How could I forget we are here to help Lily!

I inwardly chastise myself for becoming distracted and lift my chin at Gideon stubbornly.

"Of course, I heard. We need to access the archives to see if Nelinha was Lily's mother."

Gideon narrows his eyes at me and then nods grimly.

"Yes. Though, if that is the case, then we have a large issue on our hands."

I tilt my head curiously, wondering if he somehow knows that Nelinha died at the hands of a Breather. Gideon deciphers my silent question and elaborates, "The deaths of all citizens are reported to the appropriate guards so they can dispose of bodies regularly."

"All of the guards are told when people die?"

Gideon rubs the back of his neck and looks away, his cheeks slightly pink, and my eyes widen with the realisation of what he is implying. "No, only certain guards are informed and they dispose of each body. But the death of the Segment's only masseuse spread like wildfire... most guards had used her services. They will all be hoping a new masseuse appears soon."

I frown at the unsavoury emotion of jealousy unfurling in my chest, recalling the feeling from when Nelinha had come to see Xander at his home. The reaction only disturbs me because I know the emotion is derived from the thought that *Gideon* has also been with the evil woman.

I push my shoulders back and force myself not to care.

It is his business and has nothing to do with me.

Besides, I have a little girl to worry about now.

Feigning nonchalance, I raise my chin at Gideon. "I see. Well, let us first verify if Nelinha *is* Lily's mother and go from there. Lead the way."

Gideon studies me momentarily, his gaze sharp, before nodding and striding off. I quickly fall in step behind him and look down at Lily as we pass her. Her large brown eyes peer up at me and I pause, once again taken aback by how familiar the gaze is, though not like Nelinha's. Gideon must sense I have stopped following him and turns to wait patiently, his hands linked behind his back. Lily shoots me a toothy smile and my heart clenches again. "Now, can you be a good girl and sit here until we return, Lily?"

Lily nods exuberantly and I smile softly at her innocence. "Good. If you don't break your promise, we can find some treasure after. How does that sound?"

Lily's eyes brighten at the mention of treasure and locks of dark hair bounce around her face as she enthusiastically nods. Satisfied Lily will stay out of mischief, I turn to follow Gideon, abruptly stopping when I see the fervid emotion clouding his eyes as he stares at me.

No longer able to ignore his strange mannerisms, I throw my hands in the air with exasperation. "Why do you keep staring at me like that?!"

Gideon's expression immediately becomes guarded and he momentarily looks away, his jaw clenching, before turning back to answer me in his usual emotionless tone.

"No reason. Just keeping an eye on you."

He spins around without another word and stalks off. I run to catch up, silently fuming as we reach a nook deep within the library that has a section of city records.

"Shouldn't the files be stored electronically?" I ask. "The Segment has enough resources and means to do so."

Gideon grunts. "No. Most Segments will store them electronically, but the founders of this Segment wanted to preserve the old ways of civilisation as much as they could by protecting and preserving books. Implementing the use of handwriting also does this."

"Oh." That makes sense.

The room falls silent with Gideon ignoring me as he scans the various shelves and the signs protruding from them. Eventually he stops in front of a sign with indecipherable markings.

Well, Gideon can probably read it.

Sliding out his selection, he hands me a discoloured scroll without looking at me, then retrieves another and unrolls it. I hold mine awkwardly, unsure of what I'm supposed to do. Gideon glances up to frown at me, then looks down at the scroll in my hand.

"You need to read through it to look for Nelinha's name."

Heat travels up my neck and reddens my face with embarrassment, and I look down at the floor to whisper in reply. "I cannot read."

The silence is unnerving, and I glance up only to see a flicker of empathy flash through Gideon's emerald green eyes before the hard, inexpressive lines of his face soften with understanding.

"I'm sorry. I should not have assumed, particularly since you were not raised within the walls of a city."

I nod at the apology, grateful for his sincerity.

Gideon rubs his stubbled jaw then his chin as he studies me thoughtfully and I squirm under his scrutiny once again.

"I will need to teach you how to read and write. You will need these abilities if you are to be Ruler."

An unfamiliar feeling fills my expanding chest at Gideon's kindness, and I smile brightly at him, momentarily stunning him.

Xander never offered to teach me, only saying he would read to me when I needed.

Gideon is not only teaching me to read and write *but* affording me independence as well.

I push the comparison from my mind, not wanting to dwell on the past any longer, and sit down beside Gideon on the hard floor. He unrolls the ratty paper and begins silently reading through the lines of markings as I look over his shoulder. I catch the enticing scent of his earthly aromas mingled with soap and my eyelids flutter together while I inhale deeply.

My eyes snap open when suddenly comprehending my actions, and I abruptly shift away from Gideon, forcing myself to study a crack in the ceiling. Sensing his penetrating gaze burning into my profile, I turn my head to glance at him and blush at the trace of heady intrigue darkening his eyes. I gnaw my lip nervously and pause when Gideon's eyes drop at the movement. My tongue darts out to moisten my suddenly dry lips and I tense at the low groan vibrating from Gideon's chest.

Quickly darting to a standing position, I cross my arms over my breasts and clear my throat from the nervous lump lodged there. "Have you found anything that might assist us with Lily?"

Gideon remains silent as he watches me, attempting to decipher the unknown and I pace nervously to break away from his astute gaze. He snaps from his musings and briefly glances at the paper again. When he suddenly blanches from what he sees, I rush over, and he looks up at me with disbelief.

I deliver him a desperate look. "What does it say?"

Gideon's face is solemn, and he stares at me silently for a brief period before slowly answering, "Nelinha has a four-year-old girl named Lily. It is recorded with an address."

I nod my head slowly. "Okay, so that confirms our theory." My stomach still revolts with nausea at the idea of having to let the little girl know her mother has died. "What about a father or relative that can take her in? Is there anyone else within the family?"

Gideon grimaces yet nods at my question, gripping the back of his neck as he stares down at the paper.

I frown at his adverse reaction. "Why are you displeased? We found who the little girl belongs to *and* that she has a relative to take her in."

Gideon exhales sharply and rubs his hand roughly over his face before looking me dead in the eyes.

"Her father is listed as the Ruler. Xander."

I stare at Gideon with my mouth gaping for what must be minutes until the silence grows deafening. His words are too much of a shock to absorb immediately, but eventually I clumsily sink to the ground. The heaviness pressing against my chest almost suffocates me as I stare at the floor, trying to make sense of the news, and my breaths become rapid.

Gideon pushes up and strides to me quickly, sinking beside my tightly balled, rocking frame to pull me into his arms. The warmth of his hard body against mine does little to drag me from my anguish.

"There has to be a mistake," I whisper, tilting my face up to see his pained expression as he shakes his head.

"The archives are never wrong." Gideon pinches the bridge of his nose then adds, "It also explains why the men of the city were complaining about not seeing her for a time all those years ago, saying she had disappeared and that a temporary replacement stepped in. She would have stopped work as soon as she started showing."

"But how could Xander not know? Why didn't Nelinha tell him and make him take both her and his child in?" The distressing questions spew from my mouth and tears fill my eyes at the gravity of the situation. "I have to take her in and look after her, don't I?" I whisper in question and Gideon nods his head, tightening his grip on me.

"Yes. Families within the walls are most likely just scraping by with what they have and would not even consider adding another mouth to feed. You are really the only woman with the means to help. And to answer your other question, Xander would not have known as the old man that verifies all the records is not one to gossip, nor one to care about which citizens come to record newborns. He just does his job and probably would not have wanted to cause trouble for the Ruler so kept it to himself."

"So, I'm to be reminded daily of Xander *and* the woman who tried to murder me," I say, my voice breaking. Guards must gossip, as Gideon does not show any surprise at hearing the information of Nelinha's attempt on my life. Instead, he holds me tighter and affectionately runs his hand through my hair. The tender action chokes me up and a sob wrenches from my mouth as my tears drench Gideon's shoulder.

The pain and shock from the reality of the situation hinders my common sense that would typically warn me to stop clinging to Gideon. But I remain against his solid chest as he sits with me nestled in the crook of his legs. His warmth and burly arms around me are too comforting to leave.

My tears eventually subside, and I silently remain against Gideon with my face buried in his neck. As my thoughts become more coherent, I suddenly realise why Lily's eyes appeared so familiar. I take a deep breath and inhale Gideon's unique scent, then close my eyes to nestle closer into him at the comforting feel of his brawny frame embracing me.

His muscles become taut at my movement and my eyes snap open at the realisation of what we are doing, so I push off him and fall to the floor. Sliding away from him, I look down the long walkway and jump up to my feet. My face is burning, and I mumble quickly to Gideon, "I need to check on Lily," before spinning and running away.

My heart is pounding against my chest and I wipe my face to clear any remnants of tears before crouching down beside Lily, who is engrossed in her book.

The sweet vision of her brings a soft smile to my face and I momentarily forget my foolishness of being so physically close to Gideon.

He is my second in command. My guard.

He cannot be anything more.

And I love Xander still.

I force myself to be strong as Lily looks up at me, the attributes of Xander within her features now blatantly clear. My face contorts and crumples with the grief of seeing his likeness in front of me, but I paste a positive expression on my face for the sake of my new responsibility, the girl. I swallow the lump of tears down and push a strand of her thick, dark hair behind her ear, choking back a sob at her innocent question. "Did you find my mummy?"

The words become caught in my throat and I stammer, unsure of how to tell a little girl her mother has died, when Gideon walks up and crouches beside me. The press of his hand splayed against my back confuses me but offers extra strength, and I look at him with appreciation to mouth the words, "Thank you."

Gideon dips his chin at me, his face indifferent, and looks

down at Lily who is watching us both expectantly. His soft, gentle tone nearly undoes me as he speaks to the tiny girl.

"Lily, little star. Your mother has gone on a very long trip and will not return to look after you."

Lily's face falls at Gideon's white lie and her features contort with confusion as she looks at me. "But where has mummy gone?"

Tears fill my eyes and I look away, unable to answer. Gideon thankfully jumps to my rescue again and answers, his hand subconsciously running up and down my back in comfort. My sadness is too palpable to analyse his sudden change of demeanour towards me.

"Your mother died and has gone to a place where no one can return from, little sweetheart." He watches Lily with gentle eyes and waits for her to absorb his words, but her face scrunches in further confusion.

I never realised how naïve younger children were until now. How sweet it must be to live in a reality where death is not yet comprehendible.

Pushing past my own sadness in the attempt to be resilient for Lily, I lean forward to brush some of her hair back and her large, innocent eyes drift to me as I softly explain the situation. "You will be living with me, Lily-girl. How does that sound? We can look for treasures all over the big tower I live in."

Her eyes become guarded as she deliberates the offer, understandably still wanting her mother, but she eventually brightens at the idea of treasures. With a little nod and a reluctant smile, she then reaches her arms out to me. My heart clenches at the simple gesture and I place both my hands under her raised arms to lift her with me as I stand. Pulling her against me in a tight cuddle, I hold her as I make my way to the exit, Gideon following closely behind. The weight of what has transpired sits heavily on my shoulders and I take a deep breath to calm my uncertainty.

How am I supposed to raise a little girl when I do not know how?

How am I supposed to be a mother and a Ruler? And the most prevalent concern; how am I supposed to live with the reminder of Xander and Nelinha every day?

I glance over to Gideon before we exit the building to see if he has the same doubts as I do, but only see determination etched across his face.

Gideon will be my anchor through these difficult times.

Our first port of call is Alma's shop to tell her the ludicrous news. I'm baffled by her level-headed reaction as she calmly nods when I blurt it all out. Gideon plays with Lily not far from us.

"How can you be so calm about this, Alma?" I whisper incredulously, my hands erratically cutting through the air, gesturing my disbelief.

Alma chuckles and pats my shoulder. "It is very unusual news, dear, but I know everything happens as it should. This little girl has been sent to you for a reason. Perhaps a gift from Xander in lieu of his departure from this world? Who knows? But you can only accept it and move forward."

My eyes tear up at the mention of Xander, and my vision glazes for a few moments until I sigh and focus on Alma, ultimately nodding in understanding. "You are right, Alma. Thank you."

"You are welcome, dear. And it would be my pleasure to look after the little wean each day while you attend to your role of Ruler. We can eventually place her in the childcare centre."

I sigh with relief and pull Alma into a grateful hug—the burden of not knowing how to juggle both the little girl and my duties to the city now lifted.

40

GIDEON

R AE MATCHES MY PACE as we make our way to the lab and I glance down at the steadfast, beautiful woman beside me. I know a lot has been thrown at her in the past couple of weeks and have come to respect her resilience.

And trust of her as a person.

Her ability to deal with whatever has been thrust upon her amazes me, and I have not met any other woman—or even man— like her. Rae will be a great Ruler.

But that is all she will ever be to me. A Ruler.

I think back to her tenderness with Lily and a smile threatens my lips. Such natural, nurturing behaviours.

Rae will be a great mother as well.

My heart suddenly palpitates at the thought, tightening the cavity it rests in, and I frown at the unfamiliar feeling in my chest. Slightly annoyed at the fondness beginning to develop the more I'm around the stubborn woman, I rub my chest to ease the tautness.

"Are you feeling well?" Rae's soft voice pulls me from my conflicted thoughts, and I look down at her as we walk along the dusty street.

I ignore the unfurling warmth generated from her concern and ensure my expression remains hard, yet impassive. Displays of emotion are a weakness, and there is no room for that in my role as second. "I'm fine. We are nearly there."

A slight frown mars Rae's forehead at my blunt reply but it is quickly replaced with the excitement of seeing the lab looming in the distance.

A group of citizens stop and stare when they spot Rae and start chattering among themselves—realising she is the woman 'filling in' for Xander while he is *away.*

Rae does not hesitate and waves back, sending them a friendly smile. "Hello! Lovely day outside, isn't it?" The citizens gape in surprise at their acknowledgement and smiles brighten their faces as they wave back, all replying simultaneously. Rae probably does not realise it, but that simple act of kindness will spread like wildfire through the gossip chain and create a positive rippling effect. Everyone will fall in love with her.

I hold back an amused smile at her inadvertent ability of befriending locals, and my respect for her grows tenfold. For someone who apparently has barely been here a month, let alone fortnight, she already has the citizens wrapped around her delicate fingers.

Rae and I quickly reach the lab, and, against my better judgement, I grab her shoulder just before she walks up to the large metal doors.

"Rae," I say, and she turns to me with confusion. "If there is anything that makes you uncomfortable or hurts you in here, I will remove you from the lab."

My words cost me an eyeroll and I struggle to refrain from smiling at her defiance. As much as this woman is a thorn in my side, I love her spirit. It keeps my boredom at bay... but it is also a good trait for a Ruler.

"Gideon, if you pulled me away every time something hurt me or made me uncomfortable, I would be forever locked in my tower. This needs to be done. For the sake of humankind and for the city."

My respect escalates more at her selfless act; a possible sacrifice for a city of people she has never personally been acquainted with.

Inwardly cursing the feelings growing within me, I straighten my already stiff spine.

I have a job to do—if Rae will keep me as her second—and any emotions can impact my performance.

Pushing the conflicted sentiments down, I nod and keep my face impassive. "Fine. But if I think your life is in danger, there will be no argument. I *will* remove you from the situation."

Surely, she can accept that.

Rae's stunning, oceanic eyes narrow momentarily before she nods and turns to the entrance again. I key in the code to the keypad—only a select few guards know it—and we walk through the large door. The interior is much the same as the exterior, with enormous metal walls. An antiseptic smell tickles my nose and I look at Rae, who is rubbing her own to rid herself of the insistent itch.

Looking around, I notice the massive space is empty but for a metal desk at its centre. An older man with unruly white hair is hunched over it. My eyes dart to the back of the room where a narrow staircase leads mysteriously underground.

The old man looks up and scrupulously keeps his eyes trained on us, standing as we approach his desk where graphs and an assortment of data are scattered over the surface. "Can I help you?" His words are clipped, and he looks at me warily.

Rae jumps in and smiles brightly at the man. He visibly recoils from her mannerisms, taken aback by the friendliness.

"My name is Rae," she starts, and the man's demeanour transforms immediately.

Rae needs to start donning a crown of some style to indicate her position, so people respect her immediately rather than after the introductions.

"O-o-of course, welcome dear, Lucas rang to let me know we will be doing some tests on you, though he did not mention *what* tests…"

Rae pauses for a moment. I can see her bright, shrewd gaze assessing the man before her. "I have encountered many Breathers," she starts slowly, and the man's eyes expand—making his already dishevelled appearance more notable. "It appears I am Immune to their breath, so the scientists need to run tests on my blood and genetics. I believe there may be a way to create a synthetic Immunity."

The old man stares at Rae with an unreadable expression before his eyes illuminate excitably.

Ah. He must be a scientist then.

"This is amazing news, Miss! I will work alongside my best team with you!"

He gathers his papers into a black carrycase and leaves the sanctuary of his desk, quickly hobbling over to the stairs. Both Rae and I stand there dumbfounded, unsure whether we are supposed to stay or follow. The old man turns over his shoulder and gestures frantically with his free hand for us to follow him. We both jog over and descend the dark stairs.

He looks over his shoulder briefly before returning to watch his steps as he hurries down. "Excuse my manners. My name is Doctor Jörgen. I'm the lead scientist here."

After minutes of making our way down the stairs, we reach a small foyer with a maximum-security door that Doctor Jörgen walks up to. A robotic device appears out of the wall to scan his eyes. I glance at Rae curiously, seeing an expression of intrigue and astonishment cover her delicate features. All of this would be new to her after living as an outsider.

The heavily bolted metal door hisses and latches begin clicking, whirring as it slowly opens to reveal a large, underground operation of men in white coats. Various glass cases contain specimens scurrying about in their translucent prisons, and scientists watch them, furiously scribbling notes in their little booklets. The booklets remind me of Rae's needs, and I remind myself to give her a basic lesson on reading after this. I may not be overly enthusiastic on my new role as custodian, but I will always commit myself wholly to everything I do.

We follow Jörgen through the bustling room of busy scientists and reach the back where another door greets us. Jörgen waits for the door to slide open then hurries through. I follow closely behind Rae and breathe a sigh of relief at the empty, quiet room. Less people, less threats.

I quickly assess our surroundings and note our entry serves as the only exit. A large metal table sits in the centre of the room with straps at the top and bottom to contain the limbs of whatever, or whoever, is to be subjected to the scientist's studies.

Rae will be.

My shoulders rise stiffly at the idea, and I roll them back then look over at Rae. Her face indicates no fear, only curiosity as she lifts the leather straps and studies them.

"Miss Rae, if you could come over here, please," Jörgen asks as he pats a large metal chair situated next to a desk full of sharp needles, tubes, and a fancy screen.

Rae strides over and I watch the curve of her hips sway in the tight, beige pants plastered to her legs like a second skin. My groin becomes suspiciously tight and I frown at the unusual reaction, shifting on my feet to rectify the issue.

The doctor wipes Rae's arm down once she has settled into the seat and I monitor him vigilantly as he picks up a syringe, spearing it into the skin he has just cleaned. Rae does not flinch once, only observing inquisitively as Jörgen pulls the lever on the syringe and her dark red blood fills the empty vial attached. He repeats the process several times until the desk beside Rae is covered with vials of her blood. The doctor looks at each of us and smiles widely, the wrinkles of his skin becoming more prominent with the expression.

"That is all we can do for now," he tells us animatedly. "I will run tests on each of these, but the results could take up to a week to come in. If you can return the same time next week? I will come to you if we retrieve the data sooner."

Rae nods and leans over to clasp Jörgen's hand with hers, the affectionate gesture pleasantly surprising him.

"Thank you for this Jörgen. We will certainly return soon."

Jörgen smiles and lifts their joined hands to kiss hers in respect for her position, causing her to blush at the strange action. I narrow my eyes and an anomalous feeling rises in my chest.

I clamp down the aberrant urge to stride over and pummel the scientist, scoffing inwardly at my barbaric notions. He is just an old man.

I'm just being protective of her. It is my job, I reassure myself.

Jörgen leads us back out to the stairwell and leaves us to scurry back to his work—clearly keen to start running tests on Rae's blood.

As we start ascending the stairs, Rae glances behind to quietly verbalise her gratitude.

"Thank you for doing this with me, Gideon."

I pause at the soft sound of my name on her lips and my entire frame tightens in response to her docile turn of character.

My voice is more husky than usual as I reply, and I wince at the sound of it. "Any time."

Thoughts of our previous disagreement settle heavily on my chest and I sigh, knowing we need to address the issue. Once we reach the entrance foyer, I reach for Rae and turn her towards me. Her azure gaze pierces me and my breath catches in my throat at the uninhibited expression in her eyes. Mentally shaking my head to concentrate on the impending conversation at hand, I drop my hands from her feminine shoulders and hold them behind me to avoid touching her.

"We need to discuss the disagreement we had in the tower last night," I tell her quietly.

Rae nods slowly in agreement and bites her lower lip. I crush my clenched hands together to refrain from grabbing her and stealing a taste of the rosy, plump flesh.

Think of Alma's wrinkly flesh.

My lips twist distastefully.

Ah, that worked. I instantly relax.

"I agree," Rae begins softly, and her eyes fill with uncertainty as they dart to the floor then back to me. "I'm sorry I said those awful things. My temper sometimes seizes me and any of my senses."

Respite fills me at her apology, and I nod as a smile tugs at the corner of my lips. "I have come to enjoy your temper. It keeps me on my toes."

Rae's eyes sparkle but I continue, "Did you mean it when you said I may not be suitable as your second in command anymore?"

Rae's eyes increase and her hand claps over her mouth before she looks at the floor with embarrassment. "That was also my quick temper. I did not mean it. Well, I did mean it at the time—but if you are happy to still be my second, then I would appreciate it." Her earnest eyes look up at me with uncertainty and the expression sends a jolt through my stomach.

I nod affirmatively. "Yes, I would be honoured to remain as your second."

Palpable relief fills Rae's enchanting eyes and her shoulders sag as she relaxes. "Thank goodness. I do not think I could manage having to deal with another one of you all over again."

I throw my head back to laugh at her underlying insult and immediately snap my mouth shut when I realise Rae is staring at me with a mixture of disbelief and adoration.

"I love the sound of your laugh. You should laugh more often," she says, her voice a soft feather floating subtly through the air on a gentle breeze.

I clear my throat, uncomfortable with the direction our conversation is heading in, and gesture for us to walk towards the exit. "Thank you. Now, let us proceed to the tower and I can give you your first lesson in reading."

A happy squeal escapes Rae and she flings her arms around me, catching me off guard. The feel of her soft, slender body plastered against mine makes me stifle a groan and I keep my arms from sliding around her waist, hovering them awkwardly above her back.

Rae does not notice my reaction and peels off me, exaltation and gratefulness twinkling in her beautiful eyes. If I thought that her defiance and attitude was attractive—the image of her filled with jubilation is utterly breathtaking.

I'm in deep strife.

We settle into the couch at my new residence in the tower and I realise she spends more time here than above. I frown at the thought that perhaps she is avoiding Xander's old home, so she is not reminded of him.

The strange, envious feeling rises in my chest again and I clamp down my frustration, squeezing the bridge of my nose to relieve the pressure building between my eyes.

Shaking my head, I open the children's book we retrieved from the library on the way here. The pages are extremely faded or torn due to its age and usage, though it is still legible thanks to the forefathers who decided to preserve such items.

Rae nestles in closer and I stare at her leg, pressed against the side of my own thigh. The heat radiating between our connection combined with Rae's proximity causes my zipper to become painfully tight. I frown at my body's bothersome reaction.

Maybe this was not a wise idea.

But sheer rapture fills Rae's face at the animated images inside of the book, so I push my concerns aside for now.

"It's so beautiful," Rae utters as she runs her fingers over the fading gloss of the page.

I smile and nod. "It was lucky to be preserved throughout The Vanquishing. Not many items survived the downfall. I do not know how Xander's father and grandfathers managed to find all these books originally."

Rae stiffens beside me at the mention of Xander and I briefly squeeze my eyes shut, keenly aware she still loves him.

Do your job. Remain detached.

With the mantra running through my head as an essential reminder, I flip the first page of the children's book in hopes of distracting Rae from whatever grief or emotion she is suffering from.

"You will learn the alphabet initially, but I wanted to show you the pictures in this book first, just because I thought you might enjoy seeing them before we get stuck into the more tedious aspect of learning."

My strategy works and intrigue fills her face as she runs her fingers over the subdued colours that have waned over time.

"These are lovely," Rae muses and looks up at me.

Her angelic face is a breath away from my own and my eyes dip to her mouth. I nod affirmatively without tearing my eyes from the inviting rosy skin and groan when she nervously bites down on her lower lip. I purely cannot comprehend why all my sensibilities and rational thoughts fly out the window when she does that. My eyes travel up the soft features of her face, noting the smattering of light freckles across her pert nose and pale cheeks. The faint mark beside her left brow captures my attention, and I wonder how she received it along with the other various silver scars I have seen decorating her exposed skin.

My gaze drops to meet her piercing eyes, now filled with desire. The display of her need undoes me, and I grasp her chin gently, leaning down to tentatively claim her mouth with my own needy lips, giving little thought to consequences.

Little moans of appreciation come from her throat, spurring me on, and my kiss becomes more urgent. The sweetness of her is my undoing and I lay her across the couch without breaking apart from her mouth, crawling on top of her with my legs nestled in-between her own.

Rae's lips are just as softly sweet as I imagined, and my groin becomes tight with burning need, only made worse as her hips roll sensually up to mine. Her nails bite into my back as her moans become more desperate with each passing moment that I plunder her mouth. My self-control slowly slips away from me, but the last thread of common-sense wavers in the back of my mind, saving me from what could be a grave mistake for us all. *Stop. She still loves Xander. You are her second!*

Her *second* in more than one way.

The rational thought tears me from Rae as I recoil, springing up, my breath heaving and pants cumbersomely snug with arousal. I look down and groan at the glassy eyed beauty—a lustful pink hue gracing her alabaster skin. Pressing my fingers into the corners of my tightly closed eyes, I sigh with frustration at my lack of control.

I'm *always* in control.

Rae's soft voice laced with confusion pulls me from my internal war.

"What was that?" Rae asks, and I look down at her, straightening my spine.

"Something that can never happen again."

Hurt fills her eyes at my brusque answer as she sits up and wraps her arms arounds herself, but I do not make amends. It is better if she just sees me as the unfeeling second in command.

Nothing more.

I sigh and run a hand through my hair before looking back down. "Let's just concentrate on teaching you to read."

A mask of indifference falls over Rae's face and she nods. "Good idea."

We settle back down, though with a large cavity between us this time, and I go through the basics of the alphabet first. I'm impressed with how quickly she learns the letters, even drawing them with some graphite on the piece of scrap paper.

An hour passes, and we complete the lesson as our stomachs grumble simultaneously.

Rae darts up to leave as soon as I stand but I quickly grab her hand, frowning as she pulls it away; acting as if I have burnt her.

"Where are you going? You need to eat. I have food and supplies to make you supper."

Rae nervously glances at the exit before looking back to me with a pained expression. "I was going to eat upstairs at my place and then pick Lily up from Alma. I also need to obtain some rest."

I can tell things have become tense between us again, but now for a different reason.

I should never have kissed her, but I just cannot bring myself to regret tasting her sweetness, finally knowing how soft those teasing lips are.

Knowing Rae needs sustenance and probably will not bother preparing any for herself, I stride over to block the door. Her eyes narrow at me, but I maintain my widened stance, arms folded across my chest. "You will stay here for supper and *then* you can go pick up Lily and go to bed."

Rae weighs up her options, then realises there is no possible way past my large frame, so reluctantly nods her head and walks over to the kitchen.

Tilting my head to either side, I crack my neck to relieve the tension building there and follow her to the opposite side of the bench situated at the centre of the kitchen. Grabbing fresh fruit and vegetables out to make a wholesome meal, I place them all on the bench where Rae sits as she curiously watches me work. It fills me with just enough satisfaction to be content with the way things are.

I may not be able to ravish her in the way I want, and the way she needs, but at least I can feed our other hunger. And after supper, once I have ensured Rae is safely in bed, I will head to my personal residence to make her a crown, one that matches her strength and beauty.

Regardless of my feelings towards her, she will be the best Ruler of Segment One—and she is worthy of a crown that shows this. The whole world will hear of the first female Ruler who changed the course of history. I can feel it deep in my bones. And I will be the man behind the scenes, ensuring she conquers all. I will not let her down.

41

RAE

MY STOMACH IS BURSTING after the delicious meal Gideon prepared and my mind whirls with confusion at the conflicting feelings I hold for him.

I love Xander, but now I wonder if those feelings only arose from the situation that *he* forced me into. Like I had no choice but to love the man who *stole* me from the only life I knew… who stole my innocence. Well, not completely, though he did nearly *violate* me. I instantly scowl at the memory of Xander forcing himself on me during his haze of pent-up emotion.

He had demons. But don't we all?

My abdomen twists with protest, disagreeing with the thought, and I shake my head at the weak excuses I constantly create for the man who no longer exists. It was *not* okay, no matter what he was suffering from. My thoughts drift to Gideon and it does not elude me that he is a stark contrast to Xander in *every* way. More controlled, patient, quiet and considerate.

Shaking my head, I make my way towards Alma's shop and

look up at the dipping sun. The days are slipping away faster now, and I smile at the reasons behind it. I have my freedom, a purpose, a little girl, and a *good* man to keep me on my toes.

I'm brought back to reality at the squeal of happiness when I enter the shop and a little blur flings herself at me, catching me off guard. I sense Gideon's presence behind me before I feel his hand on my lower back, steadying me as Lily climbs me like a tree.

He will be your shadow from now on. Wherever you go, he goes.

It is necessary I become accustomed to his lingering presence. But after the kiss that perhaps should not have occurred, every slight touch from Gideon ignites a fire within me.

I quickly hug Lily and let her slide back down me before she rushes to Gideon and flings herself at him too. "Gig-eon!"

Gideon encircles the tiny girl with his hefty arms and lifts her up to cuddle her back.

I can see an underlying sadness in his eyes, and I remind myself to probe him further about it.

"How was your day, little star?"

"It was lots of fun!"

Gideon chuckles at her toothy smile and listens as she continues chattering away—his stony demeanour completely transformed around the sweet girl.

The contrasting image of Gideon gently holding and talking to such a tiny human causes my heart to clench with that feeling again, and I inhale deeply to calm myself. I look over at Alma who is watching the whole ordeal transpire with a keen interest, and I narrow my eyes at her.

What is she up to?

Alma spots me watching her meticulously, and she squints with a furtive technique before smiling and waves at me, pretending nothing had transpired. I walk over to her and she pulls me into a hug before letting me go, watching me carefully.

"How are you, dear?"

Her question seems odd, so I shrug. "I'm fine. We seemed to have progress at the lab today so thank you for looking after Lily."

"That is wonderful to hear, Rae. And it was a delight looking after the little girl." Alma peers at me closely, her gaze scrutinising. "Are you going to be okay tonight with her at your place?"

I realise there is an underlying note in her question and my shoulders sag, knowing her assumptions are correct.

"It will be hard at first—having *Xander's* child stay with me in *his* old residence—but I'm positive I'll manage." I'm not certain at all.

Alma nods slowly, accepting my answer, then glances over at where Gideon is playing on the ground with Lily. I narrow my eyes at the mischievous glint that enters her cloudy eyes as she looks back at me. "You know, Gideon is a complete natural with the little girl. He also seems to be watching you differently."

I cross my arms and narrow my eyes at Alma. "Your point being?"

"I'm just saying, dear," Alma chides and pats my shoulder, "try not to feel like you are tied to Xander anymore. He is gone— as much as we love him—he is just a memory now. Do not let the past hinder your future happiness. Gideon is a *good* man."

My mouth drops at the meaning behind her words and I nervously glance over at Gideon who is watching me incisively, clearly hearing everything.

I turn back to Alma, leaning over to hiss, "I know! And anyways, I owe Xander nothing since he was but a fleeting relationship I was *forced* into. But that still does not mean it is appropriate to develop feelings for a man that is to *work* for me. And so soon as well!"

Regardless of how he makes my heart race and my blood heat.

Alma nods with understanding but whispers in reply, "You cannot force feelings, Rae, but you also cannot circumvent them."

I sigh and peek at Gideon, who has resumed playing with Lily.

"You better get your rest, dear," Alma's soft words and hand on my shoulder pulls me from my deep thoughts. I nod and give her a quick hug goodnight, then wander over to Gideon and Lily.

Gideon pierces me with his dappled jade eyes, momentarily causing my breath to hitch. I clear my throat, composing myself before reaching down and picking Lily up to prop her on my hip as I keep my eyes trained on the large man below me. "Thank you for keeping her occupied," I tell him, and he nods. "I'm heading back to the tower if you are ready?"

He effortlessly rises to his feet and opens the shop door for me as Alma stands to the side and farewells us as we enter the now dark street. The three of us simultaneously shiver at the frigid air that greets us.

We walk silently, Lily slowly falling asleep on my shoulder, and I relish the rare feeling of contentedness that rises in me at this peaceful juncture.

I could become addicted to this feeling.

Gideon escorts me to the top floor of the tower and stands at my door as I adjust Lily to my other side. My breath hitches as Gideon leans down and presses a soft kiss to my cheek, and I close my eyes to remember the feeling for later. The rough pad of his finger runs across my lips and I gaze up at him as an array of conflicting emotions flash through his clouding eyes before he drops his hand, shaking his head. He clears his throat and glances away before looking back at me—the usual stone-cold expression transforming his face once again.

"I will see you in the morning."

Gideon's contradicting demeanour leaves me dazed, so I just nod my head and turn without saying another word, letting myself into the residence.

Sighing, I rest my forehead against the closed door and take some calming breaths before making my way to the bedroom where I place Lily gently into bed. I pull out the sleepwear Alma had made for me and change into the soft, loose material before sliding under the sheets next to the peacefully sleeping four-year-old.

The side of my face scarcely kisses the mattress before darkness envelops my reality.

Soft giggles slowly rouse me awake and I open my eyes to see a chubby little face peering at me closely. It is the best image I have ever woken up to and I quickly grab Lily, flipping her onto the bed with a playful roar and tickling her until she squeals, giggling uncontrollably. We tickle each other, laughing until we are both out of breath and I roll off the bed, heading to the toilet to relieve myself. I freeze at seeing Gideon standing in the bedroom doorway, watching us with an unreadable expression on his face.

My eyes dip to the shiny item in his hands and I gasp at the realisation of what it is. Lily squeals as she sees Gideon and flings herself at him before noticing the golden band he is holding and yells excitedly. "Treasure! Treasure!"

Gideon watches me carefully as he picks Lily up and gives her the precious artefact while he walks over to me. Lily studies it studiously and looks up at Gideon with confusion. "What is it?"

Gideon's eyes remain glued to mine as he answers, "A crown I made for the Ruler of Segment One."

My mouth parts in shock and I stare at Gideon as my heart flutters at the sweet and thoughtful gesture. My hand hovers over the organ thumping under my decolletage, and I sit on the bed before my knees fail me. I look up at Gideon as he crouches in front of me and hands me the beautifully crafted headpiece.

I take it slowly, my heart still pounding in my throat.

How did he make this?

Studying the intricate gold leaves on the simple band, I glance at Gideon with tears filling my eyes. "Thank you, Gideon, it is breathtaking. I will always treasure this."

His shoulders drop with relief as he places Lily down, the little girl curiously watching the entire exchange.

Gideon gently takes the crown from me and places it on my head, then stands back with a look of adoration. I laugh nervously as he drops to one knee and bows his head before looking up at me with a serious air. My smile wavers as he speaks reverently, though in his usual deep and gravelly voice.

"My queen, my Ruler. I vow to serve and protect you, for the entirety of my life."

Bumps prickle the surface of my skin at his deferential words and I exhale at the weight of what they mean. No longer able to retain from touching him, I slip down onto the ground where he kneels and take his chiselled, scruffy jaw in my hands. His body straightens but I shift closer on my knees, situating myself between his thighs and tilting my head up as I stare into his eyes.

"Those words — this crown — mean everything to me, Gideon," I say, and press my lips softly to his. His strong arms encircle me, and he lifts us to our feet as he continues to gently kiss me back. A little voice breaks us apart and I blush at Lily's outburst.

"Ew, kissy!"

I look at Gideon who smiles softly in return and crouches in front of Lily.

"We're sorry, little star, you will not see that happen again."

Lily nods exuberantly and flitters from the room, already forgetting the disturbing image of two adults kissing.

As soon as she is out of sight, Gideon scoops me up and kisses me passionately before suddenly breaking away from me.

I catch my breath; my fingers drifting to my tingling lips as I watch Gideon frustratingly rub the nape of his neck. He sighs and drops his hand to look at me with a pained expression.

"I cannot keep doing this to you. I'm sorry, Rae."

Alma's words float through the back of my mind and I lift my chin stubbornly. "Well, what if I *want* you to keep doing this to me?"

Gideon freezes at my unexpected reply and conflicted thoughts run through his eyes before his expression shuts down and he shakes his head. "No. I cannot distract you and vice-versa. Besides, I have too many... past issues. And you still love Xander. I'm *no one's* second helpings."

Ignoring the sharp pang in my chest at the mention of Xander, I tilt my head and look up at him curiously. "Can you please tell me what the past issues are? I already know it correlates to a woman."

My heart drops as a dark shadow crosses Gideon's face and he sits down on the end of the bed. "Bloody Alma," he mutters.

I settle next to him, waiting patiently as we sit in silence.

Lily sings to herself as she sits at the kitchen bench, munching on a piece of fruit, and I'm momentarily distracted by how independent she is before Gideon's voice pulls me back to him.

"I was around eight and twenty when I first fell in love," Gideon says, and I chuckle. He looks at me with a frown and I realise he thinks I'm laughing at him.

I rush to explain my thoughts. "Oh, I'm amused because that is approximately how old I am."

Gideon nods and softens at my explanation, then continues in a quiet, sombre tone, "Bronwyn was the love of my life and I was over the moon when she fell pregnant with our first child. We had only been seeing each other for a year but I was ready to settle down as a family."

I push down the jealousy rising in my chest at the thought of Gideon in love with another woman, let alone one carrying his child. Sadness replaces my envy as comprehensions dawns that he must have lost the child as well.

You have no right to feel jealous, anyway.

"Bronwyn gave birth to a healthy little girl and we were so happy for a few months. Well, I *thought* we were happy. It turns out, she was seeing another guard from a different Segment and had been the whole time we were together."

I gasp at the awful turn of events and place my hand over Gideon's own shaking one. His torment is palpable as he continues, "It turns out the baby wasn't even mine. Bronwyn left this Segment not long after and ran off to live with the father of the baby. I had fallen in love with this little girl as if she were my own and that *woman* just tore her from my life."

His story explains everything and his hot and cold actions

towards me now makes sense. I shuffle down to nestle myself in between Gideon's legs, and his deeply creased brows soften at my touch. Grasping the sides of his face between my hands, I stare raptly into his enthralling flecked eyes.

"I cannot comprehend how any woman could have left you, Gideon."

Without any warning, he pulls me against his chest and his lips crush mine as our hot tongues seductively slide together. Our lips mesh for blissful moments before we regretfully pull apart and rest our foreheads together as our heavy breathing subsides.

I deeply inhale Gideon's earthy scent as my eyes remain closed, and his hands roam my back softly. "We better get you ready for the City Hall meeting," Gideon says, his voice thick with desire.

I pull away at his news and pat down my tousled hair as I stare at him in confusion.

"What is the City Hall meeting for?"

Gideon smiles softly and his eyes travel to the gold headpiece that has miraculously stayed in place amid our passion. "The populace have all heard about your loveliness and the kindness you displayed to those few citizens yesterday. Now they all want to meet you and welcome you as their queen."

My eyes widen. "But they do not know I'm their actual Ruler! Don't they think I'm just filling in for Xander?"

Unless Alma already went to the Council members or planted the seeds amongst the people... or they think Xander is still alive and I'm to be his queen.

Gideons shoots me a sly smile and concern rises in my chest. "Today is the day we announce your legitimacy. You will be introduced to them as their new Ruler."

My heart drops at what Gideon's words mean. The city will know of Xander's death. It makes the reality of his absence much more final.

Do not live in the past.

Alma's words afford me strength and I lift my chin and pull my shoulders back as I give Gideon a resilient nod. "Fine. Lead the way."

The City Hall is packed to the brim as citizens pile in through the large entrance, and I wait nervously behind a barrier as I hear the hum of people chattering animatedly. Lily stays plastered to Alma's side as they wait nearby for me to stand up on the makeshift podium.

I see Doctor Jörgen rushing up the side as he looks around frantically with a piece of paper in his hand. My forehead crumples and concern rises within me as he spots my hiding place and comes flying over, his tone frantic. "My dear! I'm so sorry to bother you at such an important time, but I have news!"

Gideon moves closer to my side as Jörgen thrusts the paper in my face and I take it from his grip to stop the assault. "I cannot read! Can you tell me what the urgent news is please?"

Jörgen puts his finger up for me, signalling for us to wait as he catches his breath, and I pat his back upon hearing the awful wheezing sounds he makes.

"I ran the test when you left, and they instantly came up in the system with a rare genetic marker that has not been encountered since centuries ago in Ireland!"

I tap my foot impatiently and gesture for him to continue. "I know that already. What is the remainder of the news?"

Jörgen's eyes brighten and I briefly notice Alma staring longingly at him before he continues talking. "If the report is correct, we should be able to manipulate the genetic marker and artificially create it as a treatment to be administered across the world!"

The news is exactly what I want to hear, and I bounce on my toes, looking at Gideon, whose eyes are reflecting the same hope and delirium I feel. Turning to Jörgen, I clasp his hands with my own and squeeze them affectionately. "Thank you for letting me know, Jörgen. This is brilliant! The world may have hope yet."

Jörgen nods frantically and his wild grey hair flies around his head. "Yes. We can start tests on animal subjects first," he says gleefully, but then looks cautious as he turns to check no one is listening before leaning in to whisper his next sentence. "But we will need to capture a Breather to do proper testing and see if the treatment will work as a cure as well."

Gideon stiffens beside me and his hands protectively slide around my waist. "Absolutely not. That would put Rae *and* the city at risk." I look up at Gideon's warning tone and shake my head. Confusion fills his eyes, but I turn back to the doctor and nod slowly.

"Yes, I can easily capture one since I'm Immune and know what to expect. We will plan tomorrow and gather the best hunters to head out in the next few days. The sooner we start testing, the bigger the chance mankind will have."

Gideon quietly mutters a protest at the danger I'm putting myself in, but I know there is no other choice.

Jörgen bows slightly and looks up at me with a newfound adoration and respect. "Bless you, child. You will save us all."

He scurries away and I turn to Gideon. Tension is emanating from his large frame and I place my hand on one of his crossed arms to calm him. "It will be okay, Gideon. It is the only way."

Gideon shakes his head and exhales roughly. "It doesn't mean I have to like it."

I smile gently at him, secretly pleased he cares so much about my wellbeing, but know I will do whatever I want regardless.

Alma hurries over to us with Lily, and my hand clasps over my mouth with deep concern at the little girl's red-rimmed, puffy eyes. Looking at Alma, I lean to fretfully whisper in her ear, "Is she okay? It looks like she has been crying."

Alma whispers in reply, "She will be fine dear. The poor child has moments where she cries for her mother. She throws a little tantrum each time I explain her mother has died and is not coming back."

My lips tilt down as unrelenting sadness grips me, and I crouch down to open my arms for the upset girl. "Lily, sweetie, do you have a hug for me?" Her little face scrunches miserably and she looks away, causing my arms to drop at the dejectedness plaguing me, so I add, "I'm about to become a queen, so do you know what that makes you?" It piques her interest and she grudgingly peers at me, shaking her head slightly. I smile and say with exaggerated wonder, "It means you will be a princess!"

Pa told me plenty of fairy tales as a little girl before he switched to complete survival training, so I know how coveted a position as princess is. My assumptions of how Lily would react are correct because her eyes widen with awe and she steps closer to me. I smile when she squeaks in a quiet voice, "Really?"

"Yes, and we will call you Princess Lily." Her face transforms into one of glee and I ruffle her hair. "Now, how about that hug?"

She throws her arms around me and I look up to Alma who smiles and nods approvingly.

Inwardly celebrating the small but important triumph, I wrap my arms around her with a relieved sigh.

"Are you ready, dear? The citizens are waiting for you to make your speech now," Alma says with tears glistening in her milky blue eyes—eyes that would have once been identical to mine.

Peeling a now clinging Lily from me, I rise with a wide, though wavering smile, and reply with a shaky voice. "Yes."

As ready as I will ever be.

Nerves are thrumming in overdrive through my entire body.

Alma's wrinkly hands reach up and adjust the beautiful, gold headpiece Gideon created, and she stands back to look at me expectantly. I gaze up at Gideon, the affection and adoration in his eyes giving me the courage I need, and he takes my hand to place a soft kiss on the underside of my wrist.

"They already love you, Rae. You are the ray of sunshine they need."

Choking back a bittersweet sob at the words that echo my Pa's, I take a shaky breath and nod. I quickly stand on my toes and press a soft kiss to Gideon's lips, breaking away to see something deeper reflecting within his forest-green eyes.

Biting my lower lip, I turn to Lily and crouch to place a kiss on her nose. A cute giggle escapes her and has me smiling at the delightful sound. Giving her a quick hug, I direct her back into Alma's arms and stand to take a deep breath.

No more stalling.

Pushing the nerves deep down and pulling my shoulders back, my hand goes to the precious pendant around my neck and I look upwards.

This is for you, Pa.

My eyes drop to meet Alma's proud gaze and I shoot her a bright but nervous smile as I raise my chin. "I'm ready."

EPILOGUE

XANDER

THE BRIGHT SUN burns my pale, sensitive skin, and I trudge slowly in a trance across the smouldering wastelands. My memory is nothing but a whisper of glimmers from the past and the ghost of a soul that no longer exists. Something niggles in the back of my mind. Something warning that I'm not quite right anymore. I look down at my hands, not recognising the ashen flesh clinging to my partially mutated bones. A faint memory of a raven-haired, blue-eyed beauty plagues my scrap of an existence and I walk endlessly in search of her—in the hopes that she can help me. In the hopes that she can save my soul. I know deep down in the pit of my blackened heart; she's my only hope.

THE END

For now

ACKNOWLEDGEMENTS

A special thanks to my lifelong partner, Ben, for always inspiring me and giving me the strength *not* to care what other people think; I love you so much, Minnie. Thank you for supporting me with positivity and reassurance throughout this hectic journey and for keeping me grounded.

My wonderful little sister, Nadia; thank you from the bottom of my heart for being my first best friend and cultivating our creative, adventurous minds. We have had so much fun and I think we should hold hands for safety. You have been so patient with me and I love you to the moon and back!

My big brother, Dan; our daring, adventurous minds were rampant in the afternoons and on weekends so I will always cherish our escapades together with Nads (pirates, Pog & Pug & Doggy Doug Etc.). We all had so much fun growing up and my overactive imagination was certainly nurtured within time spent after school in our yard with the three of us.

Dad—thank you so much for backing me with whatever impulsive journey I had decided to embark on and always being proud of me, regardless of my failings. Your endless sacrifices of time and generosity has cultivated my being today... I will always cherish the memories us children made in every fort and cubbyhouse you built for us. Though my joints have already started aching; I will always be your little girl.

Thank you Mumsy, my mother dearest—thank you for reading to us children every night growing up; you instilled your own love for books in me and I am forever grateful for this passion. Thank you for loving me unconditionally even when I was an awful teenager… I truly am sorry for all the strife you endured! Both you (and Dad) fostered my creativity with each sacrifice of your time, money and effort; driving me to cello lessons, buying endless art supplies, allowing me to read your books and taking me to the library regularly.

I love you and Dad to the moon and back—to infinity and beyond and that love will never falter.

I am deeply grateful for our family and overtly blessed to be gifted with the childhood I had (even if we are all mad-as-a-hatter sometimes) … I wouldn't have it any other way! I would not be the person I am today without any of you. Thank you for always supporting me with whatever I am doing.

A very big thank you to my friend Shana; without your endless support and assistance, I would be a wreck! You have been so patient with my endless questions and I appreciate you from the bottom of my heart for coaching me through the tedious process of self-publishing.

A massive appreciation shout-out to my manly friend, Shalika, for always enabling me to be my own crazy self—listening to my ramblings—which has cultivated my creativity throughout our many years of friendship. You will forever be my other half—my constant—and I could not imagine a life where you did not exist.

So, thank you Shana and Shalika for being seriously amazing…

I appreciate and love you both so much.

Thank you Bazza and Joel for listening to my ideas and encouraging me during the last seven years. I will be looking forward to our Chinese celebration dinner at Simon King! You are my adopted family and I love you as if you were each my own blood.

Thank you, Leonie and Mike, for your unwavering support and endless delicious dinners. You both have been a part of this journey and I appreciate every time you listened to my rants.

Thank you my little, gorgeous niece, Claire for enabling me to play mermaids and experience childhood again. I love you with my every being, munchkin!

Thank you, big sis Veronica and my nephew Aidan for being yourselves and accepting me as I am. Even though we do not see each other that often, I cherish each visit and never fail to laugh hysterically.

Franzi (*CoverDungeonRabbit*) — you have been simply amazing and created the most spectacular cover that I absolutely *LOVE*. Thank you so much and thank you for putting up with me; it was so much fun collaborating with you. Every person who reads my book because of the beautiful covers… well that is all you, lovely!

My home will always be your home if you ever visit Australia.

Thank you to my editor, Chloe (and Aidan) for polishing my manuscript with your structural edits and clever notations; I know it would have been scrappy and entirely unreadable without either of you! I am slightly mortified you even read it at the stage you received it… but thank you, nonetheless. You are both ingenious and a great team.

Thank you to Julia for formatting my book! It is what ties everything together and I appreciate your hard work of bringing the interior of my novel to life with your beautiful designs.

This next acknowledgement is futile seeing as she cannot read this… my little Eevee. You are so special and a gift to me in place of a child—even though you bark at every trespasser walking by. I would not change a thing about you. I love you so much and I know your love for me is returned tenfold.

Thank you to my wonderful and supportive readers; I am honoured to share these adventures with you!

There will be so many others who have impacted my life such as my extended family and those who have only been fleeting encounters, but I appreciate the good and the bad; please do not feel excluded as this multiple paged acknowledgement is already stretching the limit.

Above all else, and most importantly, I would like to thank my heavenly Father; you have given me so much to be thankful for and without you, *none* of this would be possible. You have afforded me the very breath I breathe. **You created my inmost being; you knitted me together in my mother's womb. I praise you because I am fearfully and wonderfully made.**

Forgive me Jesus, for my endless failings, I know I am far from perfect. Humble me always. I lay my life at your feet.

ABOUT THE AUTHOR

Anita R. Eschler is an Australian author living on the beach with her other half and dog, Eevee. Anita's hobbies include swimming, painting, drawing and most of all, reading. There were many occasions where she found herself reprimanded during school because of reading a book held inconspicuously under the desk instead of listening to the teacher.

Follow and connect with Anita on social media and online:
anitareschlerauthor.com
facebook.com/anita.r.eschlernovels
linktr.ee/Anitaeschler
instagram.com/author_anitaeschler

CPSIA information can be obtained
at www.ICGtesting.com
Printed in the USA
LVHW090441230621
690925LV00042B/2266/J